The Way to a Man's Heart

The Way to a Man's Heart

St. Martin's Paperbacks

THE WAY TO A MAN'S HEART

ISBN: 0-312-96333-5

Printed in the United States of America

St. Martin's Paperbacks edition/November 1997

St. Martin's Paperbacks are published by St. Martin's Press, 175 Fifth Avenue, New York, NY 10010.

10 9 8 7 6 5 4 3 2 1

Contents

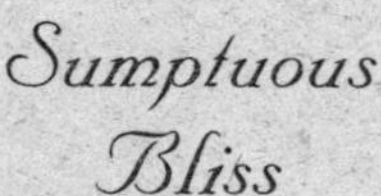

Christine Dorsey

Cinnamon's Wedding Cake

1 *cup unsalted butter*
1¼ *cups superfine sugar*
4 *eggs, separated*
4 *cups all-purpose flour, sifted*
¼ *teaspoon cinnamon*
4½ *cups dried fruit (apricots, currants)*
1 *cup candied orange peel*
½ *cup walnuts, chopped*
1 *ounce compressed fresh yeast*
⅔ *cup milk*

Cream butter and sugar. Beat in egg yolks. Mix together flour and cinnamon and add in small portions (to prevent lumping) to the sugar mixture. Then beat in dried fruit, candied peel, and nuts, again in small portions.

Cream yeast with small amount of milk and add to cake mixture. Then add enough of the remaining milk to form a thick paste. Beat the egg whites until frothy and blend them into the cake mixture. Cover and let stand in warm place for 1 hour.

Preheat oven to 325 degrees. Butter a 9-inch springform cake pan and line the bottom with parchment paper and butter the paper. Work the batter with hands to form stiff paste. Turn it into the pan and bake for 2 ½ hours, or until skewer pushed into center comes out dry. During baking, cover çake with baking parchment if it is getting too dark.

For graduated layers use different size pans and multiply recipe accordingly.

Blissful Frosting

1¼ cups butter, softened
4 cups powdered sugar, sifted
2 teaspoons rose water
1½ cups heavy cream, whipped
3 Candied flowers

Combine butter, 1 cup of sugar and rose water, beating at medium speed. Add remaining powdered sugar alternately with whipping cream, beating well with each addition. Beat at high speed until smooth.

Ice cooled cake and decorate with candied flowers.

Chapter 1

Massachusetts, 1886

"For heaven's sake, Biddy, would you hush up?" Cinnamon lifted a towel above her head and resumed slapping at the small fire on the kitchen floor. "Do you want the entire household to crash down on us?"

"Move back, lass."

"What?" Cinnamon's head turned at the sound of the unfamiliar male voice. "Who are *you?*"

"As I said, move out of the way." The man delivered the words as he tossed water from the pantry bucket onto the burning mess.

"Ohhhh!" Cold seeped through Cinnamon's petticoats, wetting her legs, soaking through her new kid boots. "What are you doing?" She looked down to see the stranger grabbing the hem of her sodden skirt. When she rapped his shoulder, he glanced up, giving her a smile that made her wet toes curl.

"Not much harm done, then," he said in a voice softened by a Scottish burr. "Only scorched the outer layer."

Not much harm done? Her gown was ruined—and her new boots with the ribbon lacings. "Look at me. I'm all wet!" Then something he'd said hit her. "Outer layer of what?" But the man, still kneeling at her feet, had turned his attention to the tumbled baking tins not far from her on the floor.

"Yer skirt," he tossed absently over his shoulder.

She glanced down at the front of her gown. "It's ruined.'' She pulled at the soaked fabric. Who was this impertinent man?

''Better a bit of silk and lace than yerself, I'd say.'' He stopped examining the charred concoction on the floor and looked up at her again, inquiry shadowing his deep blue eyes. ''Ye are all right, aren't ye?''

''Of course, I'm all right.'' She just wished she could say the same for her gown, her new boots, and her creation. ''Why shouldn't I''—she started to say as he stood—''be,'' she finished after swallowing. Goodness he was tall and broad-shouldered, dwarfing her not petite height which, of course, was no reason for her tongue to trip over itself.

''Yer hem was afire,'' he said simply.

''I don't understand how that could happen.'' She bent forward, gathering up yards of silk. ''I was so careful not to get too close to the flames.''

He shrugged as if to say she could see the proof herself which she did in the form of wet, seared yellow silk.

''Well, it must have happened when you came toward me. When I looked around,'' she added.

Again he just shrugged, a gesture she was beginning to find annoying. He used her fire-fighting towel to lift one of the pans containing the burned remains of her afternoon's work.

''What was it?'' he asked, giving her that smile again.

''A cake,'' she answered, grabbing the pan and burning her palm. She did her best to muffle her gasp of pain.

'' 'Tis still hot,'' he told her . . . a bit too late in her opinion, but she thanked him anyway. The tilt of his head showed he doubted her expression of gratitude.

''Here, let me see.''

''That won't be necessary. I'm fine.'' But her words did not stop him from prying her fingers open to examine her palm. His hands were large, sun-darkened, and surprisingly gentle.

''Doesn't look too bad, a bit red is all.''

''Are you a physician, then?''

He surprised her when he threw back his head and laughed, a deep booming sound that made Biddy, cowering by the doorway, look up. "Hardly," he answered. "Just a man who's seen his share of burns and scrapes."

Cinnamon managed a half-smile. "How interesting." He still held her hand, which wasn't unpleasant but was highly improper, as was this meeting. She pulled her hand free, then surveyed the puddled, soggy, burned cake with a sigh.

"I wouldn't think they'll be too angry with ye."

She lifted her wet skirt as she stepped around him, then paused and caught his eye. "Who?"

"Why, your employers, lass. Though I've been told Mrs. Murphy can be a bit demanding, the old captain seems right enough."

Cinnamon lifted her eyebrows. "Oh, really? That's what you've heard?"

"Aye." He smiled down at her. "But then ye would know better than I."

"Yes, I imagine I would," she agreed, amused despite his forthright comments about her parents. He thought she was the cook—in a silk gown and kid boots?

"And perhaps they won't find out," he said, waving aside some lingering smoke. "I know for a fact that Mr. Murphy is not at home, or at least he wasn't ten minutes ago."

"And just how do you know that about my . . . my employer?" Cinnamon ignored Biddy's startled gasp.

"I have an appointment with him in the library," he added a bit pompously. Then his eyes widened as if he just realized what he'd said. He muttered a curse, then a quick apology. "I'd like to stay and help ye clean up the mess"—he ineffectively swiped at the water stains on his trousers—"but I fear I may be late for my appointment. Even though it was Mr. Murphy himself who was tardy to begin with. But I suppose schedules are different for the wealthy," he said, grinning.

"You're probably right." Cinnamon gave him her best

smile. He really was handsome. She couldn't help adding, "You won't be telling Mr. Murphy what I did now, will you? I mean the fire and all."

"Well, I suppose I could be persuaded not to mention what I know—for a price."

"A price?" She cocked her head, looking at him through her lashes. Did he mean to extort money from her? Perhaps he did know who she was. Perhaps he had finally realized that no cook would be wearing yellow silk and kid boots. "Whatever could that be?"

He rubbed his chin as if deep in thought. "A kiss would no doubt seal my lips."

"A kiss?" She certainly hadn't expected that. Her smile faded.

"Miss Cinnamon ain't no—"

"Good at baking cakes," she finished for her hapless maid, who unfortunately had picked that moment to regain her tongue.

"But, miss—"

"A kiss it is," she said, quieting Biddy. Despite the fact that she'd never see this man again, she didn't want him to know she'd been making light of him. She saw no reason to embarrass him. After all, he had tried to help her. Perhaps a bit overzealously but still . . .

Besides, what could it hurt? She'd let him give her a peck like her fiancé, Lord Alfred, had. Then he'd be off to see her father, none the wiser.

She took a step closer and lifted her cheek. She caught the hint of a wicked grin moments before she was swooped against his broad chest. "Oh my . . ." The words were barely out of her mouth before firm, sensually chiseled lips covered hers. Heat raced through her—and tingles. The same sensation she'd felt in her toes at his smile now zinged through her body.

His tongue ventured along the seam of her lips and her mouth opened. When her tongue met his, pure pleasure sent her spiraling. Dizzy, she lifted her arms, grasping his shoulders for support. But soon even that wasn't enough and her hands curved around his strong neck, twining in the black curls at his nape. Delicious . . .

A noise brought reason slapping back on her. At first she thought it was Biddy, but as she pulled away from him she realized it had been she . . . moaning.

Still dazed, no matter how hard she tried to gather her wits, Cinnamon stared up into his smiling face and cleared her throat. "Well," she said, straightening her shoulders. "I suppose you should be on your way, Mr. . . ."

"Captain Ian McGregger," he said with a bow, and another dimple-revealing grin. "At yer service."

"Yes, well, good day to you, Captain McGregger." She turned away, busying herself with moving a wooden spoon from one spot on the table to another.

"He's gone, miss." Biddy crossed the kitchen and stood beside Cinnamon.

"Where did you find him, Biddy, and why in heavens did you bring him down here?"

"Well, like he said, miss, he was in your father's library. I thought Mr. Murphy might be of some help with the fire, but he weren't there, and that young man insisted I show him where it was. Grabbed my arm he did, and pulled me along."

"Oh, really?" She laughed.

Biddy didn't. "Miss Cinnamon, I don't see what you think is so funny."

Neither did Cinnamon, for that matter. But it was either laugh or try to explain to herself her reaction to Ian McGregger's kiss. And that she didn't want to do. Instead, she surveyed the damage on the floor.

"Poor Miss Cinnamon," Biddy was saying. "Look at your cake, all ruined, naught but wet ashes."

"It is a bit of a mess, isn't it? As am I." She plucked at her clingy wet skirts. "It's just too bad I told everyone about this cake." She gave the nearest blackened tin a kick with the toe of her ruined boot. "They're expecting something wonderful for dessert at dinner."

"Now, I'm sure no one will mind, miss. You aren't really expected to bake a cake now, are you?''

Perhaps. But she didn't see why she couldn't do it. How hard could baking a simple cake be? And as for no one minding that she'd failed, well, that wasn't exactly true—for *she* minded a great deal.

''Oh, Count Lorenzo, do tell us another. You are so, so amusing. Don't you think so, Cinnamon?''

''Yes, Mama. Truly,'' she agreed, though she hadn't paid the slightest attention to her sister Eugenia's husband, who sat next to his wife.

Cinnamon had heard quite enough of the Italian count's stories during their travels through Europe this past summer. Not that there was really anything wrong with her brother-in-law. He was learned, cultured, of impeccable lineage, if one didn't count several wrong-side-of-the-sheet births which, of course, would never be mentioned in the Murphy household. And even if his pocketbook didn't match his royal blood, he abided Eugenia fairly well. So all in all, he was a perfect catch. Mama was ecstatic that her eldest daughter was well married and in the autumn Cinnamon would be too.

Excusing herself, Cinnamon rose. Near the piano her younger sisters, Cornelia, Lucretia, and Philomela, took turns looking through the stereoscope and giggling. Taking a playful swipe at their posteriors with her fan, she bypassed them and headed for the window where her father stood. He had lifted aside the heavy velvet drapes and was looking out onto the gaslit street.

A large man, raw-boned and robust, he had gray hair and side whiskers and an honest, friendly face, still tanned from his many years standing beneath crisp white sails. Her mother had tried through the years to smooth his rough edges but had yet to succeed—at least to her way of thinking. Cinnamon thought her father nearly perfect, always had.

He tapped his foot absently now and rubbed at his whiskers—two habits her mother considered common.

Glancing up as Cinnamon approached, he gave her a welcoming smile. "So you're tired of hearing how the count's grandfather singlehandedly defeated Napoleon, are you?"

She hid a smile behind her hand-painted fan. "Do you suppose there's any truth to that tale?"

"I haven't the faintest idea." He let the curtain drop and lifted his wineglass, taking a sip. "But it does make him colorful."

"And the center of attention," she added. Cornelia, Lucretia, and Philomela appeared to have grown tired of the stereoscope and joined the group, chattering away like magpies, full of questions for the Italian count.

"Now, we mustn't be too critical. Your sisters haven't had the advantage of visiting the cream of European society as you have, my dear."

If she thought for one moment her father was serious, she might have felt chastised. But she knew his opinion of her trip last summer, as well as the one Eugenia took the summer before when she had met Count Lorenzo.

"You seem distant tonight, Papa. Is something wrong?"

He set his glass on the ornately carved table, next to Caesar's bust. "Wrong? No, I wouldn't say that. But there is a matter I wish to discuss with you. Should have before tonight actually."

"Why before tonight?"

"Cinnamon, Mr. Murphy, do come join us. Count Lorenzo is relating such a fascinating tale," Mama called to them.

"He and Eugenia have met our queen, Papa."

"Yes, I know, Philomela, though we must remember Victoria is not our queen."

"Oh, Papa, don't be such a fuddy-duddy."

"Such language you use, Cornelia," Mama said. "I can't imagine where you get it."

"Shall we join your mother, Cinnamon?" Patrick held out his arm. Her expression must have shown concern, for he patted her hand. "Don't fret. We'll talk later on this subject."

"I'd be pleased to know what subject you're referring to."

"Later, my dear," he said as they strolled across the drawing room toward the arrangement of scarlet settees.

Seated again, Cinnamon fluffed the folds of her wheat-colored silk gown with the Sevres blue velvet and black Chantilly lace, and wished she knew what was troubling Papa. Her lips thinned, then curved into a forced smile when her mother caught her eye. One of her daughters appearing vexed in public wasn't acceptable as far as Kathleen Murphy was concerned.

When James, the very English butler Mama had imported from London, announced dinner, her mother rose, but Papa shook his hand, waving James aside.

"Whatever is wrong with you, Mr. Murphy? We are all assembled and quite ready to have our dinner, I'm sure."

"I apologize for the delay, Mrs. Murphy. But I've invited someone else to join us." Her father flipped open his pocket watch. "Someone I am eager for all of you to meet." His eyes sought Cinnamon's.

Her mother settled down onto the settee primly. "Where is this person?"

"He'll be here."

"Perhaps he was delayed," added the count as he lifted his monocle.

"Delayed?" Cinnamon thought her mother said the word as if she'd never heard it before. "How utterly—"

"Ah, here he is now."

The parlor doors opened, and before James could announce the visitor, her father rushed forward. He took the newcomer's hand and shook it hardily, practically pulling him into the room.

"Welcome, my boy. Glad you could come. We are all assembled as my good wife would say. You must meet the family."

Her father's outburst hid Cinnamon's gasp of surprise.

She watched, stunned, while her father presented her mother, sisters, and Count Lorenzo. Though their guest appeared slightly nervous, he was nonetheless gracious, making the appropriate comments—until his eyes met hers. Then his mouth dropped open, but no words emerged.

Chapter 2

"Cinnamon, my dear, let me present Captain Ian McGregger. Captain McGregger, my daughter, Miss Murphy."

Cinnamon could almost hear the captain's thoughts exploding inside his head. The cook! No, not the cook! The daughter.

Captain McGregger muttered something she didn't quite catch. Then his gaze caught hers, and she had difficulty looking at him. She should have told him who she was before he had made those comments about her parents, before he had kissed her. Unable to stop herself, she glanced at his mouth, and heat crept up her neck.

He must have also felt embarrassed, for she noticed he tugged on his starched collar before he straightened his shoulders. It almost appeared as if he'd like to turn and walk out the door. But instead he offered his arm to her mother, who seemed hesitant to take it, and escorted her to the dining room.

The butler seated Captain McGregger between her sisters, Cornelia and Lucretia. They were pretty and young and pleasant company, so Cinnamon was surprised when the captain's gaze kept straying to her, sitting directly across the lace-covered table from him.

"Have you been to Italy, Captain McGregger?"

He glanced up from his perusal of the array of silverware bracketing his bowl of chilled soup to answer her brother-in-law. "No, sir, I have not."

"Pity. It's a lovely country. My family is from there, you know. Near Florence."

"Really." His Scottish-accented voice was laced with polite curiosity.

"Yes, they own an estate," Cinnamon added. "A villa that looks down over a lovely valley." She smiled at the captain around an elaborate silver epergne laden with fruit, while lifting the round, bowled soup spoon slowly to her lips.

"I see." The captain's sun-tanned face pinkened, but he picked up the correct spoon nonetheless.

"Captain McGregger is one of the finest sea captains in my employ." Her father set down his wineglass.

"Thank you, sir, but I'm sure I don't deserve—"

"Why not? You are the best."

"That's very kind of you, sir, but—"

"Mr. Murphy, you've spilled wine on the tablecloth. How many times must I ask you to be more careful?" Her mother said, interrupting the captain. She then turned to Count Lorenzo. "I do apologize, dear Count. We don't usually speak of business at dinner."

"I'm certain Father was simply telling us a bit about our guest," Cinnamon said in defense of her father, who simply shrugged.

The conversation then moved to other topics, mostly emanating from her sisters and centering around the count. Since her family had been in his company only briefly for Eugenia's wedding last year, her sisters were full of questions, wanting to know every detail of the count and Eugenia's recent arrival in Boston and of the round of parties and dinners planned for them during their visit.

"How long will you be in Boston, Captain McGregger?" This question came from Lucretia, who Cinnamon noticed was doing her best to flirt with the handsome Scotsman.

"I'm not certain." Cinnamon saw him glance at her father, who was busy eating his lobster and didn't meet his eye. "Until today my answer would have been simple. No more than a fortnight. Long enough to unload the shipment of spices, jute, linseed, and saltpeter, then fill the hull with manufactured goods."

"And then you'd sail to . . ." Lucretia smiled at him as she raised her glass.

"India. As I've been doing for nearly fifteen years."

What had happened today to change his plans? Cinnamon wondered. But before she could ask, Lucretia was inviting the captain to attend the ball being given in honor of Cinnamon's betrothed.

"You must come, isn't that so, Mama?"

"Of course, Lucretia. Captain, I shall see that you receive an invitation," her mother answered, though the tight-lipped expression on her fleshy face indicated that she hadn't liked saying it.

"Thank you, ma'am. But I may be in the middle of the Atlantic by then."

"Nonsense, my boy. Of course you'll come," her father said, obviously oblivious to Mama's soured expression.

The table was cleared again, and Lucretia clapped her hands. "Shall we see it now, Cinnamon? I've been so excited all day."

She turned to Captain McGregger before Cinnamon had a chance to answer. Leaning toward him, Lucretia whispered conspiratorially, "Dear Cinnamon baked a cake, if you can believe it. She tasted it the day she met her fiancé, Lord Westfield. It was at the queen's daughter Princess Beatrice's wedding. Cinnamon asked Queen Victoria's own chef for the recipe. Now she's determined to have it at her own nuptials. Isn't that right, Cinnamon?" Lucretia leaned farther toward the captain as she eyed Cinnamon.

"I didn't bake the cake today," Cinnamon said, shooting a look at Captain McGregger, daring him to contradict her. "I was too busy." Not a complete lie. She had been busy working on her father's business accounts, which was the reason she had forgotten about the cake and had left it in the oven till it caught fire.

"Oh . . ." Lucretia pouted. "I was so looking forward to tasting it. You made it sound just so . . ." She glanced at the captain through her lashes. ". . . Tantalizing. But then I thought it was perfectly absurd for you to make the cake yourself. Didn't you, Mama?"

"I didn't think she could manage it," Eugenia piped in. "And why should she even try? We do have staff for that sort of thing."

"Yes, I agree," Philomela added, nodding her head till her golden curls shook. "It really wasn't a good idea. I don't care how much you wish to impress Lord Westfield."

"I'm certainly not doing it because of that," Cinnamon blurted.

"That's excellent, because I doubt His Grace would care for his future bride slaving away in the kitchen like a common servant. Don't you agree, Count?" her mother asked.

Cinnamon didn't wait for her brother-in-law's response. "I'm baking the cake because I wish to." Her gaze met the captain's. "I can do it. I don't care what anyone says to the contrary."

"Now, now, Cinnamon, dear," her father said, his voice soothing. "Of course you can. We all know that you can do anything you set your mind to. No one doubts that and certainly not Captain McGregger. Right, my boy?"

"Nay. I've a feeling she can bake a cake if she so chooses."

"Well, I do—choose to, that is."

"Then I wish ye luck."

"Thank you!" Cinnamon realized her voice had risen considerably and her lips clamped shut. She glanced around the table. To a person, her family stared at her. She settled back in her chair, aware that she had been leaning forward, toward the captain. Why had her father dragged him into the discussion? She certainly didn't have to convince him of anything. Except that he knew the truth about her first attempt to bake the cake.

Hoping for a calm, dignified tone, she said, "I apologize for not having the cake ready tonight. Perhaps tomorrow."

"But, Cinnamon, you promised to go with me on the morrow when I visit Elizabeth Shelby. You know what a bore she is and you're the only one who can make me laugh when I'm in her company."

"Cornelia!" Her mother took in a deep breath. "We do not speak of our friends like that."

"I'll accompany you, Nellie."

"Cinnamon, her name is Cornelia, and I wish you *and* your father would remember that."

"Yes, Mama."

She decided it best not to argue the point. She could see the telltale signs of her mother's displeasure—her narrowed eyes, pursed lips, heaving robust bosom. She breathed a sigh of relief when the dessert of sponge cake and fruit was served, followed by a frozen sorbet.

With every bite, she swore to herself that she'd bake that cake. How could she not? Her father was right. If there was one thing everyone said about her it was that she always accomplished what she set out to do.

Her mother had sent her to Europe to win herself a nobleman. Perhaps Mama hadn't said it in so many words, but Cinnamon had known what was expected of her. So she'd found Lord Alfred Westfield, and she'd serve that wonderfully delicious cake at their wedding. That would make everything perfect, wouldn't it?

She raised her eyes and caught Captain McGregger's gaze. It was difficult to read his expression, but she couldn't forget that he knew of her failure. Well, she'd make that cake and sit and watch Ian McGregger eat it. Knowing it was ridiculous even to care if he tasted the result of her labors didn't seem to make her any less determined that he would.

With dessert finished, her mother rose, and Cinnamon and her sisters joined her, leaving the gentlemen to their cigars and brandy.

But only a short time later the men entered the drawing

room and Cinnamon knew it was because her father could barely tolerate her brother-in-law, whom he referred to as "that Italian potentate."

Cinnamon saw Lucretia gently pat the cushion beside her as she smiled at the captain. He dutifully accepted her invitation, and Cinnamon could barely keep from rolling her eyes. She made room for her father to sit beside her on the settee and waited for the inevitable. It took her mother no time at all.

"Philomela, dear, please play . . ."

Her sister was already in motion toward the piano before her mother could finish her sentence.

"She sings like a nightingale," Mama said to Count Lorenzo. "As a matter of fact, her name means lover of song. How Mr. Murphy and I knew what a sweet voice she would have someday is just a miracle."

Philomela managed to finish the aria and began the encore Mama requested without losing the tune. That was the best Cinnamon could say for her sister's talent. She glanced at Captain McGregger when Philomela came dangerously close to missing a note, but he seemed not to notice. Lucretia was whispering something to him behind her fan, and he nodded, his grin revealing his distracting dimples.

Cinnamon looked away, disgusted with herself. Why should she care if he was taken with Lucretia? After all, her sister was beautiful with her dark hair and wide blue eyes. Besides, most men preferred women who didn't crowd their heads with knowledge and business affairs. But that wasn't fair to Lucretia at all, Cinnamon admitted. It wasn't her fault she found the captain handsome. And Lucretia certainly didn't know, nor would she ever find out, that this same man had kissed Cinnamon that very morning. Gracious, she'd thought of that kiss again, after promising herself she wouldn't.

Not long after the music stopped, the captain said his farewells, bowing over each lady's hand in turn. When he reached Cinnamon, he managed to turn her fingers so he could see her palm. His eyes lifted to hers, and his thumb gently touched the red welt. She couldn't tell whether he meant to remind her of her baking fiasco or to sympathize with her pain.

The gesture was over in an instant, and he'd moved on to bid good-bye to the count. Lucretia called out a reminder that he was to come to their ball, and their father asked him to return for another meeting tomorrow. Then he was gone.

The door had no sooner clicked shut when her mother caught Patrick's eye. "I can't believe you invited that man to dinner."

"And why shouldn't I?"

"Why shouldn't you?" Cinnamon's mother huffed as she sat down. "He's obvious nothing but a lowly sea captain to whom you shouldn't be exposing your daughters."

"I thought he was very nice."

"You would, Lucretia. I couldn't believe your fawning over that man." Eugenia sniffed delicately.

"Just because *I* prefer handsome men—"

"Lucretia, that will be enough. Do you see what you've done, Mr. Murphy, inviting that man here?" Her mother's stare snagged on Cinnamon. "And I have no idea what you were up to with him."

Cinnamon was ready to protest, though she had some inkling as to what her mother meant. But her father's words put a stop to anything she might have said.

"Well, we all better get used to Captain McGregger's being around. I have decided that he will run Murphy Import and Export."

Chapter 3

"Are you angry with me, Cinnamon?"

"Angry?" She rose from her chair to wander about her father's library. This had always been her favorite room in their Beacon Hill home. The long arm of her mother's garish decorating hadn't extended this far. It was Papa's last bastion of authority other than his import business. At least she had thought so until last night. He'd shocked her as well as the rest of the family with his announcement.

She looked at him now, his brow creased with concern, and swept toward him. Kissing the top of his balding head, she said, "Of course I'm not angry. But I was, still am, surprised." She settled into a leather chair. "Who is this Captain McGregger anyway?"

"I can understand that this might have come as a surprise. But circumstances being as they are—"

"What circumstances?" She was out of her seat again. "Papa, are you all right? Do you feel ill?" Her palm rested on his ruddy cheek.

"Now, now, don't fuss over me," he said, shushing her away with his hands. "I'm perfectly fine. But that doesn't mean I can't use some assistance. The business has grown more than I ever imagined it would."

That was true. Her father had started with only one schooner, which he had captained, and now he owned and leased nearly twenty-five vessels. He'd made his family wealthy . . . very wealthy, and it was a lot of work for one man to oversee such a large shipping empire.

"I've always done what I could to help you." Though

Murphy Import and Export had bookkeepers, Cinnamon reviewed the ledgers. Her father relied on her abilities—at least she'd thought so until last night.

"You've been a godsend," her father said, and Cinnamon couldn't help smiling. "But I realize now I've asked too much of you."

"But you haven't." She knelt by his chair. "I've loved going to the wharf and inspecting the goods, smelling the spices—even imagining myself captaining one of your vessels to the Orient." She laughed. "You know I can't stand doing nothing all day but sit around eating crumpets."

"Yes, I know. And that's why I'd always thought that someday . . . No, never mind," he said, shaking his head. "You were quite right to accept Lord Westfield's proposal."

"Lord Westfield? What does he have to do with this? And what had you always thought? Papa, you aren't making sense."

"It's nothing. Oh, all right. I'd thought to give you Murphy Import and Export one day. None of your sisters would know the first thing about running it. And Lord knows your mother . . ." Apparently her father decided that thought was better left unfinished. "But you, Cinnamon. You are clever enough. It was your idea to expand beyond spices. You've helped make the business what it is today."

She didn't know what to say. She'd never contemplated running the business by herself, yet she hadn't considered not being around to help her father, either. Of course, Lord Westfield would wish to live at his family seat in Devonshire. They would visit Boston, surely. Her mother would see to that. How else could she show him off? But the days of sitting with her father going over bills of lading and studying the market would soon be over.

"You still didn't answer my question about Captain McGregger? When did he come to you with this plan?"

"Ian? Come to me? No, no, you have it wrong there."

"Do I?" Her eyebrow lifted. Her father was an astute

businessman but he sometimes failed to understand that some people were duplicitous.

"Aye. The boy was as surprised as you were yourself when I suggested he might help me run the company then someday take it over. He hasn't even given me an answer yet."

That sounded all well and good, but she wasn't so certain she believed Captain McGregger was as guileless as her father apparently did. But she had no time to question him further, for there was a knock at the door, followed by an announcement that the very man they discussed had arrived.

"Ah, show him back, James. Cinnamon, don't leave. This is a perfect opportunity for you to become better acquainted with Captain McGregger."

"That sounds perfectly delightful," she said as she reached for the doorknob. "However, I did promise Cornelia I'd go visiting with her."

Her father nodded. A bit sadly, she thought as she left the room.

His tall, broad-shouldered frame couldn't be mistaken even in the dimly lit hall. Cinnamon almost turned, deciding the servants' stairs a perfect way to avoid him. Then she suddenly decided against it. She had done nothing wrong. Well, perhaps she shouldn't have allowed the incident in the kitchen to happen, but, still, that was minor compared to him taking her place at Murphy Import and Export.

Standing her ground, or at least her spot on the dark maroon runner, she waited until Captain McGregger and James reached her.

"Miss Murphy," he said, bowing, with only enough sarcasm tainting his deep voice for her to notice.

"Captain McGregger, might I have a word with you?" She dismissed James with a wave of her hand.

His eyes darted toward the closed door leading to the library. "Yer father is expecting me, I believe."

"This will only take a moment."

"I'm at yer disposal, Miss Murphy," he said, bending again at the waist.

Her lips thinned. Thoroughly tired of his bowing and scraping, she crossed her arms. Her foot was tapping when he lifted his head, when their eyes met. She looked away, but she could feel his eyes on her. "Captain McGregger, I owe you an apology."

"And that is?"

This time she didn't shy away from his direct stare. "Yesterday . . ." she began. "I should not have pretended to be someone other than myself." When he said nothing, she continued, "It was rude—"

"And condescending."

She straightened her spine at his audacity, but in the spirit of her apology nodded. "Though I did not mean to be—"

"Condescending," he supplied.

"Yes, condescending." She took a breath. "I realize it may have seemed as if I were . . . to you."

"Is that it, then?"

"What do you mean?" And why was he grinning at her? She found her gaze straying to his mouth, to the dimples in his cheeks.

"I just wished to know if ye were finished, so I could accept yer . . . gracious apology."

No one in their right mind would call her behavior gracious, but she nodded just the same.

"Then allow me to offer one of my own, Miss Murphy."

"That's not necessary." She turned to leave. Perhaps she should have simply escaped up the servants' stairs when given the chance. For there was only one thing she could think of that he might apologize for and she didn't wish to discuss it. His hand snaked out, flattening on the paneled wall, blocking her retreat.

"Now, Miss Murphy, I listened to yer apology. It seems only fair ye should afford me the same opportunity to beg forgiveness."

"I didn't exactly beg." She let out her breath, wishing

she could ignore the heat of his presence, his scent.

"Aye, ye didn't," he agreed readily.

Too readily to her way of thinking.

He dropped his arm but still stood close as if afraid she might bolt at any moment. She didn't dare look at him, but instead stared at the intricately designed silver candelabra on the hall table.

"That aside," he continued. "It was never my intention to be insulting to a woman of yer stature. Ye must know I'd never have kissed ye had I known who ye were."

Well, she should think not, she decided in a huff, only to pause, not entirely certain what to think. So she was good enough—desirable enough—to kiss as a cook, but not as the daughter of the household? Somehow, she didn't find that comforting or at all flattering. She glanced around, then finally looked up at him. He apparently awaited her response.

She had the strongest desire to lean forward and press her lips to his to remind him of their earth-moving kiss. But perhaps that was simply how it had been for her. Anyway, she most certainly would not give in to any of her foolish fantasies.

Stepping back, she forced a smile and nodded. "I accept your apology."

"Good."

"And we need never speak of this again."

"Consider the entire incident forgotten."

How very gallant of him. She caught herself before she berated him for his words. After all, this was what she wanted. Now she could begin a discourse with him without those pesky fissures of guilt and embarrassment clouding the way. Or the memories of how his arms wrapped about her had all but stolen the breath from her body. No need to think on that again. Certainly not. If he could pretend it never happened, then so could she.

"Is there anything else?"

"What? Oh, yes." She swallowed. "I wished to speak with you about your decision."

"Concerning Murphy Import and Export?"

"Yes. Have you—"

"Decided to accept yer father's offer?" His dark eyebrow quirked.

"Well, have you?"

"And would it matter to ye one way or another if I did?"

"Matter?" The word came out a bit breathless and Cinnamon paused to compose herself. She thought he'd moved closer, yet he hadn't taken a step. But she instinctively backed up. "Well, of course if it concerns my father it is of import to me. That only follows. Certainly you can understand—"

"There you are, my boy. I wondered what was keeping you so long, and now I see."

"Papa . . ." she paused. "We were simply discussing—"

"Wedding cake," the captain inserted.

Wedding cake? Her eyes flashed toward him, then back to her father. "Yes, wedding cake."

"I was telling Miss Murphy how much I love cake and look forward to sampling her creation."

"As you shall, Captain McGregger." Her chin lifted. "As you shall. And it will be the best cake you've ever tasted."

"Ye've left me in no doubt of that now, Miss Murphy. No doubt at all."

"Good." She almost stamped her foot.

"Fine. And when can I count on tasting this paragon of cake?"

When? Her mind raced. She would show him she could do this—and soon. "Tomorrow," she announced. "I hope you can join us for dinner then."

"I'd be delighted."

"Well, that's settled," her father stepped forward to say. At first Cinnamon had not heard him as she and the captain stared at each other. But then Captain McGregger bowed, and she excused herself stepping around him and forcing herself to walk sedately down the hallway, when what she wished to do was run.

She heard her father invite the younger man into his library, and wished now she hadn't insisted she couldn't stay to hear their discussion. She wanted nothing more than to know what the captain had to say. Would he decide to take her father's offer? Give up the life of the sea and settle in Boston behind a desk?

She would have thought it an easy decision, since it certainly promised more financial rewards. But there was something about Ian McGregger that made her wonder which he would choose. He had the air of a rogue. She could readily imagine him garbed in a loose-fitting shirt, his black curls blowing in the wind, his eyes crinkled against the sun's glare, staring out to the open sea.

It was an image that stayed with her as she changed into a visiting gown of heliotrope foulard. Nor could she shake the mental picture later as she sat, perched on the edge of a horsehair divan, sipping tepid tea and listening to Miss Elizabeth Shelby espouse the virtues of the English countryside.

"I think it absolutely fascinating that you're to marry an English lord, Cinnamon. Where exactly did you say Lord Westfield's county seat is?"

"What? Oh, the waters off the coast of India, I should think."

There was a silence loud enough for Cinnamon to realize she'd said something utterly foolish. She swallowed, glanced toward Elizabeth, whose mouth was agape as if she were trying to catch flies. Quickly recovering, Elizabeth gently dabbed at her lips with her napkin.

"I'm sorry," Cinnamon said. "I may not have heard the question correctly."

Then using all her considerable inner strength, she vowed to shove Captain McGregger from her mind.

Chapter 4

"Two pounds of flour." Cinnamon used her forearm to brush an errant curl from her face and studied the scrawled words in Queen Victoria's chef's own hand. It did say two pounds, didn't it? She squinted trying to figure out what was written beneath a splotch of dried batter. Yes, two pounds it was, but since she was halving the recipe, she'd go with one.

"Hand me that—that thing for sifting, Biddy," she said, motioning with her head, and loosening the curl again. This time she ignored it.

"Miss Cinnamon, why don't you let me call Cook or one of her helpers out of their room. No one need know."

"I'd know." She scooped flour from the bin, shaking it through the sifter.

"But, Miss Cinnamon—"

"Do be quiet, Biddy. I said I'm . . . I'm . . . Achoo!"

"Oh, Lord bless you, miss."

"Achoo . . . achoo!"

"Goodness, miss. You've come upon a fit of sneezing. Do you think it might be the flour?"

"Achoo! Yes, of course it's the flour." She swiped at her streaming eyes. Fine particles of white hung in the air descending slowly to cover the table and her. "Achoo! Why do you think 'tis necessary to sift this stuff?"

"I'm sure I don't know, miss. I'm a lady's maid, after all."

A fact that Biddy took great pride in, as Cinnamon often noted in the past. Now her lofty position seemed to preclude Biddy even helping her mistress. That was fine, Cinnamon decided. After all it was she and she alone who insisted upon baking this cake when the staff had at least three women whose sole job was to feed the family.

If only she hadn't told everyone she could do it, she thought as she rubbed the butter into the flour—the remaining unsifted flour. It was a slow process, one that made her arms tired and her back hurt, but she persevered. For it wasn't really "everyone" that concerned her.

She'd told Captain McGregger she'd have the cake baked by tonight. She'd invited him to dinner because of it. What had she been thinking? He already knew that she'd failed once. For some reason she didn't want that to happen again.

She dragged the wooden spoon through the thick mixture with renewed determination. He would eat wedding cake tonight, and she'd make certain the captain thought it was the best cake he'd ever eaten.

Feeling more empowered, she washed the currants, setting them in the gas oven to dry. She found several cinnamon sticks, smiling to herself as she caught their scent, then began grating them. It really was very clever of her parents—her father really—to name her for the aromatic spice. As it happened, her hair was nearly the same color. And she liked her name so much better than the stuffy names her poor sisters were forever saddled with . . . "Ouch!"

"What is it, miss?" Biddy, who'd been seated at the table absently making designs in a thin layer of flour, glanced up. "Have you hurt yourself?"

It was only her determination never to raise her voice that kept Cinnamon from screaming at her maid. Instead, she clenched her jaw and stared down at her bleeding finger. "I suppose I should have been more careful."

"I should say so, miss. Do you want me to bandage it for you?"

"No." She tore a strip of fabric from her apron and wrapped it around her finger. "That's all right. As a matter of fact, why don't you go take out my green taffeta? I plan to wear it tonight."

"Oh, miss, I couldn't leave you here all alone. It's helping you, I am."

"True." She emptied the grated cinnamon into the batter. "However, I really do want everything to be perfect tonight, and I think that gown may need brushing." She remembered the currants drying in the oven, and whirled to open the door, stopping herself at the last moment, and wadding a section of her apron to use rather than her bare hand.

The currants were perfect, plump and fragrant. The sight of them forced any lingering pain from her mind. Assuring Biddy that she really could handle this alone and that she was much more concerned about her gown, she added the currants to the batter.

Candied orange peel was next and the walnuts she'd shelled and chopped earlier. More pleased with herself than she could say, she scooped sugar from a bin, blending the granules into the mix. She added yeast and set the mixture to rise, then settled back in a chair. This really wasn't so difficult. Of course she wouldn't let Captain McGregger know that. No, he must think her the most talented of young ladies to create a confection as totally perfect as her cake would be.

Deciding not to make the same mistake twice, she stayed in the kitchen, carefully watching the clock as the cake baked. Wonderful, mouth-watering smells filled the room as she removed her masterpiece from the oven.

While waiting for it to cool, she began the icing. She had a moment's confusion when she couldn't recall which was the sugar bin. The flour she could distinguish easily, but there seemed little difference between the sugar and salt bins. A quick taste was all that was needed to tell them apart, which is what she probably should have done when making the cake. But, no, she was certain she'd used the correct ingredient. Yes, of course she had, she thought as she blended the sugar and butter.

Any doubts were dashed as she added rose water, then beat the cream until it peaked prettily. Decorating the cake was not as easy as she had thought. But she decided her cake looked passably good when she finished. Besides, the test would be in the tasting, and she could hardly wait for that. She set the cake in a cool, dry spot away from the window and slowly climbed the stairs to her room.

Priding herself on her energy, she rarely napped during the day, but this afternoon she decided to succumb to the lure of her bed. No sooner had she rested her head on the pillow than she was asleep and dreaming.

Her cake. She could see it clearly, sitting atop a large table in the center of the garden. The scent of roses filled the air, vying with the wonderful aroma of freshly baked cake.

It was her wedding day, and she wore a magnificent Worth gown, similar to Princess Beatrice's. Ivory satin and Brussels lace, trimmed with orange blossoms, her gown was superb. She greeted her guests as a gentle breeze off the harbor played with the yards of her tulle veiling falling from a crown of flowers.

An orchestra began playing and her heart fluttered, for she knew her new husband would come to her. She felt his hand as he led her to the dance floor for the first waltz. She could hardly wait to feel his strong arms around her.

"Aren't they divine?" came a comment from the crowd of well-wishers. "Surely they were made for each other," another said.

She smiled, filled with joy, and wishing to share her happiness with her husband, she lifted her lashes—and froze.

Her eyes popped open and she bolted upright, fully awake. Her breathing harsh, she stared around the room, *her* room, assuring herself that it had only been a dream and nothing more. She wasn't in the garden. She wore no gown of lace and satin. It wasn't her wedding day. And she most assuredly hadn't married *him.*

Relief made her weak and she flopped back on the embroidery-edged pillow. But she feared shutting her eyes in case the image returned, for she didn't even want to *dream* that she was wed to Captain McGregger.

"I must have a word with you, Cinnamon."

Smothering a sigh, she patted her upswept hair, dressed with roses and seed pearls, and adjusted the wispy curls framing her face. She turned on the bench seat before her lace-covered dressing table to face her mother. "What is it, Mama?" she asked, after dismissing Biddy with a nod. She wouldn't need the girl until later tonight when she undressed.

Her mother waited for the maid to depart, then marched farther into the room, not stopping until she reached the row of windows on the far side. There she turned, faced Cinnamon, and clasped her hands at her waist.

"I understand it was you who invited Captain McGregger to join us for dinner this evening."

"Yes, I did." Cinnamon stood, smoothing her green taffeta gown. "I hope you don't mind but—"

Her mother sighed heavily, making no pretense of hiding her displeasure. "I really don't think he is the kind of man we should be entertaining, as I believe I mentioned the other night."

"He may be managing Murphy Import and Export."

"I realize this is difficult to understand, given that your father seems to regard him as a social equal. However, I must look out for what is best. You can't imagine what a strain it is on my nerves having five daughters.

"I worry all the time that we will be unable to provide suitable matches for all of you. Eugenia is no problem, of course. She couldn't have found a more delightful husband. And you, Cinnamon." Her mother stepped forward in a flutter of silk, taking Cinnamon's hands in her own. "A duke! Well, I simply couldn't be more pleased."

"I'm glad, Mama."

"Of course you are, dear." Another sigh. "But there are your sisters to worry about. Cornelia is not as . . . well, as attractive as she might be. Oh, I don't for one minute mean she's not perfectly lovely. But . . . Well, finding her a husband as suitable as yours and Eugenia's may prove a challenge."

"Mother, I'm certain Cornelia . . . She has the most beguiling smile."

"Yes, yes, of course." Her mother turned away. "Then there's Lucretia."

"What about Lucretia? No one can deny her beauty."

"That is exactly the problem." Her mother looked back at Cinnamon over her shoulder. "Because she is so beautiful, she is vulnerable to the wrong sort of man."

"You mean Captain McGregger."

Relief seemed to wash over her mother as she sank onto the windowseat. "Exactly. I knew you would understand why we cannot have men like him accepted into our social circle."

"Mama." Cinnamon took a step forward. "It appeared to me that it was Lucretia who . . . Well, Lucretia seemed quite taken with the captain." A turn of events that Cinnamon didn't mind in the least. At least she'd been telling herself that for two days. "I didn't note any untoward behavior from Captain McGregger."

"But then being only twenty, you are not entirely wise in the ways of worldly men, are you?" A touch of steel had crept into her mother's tone. "Lucretia did nothing but respond in a pleasant way to that man's advances."

"If you say so, Mama," she agreed for the sake of family harmony. But she had eyes in her head and she'd seen the way Lucretia had nearly tossed herself at the captain. She'd also noticed a measure of restraint on his part. But all that made no difference in the long run, for her mother demanded that she not invite the captain again, and she could do nothing but comply.

"Your fiancé's simply the most delightful man, is that not true, Cinnamon?"

She rested her fork across her dinner plate before answering, partly because she couldn't think of another way to respond other than she already had—numerous times. The entire evening was a series of her mother's flowery descriptions about a man she'd never even met.

Her mother had discussed Lord Alfred Westfield's wealth in great detail, and his family history to such a degree that if Cinnamon didn't know better she'd think him next in line for the throne. Mama had complimented his appearance, making him seem nearly as handsome as, well, as Captain McGregger. And now she strove to make him out to be the most charming of men.

As much an exaggeration as all the rest, Cinnamon admitted to herself, though to the company she agreed with her mother.

"Well, I must say you seem less than enthusiastic about the man you will wed in less than two months, Cinnamon. I was under the impression when you returned from England that you were madly in love," her mother finished petulantly.

Cinnamon felt the captain's gaze and couldn't help her own eyes being drawn to his. He stared at her with an emotion she couldn't fathom.

"Mrs. Murphy, I dare say, our Cinnamon grows tired of discussing Lord Westfield. Perhaps we should—"

"Nonsense, Mr. Murphy. How could she not wish to speak of her beloved?" Her mother puffed herself up, her ample breast expanding above the décolletage of her mauve gown. "Isn't that correct, Cinnamon? Cinnamon?"

"What? Oh." She tore her gaze away from the captain's blue-eyed stare. "Yes, of course," she agreed, though for the life of her she couldn't recall what had been said. But it hardly mattered, for the last course was being cleared and a manservant was bringing in the cake she had baked that afternoon.

Much of the icing had run down the sides, pooling on the crystal platter, but she decided that was just a minor drawback. For very soon Captain McGregger would take his first bite of her delicious concoction. Then he'd be forced to admit . . . She wasn't certain what he'd admit. But he'd know she'd done it—baked the perfect cake.

A maid sliced pieces while her father, sisters, and Captain McGregger admired her handiwork. She could hardly contain herself. She thought the portions a bit small, especially the captain's, but decided it would be worth it when he begged for a second piece.

All assembled waited until the dessert plates were positioned and Mrs. Murphy lifted her silver fork. Anticipation made Cinnamon slow to place her own bite on her tongue. She was too interested in the captain's reaction. It came about the time her own lips closed over the morsel of wedding cake.

Chapter 5

He swallowed the bite, and that was to his credit, Cinnamon thought, because that was not an easy feat. "My heavens," she managed to croak as she grabbed for her water glass.

"What's wrong with this? Mama, it tastes awful."

"There, there, Philomela, it isn't all that . . . What is in this cake, Cinnamon? I hope you don't plan to serve this to the duke."

"Of course not, Mama," she answered, after draining the water from her glass. Though she didn't know why the duke's taste buds were any more precious than hers, or Philomela's, or even Captain McGregger's. He sat across the table from her trying to hide his grin. She would have tossed the contents of her glass at him had there been a single drop of water left. She couldn't remember ever being so thirsty—or embarrassed.

"Well, what happened?" her mother demanded.

"I'm not certain. No, Papa, don't eat it. Really, it's awful."

"Cinnamon, dear, it couldn't be as bad as all that."

"Yes, Papa, it is."

But it was too late. He was already closing his lips over the fork tines. She watched until his eyes began to water, then balled up her napkin, plopped it on her plate, and mumbled a request to be excused. She made it out of the dining room and to the first step of the stairs before she heard her name.

"Miss Murphy."

She paused, her hand upon the newel and shut her eyes. Why did he, of all people, follow her? "If you'll excuse me, Captain McGregger, I really must—" Must what? She sighed as she turned to face him.

Standing as she was on the step, she was nearly level with him, could stare him straight in his mirth-filled eyes. "What is it you wish? I believe I gave everyone, including you, sufficient time to make light of my cake."

"Even me?" His dark eyebrow lifted. "Did I say anything about your cake, then?"

No, he hadn't, but he'd been thinking it. She was certain of that. Still, she tried to modulate her tone. She didn't want him knowing how upset she was. "How may I help you, Captain?"

"I wish to seek yer advice."

That was hardly what she'd been expecting. "My advice?"

"Aye. Do ye suppose we could speak privately? Could I perhaps call on ye tomorrow, or whenever 'tis convenient?"

"Well, yes, tomorrow would be fine. In the afternoon or morning." She had thought he planned to criticize her baking abilities, of which he knew better than her family, but instead he appeared perfectly serious about discussing something with her. What it was, she didn't know, for at that moment, when she would have asked, her mother appeared in the dining room doorway.

"Cinnamon?" She marched forward like a general preparing for battle. "Whatever are you doing standing in the hallway like this?"

"I was—"

"*I* was explaining to Miss Murphy what might be the problem with her cake. 'Tis a simple enough mistake really. One I've managed myself a time or two."

"You are a cook?" Her mother said it as if the words left as bad a taste in her mouth as this evening's dessert.

Strange as it seemed, Cinnamon had the strongest desire to come to the captain's defense. He didn't stand a chance against her mother. No one, not even her own father, did.

However, Captain McGregger didn't seem to realize the peril he was in. He simply smiled that smile Cinnamon was beginning to realize made her stomach feel fluttery whenever she saw it. "Not anymore, but I cooked my share when I was younger. On your husband's ships," he added.

With a "humph" her mother hustled the captain back into the dining room. Then she accompanied Cinnamon up the wide stairs to her room.

"I don't know what you were thinking, Cinnamon. Meeting with that man, unchaperoned."

"Captain McGregger was simply—" Telling her what the problem was with her cake. Cinnamon thought she had that figured out. One taste, one salty taste, had been enough.

"And that's another thing. This silly notion about baking your own wedding cake—"

"Only as a test. The actual cake itself will be—"

"I really don't care. The entire scheme is ridiculous. The very idea of you in the kitchen, beating and mixing, and . . . and . . . Well, I should think you can see now how very foolish it is."

"Foolish to mistake salt for sugar, perhaps."

"What?"

Cinnamon whirled to face her mother. "That's all I did, simply mistook one for the other. Everything else worked out. No fire, nothing."

"Fire?" Her mother settled down onto the dressing-table bench. "Whatever are you talking about?"

"Nothing, Mama, really. It's just that next time I shall bake it perfectly."

"Next time?" Her mother was on her feet. "Do you mean to say you plan to continue this debacle?"

"If you mean, am I going to bake this cake, the answer is of course I am. I said I would. I always do what I say I will. Would you have me fail at this?"

"Ohhh. Whatever am I to do with you? You are such a vexing child." She crossed her arms, then took a deep breath. "I told your father naming you Cinnamon was a mistake. I wanted Theodora, but, no, he insisted you should bear the name of a spice. A spice." She sighed. "And, see, I was right."

"Mama, I hardly think my name has anything to do with . . . well, with anything."

"Humph. I should think it does. The very idea. I can't believe I allowed him to have his way."

Cinnamon couldn't believe it, either, knowing her mother as she did. Kathleen Murphy had a way of wearing a person down. But Cinnamon was exceedingly glad Papa had stood his ground with her name. She didn't feel like a Theodora at all.

"Well, I suppose it isn't too bad. Lord Westfield didn't find fault with your name. Didn't you tell me that?"

"Yes, Mama," she answered through clenched teeth. She should hope he had no objections, with a name like Alfred Henry Charles Augustus Westfield.

"Then I suppose all is not lost," her mother said, assuming her lecture pose, her chin high, her eyes leveled on her prey. "However," she began, and Cinnamon realized she knew there would be a "however." "You must stop this foolishness with the cake. And Captain McGregger . . ." She shook her head as if she couldn't think of enough terrible things to say about him.

Then she marched toward the door, her bustle swaying in time to her steps. "Take a moment to compose yourself, then please join us in the parlor. I believe Philomela has a surprise planned for us on the piano."

That hardly induced Cinnamon to hurry. Yet she found herself, before too many minutes passed, descending the stairs, her cheeks freshly pinched, her coiffure patted into place.

But he was gone.

Not that Captain McGregger was the reason she'd hurried last night, Cinnamon assured herself the next morning. She'd simply wished a word with him concerning when she could expect his visit. She hoped it would be in the afternoon while her mother was visiting, then spent the morning fretting about why he didn't appear. He hardly seemed the lay-abed type. She could imagine him aboard ship, rising with the sun, facing the east and the new day with . . .

"Oh, drat, what do I care how he faces anything," she muttered as she read a row of figures. Each time, she got a different sum, which wasn't like her at all.

She despaired of ever reaching the correct answer when there came a polite tapping at the door.

"Captain Ian McGregger to see you, miss. Should I show him to the parlor?"

"Yes." Her hands automatically flew to her hair. "No, wait, James. Show the captain in here." Yes, the library would be infinitely better. Less likely her mother would chance upon them there. And though Cinnamon had learned years ago the best way to ensure family harmony was to do as her mother said, she also knew a thing or two about *appearing* to do as Mama said.

Cinnamon remained seated behind her father's desk, a fact that she thought brought a smile to the captain's face when he entered. Or perhaps he simply smiled at her.

"Thank ye for seeing me today, Miss Murphy."

"Of course, Captain McGregger. Please be seated."

They both acted so politely distant, it was difficult for Cinnamon to recall they'd shared a passionate kiss—until she looked at his mouth. He did have an extraordinarily fine mouth, firm lips with brackets on either side that gave him character and . . . "Oh, I beg your pardon."

"I said I realize how busy ye are, so I'll get right to my point in coming."

"Busy, yes, I am." Her gaze followed his to the desk where papers were spread. She straightened a pile only to notice the ink on her fingers. Why hadn't she washed her hands? And why did she care?

"I've come to ask yer advice and perhaps for yer help, Miss Murphy. As ye no doubt know, yer father has made me a very generous offer."

"He's told me." She also knew the captain had yet to give Papa an answer. "He seems to have much confidence in your abilities."

"Aye, he does." The captain leaned forward. "And that is where the problem lies."

"I don't understand."

His grin was self-effacing. "I'm not sure I see myself as he does. Do not mistake me. I know I can captain a ship with the best."

"Oh, really," she couldn't help injecting with a lift of her eyebrow.

He chuckled. "Would ye have me full of false modesty, then? I'd have thought ye'd appreciate a person who is aware of what he can do as ye yerself are."

"I'm hardly that."

"Oh, really," he said, mimicking her. "It seems to me a woman who can help run a business such as Murphy Import and Export, who can make up her mind to bake a wedding cake, and—"

"Let's not discuss the cake, shall we?"

"Does this mean ye've given up, then?"

"No." She realized her tone was unnecessarily firm and softened it. "No, I shall bake that cake." She opted not to add, "if it's the last thing I do," deciding it sounded too melodramatic.

"Good," he said, smiling again. "And I hope I'm there to taste the results of yer labors."

"We shall see," was the best she could do. "But I'm certain you didn't come to discuss cake."

"Nay. 'Tis my own problem that concerns me at the moment. I've had very little formal schooling since I spent most of my youth on board a schooner. And I'm wondering how good I could be in assisting yer fine father." He shifted in his scat. "He puts much store in yer skills and I was hoping ye could look at mine and give me an honest assessment."

"You wish mc to judge whether you are competent enough to accept my father's offer?"

"Aye, that's about the size of it. And if ye find me capable, a bit of help with learning the ropes would be appreciated."

She looked at him, astonished. Perhaps the man didn't realize how much she disliked him, if indeed she did dislike him. There were moments when she couldn't decide. Certainly he should never have kissed her. No, never. But then she should have told him who she was. That, however, was neither here nor there now.

It didn't matter if he'd kissed her ten times, or twenty, she would do what was best for her father, and her continuing to help him with Murphy's Import and Export would, of course, be best. But since that wasn't possible, perhaps Captain McGregger was the next best thing. And she was being given the opportunity to discover the truth for herself objectively, with a completely open mind. The idea of leaving Boston and Papa didn't seem quite so repugnant.

"Yes, of course, I shall be glad to help you, Captain McGregger." She had a sudden flash of how difficult her assignment might be. He did say he lacked schooling. Lifting a paper from the pile on the desk, she handed it to him.

"A bill of lading," he said. "From the *India Queen*, my vessel, by the look of it."

"Yes, it is." Good, then he could read. "I've been adding the numbers."

"So I see." He stared at the column a moment. "But if ye will pardon me for saying, I think ye've made a mistake.

It appears to me it should be eight thousand nine hundred aught seven.''

''Really?'' She rose and circled the desk, looking over his broad shoulder at the figures written in her neat hand.

''Aye. If ye add four hundred and seventy-two to one thousand two hundred and eighty-five then six hundred and thirty-four and nine hundred and twenty-seven . . .'' He continued down through the numbers almost faster than she could keep up. ''The answer is eight thousand nine hundred aught seven.'' He turned his head to look up at her and she realized how close they were, and how drawn she was to get closer still. She stepped back abruptly.

''I thought you said you were unschooled.''

'' 'Tis formal schooling I lack. Ciphering has always come easy. A way to spend those lonely nights at sea.'' He stood, suddenly very tall and powerful before her. ''Counting the stars in the heavens.''

Did he really do that? Stand on the ship's deck, a freshening breeze ruffling his black hair, singing in the sails, his legs spread against the ship's sway, his face turned toward the sky? She could see him so clearly in her mind's eye, could hear the gulls squawking.

Gulls? She blinked, realizing it was excited voices she heard—Cornelia's and Lucretia's. She moved away from Captain McGregger as her sisters burst through the door.

''There you are, Cinnamon. We've been looking everywhere for you.''

''Ohhh, and Captain McGregger. I didn't know you were here.''

''Stop flirting with him, Lucretia, and show Cinnamon the post,'' Cornelia said. ''It's so exciting. Do tell us again what he looks like.''

''Who?'' Cinnamon grabbed for the letter her sister waved in front of her face.

''Why, the duke, of course. Your fiancé. That's who the letter's from.''

Cinnamon's gaze caught the captain's for a moment before she looked down at the heavy vellum sealed with the duke's crest.

Chapter 6

September seventh. Cinnamon read the date again and sighed. The duke and his envoy would arrive in Boston for a three-day visit exactly one month before their scheduled nuptials. A month that he planned to spend on a hunting trip in the West. The land of savages, he called it. Alone. Not that she wished to accompany him. She was far too busy.

She lifted the watch pinned to her bodice and let the duke's letter flutter to the table. There really was no need even to keep it. She'd memorized its few lines nearly a week ago when it had arrived.

Her mother acted as if the duke's missive contained words of love and fond wishes to see his fiancée's face again. Cinnamon laughed at the very idea as she smoothed the grosgrain skirt of her afternoon dress. There was a tap at her door and she smiled. The captain was right on time.

In the library, they reviewed shipments of ice for the last year. It was normally boring work, but Cinnamon found sharing the task with Captain McGregger made it much more interesting. He sat diagonally across the desk from her, his head bent, a lock of black hair tumbling over his forehead. He'd pushed it back two times, and she resisted the urge to do it for a third.

"Do you have any questions?" she asked, trying to pull her mind back to the business at hand.

He glanced up and swiped at his hair again. "I don't think so. The cargo seems to allow for a decent profit."

True enough, and a fact she imagined he knew before

she had shown him the records. "It isn't just your questioning your ability to become my father's successor that's worrying you, is it?"

"I'm afraid I don't—"

"You're not certain you wish to give up the life of a sea captain."

His grin made her light-headed. "Very astute of ye, Miss Murphy. But then I've never doubted ye were a smart lass."

"Tell me about it. Your life at sea." She leaned forward, the ledger books forgotten.

" 'Tis freedom and adventure. No two voyages exactly alike. There are typhoons that come out of nowhere, and pirates with giant curved swords, and seas as high as this house to conquer." His eyes, bright with memories, met hers, then sobered, intensified. "And there's endless ocean and a loneliness that can swamp a man and make him long for something he's never had."

She forgot to breathe. She was so absorbed in his words that at first she could almost feel the spray on her face, taste the salt air, and experience this man's desire and pent-up passion.

"Oh." When reality returned, she sucked in air and shifted in her seat, trying to regain control. "Well, then." Her gaze snagged on the ledgers open on the desk and she flipped the page, pointing to the head of the next column. "I suppose we should get back to work."

Though he readily agreed, she could not concentrate on what she was doing. Her mind kept wandering to thoughts of balmy sea breezes—and of him.

Cinnamon checked the tilt of her green felt hat. Fetching, she would call it and just the exact shade to bring out the tiny flecks of green in her hazel eyes. Actually it was Captain McGregger who had pointed that out to her one day when she met him at the docks. But she had to agree he was right as she hurried down the stairs.

Her father was in the library, tapping his foot when she entered. "Did I keep you waiting long?"

"Well, I did tell Captain McGregger we'd meet him by half past one."

"And we shall," she said, standing on tiptoe to kiss his cheek.

But she hadn't counted on her mother descending the stairs at the precise moment they headed for the front door.

"Mr. Murphy, a word with you, please."

Cinnamon thought she saw her father flinch, but he had a pleasant demeanor when he turned to face her mother.

"Of course, Mrs. Murphy. I would be only too delighted to speak with you, but unfortunately I'm already late for an appointment."

"And you're taking Cinnamon with you?"

"She desired the fresh air."

"Fresh air, indeed." Her mother continued down the stairs. "Do you think I don't know where you two are going?"

"To the docks, Mama. We are visiting Murphy Import and Export." Her mother had never kept secret that she thought Cinnamon's involvement in the "business," as she called it, was beneath her. But her father usually won out on this front. Besides, Cinnamon made certain that she limited her activities to times when she wasn't expected to be doing something socially acceptable. At least she'd tried to do that and had succeeded fairly well . . . until lately.

"And I suppose you will meet Captain McGregger there."

There was no question in her voice, and Cinnamon feared her mother already knew the answer. It appeared her father did, too. He straightened his shoulders.

"Now, Kathleen, we've discussed this. The boy will take over running the business when I retire. It's in your best interest that he knows what he's about."

"And is it also in my best interest for him to steal one of my daughters away?"

"Mama, I don't think the captain has any interest in Lucretia.'' Cinnamon realized this didn't put her sister in a very good light and quickly added, ''Or she in him.''

''It's not Lucretia who concerns me, young lady. And do not try to shush me, Mr. Murphy. I know exactly what you are trying to do. Such a vexing husband you are, and after I've worked so hard to pull this family up to its rightful position in society.''

''What did Mama mean?''

They were in the carriage, slowed by a line of horsecars wending their way toward the docks. Cinnamon could smell the salt and the tar in the air, and she could imagine the scent of spices from far-off India.

''About what?'' Her father seemed too intent upon his watch chain stretched across his generous paunch.

''You know what I'm talking about. Mama and her remark about Captain McGregger stealing one of her daughters. It's obvious you two have had words.''

''Your mother and I are always having words, in case you hadn't noticed, Cinnamon. Her latest suggestion is that we pack up lock, stock, and barrel and move to Back Bay.''

''I'm well aware of Mama's desire to have us situated in a mansion like Mrs. Randolph's. As I'm also familiar with your desire to change the subject. We were speaking of Ian McGregger.''

Her father sighed. ''Your mother thinks I've devised some nefarious scheme to throw you and Captain McGregger together.''

''I see.'' She could hardly deny she'd ever thought of the captain in a romantic way, any more than she could deny they'd kissed. Still . . . ''I'm betrothed to Lord Westfield.''

''As I've pointed out to your mother.''

''Well, yes, I should hope so.'' She felt her face grow warm and twisted her head to the side, hoping to catch a whiff of breeze, as well as hide the blush she theorized was the cause.

''But you know your mother,'' Patrick said, stretching

his legs out as the coach started off again. "She can't seem to get the notion out of her head."

"Perhaps I should talk to her," Cinnamon offered, glancing toward him before continuing her appraisal of the granite warehouses lining Atlantic Avenue. "I'm certain I could convince her that there is . . . Well, I find no fault with Captain McGregger, certainly."

"Most assuredly," her father agreed.

"He seems an upstanding enough man."

"Courageous."

"Yes, yes, that, too."

"And certainly a fine specimen of a young fellow."

Her eyes narrowed. "No one is denying that the captain is very handsome." For the first time she wondered if her mother was right. Could Papa have planned her meetings with Ian McGregger? Shaking her head, she continued, "But the fact is I have no involvement, romantic or otherwise, with Captain McGregger—other than what benefits Murphy Import and Export." Period.

She was forced to remind herself of those words as the coach rolled to a stop and Captain McGregger himself opened the door. She'd never seen him in his maritime garb and she had to admit he was a sight to behold in his deep blue jacket, double-breasted over his wide expanse of chest. No paunch there, generous or otherwise. He looked rugged and incredibly handsome, with his black hair curling around the sides of his captain's hat.

Cinnamon felt as if the air were suddenly charged, like before a thunderstorm. But the sky was blue, with nary a cloud in the sky.

"Ah, Ian, my boy. I hope this doesn't mean you've made up your mind to return to the sea." Her father gestured at the captain's clothing as he lumbered down the coach steps.

"No, sir. I merely thought I might show Miss Murphy . . . and ye, too, sir, the *India Queen*. Miss Murphy mentioned the other day that it has been years since she toured a clipper."

"Excellent idea. Excellent. Don't you agree, Cinnamon?"

"Yes." For some reason she was having difficulty speaking. She delicately cleared her throat, deciding she needed to forget all this nonsense about Captain McGregger. Her father was incapable of devising any plot to throw the two of them together, even if he desired it. He knew she was pledged to marry another as did Captain McGregger. So that was the end of it.

Except that after the three of them spent over an hour walking through the warehouse, inspecting shipments of jute from India, and after Cinnamon assured them that she would enjoy a tour of the clipper, her father pleaded fatigue and insisted they go without him.

"Papa, I really don't think I should leave you here alone."

"Alone?" His laugh didn't sound fatigued. "I've all my workers about me. Oh, the years I've spent on these docks. No, Cinnamon, I'll not be alone."

But she would be. Alone with Captain McGregger. That was nothing new, of course. They'd been working together in her father's library off and on for nearly a fortnight. They'd talked and laughed, and she'd discovered that contrary to his lacking a formal education he was extremely knowledgeable about many things. His awareness of geography and history amazed her.

But that didn't mean she wished to walk with him steadying her arm as they crossed the gangplank.

They inspected the quarterdeck and cathead where the anchor was stored when not in use. He explained the importance of storing the sails correctly and of his fear that the days of sailing ships were limited. Cinnamon knew her father already had steamers traveling to the Orient. They were faster, could use the Suez Canal, and didn't have to depend upon the fickle wind. All in all superior vessels, though not nearly as romantic as the clippers, they both agreed.

It wasn't until they were belowdecks, in the captain's quarters, that their talk grew more personal.

"I see ye wore it. The hat," he added when Cinnamon glanced up from one of the charts spread out on his desk.

"Well, of course." She tried to keep her tone neutral. "I had to wear a hat."

"But ye didn't have to wear that one, I'll wager."

"I happen to like this hat."

"So do I. As ye well know."

Her fingers fluttered to the brim, caressing the felt, before she looked away. "It's just a hat."

"That's like saying the *India Queen* is just a boat, I'm thinking."

"Well, no one could say that," she countered, smiling. Their eyes met, held, before she forced herself to turn away. She picked up a brass telescope, put it down, then picked it up again.

"Don't you think Lucretia is lovely?" she asked after a moment of tension-filled silence, which she couldn't explain.

"Lucretia? Yer sister?"

"Yes. She's very pretty, don't you think?" She was watching him now, noting his shrug of indifference.

"Aye, I suppose she is."

"Suppose? Why? What's wrong with her?"

"Nothing. There's nothing wrong with her."

"Then I don't understand why—"

"Why I don't find her appealing?"

She sighed deeply. "Yes."

"Perhaps 'tis just that I'm not a man to appreciate dark curls. Maybe I'm fonder of hair the color of cinnamon," he said, taking a lock of her hair and twirling it around his finger.

"You mustn't do that."

"What? Touch yer hair?"

"Yes . . . I mean no." She could feel the whisper of his warm breath on the back of her neck. His nearness sent gooseflesh racing along her skin. "We aren't talking about my hair."

"I am." His fingers curved down to her chin, applying just enough pressure to turn her to face him. "And yer eyes and yer mouth." He leaned closer.

"We really shouldn't." Her body zinged with anticipation.

"Aye, ye've the right of it there."

"I'm promised to another."

"I'm all too aware of that."

"Please don't."

" 'Tis only a kiss."

"Only a kiss," she repeated as his lips pressed hers. But somehow as her body melted against his, as her arms wound about his neck, she couldn't think of what was happening as "only" anything.

His tongue touched hers and the earth seemed to tilt. His large hands molded across her back and she thought she might swoon. He whispered her name against her freshly kissed lips and she forgot all reason.

Chapter 7

Eggs.

A cake needed eggs.

Cinnamon stared at the pans of flat, gloppy goo and her shoulders drooped. Why couldn't she get this right?

Lord Westfield was expected tomorrow afternoon. She'd spent the entire morning in the kitchen, working hard, only to pull from the oven another failure. Was it too much to expect that she could bake a simple cake?

Her gaze was drawn to the basket of eggs on the table. They were right there. Why hadn't she added them to the batter?

"Oh, for heaven's sake," she muttered, whipping off her apron and tossing it to the brick floor. This was becoming ridiculous. She had an idea that she knew what the problem was—or at least what she'd been thinking about while she should have been beating eggs. Ian McGregger.

She stomped out of the kitchen. She couldn't keep him out of her mind, and she couldn't stop thinking of the kiss. But there was more. She hadn't followed through on what she said she'd do.

He'd asked for her help, her advice, and she'd agreed. She'd even decided to tell him she thought her father very clever to have picked him to run the business. Captain McGregger was perfect.

Then came that kiss. The second kiss. And because of her silly female foolishness, which she had always prided herself on not having, she had been unable to do what was best for Murphy Import and Export. For a week now she had vacillated, unable even to face the captain.

Now in her room, she sighed, then sank onto the bench in front of her dressing table. Her elbows on the polished surface, she cupped her cheeks, staring into the looking glass.

After dinner tonight she would tell the captain that he must accept her father's offer, and this would be the last time she saw him before Lord Westfield's arrival.

Her mother's excitement at the duke's imminent arrival dulled her temper toward the unwanted guest at the dinner table. She had been tolerably polite when Captain McGregger arrived, Cinnamon noted, and she hadn't even raised an eyebrow when Lucretia asked him if he had received the invitation to the ball for Lord Westfield.

When he told her he had, Lucretia batted her dark lashes at him. "Then, you will come, won't you, Captain?"

"Aye," he answered, his gaze momentarily snagging Cinnamon's. " 'Tis my intent."

"How wonderful."

"Have you ever been to Italy, Captain? The region around Florence?"

Cinnamon paused, her fork midway to her mouth, as the captain answered. Her brother-in-law had asked him the same question the first time they'd dined together and the captain's response had brought the same long dissertation on the count's illustrious family.

Was that all he spoke of? Since he had been in residence in the Murphys' Beacon Hill house, Cinnamon had heard little else from the count. Her eyes strayed to her older sister, wondering if she too had noticed this particularly boring habit and found Eugenia's attention directed elsewhere.

Did all her sisters find Captain McGregger so appealing? Somehow the idea did not sit well with her at all.

Thankfully, no one mentioned the wedding cake, or lack there of, as the dessert of pastries and custard was served. She'd mentioned it to the captain in her dinner invitation. A silly error on her part, and one she would not commit again.

As a matter of face, she was beginning to wonder if she should give up the idea of baking it altogether. Resign herself to failure. Resign herself period.

"It is difficult for me to believe that tomorrow evening we will finally meet your duke, Cinnamon. How excited you must be."

"What? Oh, yes, Mama, I am."

"Is he very handsome, Cinnamon?"

"Yes, Lucretia. Very."

"And he's very rich."

"I suppose he is, Cornelia."

"Will we have to call you Lady Cinnamon?"

She laughed. "I don't think so, Philomela."

"Do you love him, Cinnamon?"

Her fork clattered to the plate as she turned to stare wide-eyed at her father.

"What a silly thing to ask, Mr. Murphy. Of course she does. The very idea. Our Cinnamon is marrying a British duke." Her mother squared her shoulders. "A man of impeccable lineage. A man who will do our family proud. Open doors for all our daughters." Her corseted body quivered. "How could she not love him?"

That said, her mother stood, her chin high, and announced it was time to retire to the parlor. "We must leave the gentlemen to their cigars." Her eyes narrowed on her husband. "And their discussions."

As Cinnamon followed her sisters from the room, she heard Count Lorenzo launch into a soliloquy of his own heritage, and she hurried her step.

When the parlor doors opened a half-hour later, Philomela had plowed her way through most of Tchaikovsky's Piano Concerto no. 1. Papa entered, Count Lorenzo by his side, followed by Captain McGregger. Cinnamon waited until everyone's attention returned to her sister's playing, then slipped from her seat to walk toward the far window.

Spreading her painted silk fan, she sank into the closest chair, knowing Captain McGregger would come to her. Through her lashes she watched as he pretended interest in the music, then backed away. He appeared almost surprised to see her when their eyes met.

"Miss Murphy," he said, bowing. "I wish to thank you for your invitation to dinner."

He sounded stiff and formal . . . and more than a little angry. She'd refused to see him several times since their tour of the *India Queen*. Each time he visited, she had instructed James to say she was not at home, and she had little doubt that the captain had seen through her ruse. On Wednesday he'd ceased calling.

"You're more than welcome, Captain McGregger." She glanced at the group across the room. Her sisters listened with an obvious lack of enthusiasm to the count. Philomela pounded stirring chords from the piano, and her father seemed intent on keeping Mama occupied, appearing to hang on her every word as she prattled. Cinnamon supposed it was either about tomorrow's distinguished visitor or her plan to move the family to Back Bay. Whichever, she was glad for her mother's lack of attention.

"I wish to speak with you," Cinnamon said, keeping her voice low.

"Ye can't say I've not given ye the opportunity," he countered, anger coloring his tone. He stood very close to her now as he lifted aside the heavy drape to peer outside. The tulle of her skirt brushed against his pant's leg.

"I—I've been quite busy."

"Preparing for the arrival of yer duke?"

"Among other things, yes." She softened her tone. She didn't want to argue with him. "I think you should accept my father's proposal. You are more than qualified to run Murphy Import and Export."

When he said nothing, and only looked down at her, she continued, "Certainly, this cannot surprise you. Your attributes are obvious. There really never was any question of your competence." She breathed deeply. "You are familiar with sailing and the marketing of goods. You—"

"Why are ye telling me this now?"

"Why?" She fluttered her fan, feeling the need for a bit of air. His scrutiny seemed to raise the temperature in the room to beyond bearable. "Well, you asked my opinion if you recall. I am simply giving it."

"Ye wish me to stay in Boston, then?"

Hardly that. She didn't think she could manage seeing him often and not . . . And not what? She wasn't certain. But then she wouldn't be seeing him anyway. She'd be in England, in some remote shire married to Lord Westfield. She closed her eyes. When she opened them, he had looked away, again staring into the night. His strong profile held her attention.

"Ye didn't answer yer father ye know." He glanced down at her.

"It was a silly question."

"Yet one with a simple enough answer."

An answer she couldn't admit. Not to him. She lowered her head, watching as her fingers traced the fan's spine. "I tried to bake the cake again today."

"Yer wedding cake?"

"Yes." She glanced up, a slight smile curving her lips. "I forgot to add the eggs. Can you imagine? It really didn't turn out at all well."

She thought he might say something. Make light of her culinary talents, or chide her for her poor memory. Something. But he only looked at her, his eyes saying more than words could ever convey. More than she could bear to face.

Cinnamon hardly recognized him and was stunned that her memory of the duke had faded so quickly. She remembered him as taller and more broad-shouldered. How silly of her.

"Do tell us about your trip, Your Grace. That is how I should address you, is it not? I do wish to be correct."

"That will be fine, madame." Alfred Westfield lifted his teacup. "The trip was tolerable, I suppose. Long."

"I'm sure it was," her mother agreed, sending a knowing glance to Cinnamon, who sat on the settee across from the duke. "But then I'm sure anticipation of what lay ahead kept you anxious."

"Certainly." He sipped the tea, then pursed his lips. "I've always wished to see the American West. Hunt the buffalo." He leaned toward her mother. "See the savages."

"The savages? But . . . but . . ."

"Didn't I tell you, Mama?" Realization hit her that she probably hadn't. "Lord Westfield is taking a hunting trip before the wedding."

"But . . . but it's less than a month away."

"There'll be plenty of time." Cinnamon tried to keep her voice calm in contrast to her mother's agitated tone. She was beside herself, and Cinnamon felt a pang of guilt for not preparing her. She hadn't kept her fiancé's itinerary a secret on purpose. It had simply slipped her mind.

"But what of the ball? The parties I've planned? When will Boston meet you?"

"Ah, yes, the ball. I've already spoken with Miss Murphy concerning it. I will be in attendance," he added with a benevolent smile.

And as for the parties, Cinnamon hadn't been aware there were any. Though now that she thought about it, she should have known. Mama would never miss this opportunity to flaunt her royal son-in-law-to-be.

"There will be plenty of time, Mama. After we are wed." Cinnamon tried to catch her betrothed's eye, but he was busy choosing an iced cake. "Surely we won't leave for England immediately."

"What's that?" He took a bite, pursing his lips again before pushing the plate on the side table. "Oh, yes, returning to England. Mustn't stay away too long, you know. My chums want me back."

"Chums?"

"Friends. The gents I hunt with. Charming lot. I don't think you've met them. Oh, except for Lord Percy."

"Yes, I remember Lord Percy." Remembered and didn't particularly like.

"Anyway, we go to Scotland every year to hunt. Frightful fun." He went to pick up the cake, apparently thought better of it, and brushed his fingers on his napkin. "Of course this year we've had to delay the trip a bit, what with . . . this." The sweep of his hand seemed to include Cinnamon, her mother, the parlor . . . perhaps all of Boston.

"Well, Your Lordship, I'm not certain my daughter will be up to a hunting trip so soon after the ocean voyage."

"Miss Murphy? Hunting? Now that is rich," he said with a laugh. "Wait till I tell Percy." He sobered, then sniffed, wrinkling his long nose. "My dear Mrs. Murphy, there are no women invited on our hunting trips."

"But . . . but what will she—"

"Do you dislike the cake, Lord Westfield?" Cinnamon asked, interrupting her mother who seemed befuddled. "You give it such foul looks."

"It is a bit dry, Miss Murphy, now that you mention it. Nothing at all like the creme cakes at home."

"They must be wonderful," her mother gushed.

"Very." His eyes crinkled. "I can almost taste them now."

Had he contorted his face so much in England? Cinnamon couldn't recall. She also didn't know what imp took hold of her voice. Before she could stop herself, she was expounding the virtues of the cake she planned to bake.

"You? You are baking a cake? This is a joke, is it not?"

"No." Cinnamon straightened her shoulders. "Actually it isn't."

He brushed her words aside with another wave of his hand. "Well, no wife of mine will ever work in a kitchen."

"Oh, I'm sure Cinnamon would never dream of cooking once she's Lady Westfield," her mother hastened to say. "This is just a little amusement of hers. You understand how young girls can be, surely?"

The duke agreed with her mother, both chuckling, and as soon as Lord Westfield made his excuses and departed, Cinnamon rushed to the kitchen.

Chapter 8

The ball was actually given by Matilda Cowen Randolph at her mansion in Back Bay, because the Murphy house on Beacon Street could not accommodate all the *crème de la crème* of Boston society. At least that's what Cinnamon's mother lamented over and over again.

Cinnamon wondered, during any spare moment she had, if Papa would end up relenting to her mother's repeated demands that they move. Not that it affected her. She'd be far away . . . in England.

"Don't sigh, Cinnamon. It's unbecoming a lady."

"Yes, Mama." She nearly rolled her eyes but decided her mother would find that even more common.

They were upstairs in the bedroom Mrs. Randolph had set aside for their use. "It was so wonderful of my dear Mrs. Randolph to host this ball for you and your duke."

"Yes, it was," Cinnamon agreed, though she thought Mrs. Randolph's generosity had been spurred more by the idea of receiving royalty than by friendship.

"Stand back and let me look at you, Cinnamon."

"What about me, Mama?" Cornelia asked.

"And me? Cinnamon already has her duke. We are the ones you should be making sure look perfect."

"Now, Lucretia, you all are as lovely as pictures." Her gaze swept over Cinnamon and her three sisters. "And don't any of you worry yourselves about husbands. Your older sister married a count. And now Cinnamon has Lord Westfield. Opportunities for you girls abound." She fluffed the satin bow spilling over Philomela's shoulder. "Why, I wouldn't be surprised if, thanks to Cinnamon, you all wed noblemen."

This pronouncement met with the expected titters of excitement from everyone but Cinnamon. She tried to disguise her lack of enthusiasm by turning toward the cheval looking glass. Leaning forward, she examined the mauve crescents beneath her eyes. She wasn't sleeping well and didn't like thinking about the reason. But she couldn't help herself. How could she go through with this marriage to Lord Westfield? And why did thoughts of Ian McGregger confuse her so?

"I've already said you look lovely, Cinnamon." Her mother peered over her shoulder, catching Cinnamon's eye in the looking glass. "You were right to choose the apple green faille. Yes, yes," she said, her hands fluttering. "I know I advised against it. But now that I see it on you I agree completely. Truly elegant, as befits a duchess."

"I'm not a duchess yet, Mama."

Her mother's laugh was high and brittle. "Just a matter of time, dear. His lordship is obviously in love."

A statement Cinnamon thought utterly ridiculous, but she said nothing. After all, she wasn't in love with the duke. Or with anyone, she reminded herself when a pair of blue eyes and a devilish grin came to mind.

"Now come along, all of you. It's time we go down to the ball. Where is that father of yours?"

Mrs. Randolph's mansion was much larger than their own house and even more elaborately decorated, which Cinnamon usually found a bit distracting. However, tonight, bathed in candlelight and every available spot filled with greenhouse flowers, it did seem like a fairyland.

Cinnamon entered the ballroom, her mother on one side, her father on the other. Strains of a waltz played by an orchestra seated on the raised platform at the far end filled the perfumed air. As soon as they were announced, Lord Westfield excused himself from a group of young gentlemen and approached.

He looked handsome enough in his formal attire, and for a moment Cinnamon remembered how she had felt when they first met. He was pleasant, attentive, attractive. Had she really thought that that was all there was to a man?

She forced a smile, accepted his flatteries, and together they joined the other dancers. He twirled her about and she had to admit he was an excellent dancer.

"Of course we won't be using such barbaric weapons as bows and arrows, don't you know."

"What?" Cinnamon blinked, realizing she hadn't the faintest idea what Lord Westfield had said. Something about his trip, about leaving two days hence, but after that, she couldn't say. She'd been too busy scanning the dancers as she moved. "I'm so sorry, Lord Westfield. What did you say?"

"Just speaking of the savages, but no matter. It is noisy in here. Can easily understand your difficulty." He lifted his chin, glancing around in that superior way of his. "It appears our hostess did not know where to prune her invitation list."

"I believe my mother provided the list."

"Well"—he looked down at her—"there you are."

She opened her mouth to ask exactly what he meant by that, but the music stopped, the duke returned her to her family, and she decided it was probably best she didn't know.

Her father, who danced robustly, escorted her through the next set. Then her brother-in-law claimed his place on her dance card, and, still, she'd not caught sight of Captain McGregger.

Not that she was looking for him, she told herself. Yet she was surprised he'd failed to make an appearance.

The evening was warm, and more than once she glanced longingly toward the open glass doors leading to the terrace and beyond to the gardens. Hundreds of lanterns, strung from the trees, illuminated the grounds.

Her father finally suggested they step outside, and Cinnamon took her first breath of fresh air that evening.

"So, are you enjoying yourself, my dear?" Her father rested his thick hands on the balustrade and tapped his foot.

"It's a lovely ball."

"Which doesn't answer my question, now does it?"

She leveled her father a look. "Yes, I suppose I'm enjoying myself. Is that the answer you want?"

He shrugged. "I was just looking for the truth."

"You, Papa, are trying to be difficult."

His laugh shook his jowls. "I suppose you're right." He turned, lifting his head to view the mansion behind them. "Big, isn't it?"

"Quite. Are you planning to have one like it built?"

"Well, now, I don't rightly know. I'm kind of partial to the brick house on Beacon Hill, but I know your mama wants something like this." He folded his arms. "Blames the fact that we don't for some of the Brahmins not showing up tonight."

"Those old-money snobs." She laughed. "Well, they're missing a grand time." Her demeanor sobered. "I really don't care. Do you?"

"No." He leaned back. "But your mother does."

"I know. But she'll have her very own family duke soon."

"Is that why you're marrying Westfield? If it is—"

"Papa, no. My betrothal to—"

"What is it?" Her father turned to follow her gaze. "Ah, Ian, my boy, there you are. Didn't think you were coming."

"How are ye, Mr. Murphy, Miss Murphy?"

"We're doing very well. Cinnamon and I were just discussing the ball. Would you call it a success?"

He chuckled. "For a lonely sea captain from the Highlands it seems grand enough."

"And since you mentioned grand, I have to say, you look grand yourself, my boy. Doesn't he, Cinnamon?"

"Yes." An understatement if she'd ever spoken one.

"Thank ye both. And may I return the compliment, Miss Murphy. 'Tis obvious again that green becomes ye."

Her smile reflected his own.

"Now look at you two young people standing here talking with me when there's music playing and dancing to be had. Go along with you."

"Papa, I believe this dance is promised." Cinnamon fiddled with her dance card, nervous at what Captain McGregger must think having her foisted on him.

"Well, whoever it is hasn't the gumption to come looking for you so I'd say 'tis his loss."

"Would ye do me the honor, Miss Murphy?" The captain extended his hand and she had no alternative but to take it. He escorted her inside, placed a white gloved hand at her waist, and guided her into the circle of dancers.

"I fear I'm not very adept at this."

"You're doing fine."

"Strong praise, indeed."

Cinnamon raised her eyes from the front of his shirt and the corners of her lips lifted. It was hard to ignore him when his strong arm encircled her, when his scent enveloped her. And when he smiled at her that way. "Where did you learn to dance, Captain?"

"The same place ye learned to bake, I imagine. Self-taught."

"Well, you must have had a better teacher than I. Last evening I did everything right . . . I thought." She sighed. "But the cake flopped. Flat as a pancake."

"Did ye open the oven before it was done?"

"I thought I should check."

"Next time wait till ye can smell it." He grinned down at her. "Good smells, mind ye. Don't wait for the scent of something burning."

She laughed, then abruptly became serious. "I can't seem to get it right." Her eyes narrowed. "And don't tell me to stop trying. I want it perfect."

"Have I told ye to give up?" He waited till she shook her head. "And I won't. 'Tis too important, Cinnamon."

Were they talking about baking the cake? All of a sudden she wasn't certain. But they must be. What else was there? "Captain, I—"

"Ian. My name is Ian. Remember, I've given up my ship."

"Yes, but . . ." She paused and smiled up at him. The idea of saying his name was so appealing. "Ian." She tested lightly, pleased when his hand squeezed hers.

The strains of the Strauss waltz floated around them, and suddenly Cinnamon felt as if she too were floating. She stared into his eyes, those blue eyes, that reminded her of the sea, and faraway places, and freedom. She whirled about the room, safe in the cocoon of his strong embrace. Just the two of them.

Then the music died away, the last notes echoing into nothingness before they separated.

"Cinnamon, there you are."

Tearing her gaze away from Ian's, she nearly cringed when she saw her mother rushing toward her, Lord Westfield in her wake. Luckily she and Ian were near the edge of the dance floor. Still, she had the impression that people were staring.

"I told His Grace we would find you, and here you are." Her mother gave Captain McGregger a look of dismissal which he ignored. "Lord Westfield has something to tell you. Well, here she is."

"So I see." The duke stared down his long nose at her mother. "Though there really was no urgency. I simply wished to take my leave, Miss Murphy."

"So early?"

"Yes, I fear tomorrow will be busy. Plans for the hunting trip, you know."

"Of course."

"But I shall call on you in the afternoon if that is satisfactory."

"Certainly. I shall look forward to it." A movement beside her reminded her of Ian's presence, though she certainly had not forgotten he was there. "Lord Westfield, allow me to present Captain Ian McGregger. Captain McGregger, His Grace, Lord Alfred Westfield."

"Captain McGregger." The duke's tone was condescending.

"Lord Westfield." The captain's was frigid.

"I understand you're in Mr. Murphy's employ."

"He is to take over the management of Murphy Import and Export," Cinnamon rushed to say, then knew by the expression on Ian's face she shouldn't have.

"How very interesting, I'm sure." Lord Westfield gave a tight smile. "Have you ever been hunting in the West, I wonder, Captain?"

"Nay, I haven't had the pleasure."

"Well, perhaps when I return I shall tell you of my adventures."

Ian bowed stiffly and excused himself. Cinnamon wanted to tell the duke that if he really cared about adventure, he should listen to Captain McGregger. Tales of the South Seas, of pirates and mutiny, now that was adventure. But she didn't think Ian would thank her for it. So she simply watched him wend his way through the crowd, away from her, his broad shoulders rigid. She had a near uncontrollable urge to chase after him. To tell him . . . What? There was nothing she could tell him. A tight smile on her face, she turned toward the duke . . . and her future.

Chapter 9

"Captain McGregger!" Cinnamon's flour-covered hand flew to her hair. "What are you doing here?"

"It was Ian last night," he said, smiling. "And I took a chance ye might be here and came round the alley to the kitchen entrance." He waited, his eyebrow lifting as she stood in the doorway, blocking his way, staring at him. "May I come in, then?"

"What? Oh, yes . . . of course." She felt a blush steal over her already-flushed face as she opened the door wider to let him in. His presence seemed to fill the room.

She watched as his gaze swept over the kitchen: the flour spilled on the floor, the broken eggs, the oozing glob of batter seeping around the broken bowl which she'd accidently dropped. At least, she told herself, it was an accident. When his blue eyes finally lighted on her, she was near tears.

"I can't seem to get it right," she managed to choke out before his arms came around her. "I've tried and tried." She sobbed into his jacket. "But there's always some mistake." She shifted her head, staring up at him through misty eyes. "What is the problem?"

"Ye'll have to figure that out on yer own, I'm afraid." He thumbed away a tear spilling over her lashes. "But I will help ye bake the cake. If ye wish, that is?"

"You'd do that?"

"Aye, Cinnamon. For ye I would."

"That's—" She bit her bottom lip. "I don't know how to thank . . ." Her voice trailed off as the intimacy of their position hit her. Wrapped in his arms, their bodies pressed together, their lips close enough that their breath mingled, she knew exactly how he'd like to be thanked. How she would like to thank him.

"Well, then." She tried to steady her racing heart as she pushed away. "I suppose we should get started."

"Aye. Started." Ian took a deep breath. "Do ye know where a broom might be? And a dustpan? Never mind, I see one."

She almost asked why he needed a broom, but he was already showing her, sweeping up the mess covering the brick floor. When he had most of it in a pile, he motioned to her, then to the dustpan. Shrugging, she squatted to scoop up the debris.

"Where's yer little maid?"

"I sent her away," she answered as she dumped the floury mess. "Too many questions and, well, she never has liked the kitchen. Oh, no." She stepped toward Ian, reaching out to brush his jacket. "You've gotten yourself dirty."

He gave his coat a few perfunctory swipes, then took it off.

"I'd say the flour's from ye." He glanced at the bodice of her gown which was powdered white. "And I don't mind."

Of course he got himself messed up while holding her, and, of course, she hadn't minded the contact, either, though she knew she should. Just as she knew she shouldn't be watching as he stripped off his waistcoat and rolled up the sleeves of his crisp white shirt. But she couldn't seem to help herself. She found him so appealing to look at. Without the camouflaging fabric of his jacket, his muscles seemed even larger, his shoulders broader. The expanse of his sun-tanned arms, dotted with dark curly hair, nearly took her breath away.

He glanced up catching her watching him, and her face flamed. She whirled, searching for something to do, finally grabbing a wooden spoon covered with batter.

"Cinnamon."

"Yes." She could feel the warmth of his body behind her and struggled to keep herself from melting against him.

"Where's the recipe?"

"The recipe?" She glanced over her shoulder.

"Aye. Ye do have one, don't ye?"

"Oh, yes, of course." She dropped the spoon and shoved aside pans looking for the scrap of paper. She blew at the flour covering the writing, then handed the barely discernable sheet to Ian.

He scanned the list. "Currants?"

"In the oven drying."

"Good." He tilted his head ever so slightly.

"Yes, I suppose I should check them." She accepted the dish towel he handed her, wrapped it around the oven handle, and glanced inside. Smiling, she pulled out a tray of perfectly dried currants, then set them on the table to cool.

He retrieved the bowl into which she had just sifted flour, and waited while she lifted the lid of the butter crock. She added several scoops, looked to him for guidance, and laughed when he shrugged.

"Tell me the truth. Have you ever baked a cake before?"

"Ye want the truth?"

"I just said as much." She mashed the butter into the flour with a spoon.

"Nay."

"Nay?" She looked up, surprised. "But what of the stories you told me? Were you ever even a cook?"

"Cook's mate, I believe was my claim, and that, dear Cinnamon, is true. I've done my share of baking bread and the like, but cakes were not standard fare on the vessels I've sailed."

"I see."

"Shall I leave ye, then?"

"Goodness, no." She laughed. "If we ruin this cake, it shall be together."

"We shan't ruin this one, Cinnamon."

Close to responding with some good-natured quip, she stopped when she saw the expression on his handsome face. She couldn't explain it, but there was something about the set of his strong chin, the light in those sea blue eyes that told her he wasn't referring to the cake.

Ian finished cracking the walnuts while she added the currants, candied orange peel, and apricots. Then together they broke more eggs, separating the yolks.

"Do ye believe I know how to cook, now?" Ian asked after expertly beating the egg whites.

"I suppose I shall have to." She offered him a nut meat as he worked. It wasn't on purpose, of course, but her fingers seemed to linger near his mouth.

"Cinnamon." His voice was so plaintive it tore at her heart. As if she'd been burned, she pulled her hand away.

"Yes, you're right. We need to add the cinnamon." She forced a laugh. "For spice."

When she glanced back, he was laughing, too, and she sighed in relief. She didn't know exactly what he'd been close to saying or doing, but she imagined it was something she couldn't resist.

She added the cinnamon, then sat and watched him crack more nuts. Every once in a while she'd snatch one and he'd pretend not to notice. Then they'd both laugh.

"Are ye looking forward to England? What's Lord Westfield's estate called?" His questions came unexpectedly.

"Salisbury. And, of course . . . I mean, why shouldn't I? It sounds perfectly lovely." When he only nodded, she continued, "It's in the southwestern part . . . Devonshire." Still nothing but the crack of nutshells. "It sounds perfectly lovely."

"Ye said that already."

"Then it must be true," she said, nodding her head. "Yes, it must."

"Cinnamon."

"What!" she snapped. "No, don't tell me. I don't want to hear it." She lifted her floured hands, pressing them to her ears. "I don't."

"Fine then."

"Good." She sliced a scoop into the sugar, then paused, thinking better of it. She stuck her finger in the granules. But before she could taste it, Ian grabbed her wrist. She nearly swooned when his warm mouth closed over her finger. "Oh," she moaned when his tongue swirled about the tip. "Please."

"So sweet." His mouth now traveled toward her palm, and she swayed toward him.

It took all her willpower to pull herself erect and retrieve her hand. "Oh, Ian, you mustn't."

"Why?"

"Because . . ." She couldn't think of a reason at the moment other than the cake. When she said it, he laughed, pulling her toward him for one quick, hard kiss that kept her reeling through the blending of the cake dough.

"It won't be long before it's in the oven, Cinnamon." His words were accompanied by a brushing aside of a tendril of damp hair on her neck. "Then what excuse will ye make?"

Her hands, working the cake batter into the pan, stilled. "Why are you doing this to me?" She turned to face him, her fingers full of goo, her body on fire. "Are you just trying to seduce me? For if you are, you win. I surrender."

"Ye honestly think that's what this is? A seduction? That I'd have my way with ye and then leave?" He tilted his head to the side, staring at her with all the need she felt. "I'm trying to tell ye that I love ye, Cinnamon. That I can't bear the thought of yer leaving. Of yer marrying Lord What's-his-name."

"Westfield. You love me?"

"Aye." He took her hands in his, oblivious to the cake batter. "With all my heart."

"Ohhhh . . ." She sobbed, shaking her head when she saw the concern in his eyes. "No, really, I'm all right."

"I did not mean to make ye cry. Cinnamon, tell me to go away and I will."

"I can't do that. Oh, Ian, I love you, too."

"Ye do?" The beginning of a grin curved his lips.

"Yes, yes, I do." She sniffed. "I have for a long time, but I've been trying to tell myself I didn't. Oh, Ian, what are we going to do?"

"Well, first of all, ye're going to kiss me. Then, I think maybe I'll kiss ye."

"But—"

"Hush now." Ian put his finger to her lips. "We'll worry about the rest of it later."

He pulled her into his arms, taking her hands and carefully licking the batter from each finger. "Better than scraping the bowl," he declared, then leaned down to press his lips to hers.

He tasted of cake batter and Ian, and the combination overwhelmed her. His arms tightened around her, pulling her close. His hands caressed her back, and lower, driving her mad with desire. By the time he drew away, her heart raced and her breathing was shallow. She tried to think, to reason, but all that seemed beyond her.

"What are you doing?" she questioned when he moved away from her.

"The wedding cake," was all he said as he opened the oven door and slid the pans inside. Then he turned to face her. "I think it shall bake up just fine this time. But we really shouldn't stay here now. It could fall if we make any sudden noises," he said as he walked toward her.

"We wouldn't want that." She held her ground, anticipation strumming through her veins. When he reached her, she moaned, clutching his shoulders. His mouth was open and hungry.

"Where . . ." The scrape of his whiskered chin across

her cheek sent chills down her spine. ''Can . . .'' He nibbled the tip of her earlobe and her knees went weak. ''We . . .'' His large hand palmed her breast and her head fell back. ''Go?''

She couldn't think, could only feel. ''The garden,'' she finally managed to say. ''The summer house.''

Before she knew what was happening, he scooped her into his arms and headed outside.

Chapter 10

Cool shadows and whispered promises. Cinnamon knew she would always remember the summer house this way. And sweet, sweet discoveries. They sat on the wicker settee, wrapped in each other's arms, kissing, touching.

Her bodice was spread open, revealing the lace-edged chemise Ian had inched below her breasts. She moaned as he took one nipple, then another into his mouth, suckling, tightening her desire to a fevered pitch.

''Ach, ye're a bonny lass,'' he said, resting his cheek between her breasts. ''And as sweet as any cake ever eaten.'' He lifted his head, grinning when she giggled. ''What? Ye doubt what I'm saying?''

''No, no.'' She sighed. ''It just tickles when you talk against my skin.''

''Tickles, does it? Like this?'' He let his lips slide along her side, moaning himself when she squirmed down farther into his arms.

''Oh, Ian.'' She pushed his cotton shirt from his shoulders, relishing the feel of his smooth, muscled body. ''I do love you.''

"As I do ye, lass." His hands pushed up the folds of her petticoats. His hand trailed from her knee up her thigh and rested on the warm center between her legs. "And how sensitive is yer skin here, I wonder?"

"Ian. What are you . . . Oh." His warm fingers began to stroke her.

She never knew it could be like this between a man and woman. One minute she was laughing. The next she could barely breathe for wanting him.

"Please," she murmured, not knowing exactly what it was she desired. But she could tell he knew, for with every passing moment he took her closer to it.

White cotton billowed to the wooden floor. His shirt. Her pantaloons. She sat on his lap now, relishing the salty taste of his shoulder, allowing him his way beneath her skirts. Then, she shuddered convulsively, awash with erotic sensations.

"Oh my . . ." She sighed. "Oh my, my."

"That's it, then," he whispered, his voice rasping in her ear. "That's all ye have to say?"

"Mmmmm." She looked up at his smiling face. "Do you really wish to talk now? For if you do, I think I can manage to—" The pressure of his lips on hers cut off anything further she might have said, which was just as well as far as she was concerned. He'd given her a glimpse of heaven and she was anxious to see more.

The settee was small and cushioned, capable of seating two comfortably. Not made for lovers. However, a leg draped negligently over a wicker arm, a head cushioned in a corner, somehow they managed to position themselves, his weight on hers.

"Oops. Oh, I'm sorry." Cinnamon laughed. "Did I hurt you?" She'd shifted, catching the side of his jaw with her elbow. She cupped the side of his face, smiling when he assured her she could never hurt him.

"But I fear I shall not be so kind to ye."

"I don't understand." She trailed her fingers down his

wide chest, through the patch of curly hair. Her body hummed everywhere it touched his.

"It will hurt a wee bit I fear, Cinnamon."

"Just a wee bit?" His chuckle reverberated through her chest as she pulled him close. "Then I think we should get it over with quickly."

She barely noticed the discomfort at all, for soon he filled her body as he did her heart. She took him in, accepting all of him, reveling in the idea that they were one. Their loving was slow, sweet, sensual. She didn't know how anything could feel better.

Then his movements grew less languid, her own desires keeping pace, until she could hardly bear the tension spiraling through her. His mouth took hers, hungrily, their tongues mating. His hands dug beneath her, pulling her body even closer to his. Then explosions of light, sugar-fine, shot through her. Stars? The heavens? She couldn't be sure. But she did know it was meant to be, this love of theirs.

Ian felt the same way, for he told her so as he carefully maneuvered himself off the short settee. He pulled her onto the floor with him, leaning against the wicker legs and folding her in his arms.

She lolled, comfortable and replete, against his shoulder, breathing in his manly smell and thinking she'd never been happier. Until a thought popped into her head.

"The cake!" She hurried to rise, tangling her feet in her bunched-up petticoats. "How could I have forgotten?" She glanced down at him, shirtless, his eyebrow cocked, and she shook her head. "All right. It's obvious why I forgot, but now what am I to do?" She hopped about trying to drag first one leg, then the other into her pantaloons, only to stop when Ian's hands came to rest on her shoulders.

"The cake will be fine, Cinnamon."

"But how do you know? Certainly you remember the fire?"

That brought a smile to his face, but he didn't seem inclined to move much faster as he refastened the buttons of her bodice. The graze of his thumb across her breast, intentional if she read his lazy grin correctly, nearly made her forget the cake again. But she pulled herself together and grabbed his arm.

They raced through the garden and into the kitchen. At least there were no flames. With a sigh of relief Cinnamon opened the oven door. Together they peeked inside.

"I simply can't understand why Lord Westfield declined to join us this evening," her mother said for what had to be the tenth time.

Cinnamon felt Ian's hand on her knee and took a deep breath. She supposed the time had come to tell everyone. Well, not everyone, exactly. Her father knew. She glanced at him, but he was thoughtfully examining the silver scroll on his spoon. No help there.

That was hardly fair. Papa had given his blessing to Ian and her this afternoon when they approached him at the wharf. He'd also arranged the meeting with Lord Westfield, who'd taken the news surprisingly well. Or maybe not so surprisingly, Cinnamon admitted. He really hadn't cared for her overmuch. Still, she felt a bit guilty for breaking her promise—and feared what her mother would say.

Cinnamon inhaled deeply again. They were all there, Eugenia and the count, Lucretia, Cornelia, and Philomela. And, of course, Mama.

"I have something to say," Cinnamon began.

"We have something to say," Ian corrected, and Cinnamon smiled at him.

"And I'm sure we all wish to hear it, Cinnamon, dear," her father said, suddenly alert. "But look, they're bringing in your cake."

Two servants carried the perfectly iced cake and placed it near the center of the table in front of Cinnamon. She couldn't help her sudden swell of pride. It looked beautiful. But she knew the proof of the cake was in the tasting.

With a great deal of trepidation she sliced through the cake and handed out pieces. Eugenia and Philomela declined, and Cinnamon could tell Lucretia and Cornelia wished to do the same.

"I'd like a large piece, if ye don't mind, Miss Murphy."

Ian's words gave her courage. She loved him, loved him with all her heart. Nothing else mattered. Not her mother's desire to have her marry a duke. Not her sisters' wish to visit her in England and meet eligible noblemen. Not even the cake.

No, not even the cake.

Cinnamon placed the knife on the serving plate. She had nothing more to prove.

"Mother. Sisters. Count Lorenzo. Papa. Lord Westfield isn't here this evening because I . . . We are not going to wed."

It took a moment for the import of what she said to settle on her family. When it did, there wasn't a closed mouth in the room—except for Papa's and Ian's.

Her mother's voice rose, drowning the others out. "What are you talking about? Why ever not?"

"Because she intends to marry me."

Her mother seemed to notice Ian for the first time. Her eyes widened. "You?"

"Yes, Mama." Cinnamon smiled up at Ian. "Captain McGregger and I have discovered a mutual fondness—love. He helped me bake the cake today."

"It's wonderful!"

Cinnamon turned to stare at her brother-in-law. Apparently he wasn't as interested in family business as he was in his stomach, for he was busy chewing the last piece of his cake.

"It is. It's good, Cinnamon. More than good."

"Well, thank you, Lucretia."

"I love it," Cornelia added.

"Give me a piece," Eugenia said.

"What about me, Cinnamon? Can't I have some, too?" Philomela pleaded.

"Will everyone stop it?" Mama slammed both palms on

the table, sending a wineglass teetering. "This is not about cake. It's about Cinnamon—"

"Marrying the man she loves," her father said, his voice firm. "And this is the best cake I've ever eaten."

Because she hadn't cut herself a piece, Cinnamon sectioned off a bite of Ian's. Their eyes fixed on each other, they lifted their forks to their mouths, then let the sumptuous concoction melt on their tongues.

Delicious.

Perfect.

Like their love.

Chapter 11

The morning clouds blew out to sea, revealing a perfect cerulean sky. October twelfth. Her wedding day. The day Cinnamon had dreamed about since that afternoon when she and Ian had baked the perfect cake.

She smiled thinking about that day and all the happy ones that had followed and of all the wondrous ones to come.

Her fingers had just pulled aside the drapes, hoping for a glimpse of her bridegroom in the crowd gathering in the garden, when someone knocked at her door.

"Come in." She turned, smiling. "Papa, I was hoping it was you."

"Anxious to see me, or is it because I'm to escort you downstairs?"

"A little of both, I suppose." She straightened the long cordon of orange blossoms trailing down her ivory satin skirt. "Is he here yet?"

"I just left Ian, and I must say he seems as anxious as you." Her father took her hands in his. "You are happy, aren't you?"

"I couldn't be more so. Well . . . perhaps if Mama weren't so—"

"She'll come around. Even now I heard her bragging to Matilda Randolph about her future son-in-law, the famous pirate slayer." His fingers tightened. "Don't concern yourself."

"What about the cake?"

He laughed. "Now that is a different matter altogether. Your mother will never understand why you and Ian spent all of yesterday in the kitchen baking your wedding cake. Not when there are cooks perfectly capable of doing it."

But the cooks couldn't add the love, couldn't spice the batter with kisses, couldn't time the baking perfectly by making love, the way she and Ian could.

Cinnamon took her father's arm and descended the stairs. The dining-room doors were thrown open and she could see the wedding cake, hers and Ian's, reigning over the huge mahogany table. The sight added a lilt to her step as she and her father walked into the gardens. Waiting for her near the summer house at the end of the path stood Ian—her love, her perfect mate, her sumptuous bliss.

Christine Dorsey believes in love, romance, and the sensual delights of food, especially the corner piece of a frosted cake. Make that a wedding cake and her mind springs to thoughts of "happily ever after." A single bite can conjure scenes of a first kiss, shared intimacies, and growing old together.

The best-selling author of fourteen historical romances and three novellas, Christine has three children and lives with her husband of twenty-eight years in Richmond, Virginia. She writes her love stories in her treetop office and swears the crumbs you think you see scattered around her computer are all in your imagination.

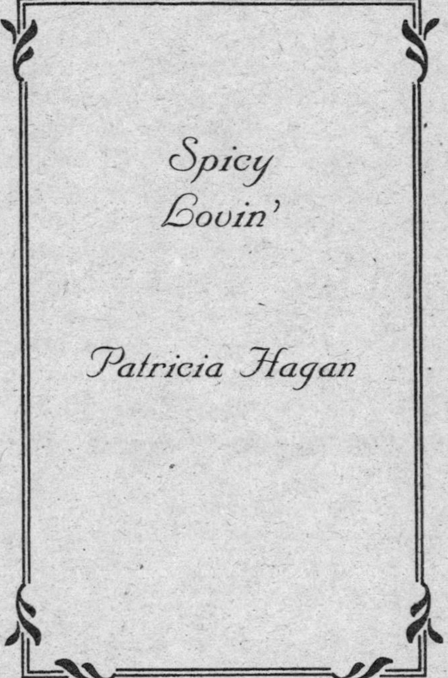

Spicy Lovin'

Patricia Hagan

Pepper's Posole

3 *pounds beef, cubed*
2 *large onions, chopped*
½ *cup olive oil*
4 *pounds hominy*
1 *cup tomatoes, finely chopped*
¼ *cup dried red chili peppers, ground*
10 *cloves garlic, minced*
3 *tablespoons oregano*
½ *teaspoon cayenne pepper*
1 *teaspoon cumin*
½ *teaspoon ground black pepper*
2 *cups water*
Dash of tequila

Take half the amount of beef, onions, and oil and brown until onions are translucent. Remove and set aside.

Repeat with remaining beef, onions, and oil, then combine both batches. In a 10-quart stockpot add hominy, tomatoes, red chili peppers, garlic, all the remaining spices, and water. Bring to a boil. Simmer 1 hour.

Add tequila just before serving.

Serve with chunks of fresh, hot sourdough bread.

Chapter 1

New Mexico, 1875

Not a breeze stirred, nor did the sagebrush and runted little junipers dotting the earth as far as the eye could see. It was as if the life had been scorched from the land as well as everything on it.

Pepper stood outside the cantina's back door, hoping for a breath of fresh air. She sighed, running her hand over her hair tied back from her sweat-drenched face. Sunset had brought no relief from the oppressive heat, which smothered the New Mexico terrain like an invisible shroud.

She pulled her damp blouse and her clinging petticoat beneath her ankle-length muslin skirt away from her heated skin. Barefooted, she preferred risking splinters to wearing her hot, constricting boots during the long grueling hours in the kitchen.

Inside the cantina, the sheep men had gathered. As they did at the end of every grueling day in the sun, they quenched their thirst with beer and tequila, only to parch their throats again by gorging themselves on Pepper's spicy cooking.

She smiled. She was known throughout much of the Southwest for her hot, piquant recipes and her special dish which had inspired her name. And that was just as well since she'd never known her real name, anyway.

As an infant, she had been the lone survivor of an

Apache raid on settlers. Kindly people had found her—sheepherder Valdiz Montez and his wife, Nina. Unable to have children, they were delighted to raise her as their own and had named her Ria which in English meant "silver mouth."

Then one day when she was about eleven years old, an old sheepherder stopped by the Montezes' hut. Having already developed a knack for cooking, she served the old man *posole*, her special chili dish. He had taken a big bite, then gasped and clutched his throat. Tears poured from his eyes as he reached with shaky hands for a glass of water. Her father had leaped from his chair at the end of the table to give the sheepherder hard pats on his back, for the old man seemed to be choking.

When he finally got his breath, he had looked at her and said, "It's wonderful. The best chili I have ever eaten. I just wasn't prepared for it to be so deliciously hot. Never have I had anything like it."

Valdiz and Nina had beamed proudly as their guest raved on, finally pounding his fist on the table, and declaring, "They named you wrong, child. It's not silver in your mouth. It's pepper. And that is what you should be called."

Her parents had thought it was funny and told everyone about it. Before long, Pepper was stuck with the name but didn't mind a bit. She continued experimenting with different dishes, all highly seasoned, and soon her new name was more than fitting. It was *her*.

Now, she walked to the rain barrel and took the long-handled dipper from the hook above. Scooping up the water, she drank deeply as she thought of her pride in running her very own cantina. But it had not come easy.

Hired as a cook by the few well-to-do people in her village of Cuchillo at a very early age, she was paid well, and her mission school training had taught her how to read and write and she knew how to handle money.

Though men pursued her hand in marriage, her father did not insist on her taking a husband. Pleased that she was able to take care of herself, Valdiz was also pleased that the money she earned helped their family.

When she was sixteen, she went to work for Diego Luigis, who owned the busiest cantina in the village. Within a short time, the other cantinas closed, because everyone flocked to Diego's for Pepper's cooking. Though Diego begged for her recipes, Pepper was smart and kept them to herself. The secret was in her spices, which she would not reveal.

When Diego became ill and feared he was dying, he gave Pepper the cantina since he had no family, no one to leave it to. But, most of all, he had told her that he felt indebted to her, that without her, he would not have profited as he had.

Drinking her fill of water, Pepper stared at the expanse of land around her and thought how contented she was, despite the heat and hard work. True, there were times when she was lonely, especially in her bed at night when she wondered what it would be like to have a man hold her in his arms and make love to her.

She had been told often enough by her would-be suitors that she was pretty and that her eyes were like turquoise. One amorous suitor had even gifted her with a pair of earrings made of the lovely stone, which he had brought for her all the way from Mexico.

Though the village men had given up on marrying her long ago and had taken wives, marriage proposals were still offered to her from time to time. Strangers passing through would fall in love with her cooking, then, learning she was unmarried, profess to fall in love with her, as well.

Some had been serious, some not. But she had turned them all down. Unlike other young women, she was not desperate or anxious to have a husband take care of her and protect her in a land that could be brutal and dangerous. She was independent and self-supporting. Besides, she could ride and shoot as well as any man . . . maybe even better than some.

So she did not really need a man, except, perhaps, to

love. But, so far, she had not met anyone who stirred her heart, and until she did, she would remain unwed. No matter how lonely the nights.

As she wiped her wet lips with the back of her hand, she heard an angry voice and then the sound of a chair smashing against a wall.

With a disgusted moan, she turned to hurry back inside. It was not even dark yet and already trouble was starting. It was the same every year at this time. Spring had turned too fast to summer, and the heat was bearing down to make throats thirsty, and too much tequila led to hot tempers.

Entering the back door of the squat, adobe building, Pepper saw that Sanchia, her waitress, had backed into the kitchen.

Her brown eyes wide with fear, Sanchia pointed to the front room. "It's a stranger. A wrangler. He says he is going to shoot Miguel if he doesn't dance for him."

Pushing Sanchia and the curtains separating the kitchen from the main room of the cantina aside, Pepper stepped through the arched doorway. The stranger, probably on his way back after finishing a cattle drive at the end of the Sante Fe trail, was drunkenly waving a gun at poor fourteen-year-old Miguel, a young sheepherder.

"I said dance, *amigo,*" the stranger roared. "Or I'm gonna blow your feet off. I want some entertainment around here. Hell, as much as I spent on whiskey, I oughta get somethin' extra."

"The only thing extra you'll get, *hombre,* is a funeral if you don't put that gun away."

The dozen or so men in the cantina backed away from the boy and the stranger. At the sound of Pepper's voice, they turned to stare at her. So did the stranger. His eyes flicked over her insolently, then settled upon her cleavage, exposed by her off-the-shoulder blouse.

The stranger's mouth twisted in a nasty grin as he licked his lips. "Maybe *you'll* give me somethin' extra, señorita. But if you're as good as you look, I might be willin' to pay you a little somethin'."

Pepper's eyes narrowed. "I said put the gun away."

He sneered. "I don't take orders from no woman, no matter how fine lookin' she is. Now I'll take care of you in a minute. But right now, this stinkin' sheepherder is gonna put on a little show."

Before he could pull the trigger, Pepper had moved with the speed of a striking rattlesnake to retrieve the knife which she kept strapped to her ankle. With a whoosh, it flew through the air hitting the back of the man's hand.

He dropped the gun and stared at the blade protruding from his blood-gushing palm. Then, slowly he raised disbelieving eyes to Pepper. "You bitch! You crazy bitch! You cut me!"

"And I will *kill* you if you don't get out of here and out of this village, right now."

Her head high, she strode toward him, grasped his wrist with one hand, and swiftly yanked out the knife with her other.

He screamed with pain as more blood flowed.

Pepper walked slowly back into the kitchen to wash her knife, and restrapped it in its hiding place. She heard the stranger stumble out the front door, cursing, and the men murmuring about her prowess with a knife, even though they had seen her in action before. She never backed down to any man.

Turning to the big woodstove, she dipped a spoon into a kettle of eye-watering stew made from cactus bits and chopped beef.

She was still standing there long moments later when Sanchia appeared at her elbow. Again, her eyes were wide with fright.

"Sanchia, what is it?" she asked irritably. The girl could be such a baby sometimes. "There's no need to be scared. The trouble is over for now."

"Not . . . not for . . . for Buck," Sanchia said, choking on her words. "For him it is just beginning."

"What's he done?" Pepper didn't like Buck Kiley, but Sanchia was in love with him, so she tolerated him.

While passing through a month ago, he had stopped for supper and then wound up staying with Sanchia in her little room behind the storage shed, at the rear of the cantina. He was a drifter, a gunslinger, and probably an outlaw, but as long as he didn't make trouble and his food and drink were paid for, Pepper let him stay.

"A bounty hunter is after him." Hurriedly, Sanchia explained that Buck had just told her that the drunken stranger Pepper had run off had told Buck earlier that a bounty hunter was on his trail. "He has to leave right away, but we need your help."

"To do what?" Pepper despised bounty hunters, for she had many good friends among the outlaws who visited the village. It did not matter to her what they did elsewhere. As long as they treated her with respect, she responded in kind. Long ago she had learned the only way to survive in this rugged country was to mind her own business.

"We have to stop the bounty hunter when he gets here to give Buck time to get away and let his trail grow cold. I thought maybe I could lure the bounty hunter to my room by making him think he could have his way with me, and then you could bang him over the head with a skillet, and then we could tie him up for a few days, and—"

"And go to jail ourselves," Pepper finished, laughing. "No, we can't do that, but . . ." She paused, chewing her lower lip thoughtfully, then snapped her fingers. "I know a way. Leave it to me."

"What are you going to do?"

Smiling, Pepper repeated, "Leave it to me."

The next morning, Pepper rode into the creekside village, where Owl Woman lived with other Apaches in their declining years, all of whom seldom ventured away from their camp. Too old to be considered a threat, the Indians were left alone to live in peace.

She found Owl Woman tending her herbs which she had lovingly planted along the creek. Her leathery face crinkled as she gave Pepper a toothless grin. "So you need more spices. Good. I am always glad to see you."

Pepper loved the old woman. It seemed she had known her forever, and it did not matter to her that Owl Woman's people were probably responsible for the slaughter of her family. That was in the past. Pepper also knew she owed the success of her recipes to Owl Woman's herbs and spices.

Giving her a warm hug, Pepper explained, "Actually I need something special. There's a bad man I must deal with."

Owl Woman did not so much as quirk an eyebrow as she casually said, "You wish to kill someone? All right. I have something in my hut. Follow me."

Pepper was right behind her, anxious to explain. "No. I don't want to kill him. I just want to make him sick for a few days. *Very* sick, so he is unable to travel."

They stooped to enter the hut. As always, Pepper was amazed by the array of pots and jugs inside. Owl Woman was the village shaman and seemed to have a potion for just about everything.

Owl Woman searched through her stock, finally locating what she was looking for in a dark corner. "Ah. I think this is it. I haven't had a need for it in so long."

Pepper took the tiny, dusty jar from her. "What is it?"

"Buckthorn berries."

"And what will they do?"

Owl Woman's eyes twinkled. "What do you want them to do?"

Pepper was used to Owl Woman sometimes answering a question with a question and patiently repeated her purpose. "I want this man to be too sick to travel for a few days."

Owl Woman flashed another toothless grin. "Oh, he won't go anywhere except to the bushes, child," she cackled.

Pepper smiled. "You mean . . ."

"I do," Owl Woman confirmed. "The buckthorn berries will give him the dreaded trots because he will trot to the bushes for many days to empty his body of them.''

''Owl Woman,'' Pepper cried in delight, hugging her again, ''you're wonderful.''

Without looking inside, she tucked the jar in her pocket and headed back to the cantina. She could hardly wait to make a batch of her famous *posole.* Only it would be a small batch—reserved for a *very* special guest.

Chapter 2

It had been three days since Buck Kiley had left town, and Pepper was glad he wasn't around. Since he and Sanchia had become lovers, Sanchia seldom showed her face before the cantina opened, which meant that Pepper had to do all the work. So it was a relief to have Sanchia's help once again.

''He should be deep into Mexico by now if he rode day and night,'' Sanchia mused aloud as she gathered cleaning supplies. ''He said it was a good place to hole up for a while. Bounty hunters don't like to go there, because the Mexican lawmen don't cooperate with them. I'll just be glad when it's safe for him to come back,'' she added wistfully.

Pepper knew it was said of her that sometimes her tongue could be as spicy as her *posole,* but she could not resist saying, ''Then I hope it's never safe.''

''Why do you say that? I love Buck. And he loves me. We've even talked about getting married. He says he'd settle down in one place if we did.''

''Sanchia, you are so pretty. You can have your pick of nice men. Why do you bother with Buck? I just don't trust him, and, besides, he has a terrible temper."

"He's good to me."

Pepper was at the stove frying beef in a big iron skillet. "I think it's the other way around. *You* are good to *him.* You let him move in with you, and lately you've been paying for his food and drinks. He's no good, Sanchia, and if I were really your friend, I'd be helping the bounty hunter instead of Buck."

Sanchia grabbed Pepper's arm. "No. Please don't do that. You mustn't. You have to help Buck . . . and me. I love him, don't you see?"

Pepper sighed. "Yes, I know, and I said I'd help you, and I will. But I'm still hoping that a miracle will happen, and you'll come to your senses and see Buck for what he is and find someone else."

Sanchia kissed her cheek. "So what have you decided to do about the bounty hunter? I still like my idea about banging him over the head with a skillet," she said, giggling mischievously.

"And I told you I have a better idea—one that will keep us out of jail."

Sanchia clapped her hands in little-girl delight. "Tell me. Tell me."

Pepper's mouth curved into a smile. "Just believe me when I say that by the time the bounty hunter feels like trailing Buck, Buck will be as far away in Mexico as he can get."

"Someday I'll make this up to you. I promise."

Pepper good-naturedly pushed Sanchia through the curtains so she could prepare for the cantina's opening in a few hours. Tables had to be cleaned and the floor swept. Beer kegs had to be checked, and bottles of tequila had to be brought from the storage room in the cellar. And glasses. So many glasses to be washed.

Pepper began chopping onions which made her eyes burn, and soon tears were streaming down her face. But she didn't care, for she loved to cook.

She added the onions to the olive oil and stirred methodically as she continued to brood over Sanchia. She did so hope that if Buck returned he would be good to her.

With the beef browned and the onions cooked, she added hominy, red chili peppers, and an array of spices.

"Oh, that smells so good," Sanchia said on her way to the cellar. "The men will be happy to know you're serving your famous *posole* this afternoon."

"This isn't for them. See that you don't serve it to anyone. Not even a spoonful."

Bewildered, Sanchia paused. "Then who is it for? Your family?"

"No. It's for our guest."

Sanchia blinked. "What guest? I don't understand."

"The bounty hunter."

Sanchia realized then what she meant and matched her smile. "Ah, so this is your secret. You're going to poison him."

Pepper looked at her, aghast. "Good heavens, Sanchia. I'm starting to think your being around that desperado, Buck, has made you as violent as he is. I'm not going to poison anyone. I'm not going to kill anyone. I'm merely going to keep the bounty hunter here long enough for Buck to be safe. Now stop such foolish talk and make sure you don't serve the *posole*, understand?"

Sanchia nodded and continued down the cellar steps.

As the *posole's* aroma grew stronger, Pepper decided she should take no chances that Sanchia might forget and serve it. After all, it was Saturday, and the crowd would be larger than usual. Some of the men would smell the *posole* and demand to have some, and Sanchia might become unnerved and not remember the warning. Should that happen, the results would be disastrous, so Pepper divided the batch into two pots, adding the dried buckthorn berries only to one.

Then she put the jar of berries away in the special cabinet where she kept similar types of jars containing all of her herbs and potions. Owl Woman had taught her many things, and Pepper was known as a medicine woman in her own right, parceling out tonics and remedies to the villagers.

When Sanchia returned from the cellar, her arms loaded with bottles of tequila, Pepper told her she had changed her mind and she could serve the *posole* to the customers. "But dish it out from the pot on the front of the stove," she emphasized. "Leave the one on the back alone. Don't serve that. Understand?"

"That's for our guest, right?"

"Exactly. And don't forget to add a splash of tequila to the *posole* once you've spooned it into a bowl."

When the cantina closed that night, the only *posole* left was that which had been set aside. "Our bounty hunter didn't show up," Pepper said to Sanchia as she threw it away. "Maybe tomorrow."

But he did not come the next day, or the next, and when a week passed, Sanchia whined that maybe the stranger had lied and there was no bounty hunter. "Buck left for no reason," she cried.

Pepper continued to make the *posole* daily just in case. Besides, the untainted batch always sold out, for it was the first thing customers asked for.

Then one night Sanchia burst into the kitchen, her face flushed with excitement as she grabbed Pepper by her arms. "He's here," she whispered. "It's him. I know it is."

"He? Who?" Pepper's attention was on the food she was dishing up.

"The bounty hunter," Sanchia hissed. "He's in there. I know it's him. He's asking all kinds of questions."

"About Buck?"

"No. About the village."

"What kind of questions?"

"What difference does it make?"

"None, I suppose." Furrowing her brow, Pepper hurried to the curtains and peered around them.

Crowding to stand beside her, Sanchia said, "See? That's him. The one in the corner."

The tall man with the blond hair did not have to be singled out. He stood out like a chili pepper in a cup of cream. His denim shirt stretched across broad shoulders and a muscled chest. Tight denim pants emphasized well-defined buttocks and strong thighs. He wore a double holster, boots, and a felt hat. He was cleanly shaven, except for a neat mustache and sideburns.

He was, Pepper decided with a little rush, a ruggedly handsome man. Not that she cared about his looks, of course. If he were indeed the bounty hunter, then she despised him.

"I'll go talk to him," she said, wiping her hands on her apron. "You finish preparing these tortillas."

He was sitting at the end of the bar nursing a glass of tequila.

"Hello, stranger." Pepper slid onto the stool next to him. "Welcome to Cuchillo. So how do you like our little village?"

He raked her with vibrant green eyes that made her shiver despite her wariness of him.

"I'm liking it better by the minute," he said lazily. "You must be the one they call Pepper. I can see why." His gaze went to her red hair.

"I'm called Pepper because of my spicy cooking," she said, her pulse quickening at the way he was looking at her. "This is my place. So who are you?"

"My name is Brand Austin." He tipped his hat.

"And what brings you to Cuchillo?" She wanted to discover quickly whether he was the bounty hunter so she could feed him the chili and be done with it. She did not like the strange way he made her feel, as if she were tottering on the edge of a yawning precipice.

"Maybe I'm a cattleman," he said quietly.

"A cattleman?" she asked sharply.

"You got something against ranchers?"

"Only cattle ranchers, señor." Her tone was frosty. "This is sheep country."

"But it's *big* country."

"It makes no difference. There's still not enough grassland and good water for both sheep and cattle.''

He took a sip of the tequila. ''Well, if everybody tried to get along—''

She slammed her hand on the counter. A few men sitting nearby jumped at the sound, but quickly returned to their meals. ''The first thing the ranchers do is put up fences,'' she said angrily, ''and if it means cutting off the water source for a sheepherder, they don't care. Besides, sheep can adapt to rough terrain and exist on foliage too sparse for cows. And they don't need nearly as much water.

''So we don't need cows here, señor,'' she finished, her face hot with her anger. ''And if you are a cattleman, then you will not be welcome in Cuchillo.''

''But you don't have any cattle. You've got this cantina. Why should you care?''

''My family are sheepherders. So are many of my friends. I have no use for cattlemen.'' She spun on the stool, ready to leave.

''Don't go. I like your company.''

''I don't wish to talk to a cattleman.''

''I didn't say that's what I am.''

''So what is your business here?''

He was quiet for a long moment, then said, ''I'm just looking around.''

Pepper's interest stirred. ''Well, if you're looking for something—or someone—in particular, maybe I can help. Everyone comes and goes through my cantina.''

He glanced around. ''Looks like all kinds, too. Sheepherders. A few cowboys working the Sante Fe Trail. Maybe even a few outlaws.''

''Are you looking for an outlaw?''

''If I were, it wouldn't be too smart of me to say so, now would it?''

''It depends.'' She made her voice as soft as a caress. ''Tell me who you're looking for. I may know him.''

He studied her for a moment, then shook his head. ''I don't think that's a good idea right now.''

She clenched her teeth. He was being cautious, not wanting to tip his hand. After all, he couldn't be sure Buck wasn't there and wouldn't take off once he knew a bounty hunter was in town. Still, she couldn't take chances, either. One of Buck's enemies—and she didn't doubt that he had a few—might have heard that Buck had gone to Mexico and then told Brand Austin.

She had to act fast.

"Are you hungry, señor?" she asked politely. "I'm known far and wide for my *posole,* a kind of chili served only here in New Mexico. My recipe is very special. You'll never forget it."

"Nor does anyone else from what I've heard," he answered. "And, yes, I am hungry. I'd love to have some."

"Well, this is your lucky day. I just happen to have a little bit left tonight."

With the sweetest smile she could muster, she slipped off the stool and hurried into the kitchen.

"Is it him?" Sanchia asked, watching from behind the curtain.

Pepper sniffed the air. "Oh, you've burned the tortillas!" Rushing to the stove, she saw that not too much damage had been done. There were a few that were still edible. "Here, go and serve these."

"But is he the one looking for Buck?"

"Yes. Now go. Leave me to do what I must."

With a swish of the curtain, Sanchia disappeared.

Unlocking her special cabinet, Pepper reached inside and grabbed a clay jar and poured the contents into the *posole* she had set aside. She stirred it a few times, then added a generous splash of tequila. She always added tequila, but it was even more important to mask any unfamiliar taste the dried buckthorn berries might have.

She put the jar back in the cabinet, then carried the baneful dish to her unsuspecting victim.

Chapter 3

Brand watched Pepper coming toward him, and thought again what a desirable woman the redhead was. Her wide hips swayed as she walked, and he knew without having to see beneath her skirt that her buttocks would be high and firm and perfectly molded. He felt a stirring in his loins at the way her large breasts bounced ever so provocatively.

He scraped the last of the chili from the bottom of the bowl. No wonder she'd bragged she was famous for her cooking. It was the best chili he'd ever had. No matter that it made his throat burn or his eyes water. It was delicious.

What did bother him, however, was that he was feeling hot in other places besides his stomach. In fact, as Pepper leaned to give him the big glass of water he'd asked for, he felt himself getting hard. She had also brought another bowl of chili, and he started eating it quickly. Maybe the hot food would take his mind off his inflamed loins.

Damn it, what was wrong with him? He wasn't some horny, young kid. He was nearly twenty-six years old and had bedded plenty of women and never went long without one, either. And, until now, he had always prided himself in having self-control, able to last as long as it took to satisfy a woman.

He was glad he was sitting down, otherwise the bulge in his pants would be embarrassing.

"So . . ." Pepper said as she sat down next to him, "you like my chili?"

He surprised himself by blurting, "Your chili and everything else." Damn it, he was even breathing hard.

* * *

Pepper bit back a smile. The way he was looking at her made her feel good. He liked her, and she found herself being strangely drawn to him as well. And so what if she were? She was a woman, and he was a man. There was no shame in her desire—even though she had never been to bed with a man.

"You like your own cooking." He nodded at her empty bowl.

She laughed and said, of course she did, glad that he had talked her into sharing the meal with him—but gladder still, that she had found a bit of *posole* left in the pot at the front of the stove. Otherwise, she wouldn't have had anything to eat, because the pot on the back of the stove contained the buckthorn berries.

"I'm afraid this is the last of it," she said, a strange tremor jerking in her belly when he stared at her cleavage.

But that odd sensation settled down as they made small talk. He asked a few questions about the village, the people, and their way of life, but mostly he devoured her with his eyes, which were almost luminous with passion.

Pepper crossed and uncrossed her legs, wondering why she felt so strange between her legs—moist, swollen—and was jolted to realize how good it felt when she squeezed her thighs together. And her nipples. They were as hard as pebbles and seemed to be throbbing, as though straining to burst from her bodice and right into Brand Austin's big hands.

His hands. Suddenly she felt him touch her knee, kneading, massaging, filling her with a searing need as their gazes locked.

It had grown late. Most of the customers had left. There were a few stragglers, draining the last of their drinks.

Pepper could hear Sanchia settling what the customers owed, trying to get them to leave so the cantina could close. As the last man left, Sanchia barred the shutters and extinguished all the lanterns, the only light coming from the candle on the table, where Pepper sat with the bounty hunter.

She knew Sanchia would not come to the table, afraid Brand might sense her loathing and know he'd been found out. Instead, she called, "I am leaving now," and hurriedly fled.

Pepper and Brand were finally alone.

He had lifted her skirt, baring her leg, and his fingers danced along her thigh, making her tremble with longing. It was as if she no longer had a will of her own, as if she were helpless to do anything except surrender to his velvet assault.

With his other hand, he grabbed the back of her head, drawing her toward his lips. He kissed her, long, hard, wet, his tongue melding with hers to lick and tease and suck, while his fingers continued their journey between her thighs.

"Feel how I want you," he murmured, pulling her hand to touch the front of his pants.

He was throbbing and hard, and Pepper moaned helplessly as she pressed against him. There was no right or wrong, no thought of yesterday or tomorrow. Only the here and now of passion awakened and demanding to be fed.

Brand suddenly pushed back from his chair to stand and pull her up with him. With deft, demanding hands, he undressed her, and when she was naked, he ducked his head to suck her breasts.

Pepper clung to him, sobbing with longing, her fingers twined in his thick blond hair. She wanted him, had to have him. "Take me," she begged. "Take me, now."

Unfastening his pants, he pushed them down and kicked them aside. With a sweep of his arm, he knocked the bowls to the floor with a clatter. Grabbing her by her waist, he sat her on the table and her fingers dug into the rock-hard flesh of his arms as he spread her thighs and positioned himself between them.

She was aching with need and praying he would end this madness. "I want you," she moaned.

He lowered her on the table, and she fought to hang onto him by lifting her legs and wrapping them around him, digging her heels into the small of his back.

He raised his head to gaze down at her as he plunged into her. The muscles in his shoulders, so wide and sleek, bulged as he supported his weight on his stiffened arms.

She arched her neck and clung to him. There was pain, for it was her first time, but she was not thinking about the agony . . . only the ecstasy of each powerful thrust.

He filled her so deeply she imagined she could feel him all the way to her heart. Every nerve in her pulsated, shivered, and burned. She felt a quickening and pushed herself against him even harder as she whimpered deep in her throat. To stifle the sound, she bit down on his shoulder and tasted blood, but he did not so much as flinch as his hands clutched her waist and held her tight, and he urgently, rapidly, moved inside her. Then he shuddered and a tremor raced through her, leaving her fulfilled but wanting more.

For long moments after, he lay across her, spent and gasping. Finally he asked, hoarsely, raggedly, "Did . . . did I hurt you?"

"Yes. No. I . . ." She swung her head wildly from side to side but did not let go of his shoulders, nor did she move her legs clasped around him. "I don't know," she said dizzily. "I only know I want you . . . again."

And he took her . . . again.

There seemed no end to their desire or their will to try and satiate the overwhelming passion that drove them. They did rouse, however, from their bewitched state long enough to find their way to Pepper's bedroom upstairs.

Again and again they made love, only to pause briefly before starting in a new way, a new position. They talked little, mostly only to convey their preferences, pleasure, or satisfaction.

Finally, they slept, their arms entwined, her head on his shoulder as he held her close.

* * *

Pepper forced herself from slumber, groggily thinking of the dream that filled her with such shame. She had never pined for a man before, not to the point of fantasizing about making love—especially love so uninhibited and wild.

She sat up and shook herself. She had overslept, and there was so much work to do. The cantina had to be cleaned, and she needed to make more chili. But more importantly, she wanted to hear any stories of the stranger who called himself Brand Austin being afflicted by the trots.

She knew he might blame her, saying her bad cooking was what had made him sick, but she would point out that others had eaten her chili last night, and she'd heard no complaints from them.

Stretching, she smiled, congratulating herself for a job well done. Yet she should not have drunk so much tequila while keeping him company, because she could not remember his leaving or her coming upstairs to go to bed, and . . .

Her hand touched something—someone. Her eyes wide, a scream locked against the terrified lump that had risen so quickly in her throat, she dared to roll over—and looked into smoldering green eyes.

"Good morning," Brand said lazily.

Her mouth dropped open, and for an instant she could only stare at him. Then she nearly fell out of the bed in her haste to leave it.

"How do you feel?"

Dear God, she thought, it wasn't a dream. It was real.

Suddenly she was aware of soreness between her thighs, and her nipples throbbed. She pressed her fingertips to her lips and confirmed they were swollen. It had actually happened.

Frowning, Brand raised up on his elbow. "Are you all right? I mean"—his grin was somewhat sheepish—"we did get kind of wild last night, but I hope I didn't hurt you."

Horrified, she swung her head slowly from side to side. Never in her whole life had she felt so embarrassed. But, beyond chagrin, she was struck by the fact that he was not sick. He should have left clutching his stomach in agony hours ago.

"Come here." He opened his arms to her.

Overcome with rage and humiliation, she began to back away from the bed, away from him. "Please just go," she cried. "I don't know why last night happened, but it won't happen again. Now go. . . ."

She turned to flee, but at his taunting chuckle she paused.

"I wouldn't run out of here like that if I were you."

With a gasp, she looked down to see that she was naked.

Chapter 4

Having sought refuge in the cellar, Pepper breathed a sigh of relief when she heard Brand leave.

"Keep on going," she whispered in the darkness. "Keep on going and don't come back."

Oh, what had come over her? Not only had she bedded a stranger but she had behaved like an animal. Remembering what they had done and how she had begged for more, she felt sick to her stomach.

She had acted like a whore. Until last night, she had been a virgin, saving herself for the man she would one day marry—*if* she ever married. So what had made her throw her virtue to the wind and allow him to have his way with her so wantonly?

She waited awhile longer to make sure he was truly gone, then crept up the stairs like a prowler in her own home.

Peeking through the curtains, she glanced around the

cantina, fearing he might have stopped to help himself to a shot of whiskey or tequila before leaving. But the room was empty.

Her gaze fell on the bowls Brand had swept to the floor in his lust to take her that first time last night. Fresh humiliation swept over her at the sight of the broken pottery. Wrapped in a blanket, she cleaned it up quickly, lest Sanchia wonder what had happened, then raced up to her bedroom. Her only thought was to bathe, then perhaps she'd feel clean again.

But she halted at the doorway when her eyes fell on the bed. She could not bear to look at it. How many times had they made love? She had no idea, but knew it had been frenetic to the point of madness.

She stripped the sheets and got out fresh, then took a cold bath, not wanting to take the time to heat the water. She wanted to wash away every trace of him, every hint of what they had done.

Yet, as she shivered in the cold water, she felt additional shame knowing she was only lying to herself. True, it was embarrassing to have given herself so easily, so freely, to a man—worse, to one whom she did not know. But it was even more debasing to admit she had enjoyed it.

Brand Austin was quite a man, and under different circumstances, perhaps feelings would have grown between them, and . . .

"Stop it!" She commanded herself out loud. "Stop it! Stop it! Stop it!"

"Stop what?"

Sanchia walked in, a bewildered look on her face. She glanced around. "Who are you talking to?"

"Myself," Pepper growled, reaching for a towel. "Now, wait for me downstairs. I have to dry myself and dress."

"But I'm anxious to know about the bounty hunter. I got up early to find out what happened, but I saw Lorenzo, the stableboy, and he says he saw him ride out of town a short while ago. Shouldn't he still be sick from the chili?" she asked worriedly. "If he's trailing Buck—"

"Then let him!" Pepper snapped.

"But the chili—"

"Yes, the chili." Pepper nodded fiercely. "I think I fed him from the wrong pot."

Sanchia's hand flew to her mouth. "Oh, no. Then he isn't sick. He *has* gone after Buck." She began to cry.

"I'm sorry," Pepper said lamely. "Somehow the pots must have got switched. We were so busy last night that I can understand how it might have happened."

"It was probably my fault." Sanchia sobbed, cradling her face in her hands. "You know how I get confused when I'm in a hurry. I even remember shoving the pots around on the stove. If he catches up to Buck, I will never forgive myself."

Pepper thought of something even worse. "What about my customers? All over the village those who ate my chili are trotting to the pots and bushes and cramping and hurting, and they will think it had to have been caused by something they ate here."

Thinking of the nightmare of having made her customers ill in addition to behaving like a *puta,* Pepper groaned and slid down into the tub of cold water, covering her head. Because, at that particular moment, she did not care if she drowned.

Days passed, and Pepper was surprised, and relieved, that no one came to her complaining about the *posole.*

Sanchia was beside herself with worry over Buck. She feared that Brand had tracked him down. Sometimes drifters would happen by on their way to Mexico, and she would give them Buck's name. She asked that if their paths crossed with his they tell him she was anxious to hear that he was all right.

Her fretting annoyed Pepper to no end, because she was not concentrating on her work. Someone would order steak, and Sanchia would take them eggs and salt pork. Or they would ask for a refill of sangria and instead she would pour tequila. Customers complained, and Pepper had to appease them, usually by saying to them they didn't have to pay for their food or drink.

So it was no wonder, Pepper decided, that the chili pots had been accidentally switched the night she had tried to make Brand Austin sick. What she still could not understand, however, was why she'd had no complaints from those who had eaten the tainted *posole?*

When days became weeks and Brand did not return, Pepper dared to believe she might be able to put her ordeal with him behind her and not be haunted for the rest of her life. After all, her monthly bleeding had come, so she was not carrying his child, thank God. And since no one knew what had happened that night except her, what was to keep her from being able to forget it?

Painfully, she acknowledged that it was her very heart that refused to let go of the memories. That one night of splendor would, despite the bizarre circumstances, live forever in her soul. Again and again, she found herself recalling his lips, his mouth, his hands, and how deliciously and wickedly good he had felt inside her.

But she told herself she had to forget about him and concentrate on not only supporting herself with the cantina, but her family as well.

One morning as Pepper was drawing water from the communal well, she was surprised to see her mother, Nina, coming into the village in her burro cart.

Pepper hurried to greet her. "I'm so happy you came," she said, hugging her. "It's been so long."

"If you would come home once in a while, I wouldn't have to go out in this heat. You know it's bad for my heart," Nina said irritably.

Pepper bit back a smile. There was nothing wrong with her mother's heart. She just liked to complain.

"We haven't seen you in weeks. Your papa was worried and sent me to find out if anything is wrong."

Pepper knew the real reason was money. She usually made the half-hour ride to her parents' adobe hut at least every other week to visit and give her father money. But between having to cope with Sanchia's erratic behavior and being haunted by thoughts of Brand Austin and her own foolish actions, everything else had slipped her mind.

"I'm sorry," she said. "I've just been busy."

"This heat will send me to an early grave. But you should come to see us more often," her mother scolded. "You spend too much time at the cantina. You work too hard."

Pepper finished filling her pails, then led the way to the cantina, anxious to get Nina into its shaded coolness and out of the broiling sun. Once inside, she poured them both glasses of water as she apologized again for neglecting her family.

"It would make your papa feel good to have you visit more often," Nina explained. "It would take his mind off his troubles."

"What troubles?" Pepper demanded, alarmed. "If he's sick, you should have sent word to me."

Nina waved away such a notion. "It's not that. It's the water. Like the other herders, he's worried about the creek drying up. You know that even though he isn't able to tend the sheep as he did when he was a young man he still has money in the herds."

Pepper knew that was only because of the money she was able to give him. It had made life easier for him in his old age to be able to buy sheep and profit from their sale rather than be paid to tend them. She took pride in having been able to do that.

"So why is he worried about the water?" Pepper asked. "There's been no problem since Jeb Daniels left town and abandoned his land. The water runs freely because he's not damming it anymore."

Nina nodded. "Yes. We have that to be thankful for. I'm sorry Señora Daniels died, but maybe that was God's way of getting rid of her husband, who made our life miserable with his cattle."

Pepper was also relieved Jeb Daniels was gone. He had

appeared one day with a deed to over twenty-five hundred acres of top land. In no time at all, he had built a house and started a herd of cattle.

At first there hadn't been a problem, but when sheep began wandering onto Jeb's range, he became angry, claiming that when they grazed, they pulled grass up by the roots, leaving the land barren for his cattle. He put up fences which the angry sheepherders tore down as fast as they were erected.

To retaliate, Jeb built a dam cutting off the water that ran from his property. Soon the sheep were dying, and the herders were begging for mercy. Jeb agreed to sell them water, only if they stopped tearing down his fences.

It was a tense time and Pepper had feared there would be bloodshed between the wranglers and the herders. The only thing that had stopped it was when Jeb's wife died. In his grief, he began drinking and gambling heavily, and it wasn't long after that his men began drifting away and his ranch fell to ruin. Finally, Jeb also left, and no one had heard from him in the past year.

"You worry for nothing, Mama," Pepper said firmly. "Papa and all the herders will have plenty of water. Jeb Daniels is gone, and he's not coming back. And the way he was drinking, he's probably dead by now, anyway."

"But nothing will bring relief from the heat. I have to cook for your papa in the communal pot, out in the open. You know I hate that, but it's better than having to fire up my own stove. Frankly, I don't see how you stand being in your kitchen as hot as it is."

Pepper smiled. "The men quench the fires of my spicy cooking with tequila. So I make money both ways—selling my piquant dishes first and then selling something to wash it down."

Nina gave a disapproving sniff. "I would rather you cook for one man only, Pepper. A husband. Soon you will be too old. Men want young wives. Strong, sturdy."

Pepper laughed. "I'm twenty-two years old, Mama. I can

hardly be called feeble. And you know how I feel about marriage."

"Only because you haven't met the right man." Nina waved her hand in disgust. "You surround yourself with drinking men, drifters, outlaws. You think you will find a husband here?"

Pepper felt the need to defend her life but kept her tone respectful. "I make good money here, Mama, and that money makes life easier for you and Papa."

"And what about children?" Nina countered. "Your papa and I always hoped you would give us many grandchildren. The Lord knows how we grieved not to have babies of our own, so it was a blessing when we found you that day so long ago. But you should marry and give us grandchildren to look after us in our old age."

"*I* will look after you as I am doing now," Pepper said stiffly.

"And who will look after you?"

"The same one who's looked after me since I left home to cook for others—me. I don't need a man, Mama."

But that was, Pepper knew, a lie. Brand Austin had shown her how pleasurable a man could be. And not just any man. Somehow she knew that if she were to bed a hundred men—no, a thousand—that not one of them could ever make her feel as he had.

"What is wrong with you?" Nina asked sharply. "You look ill. Your face is red and your eyes look like you have a fever. Maybe you should take one of your Indian potions."

"I'm fine," Pepper murmured, while wondering whether she ever would be again.

Sanchia arrived to clean, and Pepper said she would whip up a quick batch of enchiladas for their lunch, promising her mother to make enough so she would not have to cook supper.

When the enchiladas were almost ready, Pepper was dismayed to find she was out of cheese. Giving Sanchia money, she told her to go quickly to the store and get some.

A short while later, Sanchia returned, but Pepper knew at once something was wrong. The young woman's face was pale, and she stood in the back door, trembling, her lips moving wordlessly.

Pepper was glad her mother was out in the cantina waiting for her lunch, and hurried to draw Sanchia into the kitchen. "What's wrong? Have you heard something about Buck? Has something happened to him?" It was the only thing Pepper could think of that might have upset her so.

"It's the bounty hunter. He's back."

Now it was Pepper's turn to become upset, for Sanchia's words rocked her to the core of her being.

Chapter 5

Pepper helped Sanchia to a chair. "Are you sure it was him?"

"I'm sure. He was coming out of the hotel."

Located above Pepper's only competition, a rough and rowdy bar, the hotel was a joke, at best. It merely provided rooms for the bar's whores to take their customers. But it was also a place where a man could get a bath and a place to sleep if that was all he wanted.

Sanchia began to cry. "I've got to know about Buck," she said, her fists clenched in her lap. "But I can't just walk up to him and say, 'Hey, señor. Did you kill my man down in Mexico?' "

"No, you can't." Pepper's arm was around her shoulder and she gave her a brisk shake, though her own stomach was twisting like a prairie dust devil. She prayed he would not come to the cantina. Surely, now that he'd had time to think about it he would see that their lovemaking had been a mistake, something that never should have happened.

"Oh, Pepper, what am I going to do?"

"You do nothing except help me get my mother fed and out of here so we can think about it. Now, get hold of yourself, please."

Pepper hurried and finished the enchiladas, but Nina was in no hurry to leave, for the cantina was cool.

Pepper went to the windows often to look out at the dusty street for any sign of Brand. What was she going to say to him? What could she say?

Finally, with a deep breath of resignation, Pepper said, "Well, Mama, I think I'd better open for business. As hot as it is today, I can sell lots of whiskey and tequila. I also need to get busy preparing supper, but you can stay if you want . . ." Her voice trailed. There was no enthusiasm or urging in her tone.

Nina reached for her shawl. "I'll not be around drinking men. You know that, Pepper. And I wish you had another way to live."

"But I don't." Pepper took money from her pocket and pressed it in her hand. "Here. Tell Papa I love him and I will come to see him soon."

The instant Nina was gone, Sanchia began to cry. "What can we do? I have to know about Buck."

Pepper didn't care about Buck. The only thing concerning her was how she was going to face the man who had in one night of wild passion made her glad she had been born a woman.

"Pepper, are you listening to me?"

"Yes. If he comes in, leave it to me," she said more confidently than she felt. "I'll find out about Buck."

It was a busy night, and Pepper hurried from cantina to kitchen, serving spicy food that kept the men thirsty and begging for more. However, as the hours passed, and Brand did not appear, Pepper tortured herself with wondering if perhaps he didn't want to see her again. Maybe he had not enjoyed their lovemaking as she had and had found more pleasure with one of the whores at the hotel bar.

She told herself she didn't care, then promptly called herself a liar. She did care. Very much. And though she had no intentions of bedding him again, she would like at least to talk to him—for Sanchia's sake, of course.

She was stirring a special beef-and-egg dish, thick with red peppers and corn, when Sanchia appeared at her side. Digging her nails into Pepper's arm, she hissed, "He's here. He just walked in."

"Stay here and stir this and don't let it burn." Pepper took a deep breath, wiped her hands on her skirt, smoothed back her hair, and walked into the cantina, her head held high.

He was sitting at the bar, and she walked right up to him. "Señor, I must ask you something," she said, her voice cold.

"Go ahead," he said warily, the smile on his face fading.

She pressed close, so that no one else could hear. "First of all," she said, biting out each word, "what happened between us should not have—and never will again. Understand?"

"I don't force myself on women, and if you think about it, you'll remember I didn't force you."

She knew, to her shame, that was so. "Then why are you here?"

"I have business."

"What kind?"

He did not answer. He was drinking tequila and lifted the glass to take a sip, as though dismissing her.

"You're a bounty hunter, aren't you?"

He looked at her and blinked.

"We heard you were coming. You're trailing a man named Buck Kiley. You left here to trail him to Mexico, didn't you?"

He looked her up and down as if deep in thought, then murmured, "What if I did?"

"I have to know if you found him."

"And what do you care? Is he your lover?" he asked with a little sneer.

Pepper felt like grabbing the glass from his hand and throwing the tequila in his face. "You were the first man for me, and you know it."

His expression softened. "I'm sorry. So what is this man to you?"

She nodded toward Sanchia, who had come out of the kitchen carrying bowls of the meat and eggs to serve the men who had ordered them. "He's her lover, and she's worried sick about him."

"Tell her to relax. I didn't find him and I'm not looking anymore."

"Why not? You're a bounty hunter, aren't you? And there's obviously a price on Buck's head."

He turned his face from hers. "I'm thinking of settling down. I'm tired of hunting men like animals."

"That's good," she said approvingly. "Besides, I have many friends among the outlaws. I mind my business. They mind theirs." She turned to leave. "I'll go tell Sanchia you didn't find Buck."

His hand snaked out to wrap around her wrist. Unlike other men, he did not wither beneath her ominous glare. "Wait. I told you I'm thinking of settling down. Maybe here. And I could use your help."

"In what way?" She made no move to twist from his grasp, guiltily reveling in the feel of his skin against hers.

"I don't know anyone and I've learned quick that your people don't take to strangers. I ask questions and get silence and cold stares. I need someone to show me around, tell me what it's like living here. I want to know about sheep and cattle and anything else that might make me want to stay here. You can help me."

"I could . . ." she said uncertainly. His green eyes were boring into hers, and the images had begun to flash once more—his lips on hers, their tongues touching, his hands on her breasts, caressing, squeezing, his pelvis grinding against her as he thrust into her deep and hard.

She gave herself a shake and stared down at the floor, afraid he would see the desire that had to be shining in her eyes. "I don't think we should be together after . . ." She could not say the words.

"I told you, Pepper, I don't force myself on women. What happened between us was good. Damn good. I've thought of nothing else these past weeks, and I'd be lying if I said I wouldn't like for it to happen again, but I can promise you it won't . . . not unless you want it to."

Pepper pulled from his grasp then, unable to bear his touch any longer. "I never want to speak of it again."

"Very well. If that's the way you want it, fine with me. Now, will you show me around your village? Help me get acquainted?"

One part of her screamed no, not to allow herself to be so tempted, while the other part argued yes.

"There's no one else," he said quietly, his eyes searching hers.

"Are you telling me the truth? Are you sure you aren't trying to use me to help you find any of the outlaws?"

His chuckle was soft and warm. "I really want you to show me around. But tell me, why do you count outlaws among your friends? Isn't that a bit odd?"

"Not around here. There are times when things get rowdy. Sheepherders come in from the range, worn out from weeks of long days eating dust under a boiling sun, followed by nights of sleeping on the ground with snakes and horned toads on a mattress of brush. They are spoiling for fun—and trouble. One goes with the other, I suppose.

"So," she continued, trying not to think of the way he was looking at her, as if he, too, were remembering their passionate hours together, "there are fist fights and gunfights, and I am only a woman, even though I've been known to shoot or cut a man if need be."

Brand smiled and nodded.

"But there are times when I am outnumbered, and the trouble is too much even for me to handle. The outlaws step in then and clean things up. The herders are not gunmen. They run from guns, knives, and outlaws, and many times I have been spared costly damages, and lives have been saved.

"So the outlaws are my friends," she finished with a stubborn jut of her chin, "and I will never help you find a one of them."

"And I won't ask," he assured her. "So can we get started tomorrow?"

She pursed her lips, still unsure.

"Suppose we start over."

She was puzzled not only by his words but by the twinkle in his eye. "I don't know what you mean," she said suspiciously.

"We went crazy the first night we met—a nice kind of crazy, I might add. But it's obviously upset you, and since I really would like to be your friend, and really need a friend, let's just pretend we're meeting for the first time right now and forget what happened between us."

She knew that was impossible and suspected he did, too, but there was no denying that she liked him and wanted to be with him. As long as they had an agreement as to how things would be, then what was the harm?

"Very well," she said finally.

He held out his hand. She grasped it and they shook.

"Perhaps you'd like some supper?" she asked, suddenly feeling self-conscious again.

He grinned. "That would be nice—just so it's not your chili."

"But I'm famous for my chili."

His gaze was a sensuous caress that enveloped her. "Well, if you'll forgive me for mentioning it one last time, something sure set us off the other night."

She gave her hair a toss and brazenly fired back, "Well, I've been serving and eating my *posole* for over eight years and nothing like that has ever happened to me before or since, so you can't blame my spicy cooking."

"Maybe it was the tequila."

She shook her head. "No."

"You're right. Tequila has never affected me that way, either." His elbow propped on the bar, he rested his chin in his palm as he continued to devour her with his eyes. "But to be on the safe side and help me keep my promise, I think we'd better stay away from the chili *and* tequila."

"Oh, you won't need help keeping your promise," she said with a wink and grinning. "I'll see that you do. That is *my* promise to *you.*"

She flounced away, her skirt swishing, anxious to let Sanchia know she had nothing to worry about. But who was going to help her keep her promise, she wondered. Because, despite every emotion that had nagged her conscience since she had given herself so wantonly, Pepper could not deny longing to be in Brand's arms again.

Chapter 6

His arms folded behind his head, Brand lay staring up at the ceiling of his tiny hotel room. His past few weeks in the village had been a mixture of heaven and hell—heaven being with Pepper every chance he got, and hell wanting her so bad it hurt like a toothache.

He had learned just about everything he needed to know about the area, too. It was sheep country, all right. The herds were settled on established ranges, but it was a lonely life. Sometimes the men were gone for weeks with only a dog to tend as many as three thousand sheep before someone came to relieve them.

Pepper told him he had missed the shearing in the spring, which she had described as somewhat of a social season, when itinerant crews, noted for their shearing skills, followed the market northward from Mexico and traveled all the way to the Canadian border. Their arrival was a major break in the tedium of winter, an excuse to feast and drink.

"It's when I make my most money," she had boasted, then added, frowning, "and also spend the most on repairs. The crowd can get very rowdy. That's when my outlaw friends come in handy."

Brand had not missed the way she had emphasized the word *outlaw*. It was her way of reminding him that she looked upon his profession with scorn.

Profession. He laughed out loud in the empty room. Profession, indeed. He was no bounty hunter. Neither was he a gunslinger, though he had been the winner in a few unavoidable shootouts when some hothead in a bar started a fight that could only be ended with a bullet. Brand didn't like killing, but thoughts of dying appealed even less.

From below came the sounds of a tinny piano and some drunk trying to sing a song he couldn't remember the words to.

Cigar smoke, shrill laughter, whores guiding stumbling drunks down the hall to their rooms for quick pleasuring had become his world when he wasn't with Pepper or off doing some looking around on his own. He hated living like this and wanted it to end. But, damn it, he had to continue the charade, because he knew that once Pepper found out who he really was, she wouldn't have anything to do with him. So he had to try, as best he could, to win her over to his side before that time came and maybe also win her heart in the process.

The only truthful thing he had told her was that he wanted to settle down. So far there had been no direction to his life. Sure, there'd been women along the way but no one he had really cared about.

Up until six years ago, before his mother died, he'd had a family. Raised on a Texas ranch, he'd enjoyed the love and security of living with his parents and his younger sisters, Melanie and Bethany.

Then things had changed almost overnight with his

mother's death. His father had sold the ranch and used the money to move back East and start a new life, taking Melanie and Bethany with him. Brand, loving the West and feeling it was where he belonged, had refused to go with them. He had not seen them since, though he thought about them often. Melanie, the older of his two sisters, was fifteen, and she wrote once in a while. He seldom heard from Bethany. His father had remarried and had a new son, so Brand was more or less removed from their lives.

He had spent the years drifting from place to place, working cattle drives for different ranchers. He minded his own business and stayed out of trouble, while wondering where he was going with his life. He didn't want to wind up dead on a saloon floor because some kid with a quicker trigger finger had beat him to the draw on a drunken dare.

But even though he asked himself which direction he should take toward some kind of secure future, no answer came—until fate stepped in and brought him to Cuchillo, New Mexico.

Standing in his way of getting on with his life, however, was a redhead with turquoise eyes named Pepper Montez. He could think of nothing else, though he damn well tried to get her out of his mind. And not just because she was the best he'd ever had in bed, either. It was more than that. She charmed him with her grace, wit, and intelligence, and he enjoyed every minute they spent together.

He only wished he could be sure she felt the same way, but she gave no hint of having any personal feelings for him. She was friendly and polite, and he was of the opinion that her true motive in helping him was to prove to him that she wasn't the wanton woman he had bedded.

Perhaps even more so, he thought, she was trying to prove the same thing to herself. But why? She had enjoyed it. He had no doubt about that.

What puzzled him even more was knowing she had been a virgin, and it was unusual, perhaps even unheard of, for an inexperienced woman to give herself with such total abandonment to a stranger. She hadn't been drunk. She'd had two drinks with him, and even if she'd had a few before meeting him, she had certainly seemed sober when she first served him. And she had seemed sober, later, when things got hot.

So what the hell had happened? Brand didn't know, but if there were any way on earth, he intended to find out.

It was late, and he was hungry, but he had told himself he would not go near the cantina for a few days. As much as he wanted to see Pepper, he knew he had to distance himself gradually from her. That would make it a little easier on him in case she hated him when she learned who—and what—he really was.

Voices drifted through the thin walls between his room and the hall. It was a seedy hotel, but Cuchillo was lucky to have anything even resembling one. Actually, the village wasn't much more than a gathering place for herders to live between taking their turns on the range and for getting drunk and raising hell when they felt like it.

It was no wonder, he opined morosely, that Jeb Daniels hadn't tried harder to stay on after his wife had died. He had planned to have children and raise a family and suddenly found himself all alone.

Pepper had told him about Jeb, too, and Brand had inwardly cringed with each bitter and disparaging thing she had said. Lord, when she found out the truth . . .

The voices grew louder. A whore and her customer on the way to her room.

"I hope I can get my money's worth," the man was jovially saying. "I ate enough of Pepper's *posole* to make me bust."

"You'll do fine." The whore giggled. "You're already bustin' out of something else now—your pants."

The two exploded in guffaws and shuffled on down the hall.

Brand's stomach gave a hungry lurch—along with his heart. Not only did he crave Pepper's spicy cooking, he was starved to be with her, as well.

* * *

"I don't know why you are so nice to him," Sanchia admonished Pepper as she dished up yet another bowl of *posole* for Brand. "He's a bounty hunter."

"Was—not is," Pepper corrected her. "How many times do I have to tell you? He's given all that up. He wants only to settle down."

Sanchia snorted. "Ha. And become a sheepherder? If you believe that, you're crazier than I think you are. And now I'm going home. Everyone else has gone, but if you want to stay here all night and serve a bounty hunter, go ahead."

She swished out the back door, and Pepper stared after her and thought maybe Sanchia was right. Maybe she was crazy. But whenever Brand appeared with his lopsided grin and shimmering green eyes, Pepper turned as soft as churned butter.

He had arrived late, explaining that his appetite had been whetted by overhearing someone raving about the *posole*. He begged for just one bowl, but was now on his second, and, as Sanchia had pointed out, all the customers had finally drifted away, and the cantina was empty. It was also very late.

"This is all of it," Pepper said as she placed the bowl before him where he sat at the bar. Then she forced herself to add, "After you've eaten, I'll have to say good night. It's very late."

Brand nodded and started eating. After a bite or two, he smacked his lips. "It's the very best, Pepper. I can understand why you're known all over for your cooking. Anybody would think you were a true-blooded Mexican."

"Maybe I am. I don't know anything about my parents, so I've no idea where my family came from."

"Ireland, maybe. With your red hair. But certainly not Mexico."

"And you? With your blond hair? Where did you come from?"

"My mother was Norwegian. My name is also Norwegian. In Norse myths, Brand was the grandson of Woden, king of the gods."

"A Viking," Pepper cried, then, without thinking, teased, "now I understand why you swept me off my feet that first night. How I was so powerless to resist . . ." Her voice trailed off as her cheeks reddened with embarrassment. Oh, how could she have said such a thing? How could she have even brought up that night at all? In the weeks and days they had spent together, it was understood that it was behind them, never to be mentioned again, never to be repeated.

Brand's eyes widened in surprise. "But you were the one—"

"Wait." She recovered quickly from her blunder. "I'm sorry. I shouldn't have said anything. Forgive me, please."

Pushing his bowl away, he declared, "I'm sorry, too, because I see now I've just been waiting for a chance to talk about it, Pepper."

The familiar warm surge swept over her from head to toe as he looked at her with searing eyes. "No. I don't want to. We agreed . . ."

"We agreed," he said fiercely, turning on the bar stool to grab her arms and pull her to him, "that it wouldn't happen again unless you wanted it to."

Kissing her hungrily, he opened his thighs to draw her between them. His hands dropped to her buttocks, pressing her to the stony hardness of his swollen manhood. His kiss, which had begun slowly, sensually, now was bruising in its intensity as he devoured her mouth, tasting and probing her with his tongue.

Helplessly, she leaned into him, awash with longing and pressing against him. Her fingers caressed his thighs, then dug deeply to urge him on.

Lifting his mouth, he stared straight into her eyes. "Say you don't want me, Pepper, and I swear I'll stop here and now and never touch you again."

She could no more have turned from him than lassoed the sun, and, in answer, she put her hand on the back of his neck and pulled his head toward her. Then she kissed him.

Still locked in the kiss, Brand lifted her in his arms and cárried her up the stairs. Reaching her bedroom, he lowered her to the bed and yanking up her skirt, he feverishly tore away her undergarments as he whispered, "Are you ready for me, my sweet? I hope so, because I've got to have you now."

Pepper was beyond caring about right or wrong. Spreading her thighs, she lifted her legs for him, crossing her ankles against his buttocks to draw him closer. "Now," she said boldly, brazenly, "I want everything you have to give!"

Clutching her waist, he entered her.

When finally they climaxed together, Pepper screamed his name in rapturous bliss as he rained tiny kisses all over her sweat-drenched face.

Then, he undressed completely, as did she, and they lay together in bed for a long, long time, just holding each other close and letting the sensual sweetness of passion shared dance over their nerve-quickened bodies.

Sometime before morning, they made love again, and although it was slow and easy, Pepper experienced an even deeper intensity of pleasure.

This man, she knew, had much to teach her—and, oh, how she was willing to learn.

Chapter 7

Brand awoke when the fighting broke out in the room next door.

"She's my woman, damn you!" a man yelled as a chair smashed against the wall.

"The hell you say!" came another man's angry cry as more furniture was broken.

Brand was already stepping into his trousers and reaching for his shirt.

He hated the hotel more with each passing day and had lost count of how many there had been. Sleeping on the ground with nothing but a blanket between him and the lizards and his saddle for a pillow was better than being awakened at all hours by fighting.

With his holster in one hand and his boots in the other, he was out the door. It hadn't happened yet, but he wouldn't be surprised if one night a bullet came zinging through his wall.

It was early, six A.M., he noted by the clock on the wall above the hotel clerk's desk. Clerk, indeed, Brand snorted. All the old geezer did was collect money from the whores' customers. Only fools like himself used the bawdy house as if it were a real hotel.

He had left Pepper's before first light as he had done every morning since they had become lovers again, and all his good intentions to avoid Pepper had frittered away like dry dust. He felt as if he were in a state of limbo, each day passing like the one before it.

They would spend afternoons together, picnicking, riding. It didn't matter, just so they were together. Nights found him at the cantina, loving Pepper's cooking, loving being where he could just look at her, and loving *her.*

Stepping into the street, he took a deep breath and thought the air seemed a bit crisp which hinted fall was on the way. He couldn't keep dragging his heels. Time was passing, and he had to do something, damn it.

He stared down the street toward the cantina, at the other end. Pepper was probably still in bed. He wished he were with her, but she insisted he leave before anyone was up and stirring. After all, she reminded him, no one must know they were sleeping together. She had a good name in the village and intended to keep it.

He headed for the little cafe across the street and went inside and ordered a cup of coffee.

Sitting by the window, he sipped it as he watched the women begin to arrive at the well to draw their day's water. Water, Brand had learned, was more valuable than gold to the people of Cuchillo, especially to the herders who depended on the spring, which fed a small lake on Jeb Daniels's almost three thousand acres.

Brand glanced up sharply at the sound of gunfire and saw a man come flying out the window of the hotel room next to his and land in the street below.

That did it. He was not staying at that damn hellhole till he got killed by a stray bullet. And he wasn't sleeping on the ground with a blanket between him and the lizards, either. It was time he slept in his own room, in his own house, which was nice, and large, and safe.

It was also time he told Pepper the truth about who he was and the reason he was in Cuchillo.

After practically pushing Brand out the door, Pepper had been unable to sleep. She had bathed and dressed, too keyed-up to do anything else.

Foolishly, she had fallen in love with him, and during the past few weeks when he had taken her hotly, sweetly, each and every night, never once had he mentioned a future together.

In fact, it needled her that he seldom talked of anything. All he did was ask questions and probably now knew as much as she did about the village, the countryside, and sheepherding.

With the day stretching long before her, she told herself she had to stay busy so there'd be no time to fret over how deeply she cared for Brand. For all she knew, he might ride out of town without so much as a good-bye, and she would never see him again. So she was a fool to drive herself crazy this way. She had to concentrate on other things and pretend not to care.

With a blessedly cool nip in the air, she decided to make a very large pot of *posole*. She would let it simmer all day, and by evening the smell would have drifted all over and the hordes would come to buy it. Not that she cared about that. She only wanted something to do.

She began to gather the ingredients—cubed beef, hominy, onions, olive oil, water, dried and ground red chili peppers, cumin, cayenne pepper, black pepper, garlic, tomatoes, and oregano.

Oregano. Murmuring a curse, she admonished herself for spending so much time with Brand that she had neglected keeping tab on her supplies, making sure she had everything she needed. She tried to remember the last time she had been to Owl Woman for the all-important spices, and was surprised when she remembered that it was when she had got the buckthorn berries.

It would be impossible to make the *posole* without oregano, so there was nothing to do except ride out to the Indian camp. It was early. She would be back in plenty of time to have everything ready for tonight.

Owl Woman shook her head at Pepper. "I cannot believe you would run out of such an important spice. Maybe there is finally a man in your life," she added, her eyes twinkling.

"Oh, of course not." Pepper was not about to admit to something so embarrassing, especially when it was becoming more and more obvious that the only thing Brand felt for her was lust. "I've just been very busy with no time to stock my supplies."

"Well, come along. I have plenty of what you need."

Inside the hut, Owl Woman rummaged through her pots of herbs and seasonings and found what she was looking for. "I'm glad you came, Pepper. I've been wanting to hear about the buckthorn berries."

"I'm afraid there's nothing to tell. The man they were intended for got the wrong batch of *posole* by mistake, and I didn't hear any complaints from anyone else, so evidently they didn't work."

Owl Woman's brow creased in annoyance. "That's not possible. The buckthorn berries always work. You must have forgotten to add them to the pot."

"Oh, I put them in all right, because I remember hoping he wouldn't wonder why yellow beans were in the *posole*. They are unlike any of the usual ingredients, and—"

"Yellow, did you say?" Owl Woman cried.

Pepper nodded, wondering why she seemed so alarmed.

"Buckthorn berries aren't yellow. They're a deep, deep purple but ground so fine they would not be noticed, anyway. The only yellow beans I use are the mescal."

"Mescal?"

"Don't you remember? I taught you to use them in the secret potion that will drive a man mad with desire. You said a woman in your village had come to you seeking help, because her husband was too tired to mate with her and she wanted another child. You told me later she was very happy, and—" Owl Woman, startled, put her hand on Pepper's shoulder and gave her a gentle shake. "Your face is the color of the clouds, child. What's wrong?"

"Noth-nothing," Pepper stammered, frozen in shock as she remembered that when she was making the *posole* she had thought that the berries actually resembled mescal beans.

It was easy to see how she might have made a mistake, for she had never seen buckthorn berries before, and the jars for the berries and the beans were similar. So if she had used the mescal beans, then that would explain why Brand had been so amorous—and why she had matched his ardor after mistakenly eating some herself. Sanchia had said the cooking pots had been moved around, and that would explain how she and Brand could have ended up eating the same batch. But she had to be sure.

She rushed from the hut, Owl Woman right behind her protesting that she should sit down, rest, drink some cool water, perhaps have one of her potions to make Pepper feel better.

But Pepper was frantic to get back to the cantina to see if she had switched the berries with the beans. "I have to get back to start the *posole.* It has to cook all day to make the flavor right."

"Then take the oregano you came to get," Owl Woman said.

Pepper snatched it from her hand and leaped on her horse, galloping at full speed and not slowing down until she reached the cantina.

She burst through the back door and ran to the cabinet and opened it. Squatting down, she frantically rummaged through the jars, until she found the two jars that looked exactly alike. With shaking fingers, she opened one and gasped. It was full of the deep purple buckthorn berry powder. The other jar of yellow mescal beans was almost empty. There was no doubt that she and Brand had eaten the *posole* laced with the aphrodisiac.

Rocking back on her heels, she was overcome with relief, knowing that her giving of herself so wildly and wantonly that first night in Brand's arms had not been her fault. Since that night, though, their lovemaking had come naturally. It was only that first night, when they had coupled like wild animals, that had bothered her, for she had never understood her total abandonment to a complete stranger. So perhaps Brand did feel something for her, as she did for him, and . . .

"Pepper. Oh, my God, Pepper."

Sanchia burst through the back door, her eyes glowing with rage, her cheeks bright with red dots of anger.

"Pepper, it's Brand. The *bastardo.* He is *worse* than a bounty hunter."

"What are you talking about?"

"He's no bounty hunter. He's been lying ever since he rode into town. He was never looking for Buck. He came here to take over our water."

Pepper grasped her shoulders and tried to force her into a chair. "Sit down and tell me what this is all about. What do you mean he came to take over our water?"

Sanchia stood where she was, her hands clenched at her sides. Her upper lip curled back over her teeth as she snarled, "He's a cattleman. A rancher."

Pepper laughed and shook her head. "No, you're wrong. He would have told me."

"Oh, you're such a fool!" Sanchia raged. "I know what's been going on between you. I know he's your lover, because I have seen him sneak out of here when I couldn't sleep for worrying about Buck."

"That's none of your business!" Pepper snapped.

"He's been waiting until he had his fill of you before telling you why he really came here—to take over Jeb Daniels's land."

"That's crazy."

"I know of what I speak," Sanchia cried, furious. "I just came from the well, and everyone's talking about the man who rode into town this morning and saw Brand Austin in the cafe having coffee. He recognized him as the man who won Jeb Daniels's land in a poker game in Albuquerque a few months ago."

Pepper could only stare at her in wonder and horror, hoping that by some miracle there was a mistake, that she was wrong, that Brand had not been using her.

Pepper's back was to the main room, and she noticed

that Sanchia was not looking at her but past her. "He even has the nerve to come here now."

"Go." Pepper gave her a shove toward the back door. "I'll find out the truth for myself."

Steeling herself, Pepper walked into the cantina, glad it was not yet open to customers, for she would have hated for anyone to witness the coming scene.

Brand closed the door behind him and grinned at the sight of Pepper coming toward him, but his smile quickly faded when he saw her livid face and that she stood as though ready for combat—her hands on her hips, her feet apart.

"How dare you lie to me?" Pepper exploded. "How dare you let me believe you were a bounty hunter wanting to settle down in a peaceful little village? Bastard!"

He ducked in time to miss getting hit by the glass she swept from the bar to throw at him. It broke against the wall just above his head, but before she could grab another, he dove for her.

Pinning her arms at her sides, he looked as if he were performing a weird kind of dance as he lifted one foot, then the other, to escape her hammering toes as she tried to kick him in his shins.

"Lying scum! Filthy liar! You're a damn cattle rancher, and you came to steal Jeb Daniels's land."

"Now hold on, Pepper. I'm not out to steal that land. I own it. I won it fair and square from Jeb himself in a poker game."

"You lied—"

"I had to. Don't you see? When I realized how you and everyone else around here hated cattle ranchers, I was afraid to say anything. I thought maybe if I kept my mouth shut and learned as much as possible before admitting who I was that I could somehow find a way to have peace between me and the sheepherders. I also knew that if you found out, you wouldn't want anything to do with me, and don't you know by now how much I care about you?"

He tried to look at her with tenderness but could only wince at the red-hot rage mirrored on her face.

"We both know what you care about!" she spat. "It's all you wanted from me. That's why you lied, so you could come to my bed every night."

At that, his own ire flashed. He let her go. "Wait a minute. Aren't you forgetting you were so hot for me the first night we met that I took you right here?" He pounded the table next to him with his fist.

"Because I accidentally tainted the *posole* with an aphrodisiac instead of the potion with which I intended to make you sick."

His eyes narrowed menacingly as he took a step toward her. "What are you talking about?"

Pepper retreated behind the bar. "I meant to add buckthorn berries which would have torn your stomach to pieces for days. Instead, I used mescal beans which made our blood as hot as the *posole.* It had nothing to do with you," she taunted. "I ate it, too, remember?"

"Now I think you're the one who's lying, because I think you did know what you put in your damn chili. You intended to make me look like a love-crazy fool, and your only mistake was in accidentally eating it yourself."

He saw her face pale. "That's not so."

"Yes, it is. You intended to get me so horny I'd have to have a woman. Your plan was probably to get me where you could bust me over the head and then have me dragged out in the wilderness and left to die, because you thought I was the bounty hunter."

"No, I—"

"You're the fool, Pepper," he said scornfully, "because you were stupid enough to eat your own concoction."

"How dare you—"

"How dare I, indeed," he scoffed. "I'll tell you what I dare, you conniving little witch. I dare to stay here and run my ranch despite you and the rest of your cattle-hating friends.

"That," he said with finality as he opened the door, "is what I dare."

He slammed the door just in time to miss being hit by a bottle of tequila.

Chapter 8

As Brand stood on the front porch of the great house, sipping coffee, he could see for miles in all directions. Why Jeb Daniels had built such a palace in the middle of nowhere, he thought in wonder, was beyond all comprehension. He'd heard Jeb did it for his wife. She was said to have been a genteel woman, born and raised back East, and that Jeb had tried to provide her with as much luxury as possible. It made sense that that might have been his reason since Jeb lost interest in everything after her death. He had fallen apart, as had the ranch.

It had been a month since the blowup with Pepper and still she was like a daguerreotype in his mind. All he had to do was close his eyes to see her. Scarlet hair. Turquoise eyes. Dimples in her cheeks. Saucy, turned-up nose.

She could smile like an angel or put the fear of God in a man with a glare. She was anything and everything, and he cared for her like he'd never cared for a woman before in his life. Maybe he even loved her. But he didn't want to think about that.

He didn't, by damn, even want to think about *her*, but, no matter how hard he tried, he couldn't shake her from his every waking moment—or his dreams.

And she provoked so many different emotions in him. Thinking how she had intended to make him sick the first night they met made him want to turn her over his knee and blister her bottom. Sometimes he wanted to do even worse. But then his thoughts would drift to the splendor they had shared in each other's arms, making him ache to hold her again.

Holding Pepper now, however, would be like trying to snuggle a bobcat.

He stayed away from the cantina, but the few times he had seen her on the street, her eyes threatened to slice him like the hidden knife strapped to her ankle. She hated him and always would.

And while she had unknowingly taught him much about the obstacles he had to face as a cattle rancher, nothing could have prepared him fully for the sheepherders' animosity.

He had tried to get along with them. He had spread word that he had no intentions of either cutting off the water supply from his land or charging for its use. All he asked in return was that the sheep be kept off his range. He had bought a starter herd of cattle and planned for more in the spring, but there wouldn't be enough grass to feed them if the sheep ate it during the winter. The axiom among cattlemen was that everything in front of the woolly monsters was eaten and everything behind them was killed, because they gobbled grass down to the roots.

Cutting and trampling what was left with their sharp, cloven hoofs had earned them the sobriquet "hoofed locusts," and in dry areas the ground they laid bare would not put forth new growth until the spring rains. In addition, it was said that sheep left behind a smell that made cattle refuse to eat or drink.

So, as Texas ranchers had been forced to do, Brand knew the only answer was to put up barbed-wire fences to protect what was his and ensure there would be ample grazing for his growing herd.

It was costly, but he'd won a few hands of poker along the way when the stake was cash, not land, and had saved enough money to hire the men necessary to help him get started and to hire more come spring when he bought the additional cattle.

He saw his men riding in from town, led by his foreman, Kemp Howard. They had gone to pick up the wire Brand had ordered from Albuquerque, and he was disappointed to see the wagons were empty.

Kemp swung down off his horse.

"Did they say when it'll get here?" Brand asked, assuming the shipment was merely going to be late, and wondered why Kemp looked as mad as a hornet over a simple delay.

"No goddamn wire," Kemp hammered each word like a nail.

"That's nothing to be upset about."

"The hell it ain't."

"Shipments are late sometimes."

"This one ain't," Kemp sneered. "It's here and at the depot, but Joe Peblo, the son of a bitch that runs the place, has it locked up and says we ain't gettin' it till you pay a storage fee."

Brand felt the hairs on the back of his neck stand up. "What kind of tomfool nonsense is that?"

"He says it came in yesterday, and since nobody was there to pick it up, he had to pay men to haul it inside so it wouldn't get stolen and him get the blame for it if it did."

Brand had to laugh at that in spite of his blood beginning to boil. "Yeah, like somebody is really going to steal a thousand bales of barbed wire. Is he loco or what?"

Kemp stepped back as he announced, "He wants five dollars a bale for movin' and storin'. That's in addition, of course, to the money owed for the wire since you ordered it cash on delivery."

Brand roared like an enraged bull. "Five dollars a bale? Why-why," he stammered, having a difficult time speaking around the angry knot that was lodged in his throat. "That's five thousand dollars! He can go to hell! I won't pay it!"

"And you won't get the wire," Kemp said matter-of-factly. "We wondered when we rode into the village why the depot was surrounded with men carryin' shotguns and rifles but soon found out. Joe said they had orders to shoot anybody who tried to touch that wire before he gets his money.

"I know it's a pisser, boss," Kemp continued with a shrug, "but we both know who's behind it—the sheepherders. They run the village. There's nothin' we can do."

Brand slung his coffee into the yard. "The hell there isn't! Tell the men to turn those wagons around."

As they approached the depot, Brand saw it was just as Kemp had said. Men with guns seemed to be everywhere, and at the sight of his wagons rolling in, they moved in closer.

Joe Peblo stepped out the front door with a smug grin. "Ah, Señor Austin. You have come to pay your bill and get your wire, no? I am glad. I need the space." He held out a piece of paper. "Here is your bill."

Brand made no move to dismount. He leaned forward from the saddle to take the slip from Joe's hand. He looked at it, then shook his head. "I'm not paying for anything except the wire."

"It is as I told your foreman, señor. You must pay for labor and storage." His eyes shifted from side to side, indicating the gunmen. "I am sure you do not want trouble."

Brand's hands were folded atop the saddle horn. He wanted it clear he was not about to draw his guns and had told his men to do the same. "No, I don't want trouble, so I'm just going to take my wagons and go home and leave you to explain to the barbed-wire company why they've got to now pay to have their wire shipped all the way back to Albuquerque. They aren't going to like it much. And I hear they've got some real mean *hombres* working for them."

Joe's eyebrows crept into his hairline. "What are you talking about?"

"They don't like ranchers who order wire and then don't pay for it. They get nasty about it. They've been known to leave a few reminders of that fact as an example to others not to do the same. Only it won't be me they're mad at. I'm willing to pay for the cost of the shipment, and I'll see that they know that. It's your balls they'll have for breakfast, *amigo,* when they find out you tacked your ridiculous charge on top of their bill and kept them from getting their money."

Joe's eyes darted anxiously, his lips working silently, nervously.

Brand knew he was asking his comrades what he should do next. They were all in cahoots—the whole conniving bunch of them. They wanted to make things as difficult as possible so he would give up and abandon the ranch as Jeb Daniels had. But Brand was no quitter.

He raised his hand in signal. "Let's go, men."

The villagers began backing away, beginning to scatter. They had given up the fight, and now Joe was on his own.

"Wait," Joe yelled to Brand, who was reining his horse about.

Brand paused.

Joe wiped his sweaty brow. "Maybe I can lower the price."

"I told you," Brand said calmly, "I'll only pay the cost for the wire. You didn't have to move it inside, and we both know it—just like we both know what this bullshit is really all about."

"I—" Joe continued to look anxiously at his cohorts, who were leaving and also throwing warning looks over their shoulders.

"Well, what will it be? I haven't got all day."

Laughing nervously, Joe threw his hands up in a helpless gesture. "I suppose I have little choice."

"Oh, yes, you do!"

Brand's eyes cut to see Pepper coming toward them, her face tight with anger.

"You will collect the money you're supposed to," she lashed out at Joe.

"Easy for you to say, señorita," Joe bemoaned. "You

aren't the one who will have to face the fence collectors."

She pointed an accusing finger at Joe. "But you are the one who will have to face your fellow villagers if you give this bastard the barbed wire to keep our sheep off the range."

Tartly, Brand interjected, "*My* range, I should point out, and my business to fence it off if I choose."

She had avoided looking at him but now turned on him in full fury. "The best thing for you to do is take your men, and your wagons, and ride on out of here. And keep on going. All the way back to Texas or wherever the hell you came from.

"Can't you see you aren't wanted here, cowboy?" she added scornfully.

Brand leaned down from his saddle. "I seem to remember a time when I was wanted, sweetheart—by you," he whispered. He would hate himself later, he knew, for being so crass and ungentlemanly, but damn it, she deserved it, and he couldn't resist.

Angrily, she threw her long mane of hair back like a whip. "Remember it was only by accident, señor—only because I was as good as drugged. No woman in her right mind would ever want a man like you if she weren't."

Her words stung like a scorpion's tail, but he wasn't about to let her get away with making a bigger fool of him than she already had.

"If that is true, señorita," he said icily, "then people would do well to avoid eating your cooking, wouldn't they? A cook who hasn't got sense enough to add the right ingredients to her food, who would stoop to putting something in it to try and intentionally make someone sick, has no business running a cantina. Would you like for me to do you a favor and spread the word to save you embarrassment in the future?"

She swung at him but succeeded only in jumping high enough for him to reach out and catch her by her arms and pull her up against him.

"You didn't have to drug me, you little spitfire," he said

huskily as he pinned her arms at her sides and pressed her tight against his chest. "I'd have been glad to pleasure you. And I will again. You just let me know . . ."

He kissed her, hard and quick, then let her slide back down so fast she could not react.

Turning his horse around, he left her standing in the dust.

Pepper shook her fists at him, then realized people were watching her and no doubt wondering about the meaning of his words and about her anger. They were probably also curious as to why he would kiss her and then laugh at her.

She turned on her heel, her skirt swishing about her ankles, her rage making her shiver from head to toe.

Back in the cantina, she tackled her chores with a vengeance. It was Sanchia's job to wash the glasses and polish them and return them to the shelves behind the bar, just as it was her responsibility to scrub the floor. But Pepper did not care that she was sleeping late. She welcomed the toil. Later she would have plenty of time to cook the evening meal.

She would make a big pot of *posole,* too, she decided as she tackled scrubbing the tabletops. It would be one of her best batches, too, and everyone would rave about it. Maybe Brand would hear about it and know it didn't matter what he said. She was still the best cook around.

By midday, Pepper was starting to become annoyed with Sanchia, who still hadn't shown up. Though she hadn't minded doing her chores for her, it was now time to chop the onions and peppers and to prepare to feed the hungry customers sure to come.

Pepper was just about to go and drag Sanchia out of bed with a good scolding when Sanchia walked in the door looking very sleepy and happy.

Pepper did not have to wonder long as to the reason.

"He's back," Sanchia said dreamily. "Buck rode in last night, and this time, he swears he's staying for good."

Chapter 9

Joe Peblo gestured helplessly as he attempted to justify to Pepper why he had relinquished the barbed wire to Brand. "What he said was true. The people from the fence company in Albuquerque would have been very angry when they heard we refused to let him have it unless he paid labor and storage, but I"—he struck his chest with his thumb for emphasis—"would have been the one they blamed."

Pepper was at the stove, stirring a batch of *posole*. It had been several weeks since the incident at the depot, but the villagers were still angry with Joe for giving up without a fight, and he had come to her to beg for her intervention.

"They will listen to you," he said. "The herders respect you, as do all the people of Cuchillo. Now they turn their heads when I pass by, and the men call me a coward, but it is they who are the cowards. They are the ones who backed away that day, but now they say had I not given in, they would have fought."

Pepper sighed and shook her head, continuing to stir the pot. "As much as I loathe Brand Austin, I'm glad there was no bloodshed. And I don't know what I can do to help you," she continued sympathetically. "Everyone is furious over Austin's fences, and they're taking it out on you. Just be patient, Joe, and he'll leave sooner or later when he realizes just how much he's hated. Cuchillo is a village in the middle of nowhere, miles from a town. In other places, when the cattlemen move in and crowd out the sheep men, there are others of their kind around them.

"But not here. He'll get lonely, and so will his men, because there's not even a cantina where they can buy a drink." She felt like adding "or a woman," but, of course, did not. "So they'll get restless and leave."

"They have already started to do so."

"Good." Pepper wanted Brand to leave. Only then, only when she did not have to fear seeing him ever again, could her heart begin to heal. For, as much as she detested him, hated him, for his lies, there were still warm and tender emotions that would not go away.

"As I am asking for your help, he has asked for mine."

Pepper looked at him sharply. Surely she had not heard right. But Joe repeated his words, and she demanded, "To do what?"

"To talk to you. He is well aware of how highly your father, Valdiz, is regarded in Cuchillo, and knows that he will get nowhere with his plan for peace unless he has his support."

Pepper laid the cooking spoon aside and faced him, her hands on her hips. "Get to the point, Joe. What is it you're so afraid to tell me?"

Joe twisted his old straw hat in his hands. "Señor Austin has offered half of his land for *partido.* He has talked to many of the poorer herders, and they're eager to accept but haven't because of Valdiz, who tells them they shouldn't. Your father knows how you hate Señor Austin. So he will never give his approval."

Pepper was stunned. During the many, many hours she and Brand had spent together, she had told him much about sheep ranching. It angered her now as she realized that the information she had given him had been used for his own benefit, and not because he was merely interested in settling down in a quiet, friendly little village.

She wished she had never told him anything, especially about the *partido* system. It was a method of profit sharing begun in Mexico, where most men worked as hired hands.

On a few ranches, however, where owners could not afford many workers, flocks were tended on shares by herders who were paid in kind—with sheep. And each year the herders kept the newborn lambs as their agreed-upon percentage, gradually building their own flocks.

"I don't believe it. And why haven't I heard about this before now?" she asked suspiciously.

Joe smiled hesitantly. "Everyone knows you become hotter than your *posole* at the mention of Señor Austin's name. Even your father. No one dared to talk to you about it except me, because, after all, what do I have to lose? I have no friends left. Even my wife is cold to me."

"But why would Brand go to you? You loathe him like everyone else."

Joe smiled again. "He knows I am also loathed, but if there can be peace between him and the herders, then I'll be forgiven. So I need your help, and so does he, because unless you speak to your father, the herders will never accept his offer, even though it would mean so much to so many of them."

"It just doesn't make sense," she said in wonder. "Brand is a cattleman not a sheepherder. He put up barbed wire to keep sheep out, and now you say he's willing to offer *partido* and give up part of his land? What about his cattle?"

"He says he won't raise cattle. He'll raise sheep—merino rams."

Pepper's eyes widened. That was something else she had told Brand about—the highly coveted merino rams, a Spanish breed developed especially for their thick, silky coats. Full grown, they weighed ten percent more than the common *churro* breed, and produced twenty percent more wool each year, but also cost as much as a thousand dollars a head.

"It's a trick," she said, thinking out loud in her astonishment. "He thinks he can worm his way back in here, and—"

"He does not wish to call on you, Pepper."

"And what would you know about that?" she snapped.

Hesitantly, he said, "Everyone knows the two of you were once sweet on each other. You were seen together all the time."

Embarrassed, she turned back to the *posole.* "Well, it wouldn't make any difference if that were his motive. I'd never be friends with him again."

"You don't have to worry about that." He laughed.

She looked at him again sharply.

Despite all his woes, Joe's eyes twinkled. "He says he will never darken the door of your cantina again, that sometimes you put the wrong ingredients in the *posole.*"

She clenched her teeth together so tightly she felt a sharp pain in her jaw. The nerve of Brand Austin! He was still mocking her for her mistake.

She was stirring the *posole* with a vengeance now, so fast it was almost sloshing over the sides of the large pot. She was furious but knew, despite her rage, that she had to think of the villagers. If Brand was willing not only to offer *partido* but to raise sheep himself—even introducing the merinos—how could she stand in his way? It would be unfair to so many people.

She knew it would be hard, for she had clung to the hope that he would eventually leave. Now she would doubtlessly encounter him from time to time on the street, in a store. He was a handsome man. He would have his pick of young women, marry, have a family.

And all she would have on cold, lonely nights was her anger.

"What will it be?" Joe prodded gently. "Señor Austin says if you refuse, then things will just have to go on as they have been—barbed wire and hard feelings, because he will not give up and go away as Jeb Daniels did."

"So he is giving an ultimatum?" Pepper asked with a raised eyebrow. She would not be pushed into a corner.

"I don't think he meant it that way."

"I'll think about it," she said abruptly. "That's all I can tell you for now."

Joe left, mumbling to himself, disappointed she had not agreed right away.

Pepper continued stirring the *posole* as she fretted about giving her approval while still making it clear to Brand that she would despise him until the day she died. There was absolutely no way she could let him think she had given in because she cared anything at all about him, or would ever again welcome him to her cantina—or to her bed.

Glancing out the window, she saw Sanchia walking across the yard. It was about time, for it was even later than when she usually came to work since Buck's return.

Pepper readied to give her a sound scolding. Enough was enough. If Buck were going to stay, then there had to be some order. Sanchia would have to get to work on time, and . . .

Pepper's eyes narrowed. Sanchia appeared to be having difficulty walking, stumbling now and then, her hands pressed to her stomach.

Pepper hurried to meet her, fearing she was sick, then gasped in horror as Sanchia looked up at her and she saw her face. Her eyes were black and swollen. Blood dribbled from her nose, and her lower lip was split and also bleeding. There were welts on her cheeks and bruises on her neck and shoulders.

"Where is he?" Pepper asked, aching to draw her knife and plunge it into Buck Kiley's black heart.

"Asleep. He'll be leaving soon. Don't do anything, Pepper. Please. Just let him go."

Pepper helped her inside and tended her wounds, seething the whole time.

Between broken sobs, Sanchia described the horrible night. "We had just gone to bed when one of Buck's friends came. He had ridden like the wind to tell him that the real bounty hunter had heard Buck was in Cuchillo and would be here in only two days. Buck had already had a lot to drink but had even more before his friend rode on. By then he was very drunk, and I can't remember what I said to set him off, but he started beating me and wouldn't stop. I was afraid he'd kill me."

"As I hope the bounty hunter kills him—if I don't do it first."

"Just let him go, Pepper. You were right about him. I should have listened to you. He's no good. I had already begun to think that before last night."

"When is he planning to leave?"

"Probably as soon as he wakes up."

"Well, we'll see about that."

"What do you mean?"

Pepper gestured toward the *posole*. "He'll want to eat before he leaves, won't he?"

"I don't know."

"Of course he will. But let me worry about that. I want you to get out of town, because I don't want him to know that I know he beat you. Are you able to ride?"

"I think so, but where—"

"I want you to go to the Indian village and stay with Owl Woman till I come for you. You know the way. You've been there with me lots of times."

Sanchia nodded uncertainly. "I don't feel right leaving everything to you when you tried to warn me about him."

"Forget that. Just do as I say. Now go."

Once Sanchia was reluctantly on her way, Pepper stirred the buckthorn berry powder into the *posole*. Then, forcing herself to appear calm, she went to Sanchia's little hut.

"Sanchia?" she called as she entered. "Sanchia, it's getting terribly late. I need your help."

From the bed, she heard Buck grumbling sleepily as he struggled to awaken. "Huh? Who is it? What's goin' on?"

"Oh, Buck . . ." Pepper fought the impulse to draw her knife and dive for the bed and his throat. "Do you know where Sanchia is?" she asked sweetly. "I need her help."

He sat up, raking her with insolent eyes. "Naw, I don't know where the lazy bitch is."

Pepper gritted her teeth and moved closer to the bed. "Well, I guess there's no telling where she's gone. When you get dressed, come to the cantina. I have fresh *posole* made. Perhaps you'd like some.'' She smiled at him when actually she felt like gagging with revulsion for this man who could beat a woman so brutally.

He licked his lips, his heated gaze darting to her bosom. ''I'd like some of anythin' you got.''

In the past, when Buck would make such remarks, Pepper had fired an angry response to put him in his place. This time, however, she cocked her head to one side, and flashed him a tantalizing smile. ''All I get from you is promises, but then I suppose you only have eyes for Sanchia.''

''I've got more than promises for you,'' he roared, flinging back the covers.

But Pepper was already out the door, forcing shrill laughter as she ran back to the cantina.

Once inside, she paced furiously, recklessly, anxious to make Buck Kiley sicker than he had ever been in his whole life. Then, when he was completely helpless, she would summon one of her friends to help lock him in the cellar to wait for the bounty hunter's arrival.

''I'm here, my little chili pepper.''

She whirled to see Buck come through the door, an arrogant grin on his face.

''So let's have some of that *posole.*'' He smacked his lips eagerly.

And Pepper hurried to serve him.

Chapter 10

Pepper was fighting to keep from smiling as she watched Buck finish eating.

Leaning back in his chair, he wiped his mouth with the back of his hand. "I don't think I can eat another bite."

"I'll be hurt if you don't," she said. She had no idea how long it would take for the purple powder to start to work. She had to keep him there until it did—which meant he had to keep eating.

Grabbing his empty bowl, she hurried to the kitchen, calling over her shoulder, "I know you have a huge appetite. I can't let you go hungry now, can I?"

He ate one more bowl, staring at her with lust-filled eyes that made her uncomfortable. She crossed her fingers under the table in hopes the sickness would strike soon.

"Well, that's all for me," Buck said with a loud burp as he pushed the bowl away. "Now, I've got just enough time to taste somethin' else I've been hankerin' for."

He pushed back from the table so quickly his chair fell back with a bang. Pepper jumped, startled, and, at the same time, Buck's beefy hands wrapped around her wrists, yanking her to her feet.

She twisted her face from side to side, trying to escape his wet, sloppy kisses, and could hold back her revulsion no longer. "Get your filthy hands off me, you bastard!"

She tried to reach her knife, planning to hold him at bay until he became ill, but he grabbed her arm, squeezing so hard she cried out with pain.

"I know what you got hid down here." He drew the

knife from its sheath and tucked it into his belt. "I've seen you use it, but you ain't usin' it on me." He gave her a shake so hard that her head bobbed wildly. "You asked me over here, bitch. And now you're toyin' with me, and I don't like that. Now you calm down and give me some lovin', cause I got a bounty hunter hot on my trail, and I gotta get outta here, and—"

He gave a loud groan and stopped shaking her, but still held her arms tightly.

Pepper felt a thrilling rush. The buckthorn berries were working!

He threw her into a chair and wrapped his arms around his stomach, staggering back. "Oh, it hurts. My gut hurts. It—"

Pepper smiled triumphantly, and with the fury of a charging bull, Buck bellowed, "Damn you, you poisoned me, didn't you? That's how come you were flirtin' with me this mornin'. You wanted to get me over here to eat so you could feed me poison."

He started for her, but Pepper jumped and began to back away—but in the wrong direction. Horror-stricken, she found herself pinned against the bar as he threw himself at her.

"I'm gonna get you for this." He pressed against her so hard she could barely breathe. "I'm gonna fix you good. And I think now you were lyin' about lookin' for Sanchia. I think I know what this is all about—you takin' revenge for me beatin' her. Well, you saw what she looked like, but I promise she was beautiful compared to what you're gonna look like when I'm done."

He raised his fist, and Pepper steeled herself for the blow, but, instead, he let her go to clutch his stomach again.

She began inching her way along the bar. If she could make it to the door, she could run for help. Someone would help her restrain Buck and keep him there until the bounty hunter arrived.

But he saw her moving and lunged for her again, this time slinging her facedown to the floor. "You ain't goin' nowhere. You're stayin' right here till I'm able to take care of you.''

He took off his belt and tied her wrists behind her.

''I'll have my fill of you, and then I'm gonna fix that face of yours so no man will ever look at it again. I'm gonna shoot your fingers off, too. One at a time, so you won't never be able to poison anybody else.''

He pulled her up from the floor and pushed her toward the stairs. He dragged her up, her body bumping painfully on each step. In agony, she cried out. He left her long enough to go back down to the kitchen and get a rag to stuff in her mouth.

''I'm stayin' here till whatever you gave me passes, and then I'll keep my promise to you,'' he muttered as he pulled her up to her room. ''Ain't no bounty hunter gonna catch me, by damn. Hell, if I like what you got, I might even take you with me. It gets lonesome on the trail. And when I get tired of you, I can always sell you to renegade Apaches.''

He pushed her down on the bed, tied her ankles to the bedposts with a sheet so she could not run away, then bolted from the room.

Pepper was furious with herself for letting Buck get the upper hand. Her temper had done her in as well. Oh, how she wished she had listened to Sanchia and just let him go. Now, unless she could think of some way to escape, she was in real danger.

When she heard him coming up the steps, she estimated a half-hour had passed. She kept a chamber pot in the cellar for times when customers had an emergency and figured that was where he had gone.

He burst into the room, and she saw he had her knife in his hand. Her screams were muffled by the gag as she tried in vain to twist free.

''Now then . . .'' he said in a low, ominous voice as he got up on the bed to straddle her. ''You're gonna tell me exactly what you put in that goddamn *posole*, or I'm gonna start peelin' your face off, piece by piece. You understand?''

She nodded, wide-eyed, convinced he meant every word he said.

He pulled the rag from her mouth. ''Now tell me, bitch.''

His face was pale, and he was gasping, and she could even hear the angry growling in his guts as he loomed over her.

''Buckthorn berries,'' she said. ''They will give you the trots. Nothing more. I did not intend to kill you,'' she added, wishing she had the nerve to scream that she wished she had but didn't dare when she could feel the knife pressing into her cheek. She did not want to make him any angrier than he already was.

''How long?'' He pressed the tip of the knife into her flesh just enough to make it bleed. ''How long am I gonna have the goddamn trots?''

''I don't know. I've never used the berries before. I have no way of knowing.''

Suddenly his face contorted with anguish, and, cursing, he got off the bed to stumble from the room and down the steps once more.

Pepper thought this time perhaps an hour passed, and, as she lay there, helpless, she could think of no way out of her predicament. He was going to make good his threat, and there was nothing she could do about it. He would take her with him, rape her repeatedly until he tired of her, then sell her to renegade Apaches, who would make her wish she were dead. He would also shoot off her fingers.

Pepper squeezed her eyes shut against the impending horror and tried instead to think of happier times with Brand and the wonder they had shared—in the very bed where she was now held captive.

She wished there had been time to talk to her papa and urge him to give his approval for Brand's plan for *partido*. Sooner or later she knew she would have, because it would mean so much to so many families. She wished, too, that she had not been so quick to condemn Brand for having lied about being a bounty hunter. After all, she had more or less pushed him into it, and it made sense that he would allow her to think at the time that he was anything but a hated cattleman.

She could see his point, his purpose—now that it was too late.

Buck returned, looking weak, drawn. "I swear, when this is over, you will wish you were dead," he cried hoarsely, pacing beside the bed. "I'd kill you, but I want to make you suffer, and right now I'm too damn sick."

He left her again but returned sooner than he had before. That had to mean the berries were beginning to wear off, Pepper thought with dread. Soon his body would be purged, and then he could begin to make good his threat.

The day wore on, and soon the afternoon sun was streaming through the window. She was thirsty but even had he not stuffed the rag back in her mouth, she would not have dared ask for water. He would not oblige her, anyway, and it would only please him to know she was suffering.

Then he returned with a little color in his face. "I think the worst is over. We can leave soon, and it's a good thing." He was talking more to himself than to her as he began pacing once more. "Ben didn't know exactly how far behind him the bounty hunter was. Maybe a couple of days, but I need to hit the trail just in case Ben didn't know what he was talkin' about, and—"

At the sound of banging on the door downstairs, Buck froze, and Pepper's eyes widened. She seldom locked the door and hadn't this morning, which meant Buck had.

He whirled on her. "It ain't time for the cantina to open, is it?"

She shook her head. With fall approaching and the days growing cooler and shorter, she had begun waiting until much later to begin serving.

"Open up in there," a man's voice bellowed loudly.

Buck ran to the window and looked down at the street. "It's him," he whispered. "I know him. Wade Hailey. Goddamn no-good bounty hunter."

"Buck Kiley, I know you're in there," came the voice from below. "Now come out peaceful. You know I'm a fair man, and I'll take my prisoners back alive if there's any way."

"Here's my way!" Buck yelled. He drew his gun and fired.

A shot fired back.

Buck pressed against the wall next to the window. "There's a woman up here!" he shouted. "You don't want to shoot her, do you?"

A chorus of protests rang out, and Pepper, in the midst of her terror, was warmed to hear some of the villagers. Evidently they had heard the shooting and had rallied.

"Coward!" The bounty hunter cried. "Hiding behind a woman."

"I'm comin' out with her, too."

"Like hell you are."

Buck looked at Pepper. "Your friends are gatherin', and as soon as enough of 'em are here, they'll make sure he doesn't shoot when we leave. All we gotta do is wait."

Pepper squeezed her eyes shut, thinking of the nightmare before her. She also grieved for what might have been, for now her papa would never favor Brand's plan for peace. Nothing would come of it, and the trouble would continue. Neither would there be a chance to let Brand know she had forgiven him and to find out whether he might care for her, if only a little.

Time passed.

Buck made two more hurried trips to the chamber pot in the cellar. Each time he returned Pepper could hear that the crowd outside had grown larger. Buck laughed out loud when the bounty hunter's voice rose angrily as he argued with the crowd that he was not about to give up and ride out of town just because Buck had a hostage.

Then Buck aimed and fired out the window. "He's dead and now there's nobody to stop me," Buck cried in triumph. "So we're gettin' out of here right now and—" He gasped, groaned, and, holding his stomach, rushed from the room again.

When he returned, he was smiling. "I think it's over. Now don't you give me any trouble, you hear?"

He untied her quickly and yanked her roughly to her feet. With his gun pressed into her side, he began shoving her down the steps and across the cantina.

When they reached the front door, Buck unlocked it, then opened it a crack. "We're comin' out!" he yelled. "I've got a gun on Pepper, and if anybody tries anythin', I'll kill her. So get outta my way!"

Easing the door open, he held Pepper in front of him but held his gun so it could be seen.

Pepper winced, seeing her mama crying as she clung to her papa. Others cried, also.

"Don't you try nothin', neither," Buck growled in her ear. "I'll kill you, so help me, I—"

A shot rang out, followed by a chorus of screams.

Pepper felt something wet hit the side of her face, then realized it was Buck's blood as she turned and saw the blood spurting from the bullet hole between his eyes.

He fell to the ground with a thud.

There was mass confusion as the crowd surged forward. Pepper was hugged first by her mama, then her papa, wondering dizzily who among the villagers had been the crack shot able to accomplish such a feat.

Then she saw him.

Standing to one side, Brand still held the smoking gun in his hand. He holstered his weapon, then held out his arms to her, and she ran to throw herself in his embrace.

"Joe Peblo came and told me there was a bounty hunter in town looking for Sanchia's boyfriend," he said as he held her close. "I came as soon as I could, afraid there'd be trouble. Oh, God, Pepper, when I found out he was holding you hostage, I nearly lost my mind. What was he doing in the cantina? How come he didn't run?"

"He was already running," she said, softly chuckling. "He had the trots and couldn't leave."

He held her away from him, searching her face. "You mean . . ."

She nodded briskly and explained that Buck had beaten Sanchia, then described her plan to make him sick and to tie him up and hold him for the bounty hunter. Only it hadn't worked out that way. "I would've been a goner if not for you," she said, somber once more thinking of the near-disaster.

"Well, it's over now, Pepper."

The villagers converged on Brand then, and there was no more time for talking. He was pulled away from her as praise was heaped upon him for his heroics.

Pepper stood back and watched, a maelstrom of emotions whirling inside her. He no longer needed her approval. Or her papa's. The villagers were embracing him with open arms. He was now a welcome member of the community, and his plan for *partido* would make him even more so.

She turned and went back inside the cantina. She would open for the evening, as always, and there was work to be done, food to be prepared.

Life would go on as before.

Without love.

Without Brand.

Pepper was standing at the stove, stirring the *posole* when Brand walked through the back door.

"Do you still hate me?" he asked quietly.

Pepper's heart slammed into her chest at the sight of him. "No, but I did," she said with candor. "You used me, Brand. And you betrayed me. I had every reason to loathe you, but there's no denying you saved my life. For that, you have my gratitude."

She heard him cross the kitchen and stop behind her. She felt his arms around her waist and he pulled her against him. "Only gratitude?" he murmured, his breath warm against her ear. "Is that all you can feel for me now, Pepper?"

She wriggled in his grasp, torn between wanting to remain there and the impulse to run away. "You hurt me deeply—"

"And I'm sorry. You've got to believe that, but what was I to do, Pepper? If you'd known the truth in the beginning, you wouldn't have given me the time of day."

She knew that was so, yet she had her pride.

But pride won't keep you warm on a cold night, Pepper, a little voice deep inside her warned. *And he said he is sorry.*

"It was a tough time. I had a real fight on my hands, Pepper, trying to make everyone see I didn't intend to be like other cattle ranchers."

She realized then that she was not without fault, and she apologized. "I didn't make it any easier for you. I went out of my way to make them not trust you."

Suddenly, he cried, "Pepper, I love you. And I think you care for me, too. Can't we give it—us—another chance?"

Overcome with emotion, she turned in his arms and offered her lips in answer.

He kissed her until they were both breathless, then released her with a smile as he nodded to the *posole* simmering on the stove. "If you're making that for me, leave out the buckthorn berries, please," he teased. "As for the mescal beans, I'm going to lock those away to use when I need them to make you my love slave. Because"—his smile faded as he soberly declared—"I love you, and I want us to be together always."

"Oh, Brand." She melted against him. "I love you, too, and you won't need the beans, not ever. I'm yours as long as you want me."

"But I want you for my wife."

She looked up at him in wonder and knew by the look in his eyes that he meant it.

"Yes," she cried fervently, throwing her arms around him and raining kisses all over his face. "Yes. Yes. Yes."

She moved out of his arms, walked to the front door, and locked it. Her customers would have to wait for her spicy cooking, for she intended to give her spicy lovin' to Brand. This night. And forever.

Patricia Hagan, the *New York Times* best-selling author of thirty-four books, firmly believes that nothing sets the stage better for a romantic evening than a home-cooked meal.

Spicy recipes are, of course, a specialty, she says, for what is better than a meal created to add zest to the palate as well as the soul?

In addition to cooking, she enjoys reading, painting, and working in wildlife rehabilitation. She lives in the western North Carolina mountains with her husband, Erik, and their very special wirehaired fox terrier, Krystal, and a menagerie of wild "critters."

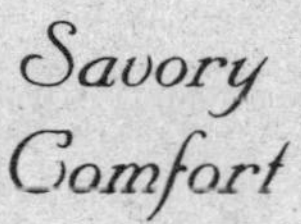

Linda Madl

Rosemary's Brown Beef Stew

2	*pounds boneless beef chuck or beef soup meat*
1	*tablespoon fat, shortening, or vegetable oil*
4	*cups hot water*
1	*teaspoon lemon juice*
1	*teaspoon Worcestershire sauce*
½	*garlic clove, minced*
1	*medium onion, sliced*
1	*small bay leaf*
2	*teaspoons salt*
2–3	*peppercorns*
1	*teaspoon sugar*
6	*carrots, quartered*
6	*potatoes, peeled, cut in eighths*

Brown meat thoroughly in a tablespoon of fat in a large heavy skillet or Dutch oven. Add remaining ingredients except for carrots and potatoes.

Simmer about 2 hours, adding water if necessary. Add carrots and potatoes and cook for about 30 minutes, until vegetables are tender. Thicken liquid, if desired, for gravy.

Makes 8 generous servings. Great served with a fruit compote or a green salad and fresh baked bread.

Chapter 1

Indiana, 1812

Rosemary had been waiting for John for two weeks, ever since she'd first smelled spring in the air. Her nose pressed against the store window, she watched the ice melting on the Wabash River, just across the street from her father's business.

It was still too cold and the days too short for green buds to sprout on the few trees along the river, and the tall prairie grasses beyond town still waved brown and lifeless in the wind. But the soft scent of spring rode the March breeze. The snow-hardened lane in front of the store had grown soft and muddy from the rain, and all of nature would soon be stirring again.

The trappers and frontiersmen would begin to trickle into Vincennes wading through the muddy streets, their moccasins caked with wet earth and their packhorses laden with shiny furs. They would come singing their melodious French Creole songs interrupted only by the shooing of the village hogs from their path.

And John would come with them—as he had come with his father and then alone, after his father's death, at the change of the seasons without fail.

She envisioned the renowned army scout, frontiersman, and trapper with his gray eyes, tawny hair, soft deep voice, breathtakingly broad shoulders, and long, strong legs.

Rosemary sighed. No man looked as good as John in

fringed buckskins, and no man had even come close to capturing her heart. Just the thought of him made her smooth her apron and touch her starched mobcap to be certain it was still crisp. She intended to look perfect the moment he walked through the door of Papa's store. Perfect.

"Where are you, John?" she whispered against the windowpane, her breath fogging its cold surface. With her finger she drew a heart on the misty glass.

She knew he'd come to see her when he arrived, as he had for the past two years. His last visit was just before Christmas, before winter set in, when he'd come to buy supplies, and she'd invited him to a supper of roasted wild duck stuffed with cornbread dressing and blackberry bread pudding. John's contentment and the look of appreciation in his eye made all her cooking worth every hour and ounce of effort.

She smiled. He'd lingered a day longer than usual to escort her to the Christmas dance. On his arm, she'd been the envy of every girl of marriageable age in town, and she'd been content with that.

But this spring she had turned twenty-four and Papa was determined to send her to Baltimore to find a husband as he had done with her sisters, Laurel and Myrtle. Nothing she said could sway him from his plan. But she was as determined to stay at home where she'd been born and raised as he was to send her away.

So this was her last opportunity to get a marriage proposal from John before her father made arrangements for her departure, and she had to make the most of it.

She knew he could arrive any day now, but hoping that John would arrive today, she had made her hearty beef stew for supper, a special dish she had not served him before. She planned that once his hunger was satisfied and he was relaxed and comfortable she would lead the conversation to the topic of marriage and hopefully John would pop the question.

Her smile faded and she rested her head against the window frame. Behind her she could hear the trio of farmers who were examining tools in the corner and the two army soldiers who were sitting by the potbellied stove sharing rumors about the possibility of war with England.

But the street beyond the window remained empty—except for Mistress Chomeau and her daughter.

Hiding her disappointment, Rosemary left the window and forced a smile to her face as she met the Creole seamstress at the shop door. Mistress Chomeau sewed for many of the town's ladies and never tired of looking at cloth, thread, and buttons.

"I'd like to see your stock of calico," Mistress Chomeau announced as she looked around the store, clearly searching for Papa, who was in the storage room. Her daughter wandered away to explore the store's treasures.

"Of course, we have some very nice colors." Rosemary tugged a bolt of calico off the shelf and bent over it as she spread the fabric.

The shop bell rang and Rosemary heard the soft pad of moccasins on the plank floor. She raised her head and bounced on her tiptoes to peer around a stack of barrels at the door hoping—praying—to see John looming in the doorway.

Red Carberry grinned back at her. "Have you heard the news, Miss Beck? Injuns massacred every last member of the Kitter family."

The red-haired trapper stated the news loudly, and the hum of the farmers' and the soldiers' conversation ceased. Mistress Chomeau dropped the fabric she'd been inspecting. White, fearful faces turned to Carberry.

Rosemary glanced around, wondering if her father, who disliked any unpleasantness in his store, had heard the trapper's news.

"Is there more?" one of the farmers inquired.

Now the center of attention, Carberry puffed out his chest and continued talking to a pair of fellow trappers, who had followed him in. "Found that poor family myself in a cabin not thirty miles from here."

Rosemary groaned, horrified and dismayed by the tragedy.

"Each of 'em scalped right in their beds, even the pretty li'l girl—hardly a hair left on her head—and no older than that little one over there."

The trapper pointed at Mistress Chomeau's daughter, whose nose was pressed against the glass jar full of Rosemary's homemade maple sugar, cream, and nut sweets. Thankfully, the little girl was oblivious to her mother's alarm and the uneasiness swirling around her.

Rosemary was about to call to her father when he came striding toward the front of the store, wearing a white apron wrapped around his tall frame.

"Red Carberry, I heard that. You take that ugly story outside or to the tavern where it belongs," Papa scolded, casting an uneasy glance in Rosemary's and the seamstress's direction. "There be delicate ears in this establishment."

But it was too late. Mistress Chomeau grabbed her child's hand and hurried out of the store. The farmers muttered among themselves, and the soldiers frowned at each other and rose to leave.

"See what you're doing to my business, Carberry," Papa said.

The trapper dismissed the complaint with a wave of his hand. "Folks should know what's going on, Beck."

"And Red's story is true, Frederick," argued one of the other trappers. "I heard about Injun trouble up north, too."

Rosemary wanted to clamp her hand over the man's mouth. Stories of Indian attacks—true or invented—would only reinforce Papa's decision to send her to Baltimore.

" 'Tis the British, I tell you," Carberry said. "And I think the folks of Vincennes deserve to know what's happening."

"Then take your story to Elihu Stout's newspaper," Papa ordered, pointing in the direction of the print shop.

"You know Stout's not printing the paper now," Carberry said.

"Then shout it from the territorial capitol steps for all I care. But I'll not have you exciting my customers, Carberry."

Grumbling, Carberry and his cronies left, and Rosemary sighed with relief. The man had never numbered among the trappers she and her father liked.

The afternoon grew late and the sky clouded over. A few more patrons came in, but gradually the store emptied as suppertime grew near.

"I better go check the stew," Rosemary said, reaching for her shawl on the hook by the door.

"Looks like we'll be alone for supper tonight," Papa muttered, rearranging some bottles on the shelf. "I'll not invite the likes of Carberry to sit down at our table."

"No, of course not," Rosemary said, disappointed that there would be no guests—dismayed that John had not appeared. She and her genteel father were known for their hospitality, and no man ever turned down a supper invitation or left without eating at least two helpings of anything Rosemary prepared. Though she loved to cook and was always prepared for guests, usually trappers, fur traders, and other merchants, this was one meal she had wanted to serve only to John.

Her father had told her more than once that she had her mother's talent for cooking and that the dishes her mother had prepared had captured his heart.

Maybe that's where Rosemary had gotten the idea to use food to capture John Winston Haley when he returned this spring. During the winter, she'd laid in all the best spices and ingredients she could find in town to make her stew. She'd even traded some precious cinnamon to Mistress Lebor for a bowl of dried wild plums for a cobbler. She knew it would be the perfect sweet after a meal of hot stew and fresh baked bread.

Wrapping herself in her shawl against the chill wind,

Rosemary hurried out the back door and picked her way across the yard on the stepping-stones Papa had laid to their house. Once inside, she found the beef stew she'd prepared earlier in the day bubbling contentedly over a low fire in the hearth. Satisfied with the savory-smelling stew, she set the table with her pewter, and checked to see that the bread had cooled and was ready to slice.

After a quick look in Papa's shaving mirror to see that her cap was still crisp and her apron spotless, she put on her shawl and headed back to the store to help Papa close up.

Halfway across the yard, she heard the unmistakable sound of a hog rooting. She halted. It was a disgrace that hogs were allowed to wander through the territorial capitol's streets damaging property, creating a hazard to animals and people, and leaving an offensive odor during the summer.

But many citizens, including their neighbor and pig owner Sam La Belle, saw no harm in a few hogs cleaning up the street garbage.

Well, this was one hog she would take care of in short order. She'd run off more than one hog in her time.

She stepped off the path. Navigating between the mud puddles, she peeked around the corner of the store, where the sound of the snorting and squealing seemed the loudest.

Sure enough a young pregnant sow had already excavated a hole right next to the store's log wall. Rosemary recognized the notch cut in the creature's ear as Sam's mark.

"Here now!" she yelled, waving the corner of her shawl at the creature. "Stop that. Shoo! Go home and make Sam feed you properly."

The hog ceased rooting and surveyed Rosemary with a beady-eyed stare, then returned to its occupation, uttering obscene squeals.

Frustrated and annoyed, Rosemary picked up a small stick and waved it at her porcine foe. "Shoo! Shoo! Get on with you now! Go!" She whacked the stick against the side of the store and hollered at the top of her lungs. "Shoo! Shoo!"

Screeching as if it'd been scalded, the hog charged Rosemary, its ears flopping, its tiny hooves splashing through the mud, its snout high in the air.

Rosemary knew a pregnant sow could be extremely dangerous, but the hog's sudden attack caught her off guard. She stumbled back, attempting to turn and run, but her heel caught in her hem and she splashed down in an enormous puddle. Muddy water showered her everywhere—across her clean skirt, her best spotless dimity apron, her face, and her freshly starched mobcap.

But she had the presence of mind to wave the stick and keep shouting, "Shoo! Shoo! Shoo, you four-legged ham!"

The hog halted in its tracks, its tiny eyes glaring at something over Rosemary's head. With a snort, the sow turned abruptly and trotted off, its curly tail flying high in fright.

Rosemary stared after the creature, amazed that she was better at dealing with hogs than she'd thought.

Slowly she became aware of someone standing over her. She tipped her head back a bit and stared into the handsome, tawny-bearded face of John Winston Haley.

Her heart sank. So much for "perfect."

Chapter 2

"Hello, Rosemary. May I help you up?"

Rosemary looked at John's hand, then tipped her head back a little farther and saw two Indians standing behind him wearing calico shirts and fringed buckskin leggings like white men. Scouts no doubt. Everyone knew Governor

Harrison hated Indians; few would be foolish enough to walk the streets of Vincennes unless they were known allies.

She looked back at John. He did not laugh, though she thought she saw the corner of his mouth working against the urge. She was certain amusement gleamed in his gray eyes. She must look a mess, not to mention ridiculous, sitting in the biggest mud puddle on Water Street.

He withdrew his hand and walked around her, avoiding the puddle. Then he leaned over and offered his broad, strong hand again. "Here, take hold."

She reached for his fingers, but then pulled back. Her own hand was dripping with mud, and she was embarrassed by her bespattered condition. "Perhaps I should manage on my own."

"Now, Rosemary, I've touched worse things than a bit of mud," John assured her, smiling at last. She couldn't resist smiling back.

Before she realized what he was doing, he caught her under her arms, lifted her from the puddle, and set her on solid ground.

"There now," he said. "See, that was easy enough."

She peered down at her filthy apron, feeling the mud splatters drying on her cheeks. Dirty rainwater dripped from the hem of her skirt and she felt the moisture between her toes. She could even smell the pig's scent in the air. What a miserable picture she made for the man she intended to marry. It was almost enough to make a less determined woman weep. Resolutely she wiped her hands on her apron—too late to worry about keeping it spotless now.

"It's good to see you, John." She held her head high and faced the Indians as if nothing were amiss. But embarrassment burned her cheeks. "Who are your friends?"

"This is Standing Tree and Cornstalk. They're Delaware scouts who've been helping me trap. They are also good trackers and loyal to the States. I've brought them to town to meet Captain Smithson at the army garrison and to offer him their services. He's been looking for good scouts since I resigned.

"Standing Tree and Cornstalk, this is Miss Rosemary Jasmine Beck."

Their faces as somber as a judge's, the copper-skinned men nodded a greeting, but to Rosemary's horror laughter danced in their shining dark eyes.

"Pleased to meet you," Rosemary said, fighting the humiliation that refused to go away. She cast a sidelong glance at John. He looked better than she remembered—taller and broader, his voice deeper, his gray eyes darker and keener. Good heavens! She couldn't give up on her plan now, not because of a soiled apron.

"Why don't you go inside?" Rosemary suggested, inspiration finally coming to her rescue. "Papa will be ever so glad to see you. Standing Tree and Cornstalk, too. I was just seeing to supper. You will join us, won't you? There's plenty."

John looked at his Indian friends, who nodded. "Wouldn't miss a meal at your table, Rosemary."

"Good, it's settled then," she said, pleased, but already edging her way toward the house. "I'll see you in about a half-hour?"

"Yes, ma'am." John's white teeth flashed in his bearded face. The only expression of his that she liked better than his smile was his laugh—provided he wasn't laughing at her.

The moment the men turned away, she dashed for the house. All she had to do was set three more places at the table and clean up. If she worked quickly, she still had a chance to impress John.

"So, John Winston, is the storekeeper's daughter as pretty as you remember?" Standing Tree asked as John watched Rosemary head for the house behind the store. Her mud-soaked skirt clung to her trim ankles and all the way up her legs to her firm, round bottom.

"Prettier," John admitted a bit wistfully.

Her almond-shaped eyes were a deeper amber than he remembered, a rich molten gold that matched her tiny amber stone earrings which she always wore. She told him that they had been a legacy bequeathed to her by her mother, who died when Rosemary was very young. From the first day he'd seen her nine years ago he'd been captivated by those tiny earrings which declared her dainty femininity.

Rosemary had been fifteen when he'd met her in her father's store and he'd been barely a man of nineteen. She'd caught his eye, but the Indiana frontier was too wide and exciting for him to tie himself to a female. So he signed on as a scout for the army garrisons on the frontier, which made him a vagrant with only his father's cabin to call home. There was no time in his life or a place in his heart for a girl, but he never forgot Rosemary.

Every time he saw her, especially these last couple of years, she had grown more beautiful. He'd often wondered how her curly sable tresses would feel between his fingers. As soft and silky as they looked? And her wide, generous mouth. Would it feel warm and welcoming beneath his lips? Though the desire to kiss her last Christmas was overwhelming, he never had and he had good reason not to. But today it almost didn't seem important.

Reaching the house, Rosemary must have felt his eyes on her because she turned, offered an uncertain smile and a small wave. Standing Tree returned the gesture.

''She's even prettier,'' John repeated to himself as much as to his companions.

''Small, busy, like a hummingbird,'' Standing Tree observed.

''Too small. She couldn't even fight off a pig,'' Cornstalk pointed out, frowning. ''My wife drove off a bear once.''

Now John was sorry he'd ever said anything about Rosemary to his friends. But when they'd neared Vincennes, thoughts of her had been so strong that the Indians had guessed that his mind was preoccupied with a woman, and their questions had begun. He'd never intended for anyone to know about his feelings for Rosemary, since the possibility of there ever being anything between them was unthinkable.

"Your wife is an exceptional woman, Cornstalk," John finally said, "and I will be forever indebted to your generous woman, who makes buckskins for her husband and his friend."

Cornstalk's head bobbed in agreement. "Friend without a wife. We will give you a new Indian name, John Winston. Friend-without-a-wife."

Standing Tree tossed his head back and laughed.

John did not find his new name amusing. He turned away from his companions' good-humored teasing and went in search of Rosemary's father to buy his supplies.

It was almost an hour before John and the Indians returned to Water Street and the Beck house.

John paused on the porch and examined his moccasins to make sure he'd remembered to brush the mud from them. His clean linen shirt was buttoned neatly at his wrists, and he rubbed his chin to assure himself that he was clean-shaven.

"We will wait out here for you," Cornstalk said, pulling his blanket closer against a sudden gust of cold wind.

During the past hour John, who had resigned from scouting after his father's death, had introduced the two Indians to Captain Smithson. The captain was in need of reliable scouts and he looked to John for recommendations. But since the war with Tecumseh and his tribes even loyal Delawares were not very welcome in Vincennes and Cornstalk and Standing Tree were well aware of that.

"No need to wait outside," John said, knowing the Indians would be welcome in the Beck house. The Becks were among the few people in Vincennes who made the differentiation between friendly and hostile Indians. "Rosemary will have places set for you, too."

Cornstalk and Standing Tree exchanged looks of disbelief.

"You heard her invite us," John said.

The Indians nodded to each other, and John rapped on the door.

"Hello," Rosemary said, opening the door and smiling up at him as he and his friends entered the house.

He noted that she had used the hour to change her clothes, too. Her fresh white cap was edged in lace. Her butter yellow calico gown set off the richness of her dark hair and the gold of her eyes. John's breath caught in his throat; thankfully he had the presence of mind to fish his gift for her out of his pocket.

"I brought you something, Rosemary." John held out the wooden comb he'd carved during the winter. It was such a humble gift and he had momentarily thought of not giving it. But the maple comb, polished to a smooth, shiny sheen, was useless except in Rosemary's hands. He'd made it for her.

Her lips parted in surprise. She looked up at him and gently took the comb from his open hand. "Oh, John, how thoughtful."

"I like to carve by the fire at night," John said, oddly annoyed with the pleasure her gratitude brought him.

"And you think of me?"

Before John could think of a denial, Frederick rushed forward to greet them. Soon the men were seated around the table, and Rosemary ladled a savory beef stew into their shallow pewter bowls. She sat down and the conversation centered on general topics for a few minutes until Beck spoke.

"Red Carberry was in today telling some wild tale about the massacre of the Kitter family up north. Anything to it?" Beck casually dunked his bread in the stew, but John had heard the concern in the man's voice.

Rosemary raised her head and frowned across the table at her father. The disapproval in her expression surprised John. Frederick doted on his youngest daughter and she adored him. Hardly a cross word ever passed between them.

"Must we talk of such things now, Papa?" Rosemary shot John a glare that made him think twice about his response, but he was not a man to soft-pedal the truth.

"Regretfully, it's true." John met Rosemary's hostile gaze and held it. He especially did not believe in lying to people he cared about. "Harrison may have defeated Tecumseh and his warriors at Tippecanoe last fall, but isolated settlers are still being murdered."

Beck shook his head. "I was afraid of that. Are the British behind it?"

Standing Tree nodded. "I talked with the Shawnee, who have met with the Redcoats. They promise guns and other gifts for making trouble for the settlers."

John relinquished his hold on Rosemary's gaze and turned to the storekeeper. "It's the old story. The British have never given up their efforts to keep the Indians warring with American settlers. A hostile Indian territory benefits British hunters and trappers while it hinders American settlement in the West.

"The truth is, if war isn't declared against Great Britain for impressment of American sailors and shipping violations at sea, it will start in the West with the Americans fighting the British and their Indian allies."

"I thought so," Beck said, shaking his head again. "Didn't I tell you this was going to happen, Rosemary?"

"Yes, Papa," Rosemary said, looking down at her bowl of stew. "But I was wondering . . . About the poor Kitters . . . Their murders could have been a renegade attack."

Beck looked at John. "I suppose a renegade raid is always possible."

"They took scalps," John said. There was no sense sugarcoating the atrocities that had occurred.

Cornstalk spoke with his mouth full. "That's the British price for the guns—scalps."

Rosemary paled slightly and put down her spoon.

"Then I am right," Beck said to her. "I don't think there's any reason to delay."

"There has always been danger around Vincennes." Pleading filled Rosemary's voice.

"Delay what?" John asked. Why were Rosemary and her father at such odds over Indian hostilities?

"I'm sending Rosemary to Baltimore to live with her sister Myrtle," Beck said, his voice firm. "And that's final. I should have done it a couple of years ago. The frontier is no place for a young woman, especially a frontier where there's a war being waged."

John peered down the table at Rosemary, whose frown had slipped into an unhappy expression. John's appetite vanished. So that was it. Her father was sending her away and she didn't want to go. He pushed his unfinished bowl of stew aside.

"It's time for her to find a husband," Beck went on, as he carefully selected another bite of beef. "No offense, John, but the pickings around here are slim. Most of the trappers are irresponsible or they already have squaw wives. The farmers are married and the garrison's soldiers are too young and penniless to boot."

John couldn't take his eyes off Rosemary now. Finally she glanced up at him, a hint of embarrassment in the flutter of her eyelashes. Their eyes met and his heart skipped a beat. What would Vincennes hold for him without Rosemary?

"She's a bit long in the tooth, but she's pretty enough and a good enough cook to find some Baltimore man with prospects who'll marry her," Beck went on, fastidiously wiping clean the bottom of his bowl with a chunk of bread.

John watched a fiery blush rise in Rosemary's cheeks. He knew Frederick didn't mean to be unkind, but neither did he have to be so blunt. Rosemary would make any man a fine wife. John knew for a fact there would be a line of Vincennes bachelors ready to propose marriage if they thought Rosemary and Frederick would accept them. But Beck was right. Damned few of them would be worthy, even if . . .

With a start, John caught Standing Tree and Cornstalk

staring at him. Unsettled, he reached for his bowl and quickly began eating again. "I think you're right, Frederick. Indiana territory won't be safe for a woman at least for a few more years. Baltimore would be a better place for Rosemary, until this war is over. I'm afraid there will be more scalps taken before there's peace."

"Makes me feel better to hear you say that." Beck handed his bowl to Rosemary, who served him another helping of stew. As she returned the bowl to her father, her gaze flickered up to meet John's once again.

In the depths of her rich amber eyes, he spied her pain. He knew he'd done nothing to help her. A spark of guilt wormed through him—guilt and irritation. He shoved his bowl aside again and glared at her.

It would be irresponsible of him if he didn't agree with Frederick's plan. Hardening his heart, John decided, like it or not, Rosemary would just have to be angry with him. Her father was right. Leaving Vincennes was for her own good.

Chapter 3

After they had eaten dessert, Papa rose from his place to search for his pipe on the mantel, and the Indians followed him.

Rosemary began clearing the table, snatching dirty dishes out of John's hands without looking at him. Helping her clean up after supper was a chore he'd assumed from his first visit to their home. It had been one of the many thoughtful things about him that Rosemary had always treasured. But tonight she was so angry with him that she didn't want his help.

To her annoyance John grabbed the same dish she reached for. Over the tabletop, they tugged on the dish.

"Rosemary?" he murmured under his breath.

The sound of her name on his lips sent a sweet shiver down her spine, and she relinquished the bowl to him, only to turn away and seize another.

"How could you, John?" she hissed.

"How could I what?"

"Agree with Papa."

"Because he's right," John said.

Then, as if they were engaged in some contest to see who could gather the most dishes, he snatched up several more before she could reach them.

She halted at the corner of the table and glared at him. "How many years have I lived in Vincennes, John?"

"All your life, as far as I know."

"That's right. And I think that's long enough for you to know that I don't belong in Baltimore."

"You belong where you'll be safe," John snapped back. "And if your father asks me again, I'll give him exactly the same answer."

Confused and discouraged, she turned away and carried the dishes to the dish tub.

"Do you fellows have a place to sleep, John?" her father asked, jarring Rosemary from her gloomy thoughts.

"I have a place at Lasselle's tavern," John answered. "But you know how they feel about Indians."

Beck cleared his throat. "I know. We've got an empty stall out in the stable, if you two don't mind sleeping in the hay. Rosemary, we have extra blankets, don't we?"

"Yes, Papa, I'll get them." She went into the adjoining room, which was her father's, and found the extra bedding in her mother's wooden chest. She also picked up the buffalo robe they used during the frigid winter nights. There was nothing warmer when the air grew blue with cold.

She came out of Papa's room with the blankets piled so

high in her arms she could barely see where she was going.

"Here, let me help you." John towered over her, taking most of the bedding from her. "Show me where you want them."

Without a word, she took her shawl, grabbed a lantern, and led the way to the small stable, where Papa kept the cow and his two packhorses. The empty stall was knee-deep in fresh hay and smelled of warm horses and sweet grasses.

"I think this will be comfortable for tonight," she said, hanging the lantern from a hook. She began to spread the blankets. John touched her shoulder briefly, and she moved away from him putting several feet between them.

"Cornstalk and Standing Tree will make their own beds," he said quietly. "They may even sweep the hay aside and sleep on the ground, but I know they're glad of the shelter. Thank you."

Over John's shoulder she saw Standing Tree and Cornstalk enter. She gestured to the bedding. "Please make yourselves comfortable."

The Indians nodded and smiled broadly at her, making her suddenly uneasy in their company. It was as if they knew something she didn't—something terribly important.

"Well, it's late and we open the store early in the morning. It's our busy season." She pulled her shawl tight at her throat and walked around John, giving him a wide berth. "I'll leave the lantern for Standing Tree and Cornstalk. Good night."

She was not entirely surprised when John followed her out the door. He'd walked her home on other occasions. But tonight she would have been happier without his company. "I'm really quite capable of finding my way to the house."

"I know," John said, taking her by the elbow. "I just don't want to have to explain to your father tomorrow why you never returned from the stable."

"Vincennes is hardly that dangerous."

"Don't be too sure of that."

"Well, I'm not afraid," she said as she climbed the porch steps.

"Perhaps you should be," John advised, his voice implacable.

"So you really do want me to go?" She stopped at the door and looked up at him. In the spring darkness she could barely make out the lines of his handsome face. His eyes remained shadowed and unreadable. But she heard him take a long, deep breath.

"I never said that, Rosemary."

She held her breath, hoping he would say more. Nothing. But his brief denial gave her courage. "It would be different if I had a husband."

"But you don't."

Even in the darkness she could see his lips thin with vexation. Her courage wavered, but not her determination. "But if I had a husband, then Papa would have to let me stay. You could make that possible, John. Just marry me."

To her dismay, she realized that John wasn't listening to her at all. He was looking past her. When she turned to follow his gaze, she saw the Indians watching from the stable door, grinning.

Roughly John seized her waist, swung her off the porch, and drew her around the corner of the house, out of their sight.

"John? What—"

"Don't pay any attention to them," he said. His eyes were dark and the twist of his mouth was unhappy, even angry.

Rosemary started to repeat her request when John cut her off.

"I heard you." His voice was husky and gruff. His fingers bit into her shoulders as he pulled her very close to him. "I heard you, Rosemary. But the answer is no. It has to be. Women like you don't belong here. This is a man's world. Women and children belong where it's safe. Where fires burn in fireplaces and the wildest things in the street are tabby cats."

"The farmers in the valley don't seem to think that," she protested, hardly believing that he'd said no when she was certain his eyes and touch said yes.

"I'm not a farmer in the valley," John ground out between clenched teeth, his hands still on her shoulders. "And I don't think you want to be a farmer's wife."

Anger flooded through her. She would have pulled away from him if his hold on her were not so strong. "Just how do you know what I want?"

"You want to be alive and safe and happy," he whispered, their faces so close now that his breath tingled against her cheek. "I can't promise you those things."

His lips brushed her cheek, sending a thrill through her belly.

"I don't care," she whispered in return, yearning for more of his touch. Shyly she closed her eyes and offered him her lips, fearful that he might reject her kiss, too.

Pressing her back against the wall, his mouth descended on hers in a hot, hungry meeting. Though she had no experience with kissing, she did not quail before the onslaught of his tongue delving into her mouth. She matched his forays. The seductive stroke of his thumb on her throat only made her want more. She slipped her arms around his waist, spread her hands across his back, and molded herself to his body. He felt so good, hard, powerful, and warm. When he released her, she gasped for air.

He groaned, whispering her name before he trailed kisses down her throat. Tenderly he kneaded her breasts. They grew taut, aching for more. She yearned to make love with John, certain that it would be magical.

The hinges on the front door creaked and she heard her father's footsteps on the porch.

Abruptly John pulled away, steadying her with his hand at her waist. Her head reeled from the sudden withdrawal of his promising touch. John pulled them out of hiding.

"There you are, you two," Papa said, seemingly unaware of the intimacy that he'd just interrupted. "I thought I heard someone out here."

"We were just saying good night and good-bye," John said. "I'm leaving tomorrow. I think Standing Tree and Cornstalk will be staying a day or two longer to trade with the fur traders and will need to sleep in your stable, if you don't mind.

"Good-bye, Rosemary," John added with a sudden huskiness in his voice that she hadn't heard before. It made her heart flutter with hope.

He took her by the shoulders once more, his long fingers gripping her firmly, almost painfully. For a moment she thought he was going to kiss her on the cheek right in front of Papa. But he released her and said, "I wish you the best in Baltimore."

Then he was gone, striding off into the darkness—alone.

She choked back tears of disappointment. She'd never felt more deserted in her life. Papa would send her away, and she'd never see John again. How silly of her to think that her beef stew, seasoned with love and simmered with patience, would have had any effect on her destiny at all.

The next morning after a fitful night's sleep, John found Cornstalk and Standing Tree waiting for him at Lasselle's back gate. Standing Tree carried a basket and, smiling, handed it to John. "For you, Friend-with-no-wife."

Cornstalk frowned. "From the maiden hummingbird with earrings. Like a good woman, she is afraid you are going to starve on your own."

"She is not my woman!" John snapped, uneasy with the Indians' assumption. But that did not prevent him from reaching for the basket he knew Rosemary would have filled with last night's leftovers of the hearty beef stew, bread, and cobbler. She'd often packed a basket for him in the past couple of years, one of the many pleasures of coming to town. But this would be the last one. He shoved the thought from his mind and peered into the folds of the linen wrappings.

"Then, she has no man." Standing Tree's smile faded into complete confusion.

"No. She has no man!" John growled, testy from his lack of sleep. "That's why her father is sending her away where she will be safe."

All night he had tossed and turned, guiltily replaying the harsh words he'd said to her, of his blunt, unkind refusal of her marriage proposal. Though he would not change his answer, this morning he wondered if he should have spoken also of the emptiness he would feel without her. Regretfully he looked down at the food so generously packed for him. She deserved a kinder farewell than he had bid her.

"Then why not speak for her," Standing Tree said, his smile reappearing. "Offer her father a bride price. Beck is a trader with white people. He will appreciate a good price."

"I cannot speak for her. I do not have enough to offer a fair bride price for Rosemary," John said, trying to explain in terms they would understand.

The Indians exchanged a mystified glance but posed no more questions to John's relief. He didn't know how to explain to them that Rosemary's value was priceless and her father knew it. That was why he was sending her away.

With his friends' help, he loaded his supplies onto his two packhorses, and then said good-bye. After tying Rosemary's basket on the top of the pack where he could reach it at mealtime on the trail, he mounted and headed out of town.

As he rode by Beck's store, he peered into the windows but did not see Rosemary. He urged his horse into a trot and soon left Vincennes far behind him. He would remember Rosemary seated at the table in her father's house with the firelight playing over her shiny hair and deepening the gold of her amber eyes, and the savory aroma of her stew filling the room. Ignoring his heartache, he decided it was best that way.

The kitten's meow sounded as forlorn and as lost as Rosemary felt. She stopped midway between the house and the store, and listened intently for the sound again. The wind was blowing with such force that it was impossible to be certain from which direction the wail had come.

She'd just taken Papa his lunch of cold venison, cheese, bread, and cider, and she was returning to the house to begin packing for her trip East. He'd ordered her to do so that morning, saying that she would be safe traveling with Gabe Rogers, who'd be arriving with his pack train any day now.

With no prospect of winning John to her side, Rosemary had lost heart. She would pack because Papa insisted upon it. But she had no stomach for the chore and welcomed any distraction—even rescuing a lost kitten. The poor creature had probably become separated from its litter and needed help finding its mother.

Once more the small, helpless summons reached her over the whistling wind, and the tiny plaintive call, impossible to resist, seemed to be coming from the stable. Clutching her shawl close, she hurried across the yard. The strong gale fought with her as she tried to pull open the door. She had to yank twice before she could get inside.

The door banged shut behind her, and the distinct smell of freshly cured skins greeted her. She stood allowing her eyes to adjust to the darkness and waited to hear the kitten again. When she could see, she gasped. There were two strong packhorses and several stacks of pelts that she knew had not been in the barn the day before.

She stroked the smooth pelt on top of the stack. Papa seldom traded in furs, leaving that to the fur company men. He only did business on a cash basis, so where had the skins come from?

She was no fur trader, but she'd lived in Vincennes all her life and knew a good pelt when she saw one. These were exceptional skins, well-cured and of the finest quality.

Another meow caught her ear, and she listened for several moments before she heard the cry again. The kitten sounded as if it were outside now, though she could have sworn it had been in the stable when she'd first heard it.

She hastily left and followed the direction of the cries.

They came more frequently now and lured her past the necessary and toward a thicket, at the edge of the grove.

"Here, kitty, kitty," Rosemary called in her most reassuring voice. "I have some cream for you. Come, come."

The mewling sounded very close, but Rosemary stopped at the thicket, daunted by the thickness of the undergrowth.

She could hear the kitten plainly now, its helpless whimper tugging at her heart. She could hardly bear the sound.

She skirted the thicket, thinking she might be able to see the creature from the other side and coax it to her. But when she reached the far side, she could see nothing, yet the cry seemed as close as before and just as forlorn.

"Kitty, where are you?" she called.

Suddenly Standing Tree jumped up from the middle of the thicket and grinned at her. With uncanny accuracy, he meowed like a lost kitten.

"You?" Before Rosemary could open her mouth to ask him what he was about, she was encased in darkness.

Chapter 4

Something heavy, soft, and leathery smothered Rosemary's yelp of surprise. A rope pinned her arms to her sides, and she could feel it being wound around her body from her elbows to her knees.

Startled, but only slightly frightened, she tried to shout questions through the buffalo robe, but the Indians—she recognized the other voice as Cornstalk's—refused to answer her. Surely she had nothing to fear from them. When she was completely bound, she was abruptly lifted off her feet and thrown over a bony shoulder.

"Standing Tree, what are you doing?" she demanded. "Where are you taking me?"

With furious kicks, she struggled against the rope and the Indian's grasp, but his hold was powerful. Exhausted, she ceased fighting. Then she heard Standing Tree laugh.

"Standing Tree?" she called again with more authority this time, determined to put a stop to this silly prank. "Put me down this instant!"

But Standing Tree did not respond to her and she could hear the Indians whispering. Then suddenly she was hefted and slipped, stomach first, across a pack saddle. She couldn't draw enough breath to scream.

Standing Tree's laughter rang out again.

"Why are you doing this?" she cried, gasping for air.

"Do not fear, Hummingbird-with-earrings." Rosemary recognized Cornstalk's voice again. "We have left your father a generous bride price. He will be proud that his daughter brought such a large sum to his lodge."

Bride price, she repeated in her head. *Bride price?*

Awakening from a dream filled with Rosemary's softness and warmth, John heard the wind whistling around the eaves of the cabin. He knew that one hell of a blizzard was coming. March storms were always the worst.

But he was prepared for bad weather. He'd returned from town with plenty of supplies—flour, cornmeal, coffee, salt, some sugar, potatoes, carrots, and onions. He'd even managed to acquire a quarter slab of beef. The cold weather would just keep it fresh longer.

He got up and dressed and saw through the window that the snow had started to fall lightly. He bundled up and went out to check on the horses and to cut some extra wood. It never hurt to have plenty of firewood, especially during a snowstorm.

By the time he finished feeding the horses, the wind was no longer whistling. It roared and the bay packhorse tossed its head and nickered. From far off John heard an answering whinny. Who'd be calling on neighbors in this weather? he wondered—unless it was an unfriendly call. He'd seen plenty of signs of Indian movements through the area on his ride home.

Putting down the feed bucket, he picked up his rifle, which was never far from him these days, and walked out of the shed to the front of the cabin. The snowfall was growing heavier, the huge feathery flakes deadening sound and obscuring visibility. A thin white mantle already covered the ground.

He was relieved, but not particularly surprised to see Standing Tree and Cornstalk ride into the clearing, leading a packhorse. But he thought the load wriggling on the horse was a curious one.

"John Winston," Cornstalk greeted.

"What have you got there, Cornstalk?" John asked, setting his rifle aside and starting toward the packhorse. He'd already realized its burden was a person. He couldn't imagine what on earth his Indian friends were doing hauling someone around.

"We bring you a gift."

"A gift for Friend-without-a-wife," Standing Tree added with a laugh.

John's heart tripped a beat when he saw dainty shoes protruding from the buffalo robe. Horrified at the thought of some poor girl suffocating inside the heavy hide, he grabbed the rope around the bundle and lifted it off the horse.

She was incredibly small and light in his arms and he began to think it was a child the Indians had found. Then she gave a muffled scream and began to squirm frantically in his arms, her struggles much too energetic for a child.

"Hold on, I'm going to get you out of there." He tried to reassure the girl as he quickly set her on her feet and began to unwind the rope. But he worked with difficulty because she fought like a wildcat.

At last he pulled the rope free and yanked away the robe to find himself face-to-face with Rosemary—and she was spitting mad.

"You!" she hissed. Her cheeks flamed red from her wild exertions—and her anger.

His survival instinct prompted John to step back to escape the full force of her fury.

"I might have known you were at the bottom of this!" Her hands braced on her hips, she advanced on him, her dark curls rioting in the wind like a madwoman's. "What in the devil's name do you think you're doing? How dare you have me kidnapped by your friends!"

"Kidnapped?" What the hell was she talking about? "You think I had you kidnapped?"

"Do you think I'm a fool? I dare you to come up with another story that explains this!" she shouted as she gestured toward the Delawares.

Standing Tree was laughing so hard he could barely sit his pony.

John turned to glare at Cornstalk. "What the hell is going on here?"

The smaller Delaware remained impassive. "Now, you have a woman, Friend-without-a-wife. And Hummingbird is spoken for by a man, so she does not have to go away as her father wishes. Best of all, I will have to listen to no more complaints from my wife about making your buckskins."

"Buckskins? What is he talking about?" Rosemary demanded.

"I don't know," John lied, understanding dawning at last. He had no idea how he was going to explain this debacle to Rosemary or Frederick Beck.

John strode over to Cornstalk astride his brown-and-white war pony. "What did you do? Did you kidnap her?"

Cornstalk shook his head and frowned as if he were offended. "No kidnap Hummingbird lady. We left a generous bride price for her father."

"John Winston, if this was not our gift to a good friend, you would owe us two packhorses and three stacks of the best pelts," Standing Tree pointed out.

"I what?"

"We knew you would offer a good price," Cornstalk added.

"What are they talking about?" Rosemary strode up behind John. "Bride price? You did have them kidnap me! You paid them to kidnap me!"

John whirled on her, his patience suddenly gone. "Now, why would I do a thing like that after what I told you last night? I refused you, remember? I said no."

Rosemary's cheeks reddened. "Well, how should I know why you had me brought here? But here I am in the last place on earth I want to be."

"That's fine with me, because this is the last place you're wanted."

She squared her shoulders and thrust her jaw forward in stubborn indignation. "I'm glad we are in agreement about that. Now, take me home."

"Gladly." John turned to the Indians again. They started this. They could finish it. "Rosemary must be returned to town. Her father will not understand the bride price. He will be afraid some harm has come to his daughter."

A fierce blast of wind wailed through the treetops and howled threateningly along the eaves of the log cabin. The feathers in Cornstalk's hair fluttered madly.

"We must ride on, John Winston," Cornstalk said, his face turned toward the lowering sky. "My family will need me in this storm."

Standing Tree nodded in silent agreement and turned his horse into the forest.

"If you wish her returned, you take her, John Winston," Cornstalk said, reining his horse to follow Standing Tree. "Perhaps she will travel better with you and make less noise."

His hand raised in farewell, Cornstalk disappeared behind Standing Tree into the woods.

John swore softly in frustration. There was no arguing with his Delaware friends once they decided their course.

"Where are they going?" Rosemary cried, following the Indians a few steps before she turned to John again. Her anger seemed to have deserted her, replaced by bewilderment. "I want to go home."

"They are going to their own families. I'm afraid they're right, Rosemary. You're not going home, at least for a while." Though John longed to send her back as much as she wanted to go, the bitter cold posed a greater danger than Frederick Beck's wrath. "Look at the sky. This is no time to travel, no matter how urgent the need."

She looked up at the sky. John watched snowflakes shower down on her, sparkling against her sable tresses like diamond dust against rich brown velvet. Her shoulders slumped, and an expression of confusion came over her face, touching—and annoying—him at the same time.

"Let's get out of the cold," he said, reaching for her arm.

Rosemary pulled away and hugged her shawl more closely to her, her eyes wide and troubled. The wind raged relentlessly; sharp fingers of cold stung John's cheeks and Rosemary's apron and dress were plastered against her body. He couldn't believe she was refusing to come. She had to be freezing.

"I'm sorry about this situation," he said, wondering if that would make her feel any better about staying with him. "But we have no other choice except to wait out the storm."

She nodded slowly as if she understood and he turned and started toward the cabin alone. A moment later his keen ear caught the sound of her footsteps on the frozen ground behind him. He never looked back, but when he got to the door, he swung it wide and strode in. Rosemary followed him without a word.

"You mean Cornstalk and Standing Tree thought they were doing you and me a favor?" Rosemary asked, astonishment bringing her up off her fireside stool at John's explanation of the Indians' behavior. "Then the horses and pelts I saw in the stable are my bride price." The whole situation was ludicrous and humiliating.

"Yes, the Indians consider it a favor and I think perhaps I prevailed on Cornstalk's wife to make buckskins for me once too often," John admitted as he threw another log on the fire. Sparks flew and the roar of the flames almost covered the whistling wind outside. "There, that should warm you up."

"Yes, thank you." Rosemary settled on her stool once more and cast John a sidelong glance. He was frowning as he stared into the fire, clearly no happier than she. He'd made it very clear last night that he had no intention of making her a part of his life. Now, here she was in the middle of it. No wonder he was angry but so was she.

Yet as enraged as she'd been when John unwrapped her from the buffalo robe, she'd also been relieved. After having been jostled around all night, she'd had plenty of time to envision being delivered to hostile Indians—or worse, to British soldiers.

"As soon as it stops snowing, we'll ride back to town, right?" she asked, breaking the uncomfortable silence between them.

"Yes." John restacked the logs by the fireplace. "But that's a hell of a blizzard out there. We might as well face the fact that it's going to be a couple of days before we can leave."

"A couple of days! But Papa will be frantic," she cried, rising from her stool again.

John knelt down to stuff a fur rug into the crevice between the door and the dirt floor. With a flutter of panic, she felt as if she were being sealed off from the world.

"He won't understand that Cornstalk and Standing Tree meant no harm."

"I know, but he's not going to be able to search for you, either," John added, moving to the single window to check the draft around it. It was a glass window, Rosemary noted. How like John. No hole covered with oil skin for him.

He pulled a pelt pegged to the wall down over the window, and the flickering fire dimly lit the one-room cabin.

"I know this is awkward. But can we make our time together bearable?"

A couple days? She sat up a little straighter on her stool. A lot could happen in that time—like a man having a change of heart. Turning to survey the cabin that smelled of good leather and woodsmoke, she scrutinized it with renewed interest.

She noticed the hutch next to the fireplace held several rusty cooking pots. A couple of rifles, a shot pouch, powder horn, and snowshoes hung on the walls. Skins covered the packed dirt floor. A small rough-hewn table with two log benches stood in one corner near the window and in another was a big chest which she assumed was for clothes and bedding.

In a third corner lay a pile of junk, and behind her a narrow bed was attached to the wall and covered with more furs, much nicer than the ones on the floor. She certainly had her work cut out for her and not much time to do it in.

"How do you think we can arrange to make that time bearable?" she asked innocently, without smiling too broadly. It was best not to appear too hopeful.

"You can see I live pretty simply," John said. "You can sleep on the bed and I'll make a pallet near the fire."

"Oh, yes, that will be fine," she said, wondering where she would go to dress and wash. "Perhaps we could hang a blanket between us."

John blinked at her. "Do what?"

"I'll need some privacy," she explained, trying to ignore the heat rising in her cheeks. "To dress and undress and, you know, to use the chamber pot. By the way, where is it?"

"Chamber pot?" John repeated.

"Yes, you know, the necessary," she said, annoyed with him for embarrassing her.

John made a sound, suspiciously like a derisive laugh. "I don't own a chamber pot. I'm afraid this isn't like your house. There's only one room, no chamber pot, and no necessary just outside the door, either."

She stared at him in disbelief. "Then what do you do? Surely you don't just walk around the corner of the cabin and—"

John nodded, a satisfied smile spreading across his face. "Yes, I do."

"Well, *I* can't do that." She primly folded her hands in her lap. "It's inconvenient for a lady to . . . Well, you know what I mean."

His infuriating grin faded and he looked a bit perplexed. "I know. I've got to bring in some wood."

Puzzled by his sudden decision to go out into the storm, she watched him put on his bear coat. Then he kicked the rug out from beneath the door and threw the bolt. When he pulled open the door and snow swirled into the room, she jumped up and ran to close the door behind him. Without a word, he disappeared into a white wall of swirling snow.

She latched the door and hastily tucked the rug beneath it as she'd seen John do. Then she turned back to the room.

Clearly this was an intolerable situation and no amount of complaining or blaming would change anything—though she'd have a few things to say to Standing Tree and Cornstalk when she saw them again. But John was right. They were going to have to make the best of it.

She contemplated the hutch and wondered what supplies John had laid in. For the first time she realized they might have more serious concerns than the lack of a chamber pot. But she wasn't worried. John was an experienced frontiersman and she had complete faith in him. He'd assured her the storm would probably last only a couple of days.

A smile spread across her face. *Two whole days!*

Chapter 5

Trudging to the shed, John cursed. What on God's green earth was he going to do with that woman sleeping under his roof for the next two days? This was nothing like his giving shelter last winter to that homeless Indian squaw with her half-starved baby. This time a tiny, soft woman who could touch his heart with her cooking and make his groin ache with her smile would be sleeping in the same room with him.

Inside the shed, he rubbed his cold ears to get the blood flowing back into them. In his rush to get out of the cabin, he'd forgotten to put on his coon cap. He muttered another curse and groaned, thinking of Rosemary's father who had to be out of his mind with anxiety. He wouldn't know what to think of two packhorses and three stacks of pelts. That was an astronomical price for an Indian brave to offer for a bride, but that would not impress the storekeeper. All he would think is that he'd lost his favorite daughter to the Indians.

John cursed aloud again. When this storm was over and he managed to get Rosemary safely home, there was going to be a lot of explaining to do.

He checked the animals and after locating the bucket he wanted, he went to the wood pile and loaded up on firewood.

By the time he left the shed and reached the cabin door, he'd convinced himself that he could live with Rosemary under his roof and never touch her. All he had to do was be cool and distant. He'd act as if being near her didn't affect him at all. As if her golden eyes didn't make his heart beat more rapidly or her sweet lavender scent didn't make his hands sweat. For her sake, he had to do it.

The moment he pushed open the door, the tantalizing fragrance of simmering vegetables and coffee brewing assailed him. His new resolve threatened to desert him, and steeling himself, he frowned and went straight to the wood box.

Rosemary was stirring a pot hanging over the fire and she looked up at him and smiled her beautiful wide smile. She'd tied her dark curls back from her face, and in the firelight her eyes shone a burnished gold and her amber earrings glowed. John noted that cooking had restored the pretty peach blush to her cheeks.

"I thought you might be hungry," she said.

Not answering her, he dropped the firewood into the box and then hung up his coat on the peg by the door. He reminded himself of Rosemary's faults. She was small, helpless, and naive *but* she was a damned fine cook. How difficult would it be living with a woman who knew how to put a good meal on the table?

He'd done harder things like trap wolves or track Redcoats. He'd done more dangerous things like wrestle a bear and he'd survived a snake bite. So enduring two days in a one-room cabin with Rosemary would be no problem at all.

At the sight of John's fierce scowl and lack of response, Rosemary's heart sank. She'd hoped that a hearty meal would improve his mood. It was only natural that he might feel a little trapped with her being there. He hadn't expected to have a guest dumped in his lap.

"That's all right if you're not hungry," she hurried to say, though she was annoyed, too. She hadn't exactly expected to be trapped with him, either. "It needs to simmer another hour or so to be at its best anyway. Maybe by then . . ."

Suddenly he thrust a bucket at her. "Here."

She stared at it. "Did I ask for a bucket?"

"Your chamber pot." His words were crisp, terse.

"Oh, yes, thank you." She took it from him, touched in an odd way that he should come back from his chores with "her" chamber pot. She set the bucket down. "I hope you don't mind, but I took the liberty of going through the bedding in the chest."

"Take whatever you need," he said.

"Well, thank you. I found this beautiful, unfinished quilt that would be perfect to hang across the corner of the room for privacy. It also would brighten things up a bit."

"What quilt?"

His voice was so loud and harsh, she cringed. "The red, white, and blue one."

She went to the bed, where she had spread the quilt to examine it more closely. "It's quite lovely, though the edging isn't complete. I don't think hanging it over a rope will harm it."

"No, don't use that!" John snapped. "My sister and mother made it. Put it away."

"Of course," she said, puzzled by his angry reaction. She refolded the bed cover, realizing that nowhere in the cabin had she seen any keepsakes or miniatures of his family. Certainly nothing feminine besides the quilt. "Your mother and sister did fine work. A quilt like this needs to be aired and used with love and care."

"I don't want to use it." John turned toward the fire. "Is the coffee ready yet?"

"Yes, it should be."

She heard him pour himself coffee as she replaced the coverlet in the chest. Thousands of questions formed in her mind. She'd found the quilt lovingly folded, sprinkled with herbs to ward off insects, and wrapped in tissue at the bottom of the chest. She was certain it was special to the Haley family. She was not offended that John refused to allow her to use it, but she was curious.

Quietly, she joined him by the fire, where he sat staring into the flames, hardly aware that he was sipping his coffee.

She poured herself a tin cup of coffee and sat on the other stool by the fire. "You know, I remember when a trapper brought the news to us that your father had died. It's almost two years now that he's gone."

"My father died of old age, at peace in his bed," John muttered. "Nothing much to grieve over."

"I suppose not." The coolness of his answer surprised her. "Over the years Papa got to know your father pretty well. Both of you joined us for a meal nearly every time you came to town. He talked about your mother, who had died in Virginia before you and he arrived in Indiana. But it's strange he never mentioned a daughter—your sister. What happened to her?"

"She died on the trail coming here." John sipped from his cup again, clearly unwilling to say more.

Rosemary wanted to respect his feelings, but she needed to know more. "Older or younger?"

"Older." He drained his cup with a toss of his head.

"What was—"

"Her name was Georgeanne." Abruptly John rose from the stool. "I don't want to talk about her. Now, where do you want to hang that curtain?"

"I thought right over here would be best," she said, also rising and pointing to the corner she had in mind. She decided to drop her questions, but she suspected that knowing more about Georgeanne would tell her a lot about John.

John didn't much like hanging a curtain in his cabin. It would make the place smaller and throw shadows in the corners, where the firelight had always reached. But Rosemary thought it would give her privacy. Maybe if she had some privacy, she'd give him some. Had she always asked so many questions?

"I can tie the rope to this peg here and tie it off over there," John explained.

Rosemary held the coil of rope in her hands and eyed the two spots he pointed out. Thoughtfully she tapped her finger on her chin. ''What about starting over here and tying it up there?''

''But I already have a peg in the wall here,'' John reminded her, trying to be patient.

''Yes, I see,'' she agreed, moving closer to him, while she studied the far wall where he'd suggested tying off the rope. He could smell her sweet fragrance.

Suddenly she thrust one end of the rope at him and he took it. ''You hold the rope here and I'll hold it over there, and we'll see.''

She scurried across the room, dragging a stool with her. What on God's green earth was she doing now? John wondered. When she climbed on the stool and held up the rope, the bodice of her soft cotton, blue gingham dress stretched tantalizingly across her breasts, and the hem lifted, giving him a stirring peek at her trim little ankles. All John could do was stare.

''Pull it up,'' she said, scowling at him.

''What?''

''Pull up your end of the rope.''

''Oh, sure,'' he answered, realizing that she was trying to see if she liked the effect. He shifted his weight from one moccasined foot to the other. This kind of thing was just one reason why he had no intention of taking a wife. Even the simplest of chores became complicated, very complicated.

She dropped her arm and scrutinized the corner, obviously dissatisfied with what she saw. ''You know, you really need a loft.''

''I need what?'' Surely he hadn't heard her properly.

''A loft,'' she repeated. ''If you had a loft, it would be just like having another room. All you would have to do—''

''I like my cabin just the way it is,'' he said, thankful that she hadn't raised her arms again. ''Do you want the rope tied here or not?''

''Yes, that will do,'' she said, her feelings obviously hurt. ''I was only making a suggestion.''

He inwardly cursed his impatience and his body's wayward nature. He only had to be strong for a couple of days, he promised himself. *Two days.*

Reaching up to the peg, he began to tie the rope. "So how is your father sending you to Baltimore? By river or land?"

Finished knotting the rope, he turned to her and saw the disappointment on her face.

"With ole Gabe." She avoided his gaze. "Papa thinks I'll be safest with one of Gabe's trains."

"Yeah, the Indians won't bother Gabe," he agreed, relieved to know that her father had chosen well. Holding the rope taut, he walked across the room to the other peg.

Rosemary suddenly looked so woebegone that John thought she was going to be sick. "Are you all right?"

"No. Yes, I mean, it's just that I can't bear to think of going away." Her voice was little more than a sigh.

Her eyes had grown round and he swore silently to himself when he spied tears welling in them.

"I've visited before and I hated it. What will I do in Baltimore?"

"You'll be safe." He turned away, refusing to let her misery touch him. "You'll have your sisters and your nieces and nephews. There will be parties and shops and lots of new people to meet."

He turned his back on her and tied off the rope. *New people and men!* The thought of a smug Easterner stroking Rosemary's hand turned John's fingers into fumbling appendages. Tying a familiar knot suddenly became a challenging task. No coxcomb could ever appreciate Rosemary's acceptance of people on their own merits or the sweetness of her loving generosity. Nor would he have enough sense to cherish the contagiousness of her laughter—or the soft warmth of her lips. John's body began to ache once more and his knot untangled. Swearing under his breath, he attempted to retie it.

And what about her extraordinary cooking? Her talent would be wasted on a citified gent who had no idea how difficult it was to make a cup of flour and a few handful of berries taste better than any French pastry. John struggled with the knot and finally it fell into place despite his bungling fingers.

"There. Now, let's hang the sheet that you got from the chest."

Rosemary picked it up from the table. Handing one end of it to him, she moved away, opening the fabric to its full size. For his sanity, he avoided watching her stretch to toss the corner over the rope. He was rapidly concluding she was right about the need for having privacy in the cabin.

When they finished hanging the curtain and he had determined that the edge cleared the floor, he stepped back from it and prayed she was happy. "Will this do?"

"It's wonderful." She smiled, looking at the sheet, apparently well pleased with their effort.

She ducked behind the curtain and John noted that the candle she'd set on the shelf above the bed cast a remarkable shapely silhouette of her against the sheet.

"Wasn't that easy? This will give us all the privacy we need."

"Sure," he answered, unwilling to say anything that would result in the ordeal of rehanging the sheet.

"See, it's not going to be as difficult to share your cabin with me as you thought," she piped from behind the curtain.

He studied her luscious shadow. "You know, I think you're right."

Chapter 6

Rosemary awoke the next day determined to make herself indispensable to John. She had slept soundly, but she heard him as soon as he began moving around on the other side of the curtain. Immediately, she rose, dressed hurriedly in the cold, and ducked beneath the curtain to start breakfast.

John had already thrown wood on the fire and had a good blaze going. After brief morning greetings, they did their chores in silence. Rosemary soon had coffee boiling and bacon sizzling in the fry pan.

"I'm going to string a rope to the shed this morning," John said as soon as breakfast was finished. He shrugged into his bear coat. "Then I can get out to the horses or the wood pile when needed."

"Of course." Rosemary lifted the skin over the window and peeked out between the fingers of frost spread across the glass. Beyond the window swirled a wall of white. "Will it take long?"

"I don't think so."

John went to the far corner of the cabin and rummaged through the items stacked there. He seemed to know what he wanted, but she couldn't imagine how he could find anything. A few moments later he went to the door carrying a rope.

"Stay inside and wait for me. If it takes longer than you expect, *don't* come after me. I'll be at the other end of the rope and I'll get back. Do you understand?"

"Yes." She bristled at the tone of his voice. Did he think

she was some heedless child? "I've faced winter storms before. I'll be waiting right here."

With that, he left and disappeared into the white world outside.

The wailing wind sent a shiver of fear down her spine, and for a moment after he was gone, she nearly grabbed a coat and followed him. On the other hand, this was the perfect time to get to work. She could act freely without John's interference. If she worked fast, she would have everything done by the time he returned. He would hardly recognize the place when she finished.

She turned to the stack of gear piled in the far corner. Taking the broom from the fireside corner, she attacked the heap of equipment.

By the time John returned, carrying in a load of firewood, she was sweeping the cobwebs from the empty corner. She'd laid the traps, chains, ropes, and tools on the floor. She'd put the smaller things on the table.

"What in the world are you doing?" he demanded as soon as he'd dropped the wood into the box. His cheeks were ruddy from the cold and snow clung to his eyebrows.

"I'm just straightening up, so you'll know where everything is." She set aside the inadequate broom and reached for his coat. "Any sign of the storm blowing over?"

"Not a bit," he said, peeling off his mittens and shrugging out of his coat. He nodded to the items strewn across the floor and the table. "What is all this?"

"It's your inventory. Did you know you had all these traps? I know how to set rabbit traps, and I have an excellent recipe for rabbit, if we run short of food during the storm."

"We're not going to be snowed in long enough to need rabbit traps."

"I can load and shoot a rifle, too," she added.

"You'll be home before there's any need of that." John sat down on the stool to pull off his snow-caked fur boots.

"Well, the cabin will be better for my stay." His indifference to her skills miffed her. "By the way, you need a new broom. This is worn down to nearly nothing. I'll hang the traps from this peg. Chains and ropes can go in this basket.

"What is this?" She held up the small length of hollow reed she'd found. Holes had been drilled in it and a rawhide thong decorated with beads hung from it.

John gazed at it for a moment before he answered. "It's an Indian flute. A flageolet."

"Really?" She studied the musical instrument more closely. "I thought Indians only played drums and rattles. Where did you find it?"

"It was a gift from an Indian when I traveled west a couple of summers ago," John said as if there were something about the trip that he did not care to reveal to her. "Some of the Plains Indians play a flute to, ah, well . . . to woo their sweethearts."

"Oh." She stared at John. She'd never thought about the possibility of another woman in his life—even an Indian maiden.

Rosemary's heart sank a bit. Many of the trappers—scouts, too—took Indian wives, because the women were self-sufficient and independent. She dropped down on the bench by the table. "Did you court a sweetheart among the Plains Indians?"

"No, nothing like that," John said, but he would not meet her eyes. "I just admired the flute and my host gave it to me—along with a few lessons. Here, I'll show you."

She walked across the room, sat down on the other stool, and handed the flute to John.

After wiping the flute across his breeches, he put it to his lips and produced a simple, sweet, haunting tune.

"Oh, that's charming." The sound delighted her. "I can see how a woman might be beguiled by that."

"That particular song is called 'I Am Here Waiting for You.' "

"How romantic," she said, hoping that he would play it for her again.

John shrugged. "It's just a melody I remembered from my lesson."

Though she longed to attach some meaning to the music, she knew better. "I didn't know you'd lived among the Indians."

"Only that one summer," John said. "I learned a lot from them. They are a proud people with their own standards of honor and courage. I found myself ashamed that we have not always dealt honestly with them. But they can be savage, too."

She nodded, not entirely surprised by John's sentiments. Often those who had lived among the Indians were not so quick to condemn them as were the citizens of Vincennes. "So where will we hang the flute? Or maybe you'd like to play some more songs."

"No," John said. "I have no use for it."

"Why not?" she asked, realizing she was treading into dangerous territory. John would agree to nothing that smacked of courtship. "You could make up your own tunes. I like the sound of the flute much better than the howling of the wind."

"Here then." He scowled and thrust the musical instrument toward her. "You play it and leave my gear alone."

"I was only trying to help."

Disappointed that John was unhappy with her efforts, she snatched up the flageolet and put it to her lips. It was easier to play than she'd expected, and she soon contented herself with coaxing "Yankee Doodle" from it. A happy tune, and ever so much more pleasant than the sound of the wind—but hardly as romantic as the song John had played.

On the third morning of the blizzard John found fresh moccasin prints in the snow as he left the shed. The scars in the layer of white ventured only as far as the edge of the cabin's clearing, then turned away.

Squinting against the white glare, he peered deeper into the woods trying to catch a glimpse of the silent callers—intruders? The snowfall had lightened considerably. He could see ghostly tree trunks where he'd seen only a white wall the day before.

Apprehension flooded through him as he realized he'd left his rifle in the cabin. He'd left it only because carrying a gun limited the amount of wood he could carry, and he didn't think that any sensible man or creature would be out in this weather. But they'd had visitors and they might still be close by.

He studied the tracks again, muttering aloud. "Six, I think. Men. No women or children. Warriors."

The falling snow had barely softened the edges of the imprints. Hell, they had probably watched him come out of the shed. That realization made him especially uneasy. If the visitors had been friendly, they would have greeted him and sought shelter by his fire.

He glanced at the trail again. It curved back into the deep woods, southward. But nothing moved among the trees. Six! He could take care of himself, one way or another, but against such odds, how could he protect Rosemary?

Cursing under his breath, he trudged back toward the cabin. The notion of patrolling the edge of the clearing had seized him as he was feeding the horses. He'd obeyed it mostly to put off returning to the cabin and Rosemary.

She was driving him mad—not intentionally, of course. She'd rearranged his few pieces of furniture and all his gear, and he'd never find anything now.

And the flute—she had no idea how her delight in it had touched him, though he was thoroughly sick of hearing "Yankee Doodle." Nor did she know that the lighted candle on her side of the curtain cast provocative shadows as she undressed for bed. After watching her strip down to her shift, he'd lain awake half the night, his body aching for release. But he had no intention of telling her about the candle or the shadows.

Nor was he inclined to tell her about their mysterious visitors. The Indians knew he lived alone. He was certain if this war party was looking for scalps, it wanted more than one and it wanted scalps easier to take than his. Hopefully they had moved on to more promising hunting grounds. Still, he was more determined than ever to get Rosemary out of there. He wanted to do it as quickly as possible and without frightening her if he could.

Inside he found Rosemary standing over the fire, cooking again. She smiled at him and stirred the kettle. He sniffed the air and pulled off his coat. How easy it would be to get used to returning from chores to a room snug and bright with candlelight instead of the cold darkness. The air was filled with the delicious aroma of bread baking in the Dutch oven she'd scrubbed clean and seasoned over the fire the night before.

"What are you making?" he asked.

"My beef stew," she said. "You seemed to like it when you had it the other night. I found the beef in the lean-to and the other fixings in your stores and thought you might like having it again."

"Yes, it was good," he said, his mind only half on Rosemary's chatter about food. He reached for his rifle, trying to appear casual. Satisfied that it was loaded, he set it by the window and reached for the other gun.

"Are you going hunting?" Rosemary asked, eyeing him and the guns. "That slab of beef is good for several more meals."

"Yeah, well, I thought I'd be prepared. Did you see any jerky in the stores?"

Rosemary stopped stirring. "Yes, I did, but the storm will be over before we need to resort to that."

"I was just thinking about food for the trip back to Vincennes," he said honestly this time.

"Oh, I'll pack us a basket with something better than jerky." The lilt of a good cook's pride brightened her voice.

"Fine." He turned away to check his gunpowder supply in his powder bag. If the storm broke, he wasn't going to wait on any basket-packing. He would throw her on one of the horses and hit the trail.

"Ooh. Ooh!"

The distress in Rosemary's voice brought him around slowly. He'd heard her react like that at the sight of a spider she'd disturbed when she was cleaning one of the corners. "What is it?"

"Ooh."

"Rosemary!" He dropped the powder bag. Flames from the fireplace ate at the hem of her skirt and licked up the front of her apron. He froze. The old, vivid nightmare paralyzed him.

Rosemary stepped back from the fireplace and spoke with amazing calmness. "John, hand me one of those skins."

He could do nothing but stare in horror. He'd seen this before—Georgeanne turning into a pillar of fire.

"John?"

The sight of her dropping to the floor on the other side of the table galvanized him. He knocked the table over to get to her side. He fell to his knees, dragging a skin from the floor. She had already managed to throw a pelt over her burning skirt. John threw another skin across her apron, beating at the flames to smother them.

Quickly the fire died. Rosemary began to cough, choking on the smoke. The stink of burned cotton and singed fur hung heavy in the air. John found his mouth had gone as dry as cotton in the sun.

"Whew, that was close." She spoke as if she nearly burned to death with every meal she cooked. She pushed a lock of hair out of her face, then looked up at him, and he saw a smudge of soot on her nose.

He drew in a deep breath and pulled the skins away from her legs. His hands trembled with the fear of what he might find. "Are you burned?"

"Not much." She peered down at her ankles.

He studied the damage. Her apron was eaten away and so was much of her skirt. Her petticoat was in shreds, but he was most concerned about her legs. Though her stockings were pockmarked with black-edged holes, she appeared to be all right. She might suffer a blister or two, but little else. If she had not acted so quickly, the burns might have been much worse.

"My clothes and stockings are ruined," she lamented.

"I think that is the least of our worries," he grumbled. "Why do you wear cotton anyway?"

"I like cotton," she said, a shadow of astonishment and pain in her eyes.

"That's ridiculous. Worse, it's foolish!" he snapped. "There's a good reason why the blacksmith wears a leather apron, you know."

"It's not quite the fashion for ladies!" she snapped back. "But if I ever become a blacksmith, I'll consider wearing a leather apron."

Her sharp words and the image of tiny Rosemary slinging a hammer over an anvil cleared his head. He passed his hand over his face. He must sound like a fool.

"What's wrong with you?" Rosemary asked more gently. "If I didn't know better, I'd think you just saw a ghost who made you angry."

He shook his head. She was right. He had seen a ghost, but she didn't need to know that.

"It has something to do with your sister, doesn't it?" she asked, her voice low.

Damn women and their instincts. "It's not important now."

"Did her skirt catch fire?"

"Rosemary—"

"Was she cooking?" Rosemary stared at him expectantly and he knew there would be no peace until he told her what he and his father had never talked about.

"Yes, we'd made camp near a spring," he said, the memory taking shape in his head. "Just like we'd done day in and day out. The corner of her apron caught fire. Fire had popped at her before, but this time she panicked. The flames leaped in her face and she tried to turn away from them. She ran toward the spring. I guess she thought she could douse the fire."

"You tried to help her, didn't you?" Rosemary touched his hand sympathetically.

He pulled his hand away. "Pa and I were with the horses, but I grabbed a blanket and ran after her." His throat began to close, choked with emotion he thought he'd conquered. "By the time I was able to throw her to the ground, she was engulfed in flames. She died three days later."

He closed his eyes against the ugly memories. She'd died after days of incredible pain and burning fever. He'd never been able to stop blaming himself.

"It wasn't your fault," Rosemary said.

"Pa and I were foolish to drag a woman to the edge of the frontier." His grief solidified into safe, familiar anger.

"Did you force her to come with you?"

"No, but we should have never allowed her to come," he answered. "There are so many dangers. Indians. Weather. Wild animals. Flooded river fords. We could have sent for her later."

"But the fire could have happened at any time or any place, John. It might have happened in your family kitchen in Virginia."

"I don't believe that, Rosemary," he said, amazed that she did not understand what he was telling her. His father and he had been obligated to protect Georgeanne. They'd neglected their responsibility. They'd been careless and had put Georgeanne in danger. "My sister suffered for our carelessness. That's as clear as daylight."

Rosemary stared back at him. "You're as impossible as Papa." Her frustration was evident in her voice.

"Women need to be protected," he said. "They're weaker and more delicate. They have the right to be protected. That's a man's job."

"I can take care of myself."

He guffawed. "You can't even scare a pig."

She gasped. "John Winston Haley, that's unfair. I would have been all right if you hadn't come along!"

"Yes, of course." Annoyed, he got to his feet and offered her a hand. "I think we'd better find you some clothes."

"Fine and then I'll finish cooking dinner." She cast his proffered hand a loathsome look, then got to her feet on her own. "Just because something has risks does not give you the right to decide I shouldn't do it."

"We'll never agree on this," he growled, his emotions raw from reliving the horror that had befallen Georgeanne—from the terror of not being able to protect Rosemary, either. "You can forget any silly notions you might have of changing my mind. When the snow lets up, we're on our way back to Vincennes and I'll help your father send you off on Gabe's pack train to Baltimore if that's what it takes."

Chapter 7

So how do you change the mind of a man like John Winston Haley? Rosemary wondered as she returned to her cooking. The storm had proved stronger than John had forecast, and they were about to spend their third night under the same roof. But she was probably further from changing John's mind than she'd been on the day she'd arrived.

After discarding her burned clothing, John'd provided her with one of his shirts, which she wore with the sleeves rolled to her elbows, and a pair of his shrunken buckskin breeches that he'd shortened with his knife. The clothing proved surprisingly warm and comfortable. But her mind was in turmoil over the disagreement they'd had.

The fire plainly had shaken John, and silence hung between them like a sheer curtain only stirred by necessary words. Jumpy and cross, John occupied himself with sharpening his knife and looking over his gear. His eyes darted in her direction every time she made a noise or a quick move. His sister's tragedy had left a wound that had not healed even after all this time, and Rosemary wondered if it ever would.

When the early-winter darkness began to gather beyond the window, John put on his coat and stopped at the door. "I'm going to check on the horses. Drop the bolt behind me."

Rosemary studied him. He'd always latched the door but never requested that she drop the bolt. "Why?"

"Just a precaution, and don't open the door until you're sure it's me on the other side."

"Is something wrong?" She followed him to the door to do as he said.

"Just bolt the door," he repeated firmly. This time he met her eyes with a quelling glare. She decided not to press the point.

Once he was gone she sat down at the table. With her heel on the edge of the bench, she rolled up her breeches and rubbed some more smelly salve on the stinging burns. They weren't serious and probably wouldn't even leave a scar, thank heavens. She'd been lucky. Little harm had been done, but the fire had made her understand the reason for John's rejecting her marriage proposal. His foolish belief that a woman needed protecting would never be changed by all her best meals or her efforts to make his cabin homey and neat.

Only one tactic remained, one last powerful, but dangerous, ploy. The daring thought made her spread her hand across her heart. Seducing John could backfire. As for her father, well, he would be outraged. But she had to take that chance, and she knew what to expect when the time came to convince John to make love to her. Her best friend, Frannie, married with two children and pregnant again, had shared much about the intimacies of married life with Rosemary. So she had some idea of what to do and how to tempt a man. And it was time she tempted John.

When John returned from the shed, Rosemary let him in as soon as he knocked and called to her. Once he was inside the door, she returned to her cooking and he hoped she wouldn't ask any more questions, because he'd run out of lies. He'd found more footprints in the snow. If she asked, he'd have to tell her the truth: Hostile Indians were on the prowl.

He watched her set the table with his modest wooden bowls and tin spoons while the smell of fresh ground coffee filled the room. He marveled at how he'd already come to think of this as "normal."

"Was everything all right with the animals?"

"Fine," he answered, throwing his armload of firewood into the box. He noted as he arranged the wood that she'd piled her brown curls on top of her head with tantalizing wisps clinging to her neck.

"Is the snowfall still heavy?" she asked, measuring coffee into the coffeepot.

"About the same. Maybe a little lighter." He hung up his coat and kicked off his boots. And the footprints in the snow revealed the same six Indians had returned to observe them. But he didn't say that aloud. "If it's as light as it is now in the morning, we're heading back to town tomorrow."

"Oh." Rosemary stopped spooning the coffee into the pot. "Tomorrow?"

"Yes, we can't let your father go on not knowing that you're all right," he said.

She resumed measuring the coffee. "Well, if we're leaving tomorrow, we'd better eat well and get a good night's rest. I'll get supper on the table."

Rosemary served the meal and they sat down to eat. For a few minutes only the sounds of bubbling coffee, their clinking forks, and the fire popping filled the room. John was relieved when Rosemary broke the silence.

"So tonight is our last night together. I imagine you'll be glad to have your bed back when I'm gone."

"It's no trouble sleeping on the floor." Sleeping on the pallet had been among the least of his discomforts during her stay.

"I was just wondering since this is our last night if maybe you'd play the flute for me again."

He paused, his spoon halfway to his mouth. It seemed an odd request, but innocent enough.

"I'm tired of playing 'Yankee Doodle,' " she said, as if she feared he would refuse her.

"I'll play if you want me to. Maybe I can remember some other songs my friend taught me."

"Thank you." A slow, sweet smile spread across her face, warming his heart and making him feel like a fool for being so eager to rid himself of her company.

Soon they cleared the dishes, and while Rosemary washed off the table, he took the flute down from the peg, where Rosemary had hung it. He sat on the bench and began to play.

She sat down beside him, looking amazingly feminine in his oversized shirt, her amber earrings flashing gold in the firelight. He noted, but tried not to see, how the garment threatened to slip off her shoulder and reveal the sweet swell of her breasts he'd already held in his hands.

After the first song, she smiled at him. "Tell me about how the Indian braves court their girls. When do they offer the bride price?"

"The bride price is for the girl's father," he explained, amused by her curiosity about Indian courting customs. "First there is the exchange of looks. Batting eyelashes. They flirt when the girls carry water or collect firewood. Those are women's jobs in an Indian village."

"So they flirt just like we do?" Rosemary seemed delighted with the discovery.

She scooted closer to him on the bench so that they sat nearly thigh to thigh, and touched his arm—a light spontaneous gesture but it burned through his buckskin shirt.

''Do the braves do things like you did at the Christmas dance? Remember when you cut in on Billie Hogan, who was dancing with me?''

John hesitated, recalling the incident. Hogan had been as drunk as a skunk in a cider barrel and had no business dancing with a lady—especially not with Rosemary.

She smiled at him shyly, her dark lashes fluttering against her cheeks and a blush heightening her color. She brushed her hand against his thigh as she pulled away from his arm. Her touch burned through his thick buckskin breeches.

With a jolt John knew what she was up to. She was trying to seduce him! As if she hadn't been driving him mad without trying all along.

Anger seared through him. He'd always been attracted to Rosemary, from the first day they'd met years ago. But over the last year he'd come to think of her as something special to him. Thoughts of her often tugged at his heart and strayed into his dreams—some rather provocative dreams. And now, she was going away and trying—with her naive, but appealing wiles—to seduce him into marriage. As much as he wanted her, he was not about to be maneuvered into something he didn't think was right.

''Yes. Indians flirt something like white men do.'' He tried to keep his anger from his voice.

''John? Did I say something wrong?'' She lifted her face to his and leaned closer, allowing her breast to brush against his arm. Her golden eyes were wide and guileless. ''What troubles you?''

''Nothing.'' He laid the flute on the table and took her face between his fingers. ''You know, you're not very good at this.''

Wariness shadowed her eyes. ''What do you mean?''

''You know exactly what I mean,'' he said. Then he kissed her hard. It was what she wanted, and heaven help him, it was what he wanted, too.

His tongue probed and prodded until she parted her lips, softly moaning. His lips rubbed kiss after kiss upon hers. His hand fell from her face and he wrapped her in his arms, savoring the feel of her narrow back. She slipped her arms around his neck pressing her ripe breasts against his chest.

It was his turn to moan. He moved his hands up and down her body stroking her ribs and cupping her breasts in his palms.

"Yes, John, yes," she whimpered. "I've been waiting for you."

Those were the sweetest words he'd ever heard. He knew her body was the most desirable he'd ever touched, but what she wanted was impossible.

"It's not going to work, Rosemary," he murmured, kissing her ear.

"What?"

"You're not going to seduce me," he vowed, though she had already.

"Why would I do that?" she asked, resting her forehead against his. Her lashes fluttered against his cheek, tingling and sweet, like a butterfly's kiss.

He groaned, wanting so much more from her than just holding her in his arms. Slipping his hand under her knees, he lifted her, kicked the bench aside, and headed for the bed. He lowered her gently onto the furs. Kneeling over her, he sank his fingers into her hair. He angled her head back and kissed her mouth, then her throat, then her mouth again. Between each hot kiss he whispered her name.

Engulfed in mindless pleasure, Rosemary tossed her head back and arched her body beneath his hands. His fingers seared her skin through her coarse cotton shirt. It seemed sheer and insignificant against the demanding quest of his hands. But she longed to be free of the garment and wrapped in the power of his passion.

His kisses gentled. His tongue played in and out of her mouth teasingly, provocatively. Suddenly he seized her by the waist, pulled her across him, and stood her beside the bed. She faced him in astonishment.

"Undress for me," he demanded in a hoarse whisper.

Inside she quailed. Her head was spinning from the impact of his kisses and her knees were weak from his caresses. Now that he demanded something she'd never done for any man, she became uncertain.

"You made me watch you undress from the other side of this damned curtain for the past two nights," John rasped, propping himself up on his elbow.

She gasped. "You could see me?"

He nodded. "But tonight I watch from this side."

Her gaze flicked over the bulge in his buckskins. Longing to be free of her shirt only moments ago, now she was having second thoughts. But a bit of her courage returned. She slowly pulled the shirt over her head and he took it from her. She stood before him, her shoulders bare and only the thin cotton of her shift covering her breasts. They had become heavy and sensitive. When she looked at him again, he was studying her face.

He beckoned to her and moved over so that she could perch on the edge of the bed facing him. "Now, off with the shift."

She reached for the thong that held up the buckskins she wore, but John stayed her hand. "Just your shift."

He helped her pull the undergarment from inside the waist of her breeches and up over her head.

The cold air tingled across her bare skin, tightening her nipples. John murmured sounds of gratification at the sight of her and some of her fear and embarrassment slipped away. She leaned forward offering herself to him. He bent his head and laved her breasts quickly with his tongue. His hand pressed against the small of her back as he drew one breast into his mouth and sucked firmly.

A new sensation seized her. As if some dam had broken, heat flooded through her leaving her warm and moist and helpless. She laced her fingers through his tawny hair and sighed with pleasure.

He groaned as he took her other breast into his mouth. Then he grabbed her and pulled her across him and down onto the bed again. He never stopped suckling her. She didn't want him to. Once on her back beside him, she gave herself up to the pleasure of his mouth on her breast and the stroking of his hands across her belly.

She felt him loosen the thong of her buckskins and suddenly his calloused palm slipped gently over her bare hip and then rested lightly atop the curly triangle of hair between her legs.

Then he rose above her, working the breeches down over her hips and legs. He threw the clothing aside and returned to her, stroking her thighs.

"By tomorrow morning you will know what it's like to lie with a man who loves you," he whispered, his eyes hooded and dark with passion. "I'll show you. I'll give you what you want."

She smiled languidly, pleased to feel his eyes caressing her naked body, thrilled to know that he loved her. She gazed up at him, wondering vaguely when he was going to take off his clothes and reveal to her that intriguing bulge in his breeches.

"But, Rosemary, make no mistake, you are going to Baltimore, just as your father wishes."

Her warm cocoon of pleasure vanished. "No."

John rolled atop her, pressing her against the bed. His knees worked their way between her thighs until she lay naked and open beneath him.

"You do want me?" he demanded.

"Oh, yes, John," she whispered. "You know I do."

He braced himself so that his weight no longer weighed on her and he kissed her, inching his way to her neck and chest. She gripped his shoulders tightly as he suckled her breasts once more until her nipples were stiff and aching. He nuzzled her belly, his tawny beard pleasantly scratching her sensitive skin. His tongue flicked over her navel until she gasped.

She sucked in a sharp breath when he planted a hot, wet kiss on the delicate skin of her inner thigh. She could hardly breathe as more kisses followed.

He slid his hand beneath her bottom, parted the tender folds of her flesh with his thumb, and drew her against his open mouth. He tasted her gently, clearly enjoying her as much as she enjoyed being tasted, then his tongue moved mercilessly over her sensitive bud.

She arched off the bed and clutched his hair. "Oh, John. No."

She drifted, poised on the edge of something wide and yawning, something that would swallow her up.

"This is what you wanted." His lips brushed against her throbbing flesh.

She fell back on the bed unable to stop any of the sensations that were washing over her. She hardly heard the scream she uttered as a wave of unbearable pleasure swept over her and she clung to John, her only anchor in this maelstrom of indescribable ecstasy.

When the last of the storm of sensations receded, she opened her eyes. His face was close to hers.

"Now," he whispered, stroking her hair away from her damp brow, "no matter who you wed in Baltimore, you will never forget me."

"Never," she repeated, still wrapped in the warm haze of pleasure and fulfillment he'd awakened inside her.

Yet the awareness grew as she lay in his arms that they had not truly made love. John had touched her intimately., had definitely touched the woman in her, but he'd left her a virgin. She moaned. Her seduction had failed, but she didn't have the energy to think any more about it as sweet exhaustion overcame her and she fell asleep.

Chapter 8

The next morning John tightened the cinch on the packhorse and glanced out the door of the shed once more. The snowfall had lightened to little more than a flurry. Visibility was good, but the wind remained gusty and bitter cold. The freezing temperature would be their foe on the trail—and the Indians.

When he had made his way to the shed, he had seen the footprints again and knew that the six warriors had come during the night without making a sound. He would have heard them, since he'd kept watch all through the wee hours, sitting on his pallet by the fire, wanting Rosemary, tormented by his fear that he'd done the wrong thing by her.

At daybreak, however, reality had set in and his regrets had evaporated. She would go to her marriage bed a virgin; he had not robbed her of that. But she was a woman now and she'd become one in his arms. The thought had brought a satisfied smile to his lips, if not satisfaction to his body, because even now he still ached for her.

Finished with saddling the horses, John slapped the packhorse affectionately on the rump and headed for the cabin.

Inside he pulled back the curtain to wake Rosemary. Instead of finding a sleeping beauty, he found her sitting on the edge of the bed, clutching her clothing to her bare breasts. The firelight made a glittering halo of her dark hair and limned the sweet contours of her bare shoulders.

His loins tightened and his gaze lingered on her, taking in every soft, warm curve that he had caressed and kissed.

A strong urge overcame him—stronger than possessiveness or mere responsibility. It rose inside him, a deep perception of owning and caring and belonging, a power-huge, invisible, and potent. It was *love.*

Rosemary stared at him, her amber eyes large and luminous in her surprise. "It must be late. I don't usually lie abed like this. I'll be dressed in a minute."

"No, it's early, but you should get dressed," he said, without looking away. "The snow has nearly stopped and we need to be on our way. It's a twenty-five-mile ride back to town and the daylight hours are short."

"But we don't have to go today, do we?" Hope tinged her voice.

He sighed. She had not abandoned her purpose.

"Wouldn't tomorrow be soon enough? The weather might even be warmer."

"No." He shook his head and decided now was the time for her to know. "I've seen signs of unfriendly Indians in the area."

"Indians? I see," she murmured distractedly. No panic, no fear glinted in her eyes. "Would you be so quick to leave if I weren't here?"

"Yes," he said, prepared for her question. She'd be angry if she thought he was shuffling her off to safety for her sake alone. "Captain Smithson has got to know about the Indians' movements so he can protect all the settlers near Vincennes. I may not be scouting for him any longer, but it's my responsibility to tell him."

"Oh. You're right then, of course. We should get to town."

He nodded, glad there would be no argument, relieved that she'd brought up no recriminations about their passionate interlude.

"We'll leave as soon as we can. Put on every layer of clothing you can find. It's going to be a long, cold ride."

He let the curtain drop as he turned away.

* * *

Half an hour later they rode into the gloomy woods. John led the way, uneasy about Rosemary riding behind him on his number-one packhorse. He'd rather have had her ahead of him where he could keep an eye on her. But it was not safe for her to lead on the trail, either.

When he glanced back at her, he could almost believe that a boy was riding behind him. The disguise had been her idea and since she was dressed in buckskins already, he decided she might be right. Attacking two armed males was bound to be less appealing to the Indians than attacking a man and a defenseless woman. So they'd wrapped her up in his blanket coat with her shawl underneath to broaden her shoulders. Then they'd pulled an old coon cap down over her ears and tucked her hair into it. From a distance the Indians might be fooled.

"You all right?" he called to her.

With his second rifle slung across her back, she seemed comfortable on horseback and nodded. "I'm fine."

John turned forward again to look down the white trail twisting through the black and white woods ahead of them. He put his heels against the sides of his pony, demanding a fast, steady pace. He didn't want to get caught in these woods after dark.

For hours they heard only the creak of saddle leather and the crunch of their horses' hooves on the snowy trail. All they saw were straight tree trunks ebony against the pristine blanket of white.

But they made good progress. By midday they had covered nearly half the distance to town, and John was beginning to feel they might be out of danger. He'd seen no movement in the woods, wildlife or Indian. Chances were good that the closer they rode to Vincennes and to the well-armed army garrison the safer they were.

"John?" Rosemary called.

He turned.

"Can we stop for a rest?"

"There's a creek at the bottom of the next hill," he said, secretly surprised that she hadn't asked to stop sooner. So far she'd been as easy to travel with as most men. But he could see that she was wearing out. He was pushing it and she was bound to start tiring.

They dismounted on the banks of the clear, babbling stream.

"Don't go far," he warned her as she disappeared behind a tree. While he allowed the horses to drink, he began to regret his choice of resting places. They were in a hollow, surrounded by high ground which made them an easy target for an ambush.

"Rosemary?" he called, surveying the top of the rise ahead. "Don't dawdle."

"I assure you, I am not dawdling." After a moment's pause she called his name.

He didn't like the soft ring of alarm in her voice. Dropping the horses' reins, he started toward her. "What is it?"

She came sliding through the slippery snow toward him, from behind the tree. "I thought I saw something move back there. See, near that deadfall."

He saw nothing, but it was a good hiding place. He glanced back at the rise again. Nothing there, but the hair prickled on the back of his neck. Something didn't feel right.

"Let's go." He spoke softly, trying not to convey his concern. Nevertheless, the moment she was within arm's reach, he seized her waist and threw her onto the packhorse. Then he vaulted into the saddle and led them splashing across the stream.

Silently he prayed his gut was wrong, but he pulled his rifle from across his back anyway. There just might be a passel of Indians waiting for them at the top of the rise.

Rosemary clung to the saddle and urged her mount up the hill after John. When she saw him pull his rifle from his back, she knew he expected something to happen. She wished he'd told her what it was. Twisting in the saddle, she looked behind her in time to see two Indians appear from the cover of the deadfall. Red and black war paint streaked their faces. To her horror, two more Indians trotted from behind the far end of the heap of fallen trees.

Four! And two of them carried rifles. Small strange pelts swung from the waists of their buckskin leggings. Rosemary's scream caught in her throat. Not pelts—scalps. Scalps swung from their clothing. One of the scalps was blond, fine and silken even in the dull daylight. Scalps were what the Indians wanted from John and her.

"John!" The sound came out a croak.

"I know, Rosemary. I saw them." His voice floated back over his shoulder. For the first time it was full of urgency. "Keep riding. Keep putting as much distance between us and them as you can."

The only advantage they had against four warriors were the horses. Rosemary pressed her heels against the packhorse's sides, and the animal quickened its pace.

Rosemary reached around to pull her rifle from her back, also. The weapon was long and unwieldy in her hands. John had loaded it for her before they left the cabin. She knew she could never hit a target while she was on horseback, but she was prepared to try.

When they reached the top of the rise, a war whoop shattered the woodland silence. The screech sent shivers down her spine. A fifth warrior jumped into the trail and swung a tomahawk at John, whose horse shied.

Rosemary's mount reared and backed down the hill, nearly throwing her. She struggled to stay in the saddle and to regain control of the animal.

A shot rang out. The whoop ceased.

Terrified, she turned to see the tomahawk-slinging warrior fall to the ground. But another shriek rent the air. A sixth warrior charged from the woods near John. He grasped his rifle by the barrel and rode toward the Indian.

The warrior ducked and turned, prepared for John to swing around. John swung the rifle butt backward. The wood stock caught the warrior under the chin and dropped him.

Rosemary looked back to the four warriors racing up the

hill behind them. One had stopped and raised his rifle taking aim at John's back. She had to do something.

Struggling with the bridle reins, she rested the long-barreled rifle across the saddle bow. Her fingers trembled as she pulled back the hammer. The barrel wavered. Hastily she steadied the stock against her hip and pointed the gun in the direction of the Indian rifleman. He had John in his gun sights. She took a deep breath and squeezed the trigger. She closed her eyes, and with all her might she willed the lead ball to find its target.

Gunpowder flashed, and the recoil knocked her halfway out of her saddle. The thunder deafened her. Smoke curled into the frosty air. Its eyes rolling, her horse pranced sideways up the hill. The pack saddle offered no stirrups for footing so she grabbed the horse's mane and hoisted herself back into the saddle. Centering herself again, she turned and saw the yelping Indian fall to the ground, thrashing in the snow.

The remaining three warriors halted.

"Nice shot," John said. Rosemary swiveled at the sound of his voice and he grabbed her horse's bridle bit.

One of the warriors backtracked to his comrade's side. The other rifleman raised his gun to his shoulder.

"But no time to gloat over marksmanship."

John pulled her horse around. Spurring his mount into a headlong gallop up the slope, he led them out of the hollow. Clinging to her horse for dear life, she leaned low over the saddle bow. Gripping the gun until her hands ached, she prayed that they were outdistancing their attackers at last.

At the top of the hill, a ball whistled just over her head. Then she heard a shot which echoed off the hills behind them. She never looked back. John did, but only long enough for her to assure him she was still in the saddle. As soon as they dropped over the rise, he slowed the pace to a steady canter. He signaled for her to ride on ahead of him.

"You know this part of the trail?" he called as she moved in front of him.

"Yes."

"Good." John glanced over his shoulder, then turned back to her. "I think we're clear but keep your eyes open. Let me know if you spot anything."

She nodded, then pressed her heels against her horse's sides, urging it on toward home, nearer to Papa and safety from the Indians—and closer to losing John forever.

Chapter 9

The muddy street in front of Papa's store was clogged with horses, buckskin-clad trappers, and blue-coated soldiers.

Eager to find her father, Rosemary reined her horse through the crowd, wondering what all the commotion was about. John followed her.

Someone called her name, and she turned to see who it was.

Sam LaBelle waved. "Look, Haley's got Rosemary. He's saved her from the Indians."

It took the crowd a moment to recognize Rosemary in her disguise. When they did, a cheer rippled through it. Friendly hands seized her horse's bridle and helped her out of the saddle.

"We thought the Indians had your scalp by now for sure," Sam told her, flashing his single-toothed grin. "Your papa is near beside himself with worry. We were just ready to head out to search for you."

"I was quite safe with John," Rosemary said, exchanging a glance with him. He had not dismounted yet.

The crowd fell silent and turned expectantly to John.

"Rosemary! Rosemary!" Papa bolted out of the store,

his gray hair flying in all directions, his eyes dark-circled, and his face pale and drawn.

"Papa!"

Rosemary ran up the porch steps and threw herself into his arms. He crushed her against him, and she pressed her face into his shoulder and clutched his tall, spare body. His scent was familiar and safe. She was home. She choked back tears of relief and gratitude for being where she belonged at last. "I'm all right. Really I am."

"Oh, girl, I was afraid I wouldn't see you alive again," Papa whispered against her hair, his voice full of emotion. "What happened to you? You're wearing breeches? You've never worn breeches in your life, child."

"John and I can explain everything, Papa," Rosemary said. "It was the Indians, but not like you think."

Captain Smithson stood in the store doorway, a scowl on his face.

John stepped up onto the porch. "I'll fill you in, Captain, and if it's all right with you, Frederick, why don't we all go to your house so we can talk."

John was right, Rosemary thought. The story was too complicated and personal for everyone in town to know.

An hour later the captain was satisfied with John and Rosemary's explanation of her kidnapping, and asked John to come to the garrison as soon as possible to tell him about the war party they'd encountered on the trail. As the captain got up to leave, John promised he would.

Papa sat down by the fire and pulled Rosemary down on the settle beside him. "I tell you, girl, you gave me a start there for a few days."

"It's over, Papa," she assured him, hoping he wouldn't ask many more questions. "And no harm was done."

"And I thank you for that, Haley," Papa said, turning to John. "I'm grateful for your taking care of my girl."

"No need to thank me, sir." John cast Rosemary an inscrutable look. She wondered if he was as apprehensive as she about more questions.

"Can I fix you something to eat, Papa?" she offered.

For the first time she noticed that a kettle was already on the fire.

"Mrs. Chomeau brought over a pot of beans and ham," Papa explained. "But I'm not hungry. Right now I'd like to hear what John has to say to me. You go clean up. Change your clothes and brush your hair."

Panic fluttered in her belly and she turned to John. "Papa—"

"It's all right, Rosemary," John assured her, his face grim. The line of his jaw seemed suddenly unyielding.

She glared at him. He wasn't the only one who had feelings about what they'd shared in his cabin. "If you two have something to say about what happened out there between John and me, you can say it in front of me."

Papa stared at her then at John. "John, I know your pa raised you to be an honest, honorable man, but you two were alone together for three nights."

"Papa!" Rosemary's face grew hot.

"Your daughter's virtue is intact." John locked gazes with her, challenging her to contradict him.

She glared back at him. "Just barely," she wanted to cry, but she bit her tongue. Not because she was ashamed, but because she knew revealing their intimacy to Papa would serve no purpose. She could not force John's hand now. Nothing she could say would change anything.

"Rosemary, is that true?" Papa asked. "Your future and a man's reputation is at stake."

"So is my heart," she whispered, surprised to find tears threatened to spill from her eyes. She looked from one to the other of the men she held most dear in life. Did neither of them understand? They were not heartless men, but they could not seem to comprehend that her heart lay in Vincennes with them.

Abruptly John rose, avoiding Rosemary's eyes. "If that's settled, I best be on my way to talk to Captain Smithson. He will be eager to begin tracking that raiding party as soon as it's light. He'll need my help. Unfortunately no one is going to trust Cornstalk and Standing Tree."

"Of course," Papa said as he rose from his chair. "I've got to see to locking up the store. You two say your farewells now."

Rosemary's tears had dried by the time Papa closed the door behind him. She turned to John, her mood resentful—and frightened. She realized as she looked up into his face that she'd never really believed he would not come around to her way of thinking.

"Rosemary . . ." he began, without looking at her.

Suddenly he reached for her, pulling her close and studying her face. She allowed it only because she did not have the strength to resist him.

"We lied to him."

"Yes and no," John admitted. "Your virtue is untouched."

"But not my heart. If you planned to send me away, why last night?"

He bent closer to her. "Because it was what you wanted. Admit it."

"Yes, but I wanted you to make love to me. Real love."

"But if we'd crossed that threshold, I would never be able to let you go. I would want more and more of you."

A hopeful thrill fluttered through her. She looked up into his face willing him to look into her eyes. "Would that be so terrible? Haven't I proven myself to you? Look what happened to us on the trail. We fought the Indians off successfully—together."

"You probably saved my life, Rosemary—"

"Then tell Papa—"

"Hear me out. I'm grateful for your fast action, but that's not enough. Think about what would have happened to you if we hadn't been successful."

"John, every woman on the frontier has already faced that thought."

"I want better than that for my wife." Anger glinted in his eyes and he released her so abruptly that she staggered back from him. He turned to reach for his coat on the hook by the door. Avoiding her gaze, he added, "I wish you every happiness, Rosemary, and a safe trip.''

She bit back a sob and vowed she would not beg. But the plea escaped her anyway. ''John? Don't leave like this.''

He turned to her, his face a hard unreadable mask. Without warning, he swept her up in his arms, his hand clamped against the back of her head. He bent to kiss her—a deep, angry, ravishing kiss—and she was helpless against his strength, unable to free herself, even if she'd wanted to.

He let her go, just as abruptly as before, and she reached for the edge of the table to steady herself, but her knees almost buckled.

He pulled his cap over his tawny hair. ''Good-bye, Rosemary.''

A gust of bitter cold wind filled the room as he let himself out.

Tears rolled down her cheeks. Her plan had failed, but that was not what broke her heart. John didn't love her. Not enough anyway. She knew with a certainty she could hardly bear to face that she would never see him again.

During the next three days John joined Captain Smithson and his company of twenty men to scout out the trail of the Indian raiding party that had attacked Rosemary and him. Though they were unsuccessful, their presence and strength in the area was made known to the British as well as the Indians.

On the evening of the third day, John rode into his cabin's clearing, glad to be home again after a grueling thirty-six hours in the saddle.

The snow had melted away, and twilight lit the sky. The orange sunset reflected off the cabin window. No welcoming smoke rose from the chimney, but the place looked good to him and coming home to a cold hearth was nothing new.

Once his horse was rubbed down and fed, he carried wood inside and started the fire. The air was cold and something smelled stale and rotten. As flames leaped in the hearth, he saw a pot on the table which Rosemary had not had time to take care of. He'd allowed her only enough time to pack the buffalo robe she'd been delivered in.

His belly growled with hunger and he eyed the pot speculatively. A hot meal would taste good at the moment. Maybe if he warmed it up . . . Optimistic, he lifted the lid and took a sniff. The odor of rotten meat swirled up into his face, and he choked.

"Whew!" He drew back and dropped the lid back on the pot. This pot of savory stew wouldn't do him any good now.

He carried it outside to the dumping pit just beyond the clearing, and as soon as he reentered the cabin, he tackled the curtain. There was no reason to live with it any longer.

He folded the sheet and coiled the rope. Then he put the table back in its corner. She had insisted on putting it closer to the fire—for light she said.

With his furniture back in place, he began to pull his traps and ropes off their pegs and tossed them back into the corners she'd swept out.

But when he came to the peg where the Indian flageolet hung, he stopped, his hand poised in midair. He pulled back, staring at the musical instrument. He was unable to bring himself to throw it back into a corner with the other clutter. Somehow, the flute belonged where it hung. He backed away from the instrument, uneasy with his reaction to this change Rosemary had made—the one change he could not bring himself to undo.

Plucking the flute off the wall, he put it to his lips and played "Yankee Doodle." He groaned, then chuckled at the memory of Rosemary practicing that tune.

The fire had lit her hair with deep gold and red lights and her pretty, wide mouth had pursed into a kissable bow as she coaxed the melody from the Indian courting flute. The poignant image left John nostalgic and moody. She'd played that damned song until she'd driven him from the cabin. Until she'd driven him mad. With a strange tingle in his gut, he realized he longed for that madness again.

He shrugged and replaced the flute on the peg. Then he turned away to look for some beef jerky. It wouldn't make as tasty a supper as Rosemary would stir up, but it would suit him fine.

After he'd eaten, he began to clean his guns, amazed at how quiet the cabin seemed. If Rosemary were there, the silence would have been filled with feminine chatter and the clatter of pots, pans, spoons, and bowls.

He liked the silence, he thought, looking around the cabin. But he knew that wasn't true. Maybe a dog would be nice. Something to talk to—and hunt with.

But that thought did not inspire visions of floppy ears, friendly brown eyes, and a long, wet snout. Instead, Rosemary's leaving was on his mind. Annoyed with himself, he finished cleaning his guns and decided to go to bed.

Pulling off his boots and his shirt, he relished the thought that he didn't even have to wash up if he didn't want to. He could leave his razor untouched for weeks if he wanted.

Stretching out on the furs, he drew his buffalo robe over him, and closed his eyes. It'd been nearly a week since he enjoyed the luxury of sleeping in his own bed—what with giving it up to Rosemary, then being on the trail for three days. The bed ropes creaked as he relaxed, his weary muscles glad to rest on something softer than a straw pallet on the floor.

He drew in a long, deep breath, ready for a peaceful night's rest. But a heady scent ambushed him. Lavender filled his head. His body stirred. He sniffed again. Beneath her familiar fragrance he detected the musky scent of a woman ready and willing to give herself to him.

He grew hard and groaned at his body's reaction. Three days of hard riding should have cured him of this agony. He faced the wall, squeezed his eyes shut, and willed himself to sleep. But images of Rosemary swam before his eyes. Rolling to his other side, he stared at the flames in the fireplace. The softness of the fur beneath him reminded him of the silkiness of her hair, the smoothness of her skin.

Throwing aside the buffalo robe, he jumped out of bed

and stalked to the door. Despite the brisk night air, he strode, shirtless and bootless, straight to the well. In the moonlight he stripped off his buckskin breeches, then tossed the bucket into the well. As soon as he heard it hit the water, he drew it up. Water sloshed over the rim as he turned it over his head. The icy liquid cascaded down his body taking only a little of the unbearable fire with it. The agonizing ache remained.

He threw the bucket back into the well again. The next dousing made him gasp, and the third sent a chill through him making him shiver. He threw his head back to stare at the starry sky and to breathe in the cold night air.

The fourth soaking brought some relief to his body, but his heart still ached. He threw the bucket into the well once more, resolving to continue dousing himself until he'd washed away everything. All the guilt about Georgeanne—and every last yearning for Rosemary.

Chapter 10

''Don't look so daunted, girl,'' the gray-bearded Gabe Rogers said, cheerily smiling at Rosemary and touching her shoulder.

She liked the short, sturdily built Gabe. She had always looked forward to his arriving with his endless train of packhorses carrying a wealth of surprises and novelties shipped west from Baltimore's stores and docks. Until today.

''The trip will go fast. You'll see, Rosemary,'' Gabe assured her.

Papa nodded. ''Before you know it, you'll be throwing

yourself into Myrtle's arms. There will be shopping for new dresses and shoes and all sorts of frippery."

"Yes, I'm sure you're right," Rosemary said, with little interest in frippery. Gabe had arrived only a week ago and already he'd rid himself of his goods and was ready to return East for another shipment.

The day was cloudy and would be dark, even when the sun was fully risen. With growing dismay she surveyed the line of packhorses lined up nose to tail along Water Street. She would ride in the lead with Gabe, and he, his drovers, and these small strong animals would be her only company during her journey into exile. That's how she felt, banished from the land of her birth.

"I'll keep a close watch over her, Frederick," Gabe said.

"I know you will." Papa put his arm around the shoulders of his long-time friend and led him away from Rosemary. "By the way, would you mind seeing that this letter gets to . . ."

Rosemary ignored their conversation. It was clearly not intended for her. She wanted to use her last minutes in Vincennes to memorize the details of the whitewashed houses and thatch-roofed stables. The stately red-brick Vincennes Seminary and the log church with its modest belfry. The graceful limbs of the trees and the quiet surge of the river. The square print shop and the tall, two-story territorial capitol. The great sprawling community garden below town. It was all so dear, even the town's smelly pigs. She turned back toward the store, suddenly longing to confront Sam's silly sow again.

"See if you can get some more of those Irish linens and that French silk taffeta. Bright colors. The ladies like that," Papa was saying to Gabe.

Rosemary listened with half an ear until she realized she was also hearing music. The soft melodic sound of a flute. The song seemed much like "I Am Here Waiting for You."

Her heart thudded and she whirled in the direction of the music. John was riding down the street toward her playing the Indian flageolet. Their eyes locked. She forgot about everyone and everything around her. Only John filled her vision. She was afraid if she looked away, he would disappear.

Only when his horse halted in front of her did he stop playing. He swung down from the bay without a word.

"I thought you two said your good-byes already," Papa said, casting an uneasy glance at John.

"Rosemary forgot something at my cabin," John said, offering her the flute. In a soft, husky voice he added, "And I want you to have it."

She stared at the flageolet in his open palm. She looked into his face, mystified by the dark circles under his eyes and the uncertainty in the depth of his gaze. She sensed that he'd been on the trail all night.

"Why should I take this? It was a gift to you."

Papa lingered, nearly standing between them.

"Frederick, may I talk to Rosemary alone?" John asked, his tone polite, but his voice suddenly stronger as though he'd settled on his course at last.

"Gabe's train is leaving soon," Papa warned.

"I know," John said, his gaze holding Rosemary's once more. "I won't take long to say this."

"Fine. As long as you understand that." Papa hooked his thumbs in his apron strings and strolled away.

Rosemary reached for the flute, but when she touched it, John seized her hand.

"What's wrong?" She struggled to free herself, but his hand tightened around hers.

"Nothing. Just hear me out. I've been thinking a lot about what you've been telling me. About wanting to stay here."

"About staying where I was born and with the people I love?"

John's gray eyes searched her face again. "I remember that Georgeanne came with Pa and me because she wanted to. We even had a big argument about it. She had a chance to stay with a neighbor family. Good friends with whom she would have been safe and comfortable. But she wanted to come with us, though she knew it would be a hardship."

"Did she ever complain about the hardship?" Rosemary asked.

"No, never," John said. "Never. I remember that clearly. She never complained."

"Thank you for bringing me the flute. I shall cherish it, but I really must—" She pulled against his grasp again, but he would not release her.

"Rosemary, you asked me to marry you once, and I refused you."

She stared down at their hands clasped around the Indian courting flute.

"Well, now I'm doing the asking and I'm praying for a better outcome than before." He took a deep breath.

She looked at him, certain that her heart stood still.

"I love you, Rosemary. I always have. And I'm asking you to marry me."

She stared at him in disbelief. "Are you certain about what you just said? Maybe you'd like to think it over."

"I've never been more certain of anything in my life." John smiled and shook his head. "Don't torture me, woman. I want to finish what we started—that night."

She looked away as heat flooded through her. She knew exactly what he meant. She wanted to finish what they had begun, too. She'd daydreamed every day and lain awake every night since he'd brought her home, beset by the vivid memories of his touch. She yearned for his caresses, his kisses. She longed for him to become a part of her.

"You know I can't even defend myself against a pig."

"No, just Indian warriors." John stepped closer. "Are you going to say yes, so I can start arguing with your father before he sends you off with Gabe?"

She spread her hands across his chest and tipped her head back farther to hold his gaze. "Yes. Oh, yes."

Frederick proved less of an opponent than John anticipated, but then he'd always known the storekeeper doted on his youngest daughter. That probably was the only reason Rosemary hadn't been sent off to Baltimore years ago. The only condition Frederick demanded in exchange for his blessing was that Rosemary have a church wedding and John agreed.

So on the morning of March thirtieth, John, standing at the altar of Saint Francis Xavier log church, watched his bride walk down the aisle—a blushing beauty dressed in rosebud-sprigged English muslin. A white lace cap crowned her dark curls, and a handful of ivy tied with pink ribbons served as her bouquet.

Though she had approved of his wearing new buckskins, John had borrowed a cutaway jacket of burgundy broadcloth, buff breeches, and black leather boots. He wore the new, white ruffled shirt Mrs. Chomeau made for him, and the proud gleam in Rosemary's eye told him he looked fine as he waited for her at the altar

The ceremony was brief, but the celebration in Lasselle's banquet room wore on longer than John liked. When Billie Hogan appeared, drunk as usual, with his lips pursed to kiss the bride, John was ready to take Rosemary home.

After they said good night to Frederick, they slipped away to the fresh horses and change of clothes John had waiting in Frederick's stable. They quickly dressed, mounted, and headed for home.

The sun had begun to descend so quickly that they pushed the horses to reach the cabin before darkness fell. Only a strip of the vermilion sunset silhouetted the woods against the horizon when they rode into the cabin's clearing.

John was still a bit apprehensive about their safety. Though Captain Smithson had promised the area would be patrolled, there were still other dangers besides Indians like bears, wolves, and wildcats.

But he shook off his concern when he looked at Rosemary. Proud and pleased to have her to himself again, he helped her off her horse and kissed her—quick and firm. "Welcome home, Mrs. John Winston Haley."

"Thank you, Mr. Haley."

Her smile gave him a sense of strength that warmed him and he swept her up into his arms, and carried her into the cabin.

"The fire is laid," he said as he put her down.

She turned toward the cold hearth. "I'll get the fire started and warm up the food I packed while you take care of the horses."

John kissed her again. "I'll bring in your bag and the food basket, but don't fix much. I'm not hungry."

"Me, either." She turned to him once more. A soft smile played across her lips. "But I think we may need sustenance later."

"Good thinking." John studied her face, trying to understand how his life could transform so quickly from lonely day-to-dayness into a whole new world of pleasurable possibilities. "I won't be long."

He returned and set her bag by the bed and the basket on the table. He then hurriedly left to tend the horses.

The fire blazed bright in the hearth when he returned. Rosemary looked up at him and smiled as she arranged the tablecloth, and set the table with her pewter and crockery. She'd obviously packed more than food in her basket. She'd also dragged the table out of the corner and closer to the hearth.

He noticed one more thing: her dressing gown. His body reacted swiftly and painfully. To hide his obvious response, he turned away to hang up his coat and cap. When he turned around, her hands were clasped primly before her. The soft wool stretched across her breasts revealing she was naked beneath the gown.

John quickly crossed the room, swept her up, and carried her to the bed. As soon as he placed her on the furs, she scrambled beyond his reach. Firelight caught the gold of her earrings. Desire gleamed in her amber eyes. "Tonight, sir, I watch you undress."

"I see." He recalled ordering her to strip for him during

their last night together. Her boldness surprised and pleased him. "Fair enough."

"Not just your shirt, either," she reminded him with a sly smile. "Everything. I wish to avail myself of my full wifely rights."

"Far be it from me to deny you your full wifely rights."

He watched her as he pulled off his shirt. Her eyes, bright and solemn with womanly curiosity, followed his every movement. When he tossed his shirt aside, she leaned forward and slid her hand up his belly to comb her fingers through his chest hair.

Her touch increased his arousal. "Do you like what you see?"

She smiled shyly and nodded. He noted that her gaze had drifted down to the bulge in his breeches.

He untied his belt and slowly began to lower his buckskins over his hips. When his manhood sprang free, Rosemary's eyes widened a bit. He quickly stepped out of his breeches and stood straight and tall before her, allowing the firelight to reveal him completely.

"Oh my," she murmured.

He knelt on the bed, and the ropes creaked under his weight as he reached for her. She came willing into his arms, and he pulled her down onto the furs. Her breath was quick and shallow as he peeled her dressing gown from her shoulders.

Impatiently he freed her arms of the sleeves and admired her breasts. Under his scrutiny, her pink nipples grew button-hard.

"Beautiful." He bent over her to stroke one then the other with his tongue. She moaned and arched her back, and he touched her again and again with his tongue and his fingertips.

She smelled wonderfully of lavender. When he lifted his head to take a breath, she clutched at him. "It's so exquisite, John."

He kissed her mouth. "Tell me what you feel."

She let her head sink back against the furs. "A burning

and need and something wonderful in my belly. I want you to touch me.''

''Like this.'' His hand cupped her triangle of hair and his fingers began to part the soft warm, wet petals of the secret place between her legs. She was already hot and wet.

''Yes, oh, yes.''

She was tight, and she winced. He tensed and halted his eager explorations. ''I don't want to hurt you, darling.''

''I know.''

He kissed her, tasting and caressing her lips until he felt her body settle against the furs once more. Gently his fingers sought her wet heat again, and he stroked her until she moaned and arched against him.

His own need had grown painful. He could hardly resist the yearning to bury himself in her softness. Rising above her, he knelt between her thighs and entered her slowly at first. He found resistance and suddenly she lifted her hips to meet him. He felt her wince again ever so slightly, but he could not keep himself from sinking deep into her sweet, dark warmth. Concerned for her, he chanted her name.

Her small hand stroked his back reassuringly. With a cry of pleasure, he surrendered to the desire to drain himself into her. Astonishingly she came with him. Her head thrown back, a soft sob of release escaped her lips. Small spasms deep in her body milked the last of his strength, and he sank against her neck, careful to throw his weight to one side of her.

When he could move again, he rolled onto his back and pulled her to him. To his relief, she snuggled against him.

''Are you all right?'' he asked, concerned for her comfort and welfare.

''Fine,'' she whispered, her voice thick with sleepy contentment.

''Don't fall asleep yet,'' he warned. ''I have a gift for you.''

''You mean there's more?'' she murmured.

He smiled. ''Yes.'' He reached under the bed, found the bundle, and handed it to her.

Rosemary leaned on her elbow to unwrap the oil cloth from around the gift. Slowly she unfolded it. John waited patiently. When she recognized what it was, she began to laugh and fell back against the furs.

He did not think it was quite that amusing. "It's very practical and I want you to use it."

Rosemary struggled to sit up. Her dark curls fell across her shoulders, and firelight revealed her shapely feminine body flushed with sexual satisfaction.

Biting her lip, clearly to hold back her laughter, she held up the leather apron that John had lovingly made for her.

When she saw that he wasn't laughing, she bent over to kiss him—a sweet tasting of lips. She paused before she withdrew, allowing her lashes to brush like butterfly wings against his cheek. His heart skipped a beat and his exhaustion disappeared.

"Are you hungry?" she asked, slithering away from his grasp to perch on the foot of the bed, beyond his reach.

"Well, yes." He thought a little sustenance might serve him well later.

"Then bring me a piece of that beef quarter you have hanging in the storeroom and I'll fix us my stew."

John didn't take long to pull on his breeches and coat and head outside for the beef in the lean-to at the side of the cabin.

Back inside, the sight of Rosemary at the fireside brought him to a halt.

"John, close the door," she said, rubbing her arms. "It's cold."

He slammed the door without taking his eyes from her. "What in heaven's name do you think you're doing?"

"Fixing us supper," she answered as if she always cooked naked, save for a pair of earrings and a leather apron.

Occupied with taking in every detail of his new wife's apparel, he hastily managed to drop the bar into place.

The dark leather apron bib stretched tight across her breasts, plumping them so the firelight glowed off their smooth roundness. The thong ties pulled the apron snug around her ribs and waist. His gaze traveled downward to the taut leather tugging across her thighs, hinting at the sweet warmth between her legs. His body began to strain against his breeches again.

"You wanted me to wear this, didn't you?" She turned sideways, offering him a view of her back.

John devoured the tempting lines of her body with his eyes. He envied the bow knot she'd managed to tie. It fit tight against the small of her back. The apron strings dangled tantalizingly against her bare bottom.

"Let's forget about supper." The ache in his loins was more insistent than the gnawing in his belly.

"Oh, no." Her eyes sparkled with mischief. "I already have the potatoes and onions ready to go into the pot. All I have to do is cut up the meat and carrots. Take off your coat and help me."

He hung up his coat and eased himself down on the bench to help her with the last of the preparations. Standing on the other side of the table, Rosemary sliced the carrots. He was supposed to cut up the meat. But every time she leaned over to reach for something, her breasts pressed against the apron bib made his loins throb and his mind go blank. But before long he managed to accomplish his task without cutting himself.

They sat across the table from each other, sharing their first meal as man and wife. John found he was hungrier than he'd thought, but he still couldn't take his eyes off Rosemary.

"You will wear the apron whenever you are working around the fire," John said, suddenly more aware than ever how vital her welfare was to him. "I did not give it to you in jest. The leather will protect your clothes from the fire."

"I know it's no jest, John," she said, "but I don't know one woman who wears leather when she cooks."

"Rosemary, I don't care what other women wear." He reached across the table and took her hands in his. He had to make her understand. "Promise me you will wear the apron when you're working around the fire.''

''Thank you for the thoughtful gift.'' She freed her hand and touched his cheek.

Her touch was warm and gentle, but he would not succumb to its lure until he heard her promise—a promise more meaningful than any vow she had made in church. ''Rosemary, this is important to me.''

''I know it is,'' she whispered. ''I know exactly what it means to you. It is a gift of love. I promise to wear this apron when I'm working around the fire. Because I love you, too, John Winston Haley.''

He could live with that promise. He got up from the table and pulled her into his arms. ''I'm glad that's settled.''

He kissed her, his hands pressing against the small of her back, his fingers already untying the leather apron strings. . . .

Award-winning writer *Linda Madl* is a realistic romantic who believes there is someone for everyone. However, the path to true love can be rocky, regardless of the century or the setting.

But Linda thinks that there is nothing quite so likely to help smooth that road as a good meal, which is spiced with just a dash of savory, simmered with a generous amount of love, and served up with an imaginative garnish. An irresistible combination to satisfy a man, body and soul.

Gardening, travel, and family fill Linda's non-writing hours, and she currently resides in the Kansas City area with her husband and daughter.

Sinfully Sweet

Penelope Neri

Honey's Glazed Double-Chocolate Torte

Torte (all at room temperature)

20 *ounces semisweet chocolate*
10 *ounces butter*
2 *teaspoons vanilla*
1 *tablespoon coffee liqueur*
6 *eggs*

In a double boiler, melt the chocolate and butter, stirring till smooth. Remove from heat. Add vanilla and coffee liqueur.

Whisk eggs until tripled in volume. Fold ¼ of the egg mixture into the chocolate-and-butter mixture. Fold in the remaining eggs. Pour into buttered 8 ½" springform baking pan.

Place watertight springform in a larger, shallow pan containing 1 inch of hot water. Bake at 400 degrees for about 18 minutes. Remove springform from oven and allow torte to cool for at least 1 hour.

Glaze

1 *cup heavy cream*
6 *ounces semisweet chocolate*

In a heavy pot, heat ½ cup cream to simmering point. Add chocolate, then remove from heat. Cover, then cool for several minutes. While still warm, stir glaze then spoon over torte. Chill to set, before removing springform. Use ½ cup of remaining cream for garnish.

Raspberry-Amaretto Sauce

1½ *pounds fresh or frozen raspberries*
3 *ounces granulated sugar*
1½ *tablespoons lemon juice*
2 *tablespoons Amaretto liqueur*

Reserve ⅛ cup fresh raspberries for garnish. Mash the remainder, straining the juice into a small pot. Simmer until the liquid is reduced by half. Add sugar, lemon juice, and raspberry puree. Stir well. Cool thoroughly, then add the liqueur.

To Serve

Slice the torte into the desired number of wedges. Garnish with whipped cream and chocolate curls. Serve on a plate dressed with a generous swirl of raspberry-Amaretto sauce. Finish with a scattering of fresh raspberries.

Chapter 1

Louisiana, 1840

"Good morning, my pet!" Honey's mother murmured. Unfastening her opera cloak, she handed it to Remy, who scowled, taking it with her floury hands. "Mmm, that coffee smells heavenly! Pour me a cup, Mammy. I have such a dreadful head!"

"Poor *Maman.* Finish the kneading, Remy. I'll do it," Honey offered.

Turning from the pan of bubbling fat, she lifted the coffeepot from the spider and poured. The roasted fragrance of chicory coffee mingled with the smell of fried beignets and the pungent scent of the onion, garlic, and pepper strings that hung from the kitchen rafters.

"How was the *Barber of Seville* last night, *Maman?*" She handed her mother a dainty demitasse cup and saucer.

"The Figaro was marvelous—and my Don Carlos even more so!" Perched on a low stool beside the enormous hearth, she wore a dreamy expression as she sipped her coffee and gazed into the fire. "What an old darling he is! He could never replace your papa in my affections, but . . ."

"But what?" Dredging another beignet with sugar, Honey added it to those in the basket.

"But he has charm and wealth, thank God! If he asks me to marry him, I shall accept. Then the tedious question of our livelihood will be solved and I shall be able to order some new gowns. *Alors!* Look at this rag!"

Honey shook her head. The "rag" had cost Papa a small fortune five Christmases ago. "I shall ask Saint Jude to answer your prayers, *Maman,*" she promised, wishing the saint would answer a few of her own. Since Papa's death, so many people depended on her for their financial security and she couldn't let them down.

Blinking back tears, she gazed through the long, white-framed window to the courtyard beyond.

Above the brick walls draped by wisteria, the last stars were paling. To the east, dawn painted streaks of sulphur over the levee and revealed the Mississippi's inky waters. Her throat tightened. *Cher* Papa! On mornings like this, when her world was falling apart around her, she missed him so!

It was from Papa she had learned to cook. From him, too, she'd learned the priceless secret that had brought her such success as a pastry chef: If food was cooked with love, the great love in the cook's heart flavored every delicious morsel. Papa had believed that love made the difference in everything one did.

Even as a little girl, she'd known he was right. Nothing had ever tasted as wonderful as the scraps of fried dough he lovingly had popped into her mouth. "Sweet as honey to the bee. That's what Melisse Marie is to her papa. His little honey," he'd said, and ever since, she'd been called Honey by everyone but *Maman.*

And then, the summer when she was sixteen, both her parents had fallen ill with yellow fever, and everything had changed. Fearing her mother would follow him to heaven, Papa'd left the restaurant to Honey and after his funeral, standing before his vault in the Saint Louis cemetery, she had sworn never to marry until the restaurant was everything she and Papa had dreamed of. She had promised to cook with love as he had taught her.

She had kept both promises. Her mouth-watering desserts had made Armand's one of the most fashionable places to dine in the French Quarter. Her creations had also earned her an enviable reputation as a pastry chef. Most nights the restaurant did not have an empty table to spare, even in the ladies' dining room, which was, of course, separate from the men's, except during the more relaxed week of Mardi Gras.

But now her good fortune had ended. Last year's hurricane in Madagascar had destroyed the vanilla bean harvests, and only weeks later an early monsoon in India had rotted the cinnamon trees' barks, leaving the groves devastated, unfit for spices. As if that were not enough, during a terrible storm the Italian vessel carrying the luscious European liqueurs that gave richness and body to her desserts had sunk off the coast of Florida. The crew had all died and Honey lost every single cask of her cargo.

In the wake of those natural disasters, the price of those ingredients had skyrocketed, yet she had not dared to pass on the increased costs to her patrons, for fear they would dine elsewhere. Forced to cut corners, she had fallen three months behind on her grocers' bills. Now, her creditors were demanding payment in full by the last day of February.

She sighed. Ever since her banker, Monsieur Henri Bienville, told her the bad news yesterday, her thoughts had chased themselves like a mouse on a treadmill. A month! She had only one month to come up with the money, or lose the restaurant! Unable to sleep last night, she'd come down to the kitchens to forget her problems doing what she loved—cooking.

The delicious smells, the cozy warmth of the faded brick fireplace, the gleaming copper pots hanging from racks on the walls brought back happy memories of watching and learning as her papa cooked. The German butter pats, cake tins, and cookie boards that *Grandpère* Jerome Armand had brought to Louisiana from the first Armand's in Paris were like old friends.

"Ooh, my aching head!"

"What is wrong, *Maman?*"

"I am dying, *cherie!*"

"Oh, pish. You ain't dyin', Miz Estelle. Your head poundin' cuz you bin out all night." Without looking up, Remy continued kneading bread dough on the huge, bleached table.

Nobody made bread like Remy, Honey thought, watching her mammy's deft brown hands working the dough. Those hands could cradle a baby as gently as an egg, or soothe a little girl's hurt as lightly as an angel's kiss.

This morning, as always, Remy had tied a madras tignon around her head rather than the flowered silk squares Honey had given her. Still, on Remy, who carried herself like a Nubian queen, even cotton had a regal air. Her neat yet faded guinea blue dress and ruffled white apron were so stiffly pressed and starched, they could have stood up on their own.

"Oh, Mammy, don't scold. The pain is like a—a hammer. *Pom! Pom! Pom!*" Estelle grimaced. "A cloth soaked in cologne would help. . . ."

"What'd help is a good night's sleep, missy. Up till all hours, dancin' with them mens, drinkin' champagne like a Choctaw at a tradin' post, then sashayin' home at dawn!" Remy's brown eyes flashed disapproval. "Ain't no wonder you got the headaches, chile. You ain't no sweet young thing no more."

"Can I help it if I've been delicate since Louis passed on?" *Maman* demanded, tossing ringlets the same corn silk color as Honey's.

Despite the difference in their ages, everyone agreed that she and her mother could have been sisters, except that, while *Maman*'s eyes were aquamarine, hers were chocolate brown like Papa's. Fortunately for Armand's, however, their likeness did not extend to their personalities. Honey was more practical than her mother had ever been. But then, she'd had to be with no one but Bienville and Remy to advise her in the running of the restaurant. Certainly *Maman* was no help! Among Creole ladies of her mother's class, it was considered vulgar to discuss business or—horrors!—money.

Estelle flounced to the door, taking her coffee cup with

her. "How am I to find a new husband, unless I accept invitations to balls and the opera, tell me that!"

"You don't have t' eat all the pickles in the barrel t' know they good, missy," Remy pointed out. " 'Sides, this chile needs your help. The restaurant's in big trouble, Miz Estelle, unless Miz Honey can come up with a heap o' money!"

"That *word* again." Estelle pursed her lips in displeasure. "I declare, it's all you two think about! I should have known I'd find no sympathy here. You'd like to keep me a widow forever! I will leave you to your vulgar discussion, Melisse, my pet, but remember what I told you. There's only one acceptable way for a woman to attain wealth. She must marry it!"

"I'll remember, *Maman.* But at Mass this morning say a tiny prayer for Armand's, will you? Just for me?"

"Mass?" Remy snorted. "Your mama ain't goin' out, chile. She comin' in! You hear them bells? That's the Angelus chimin'—and she ain't bin to bed yet. Leastwise, not her own!" She rolled her eyes. " 'Sides, if Miz Estelle went t' Mass wearin' that gown, lightnin' 'ud strike her dead, sure as my name's Remy Valoir!"

"Oh!" Two spots of scarlet bloomed in *Maman*'s cheeks. Stamping her foot, she flounced from the kitchen.

Honey couldn't help smiling. Only Remy would dare comment on *Maman*'s gowns. Hearing the two of them argue, a stranger would never guess that there was genuine respect and fondness between mistress and slave.

Years ago, Papa had bought Remy and Tobias Valoir, Remy's husband, from Monsieur Paul Valoir, the old master of Belle Refuge plantation out on Bayou St. John. Remy's sisters, Thalia and Maddy, were still slaves there.

Honey swallowed. If her creditors took the restaurant, the Valoirs and their six children would be sold off as slaves to cover her debts. She couldn't imagine losing the youngest, little Hepzibah, or pigtailed, sassy Minna, or pretty Harriet who was so like Remy. Then there was soft-spoken Raoul who was Armand's head waiter, and beefy

Hannibal with his heart of gold and shy, quiet Samuel, Remy and Tobias's two oldest boys, who did the heavy work around the restaurant.

Just the thought made her heart feel like breaking. She'd seen slaves being sold like animals on the auction block, a sight that had turned her stomach. She would never let such a dreadful thing happen to the Valoirs. She'd free them all, somehow, just as she'd promised. . . .

"Miz Estelle should be findin' you a husband, 'stead of givin' the gossips somethin' to jaw about," Remy said, gaining Honey's attention as she plaited long strips of dough.

Then Remy brushed the loaves with melted butter and set them by the hearth to rise. They would be baked in the four brick ovens in the whitewashed wall opposite the work table.

"What do I need a husband for? To pay my debts?" Honey snorted as she strained sizzling fat through a slotted ladle. "Thank you, but no! I'll find another way."

"I want you t' have a family, chile. A man in your bed and a babe at your breast. Not be breakin' your back in this kitchen night and day. This here ain't no proper life for a fine Creole lady."

"But I love running the restaurant, and I love cooking! And this 'fine Creole lady' doesn't want anyone in her bed, *merci!*" It was true. She was not ready to become any man's wife.

Having the distinguished title of Madame Armand rather than the ordinary mademoiselle of an unmarried woman had given Honey an independence she cherished. While most Creole women were pampered and protected, like *Maman,* as a respected pastry chef and restauranteur, Honey was free to live her life almost as she pleased. And what she pleased did not include taking a husband or birthing babies! For the second time that morning she pinched the bridge of her nose.

"You look peaked, chile. You got the headaches like your mama?"

"*Oui.* Only I call my headaches 'debts'!"

Remy wiped her hands on her apron. "It that bad, baby?"

"Worse!" She swallowed. "Monsieur Bienville says I have only thirty days to come up with the money."

"Only thirty? Lordy!" Remy frowned. "You reckon Monsieur Bienville's clerk made a mistake someplace?"

"No." She sighed. "But I'll stop by his office on the way home from the market on Monday and ask to look at the books anyway." Perhaps she'd find a mistake in her favor.

"You cud ask Massa Nick to back you, like I said before."

Honey pursed her lips. "I could but I won't."

"Oh, I know it sticks in your craw, but you're gonna have t', sugar. Pride cain't pay off that big ole debt—but Massa Nick surely can!"

Since last June, Nicholas Sauvage had become a frequent patron of Armand's. He'd also become Honey's frequent escort. They'd attended church together, several parties, the opera, Mayor Poudreux's Christmas ball, and most recently a New Year's Eve ball.

Maman had protested that, despite his fortune, Nicholas was of questionable background and certainly no blue blood, and had no interest in meeting him. But Honey had accepted his invitations anyway. She'd claimed her refusal could mean losing a valuable patron. But in all honesty she was drawn to the dashingly handsome, dark-haired, wealthy planter like a moth to a dazzling, dangerous flame!

Though always the perfect gentleman in both manners and attire, Nicholas's dangerous edge secretly excited her. Ever since the New Year's Eve ball at the Cabildo, when they'd stood side by side in the starlit place d'Armes, their bodies touching as fireworks exploded, church bells pealed, and champagne corks popped to usher in the New Year, she'd dreamed about the dark-eyed Nicholas every night—and sometimes during the day, as she created desserts for the new year's menu.

Such marvels had sprung from her fantasies! Whimsical meringue swans. Caramel-frosted banana gateaux, exquisite, airy souffles of luscious imported chocolate—Nicholas's favorite flavoring.

Her recent creations had impressed even her sternest critics. *The Picayune*'s epicurean had raved, "In this reporter's opinion Mme Armand's love for the culinary arts is the 'secret ingredient' that goes into every luscious spoonful the lady creates."

He was right. Everything she cooked was flavored with happiness and love. Lately, however, her dishes had been liberally seasoned with tears.

"If I ask Monsieur Sauvage for his backing, do you think he'll give it?" She heard the doubt in her voice.

Remy shrugged. "Way I see it, the worst he can say is no, chile. If he do, you ain't no worse off than you is now."

Honey nodded. What choice did she have, really? If she let her creditors take the restaurant, she, her mother, and the Valoirs would be out in the gutter!

Still, just thinking about asking Nicholas Sauvage for his financial backing sent tingles down her spine. What might such a rogue demand in return?

What, indeed?

Chapter 2

Nicholas concealed a scowl as he watched Honey greeting her well-heeled patrons.

"I'll be! If I hadn't seen her with my own eyes, I'd never believe she'd been out all night, would you?" his factor and friend, Jean-Pierre Delacroix, observed. "No dark circles. No bloodshot eyes! Your little Widow Armand looks as fresh as a daisy, don't you think, *mon ami?*"

Nick thought it—and more. Honey not only looked daisy-fresh, but so damned lovely she was drawing the eye of every man in the room!

The first time they'd met had been on an evening like this, he recalled. A Saturday last June, when every table in the restaurant had been filled.

He and Jean-Pierre had been celebrating the sale of a bumper cane harvest with a top-notch dinner, much as they were doing tonight. They'd chosen Armand's in the French Quarter because Jean-Pierre had heard its beautiful female chef specialized in the desserts and pastries Nick loved.

He'd not been disappointed. The excellent meal and refined atmosphere had outdone Jean-Pierre's promises. And then, over an after-dinner brandy, had come the *pièce de résistance.* He'd locked gazes with a fair-haired, brown-eyed beauty, who'd stolen his breath away.

A little over five feet five inches tall, she had skin like creamy magnolias, a mane of lustrous corn silk hair, and a voluptuous figure that could fuel any man's fantasies—his own included.

Pointing her out to Jean-Pierre, he'd demanded to know her name. His friend had squinted at the three women conversing by the potted palms. One had been a tall Negress who carried herself like a queen. The other two women had the same golden hair.

Jean-Pierre had said she was none other than Madame Armand, the pastry chef whose confections they'd enjoyed. He'd added that the lovely widow had lost her husband in the yellow fever epidemic of thirty-five and that fortunately for her, the lady had several wealthy admirers to console her in her loneliness. Nick had decided then and there to make Honey Armand his mistress.

He'd dined at Armand's every Saturday since, enjoying the restaurant's best table and the exotic desserts Honey sent him. They were, he knew, her way of welcoming him to her restaurant. How much longer, he wondered, before she welcomed him into her bed? Although he'd escorted Honey to the opera, the theater, to Masses, balls, and several other social occasions, they'd not been intimate—yet.

Most recently, they'd sipped rum punch and waltzed the night away at the New Year's Eve ball, under the watchful eyes of dozens of Creole misses and their ambitious mamas.

Over Honey's head, he'd seen the society matrons whispering behind their fans, and guessed he was the subject of their gossip. Old hypocrites! They despised his background. But he knew that on behalf of their daughters they coveted the fortune he'd amassed by gambling, then investing his winnings in cotton, tobacco, and sugar.

Well, he'd not change to suit them. He was who he was—the son of Natchez gambler Jacques Sauvage, who'd drunk himself into an early grave, and of Lucia, a Spanish saloon gal, who'd run off with another man, leaving her infant son to be raised in a Natchez bordello.

He offered no excuses, no apologies for having been a gambler or for not being a blue blood. He'd turned his life around and was proud of it.

For the past two years, he had worked long and hard to put his past behind him and to learn everything he could about growing sugar cane. The plantation, Belle Refuge, belonged to him now, and the pedigree of the blooded Thoroughbreds in his stables put his own to shame. He possessed the finest carriages, the costliest European furnishings, well-cut garments, English-made boots, diamond stickpins, and pearl collar studs. He now had everything his checkered beginnings had denied him, except a family and that he could do well enough without, by God!

What he did need, however, was a beautiful mistress. He'd decided to take one once the plantation had produced a handsome profit, and to set her up in an elegant *pied-à-terre* in the French Quarter until he wearied of her charms.

To that end, he'd purchased the townhouse on rue Orleans, installed a housekeeper, and started his search for the perfect woman to grace its elegantly furnished rooms. A worldly, sensual beauty who would satisfy his needs, as well as her own, yet have no expectations of love or marriage.

The Quadroon balls at the Orleans Theater had proven an amusing diversion on Friday evenings. But, alas, the beautiful women Jean-Pierre had introduced to him were only *café au lait* counterparts of their sheltered Creole rivals. They had been peerlessly gowned and coiffured, accomplished at flirtatious conversation, but precious little else.

No woman in New Orleans had sparked his fancy—or his lust—until the evening he'd spotted the lovely blonde across the crowded room. A single plunge into Honey's dark-lashed, chocolate-brown eyes had been enough, and the unique blend of experienced, worldly widow and demure, innocent miss was an alluring, heady combination.

He scowled. But he was no closer to bedding Honey now than he'd been that first night seven months ago. Oh, he was almost certain that he could have sweet-talked her into surrendering long ago. But he had to admit that though he was accustomed to women who yielded to him at the drop of a hat, the lazy escalation of his and Honey's relationship had proven an exciting, stimulating novelty. Their brief, charged encounters were like sips of a fine aperitif before what promised to be a superb meal. He had only to look at Honey, and he grew hard. And, despite her efforts to mask it, he'd seen his own hunger mirrored in her beautiful eyes. Beneath her sweetness burned pure fire!

"*Mon Dieu!* You're scowling tonight, Sauvage! Not brooding about this morning, are you?" Jean-Pierre asked, jerking Nick's thoughts smartly back to the present. His friend's myopic eyes were merry as he awaited Nick's response.

"This morning?" Nick repeated, although he knew what Jean-Pierre meant.

On the way back to his townhouse for breakfast after a night of carousing, Nick's carriage had crossed the place d'Armes as the Angelus chimed. As they passed the Cabildo and Armand's, he and Jean-Pierre had seen Don Carlos de Rozier y Castellanos handing a woman down from a carriage. Though Nick had not seen her face, there had been no mistaking those gleaming gold ringlets. The woman with the stout Spanish gentleman had been Honey.

"Should I be? Brooding about it, I mean?" he inquired casually.

Jean-Pierre's mouth quirked in a grin beneath his clipped, blond mustache. "I'd say so, yes. You seemed rather . . . disturbed when you saw who Castellanos was with. And who could blame you? It could mean only one thing, at that ungodly hour . . ." He gave an eloquent shrug.

Nick restrained the urge to punch his friend's clean-shaven jaw.

"You're, er, not thinking of challenging him for your widow's charms, are you?" Jean-Pierre asked.

"Duel over a woman? Hardly! Besides, Madame Armand is not 'my' widow." He drew on the cheroot clamped between his teeth, exhaling a thin ribbon of smoke that rose to join the blue-gray haze around the brass chandeliers.

"So you claim, *mon ami*. However . . ." Jean-Pierre fished in his inner pocket. "I have ten dollars here that say otherwise!" He fanned the banknotes and winked. "I predict a mistress for Belle Refuge by year's end, 'else I'm a Dutchman! Have we a wager, then?" His sandy eyebrows rose.

Nick snorted and stubbed out his cheroot. "The devil we do! If I hadn't sworn off gambling, you'd lose your shirt. Me, take a wife? Perhaps—when hell freezes over!"

Despite Nick's cool indifference, Jean-Pierre's innuendo had touched a nerve. Was he jealous of Honey's other admirer? If it wasn't quite jealousy, it was pretty damn close! Seeing her with another man *had* disturbed him. He hadn't realized how deeply until he'd seen her across the dining room tonight.

"Ahem. Nick?" Jean-Pierre's discreet cough drew his attention.

A shapely shadow had fallen across the tablecloth. He

glanced up to find Honey standing there, as if summoned by his thoughts.

The chandelier's myriad candles gleamed in her corn silk hair and lent a golden sheen to her chocolate brown eyes as she inclined her head to him.

He stood. "Madame Armand, *je suis enchanté!*" Taking her slender hand, he bowed over it. As his lips brushed her knuckles, the fragrance of vanilla, strawberries, and warm, sensual woman teased his nostrils. His stomach muscles clenched.

"Good evening, Monsieur Sauvage. I'm delighted to see you." Her voice was low, husky, and as sweet as molasses.

"And I you, *chere* madame. May I compliment you on the Meringue Melisse? Once again, it was mouth-watering—yet another of your triumphs."

"I am happy to hear it, monsieur. I was afraid it was only my chocolate gateaux that you craved." Her brown eyes were teasing as she smiled at him.

"Rest assured, madame, it is not only your desserts that entice me." He stared at the delectable pout of her lower lip, wondering idly if she would taste of vanilla or honey when he finally kissed her or deliciously tart like wild strawberries. "Come, madame. Join me, just this once. Over a glass of wine, I shall tell you what other . . . confections . . . whet my appetite." His tone was a lazy purr.

As he'd known it would, the color in her cheeks deepened. "I regret I must decline yet again, monsieur. You know that for me to sit at your table in the gentlemen's dining room would be most improper."

"I know, but you're an unconventional woman, madame. A successful restauranteur! Surely you're in a position to scoff at propriety—if only for tonight."

"If only I could afford to! But, *alors*, my success is due, in part, to the respect I have earned from my patrons. So forgive me, but yet again I must refuse.

"Raoul! More coffee for Monsieur Delacroix. Hannibal, a light for Monsieur Sauvage's cigar, at once!" She inclined her lovely head, cool, gracious—and as sexy as hell.

"Please, be seated, monsieur. I did not wish to disturb you."

"You always disturb me, madame," he countered, adding, "as well you know, I fancy." His gaze met hers, lingered.

She lowered her lashes and looked away. The seductive gesture made his groin tighten. Her graceful hand smoothed the heavy chignon at her nape, while the rise and fall of her bosom quickened beneath a row of buttons he itched to free with his teeth. He hardened his jaw, imagining the swell of her creamy bosom hidden beneath the prim silk, the ripe coral nipples . . .

"If you will excuse me, I have other guests." She sounded breathless. "Enjoy the remainder of your evening, monsieur."

He wanted to do more than excuse her. He wanted to take the combs from her hair, to kiss her bare shoulders, to remove her frothy undergarments, layer by layer, until she wore only a blush. To press her down onto cool silk sheets and explore the mysteries of her lovely body again and again. . . .

Time to play his hand, was it not?

Clearing his throat, he called after her. "Madame! A word, if you please."

"Monsieur?" She turned back wearing a curiously unguarded, hopeful expression. Framed by walls of crimson damask, blue cigar smoke wreathing about her, she looked like a golden-haired angel who'd stumbled into purgatory.

"Forgive me if I'm wrong, but I flatter myself that you've enjoyed our little outings, have you not?"

Her expression of cautious hope deepened into one of undisguised pleasure. "Very much so, monsieur. Especially the opera. I have become quite the aficionado."

He gritted his teeth. Is that where that old goat, Don Carlos, had taken her last night? To the Orleans Theater—then to his bed? Did that explain Honey's fondness for the opera?

"Splendid!" he murmured, masking a scowl. "Then you will allow me to escort you again, yes?"

"I would be honored." She favored him with a shy, sweet smile. "What did you have in mind, monsieur?"

He bit back a snort. If he told her, she'd slap his face! "Balloons, madame. What I had in mind are balloons!"

Chapter 3

"Balloonin' ain't natural! If the Lord meant us t' fly, He'd 'a given us wings!" Remy exclaimed.

Behind her mother's back, Harriet tucked her hands under her arms and flapped them. "Want me t' put some chicken in the basket, Miz Honey?"

"Please." Laughing at Remy's daughter's antics, Honey tucked a bottle of wine and a corkscrew into the picnic basket herself. "Did Hannibal pack that barrel with ice yet?"

"Yez, Miz Honey. It's keepin' cool in the larder here," Harriet confirmed. "You jest have t' pop in that banana-rum cream pie, an' you set."

"Perfect! You're sure Philippe can manage, Remy?"

"Chile, he bin tryin' t' get this kitchen to hisself for a year now! It's you I'm frettin' on."

"Why, I thought you were pleased that I'm still seeing Monsieur Sauvage. He's everything you or *Maman* could want in a beau. Handsome, rich—and the perfect gentleman."

"Humph. I ain't never thought 'bout him bein' your beau or else I'd 'a never told you to sweet-talk him into backin' you. Alls I know is that my sister Thalia seen Massa Nick rifflin' a deck o' cards like he was born with 'em in his hand!''

''That doesn't mean anything.'' Honey tied the ribbons of a flirty leghorn straw, decorated with red silk poppies, beneath her chin. ''Lots of gentlemen play cards.''

''Then Thalia overheard Mister Delacroix's servant tell my niece, Suki, that Massa Nick was a riverboat gamblin' man, 'fore he bought Belle Refuge from the ole massa's heir.'' Remy frowned. ''If she right, that man ain't fit company for no convent-school miss like you.''

''Oh, pish! Tell Thalia to tend her kitchen and stop spreading gossip,'' she scolded. ''Besides, I've been handling Monsieur Sauvage for months now, haven't I?''

''Maybe, chile. But you got a look to you lately that's got me worried.''

Honey's cheeks flamed. Remy was always detecting ''looks'' about people. Honey should have known she couldn't hide her feelings for Nicholas from her. Remy knew her too well for that.

''That's why I'm sendin' Harriet along t' chaperone you. Minna can redden the front steps, instead.''

''Do I got t' go up in that balloon, too, Mama?'' Harriet asked, her expression mirroring Remy's doubtful one.

''Great day in the mornin', I hope not, sugar! Both you childrens flyin' don't bear thinkin' about!''

At ten, Nicholas called for Honey in a smart yellow-wheeled buggy pulled by a showy bay. They traveled the pretty trace through St. John's Parish for just over an hour, before reaching the first of Nicholas's fields on Bayou St. John.

In the shade of a live oak grazed a dray horse, harnessed to a wagon, and in the center of the meadow, a gaily striped balloon bobbed above a wicker gondola. The meadow sloped down to a wooden jetty where a pirogue was moored. Beyond beckoned the bayou, cool green and mysterious.

Nicholas introduced the balloon pilots as James and

Charles Goode of London, England. Their plaid jackets, knickers, goggles, and leather helmets would have sent her fashion-conscious *Maman* into gales of laughter, Honey thought, trying not to laugh herself.

Charles Goode explained that he and his brother traveled across America giving demonstrations of ballooning. "It's a frightfully safe method of travel, madam," he assured her.

She prayed he was telling the truth.

Moments later, Nicholas lifted her over the edge of the wicker gondola, then sprang in after her. Since no amount of bullying could induce Harriet to join them, she was left behind. Returning her wave, Honey wondered if Harriet didn't have the right idea, after all.

"Relax. Think what an adventure you'll have to share with your children someday," Nicholas murmured.

But she was too distracted by Charles Goode's bellowed, "Brace yourselves for the ascent, madam, sir!" to appreciate his reassurances.

Moments later, the balloon shuddered, shifted. Honey closed her eyes, her fingers digging into Nicholas's wrists as it rose into the air. In just seconds they were drifting among the clouds.

"Look below, *chere* madame! It's beautiful!"

Her heart in her mouth, she opened her eyes and risked a peek over the gondola's wicker rim. He was right. The view was breathtaking!

Far below, the curve in the broad Mississippi that had given New Orleans the name Crescent City, flashed like a mirror in the sunlight. A paddle-wheeler plowed through the muddy waters, churning bright cascades of wash as it skirted the sandbars. Beyond the city and the levees gleamed the mysterious bayou's green waters. Veils of misty Spanish moss draped the live oaks along its banks, while among the cypress "knees," palmettos, and reeds, white egrets engaged in an elegant courtship dance. Diamond drops of water sprayed all around them as they beat their snowy wings.

Directly below was Belle Refuge, where as a child

Honey had gone to visit Thalia and Maddy and had enjoyed the delicious gingerbread men Thalia made just for her. Although Nicholas was master there now, everything looked much as she remembered it. From immaculate English gardens abloom with roses, the mansion rose like a little palace of royal icing, perfect from its iron-laced balconies to its shady verandahs and stately Corinthian columns.

To the rear, she could make out the kitchens, the stables, the row of slave cabins, and beyond those, the sugar mill. Its chimney thrust skyward like a brick finger. Both house and field hands looked like toys from this elevation.

''Don't be afraid.'' Nicholas chafed her chilly hand between his own. When she made no attempt to withdraw it, he hooked his arm around her waist and pulled her against him.

They were close now—closer than when they'd waltzed at the balls. Closer than when they'd stood side by side to watch the fireworks display on New Year's. ''Remove your arm, monsieur!''

''This little old arm, right here? Why, it's there for moral support. Nothing improper intended, I assure you,'' Nicholas insisted in a most improper, very husky voice.

Though far from reassured, she laughed and leaned against him, enjoying the feel of his powerful body pressed to hers. He smelled of Cuban cigars, bay rum, and gentleman's soap, scents that made her pulse race!

Was it the way he was smiling down at her with heat in his dark eyes that made her shiver so? Or the way his arm banded her waist, his thigh rode against her hip, its pressure felt through layers of ruffled linen? Or was it simply her fear of flying that made her foolish heart thunder so? *It's him!* her conscience accused. *Admit it. You're in love with him!*

''I must be!'' she murmured and heaved a sigh. ''Why else would I feel like this?''

''Feel like what?'' His eyebrows rose, and he hastily stepped back. ''You're not going to be sick, are you?''

"No! It's the, er, balloon, I expect. I never dreamed it would rise so—so quickly!" She shivered.

Her heart turned cartwheels as he removed his frock coat, draped it about her shoulders, then drew her back against his waistcoat of figured satin. "Warmer now, *cherie?*"

Cherie. Was that how he thought of her, as his darling? "Much, thank you. However, monsieur, I do not think it is at all proper for you to—"

"Hush, *cherie.* It's another world up here, in the clouds, *non?* One with very different rules from those down there. Forget your little games. Forget propriety. Just close your eyes and enjoy!"

He must mean the balloon ride, surely? Yet his tone implied something else entirely. Something she didn't quite understand but that stirred an excited quiver inside her, nonetheless.

When he drew off her poppy-trimmed straw hat to take her in his arms and kiss her, she was not entirely surprised. And when he held her firmly against his lean, hard body and his kiss deepened, she murmured in pleasure several times before she remembered to protest. By then, it was far too late to pretend she was in any way outraged—far too late to do anything but enjoy as he'd urged her.

He held her so close, the butterfly flutter in her stomach became the fierce, sweet ache of desire. At school, the nuns had warned that when sin reared its wicked head, a girl should think about embroidery, pressing flowers, or other less inflammatory subjects. Her eyes tightly closed, she tried to think. She'd meant to ask Nicholas something. What had it been?

About him backing her restaurant, that was it! How could she have forgotten when the future of Armand's, of everyone she loved, was at stake?

She pulled away. "Monsieur, please. We must stop. There is something I must discuss with you. A matter of great importance."

"Nothing's as important as this, little one," he drawled,

trailing a tanned finger down her cheek. "Ask me later. *Much* later."

She could not escape him, not up here, even if she'd wanted to flee.

"Hmm, you taste so sweet, *cherie,*" he murmured, grazing his lips over her earlobe and down to the hollow of her throat, where her pulse throbbed. His hot breath, his lips, made ticklish goose bumps shimmy down her arms, her spine. "A confection as luscious as any on your menu . . ."

She could find neither the words nor the will to respond. Her lips were swollen from his kisses. Her skin tingled. She felt flushed, disoriented, in the grip of some wild, sweet fever she could not—would not—throw off.

"Monsieur," she whispered in a last, desperate bid to restore propriety. "I beg you to remember we are not alone!"

"Hmm? Ah, yes. The Englishman. I'd forgotten." Nicholas glanced over his shoulder.

She saw that Charles Goode pointedly turned his back. He was staring at the sky as if his very life depended on it.

Nicholas's grin deepened. "Say it, then! Insist that I stop—and I shall." Cupping her breast, he boldly teased its stiffened peak through her striped taffeta gown.

She gasped as an exquisite sensation sizzled from her breast to her loins. Distracted by its pleasurable eddy, she waited a moment too long before slapping his hand away. "Stop it! Stop it at once! What sort of woman do you take me for, monsieur?"

He gripped her chin between his fingers. "A lovely little tease, that's what! Admit it, darling. You don't want me to stop any more than I do."

"You're mistaken, monsieur," she insisted, but it was a lie. She didn't want him to stop. She wanted more. More than kisses, more than caresses—and he knew it. "Stop, or I'll scream."

"Scream? *Mon Dieu!* You will drive me to distraction, madame!" His voice was hoarse. His eyes were a hot, smoky black. When he freed her, he was breathing heavily, and his fists were knotted with the effort to master his emotions.

"It is high time we descended, I believe, Monsieur Sauvage." She straightened her skirts and jammed her straw hat firmly on her head. Her palms were damp inside her gloves.

He squared his jaw. She could not read his expression, but could guess the thwarted emotions seething beneath it, for they were her own!

"Very well, madame. If that's what you want. Pilot Goode? Take her down, if you please!"

"Right-o, sir!"

"What in the world's eatin' you, chile! You bin bangin' 'round down here, half the night! I thought them pesky raccoons had got into the—oh, my Lord!" Remy gasped as Honey stepped aside, revealing the fruits of her night's labors.

The long table behind her was covered with puddings, cakes, meringues, mousses, tarts, pies, and compotes. Some were topped with powdered sugar or whipped cream, others with toasted coconut, caramel, brandied peaches, or cherries. Still others gleamed with ruby-red or golden sauces, or boasted curls of chocolate or ground nutmeats.

"The days are flying by, yet I couldn't do it, Remy," she confessed miserably. "There we were, up in the clouds, with no one to interrupt us, and I couldn't ask Nicholas a simple little question." She licked the last of the chocolate from the back of her wooden spoon, and yawned. "I do believe I can sleep now, though."

"I reckon you will, chile, after all this!"

She shrugged. "I couldn't help it. You know how I am. I was so upset last night. Cooking makes me feel better."

"That gamblin' man got your blood fired up just like I thought, don't he, missy? Don't you go tellin' me no, chile! I seen the look on your face 'fore you left here yesterday mornin'!"

She pouted. "Perhaps, just a little."

"A little! You in love with that no-good gamblin' man, ain't you?" Remy whispered triumphantly. "That's why you down here cookin' up a storm! It's get cookin'—or burn!"

"Don't be ridiculous!" she scoffed, furious that Remy had read her so easily. "I was upset, so I decided to try some new recipes. You'll be glad I did come morning," she added defensively. "We won't have to make desserts for a day or two."

"A day or two?" Remy rolled her eyes. "Sugar, we won't have t' fix nothin' for a *week!*"

At a small wrought-iron table in the courtyard, behind the restaurant, *Maman* sipped chicory coffee and nibbled beignets with Don Carlos, who was now her constant escort. Their voices carried only faintly to Honey and Remy in the restaurant kitchens, where preparations were underway for Saturday's dinner.

"So? What do you think? Will he like it?" Honey watched anxiously as Remy sampled a mouthful of glazed double-chocolate torte, garnished with a swirl of whipped cream. The crystal plate that held the torte was dressed with a ruby-red sauce.

Honey had experimented for hours, until the ingredients' proportions for both the sauce and torte were perfect. The result was a luscious raspberry-Amaretto sauce that complemented the crumbly chocolate torte to perfection.

"Hmm! It tastes rich an' dark, somehow. Then there's that li'l ole cloud o' fresh cream on top." Remy chuckled. "Reminds me of my Tobias, come to think on it! Dark and sweet as brown sugar—then white an' fluffy on top!" She tapped her head and chuckled. Tobias's hair was woolly and white.

"And the sauce?"

Remy smacked her lips. "Hmm, fresh raspberries an' smooth Amaretto. It sure tastes like a winner to me, chile. Fact is, it's sweet as sin!"

"Sweet Sin. That's perfect! Do you think Nich—Monsieur Sauvage will like it?"

"If he don't, there's somethin' wrong with him. 'Sides, he's liked everythin' else you set in front of him." She rolled her eyes.

Honey flushed. Remy knew there'd been more to their ballooning than flying high over the bayou. Truth was, she'd been walking on air long after Charles Goode had returned them to solid ground. She was in love with Nicholas Sauvage! The knowledge sang inside her. Being in love had made everything she cooked taste superb! Ripe pears poached in brandy. Apples stuffed with honey, raisins, and cinnamon, then wrapped in a flaky crust. Bananas fried in golden-brown fritter batter, served with molasses and cream . . .

"He has, yes," she told Remy. "But I want this to be extra special. My best ever! You see, if all goes well, Sweet Sin will be part of a celebration."

"Then this ain't the Mardi Gras dessert you was fixin' t' make?"

She shook her head. "*Non.* I created it for Monsieur Sauvage. Tonight, I'm going to ask him to help me. And this time I won't get cold feet."

"You can do it, baby, I know you can." Remy came around the table to hug her.

"I'm not going to ask him to back me." Her eyes met Remy's.

"You ain't?"

"*Non.* I'm going to offer him a full partnership." She braced herself for the argument that was sure to come.

She wasn't disappointed when Remy's eyebrows lifted. "A partnership, chile?" She sniffed. "I don't reckon that's such a good idea."

"I disagree. With Monsieur Sauvage as my partner, I could pay off my creditors by the end of this month and have someone to advise me about the business."

"A partnership all you're offerin' him, missy?" Remy asked sternly, her snapping brown eyes narrowed. "Cuz if that black-eyed rascal's laid a finger on you, I'll find a conjure woman t' hex him, just see if I don't! I won't have you losin' your heart to that no-count gamblin' man!"

"Too late," Honey whispered with a smile.

Remy snorted. "That's just fine. But he touches a hair on your pretty head, it ain't his heart he'll have to worry about. It's somethin' a mite farther south!"

"Remy! What sort of woman do you take me for?"

"A desperate one, chile," Remy returned gently. "I know how you bin frettin' about losin' this place. Don't do somethin' you'll be sorry for later."

"I know what I'm doing."

"I sure hope so, cuz once you got yourself a partner, it's like bein' married. You cain't be doin' things your own way anymore. You'll have to answer to Massa Nick, like it or not. Unless I miss my guess, that man ain't used to takin' no for an answer—an' neither is you."

Honey laughed. "Oh, Remy, all he cares about is growing cane. Being my partner wouldn't change that."

"No? You really think that man gonna put up the money an' keep his nose out?"

"That's exactly what I think." Or rather, what she hoped.

Remy laughed. "From what Thalia tells me, Massa Nick don't strike me as a fool. Maybe you should ask someone else t' back you. Don Carlos, maybe. He's mighty sweet on your mama. She expectin' a proposal any day now."

Her chin came up. "I can't. I'm almost out of time—between the devil and the deep blue sea!"

"Well, if the way to that handsome devil's fortune is through his belly, your Sweet Sin will win him over, sugar!" Remy framed Honey's face between her brown hands. "God bless you, chile, you've worked so hard these past five years. Your papa would be proud of you. I know I is."

Chapter 4

"Yes, Raoul, what is it?" Nick looked up to see the tall, black head waiter at his elbow. He carried a silver tray on which lay a small cream-colored envelope.

"A note for you, Monsieur Sauvage. I'm to wait for your reply, suh."

"*Merci.*" Nick waved the envelope beneath his nose. Vanilla and strawberries. He knew at once who had sent it and smiled. He'd been hoping to see Honey tonight. His wish was about to be granted. Who knew what others might be granted after that?

"A *billet-doux, mon ami?*" Jean-Pierre asked, grinning.

Nick tore open the envelope and scanned the script. It was as elegant and feminine as the lady herself. "On the contrary. It appears to be a matter of business."

"The devil you say! I doubt mere business could put that gleam in your eye." He sighed. "I suppose you expect me to make myself scarce?"

"Your head for business is matched only by your discretion, *mon ami!*"

"All right. I'll leave. But you owe me dessert, Sauvage. I intend to collect next time."

"It's a deal! Raoul, have Monsieur Delacroix's carriage brought around, then inform Madame Armand that I would be honored if she would join me."

"Certainly, monsieur."

Honey appeared as soon as Jean-Pierre had beaten a hasty exit. Instead of the sober colors she usually wore in the restaurant, tonight her gleaming satin gown was the color of butterscotch. Its huge puffed sleeves and low neckline left her ivory shoulders bare. Narrow topaz ribbons threaded her corn silk ringlets, matching the color of her teardrop earrings and the larger teardrop nestled between her breasts on a delicate gold chain. How he envied that teardrop!

Ever since their balloon outing, he'd been unable to forget the kisses they'd shared. He'd savored his first taste of her lips over and over again, the elusive fragrance of her skin, warmed by desire, and the way her exciting curves had pressed against him. Each night she had danced seductively through his dreams, always just out of reach, trying his patience, bewitching his senses, fueling his lust. By being elusive, playing hard to get, she'd made him want her more than any other woman—as well she knew, the tantalizing minx!

Standing, he bowed over her hand. His lips brushed her knuckles, lingering a little longer, pressing a little more firmly than etiquette deemed proper. "Madame. I'm delighted you could bend the rules to join me tonight."

"As am I, monsieur. I'd not dared to hope for such a prompt response to my request."

Despite the innocuous exchange, a current crackled between them like the electrical charge in the air before a storm. "Please, be seated."

He stood behind her chair until she'd arranged her billowing skirts, then signaled to Claude, the sommelier. "A glass of wine, my dear? You seem a trifle . . . nervous tonight."

"Just a sip for me." When they were alone again, she continued, "I apologize for joining you at your table."

"Think nothing of it. This close to Mardi Gras, society's conventions are a little more relaxed, *non?* Besides, I gathered the business you wished to discuss is somewhat urgent, is it not?"

"Very, monsieur." Favoring him with a nervous smile, she took a sip from her glass. Almost immediately, her face grew flushed. Her chocolate-brown eyes brightened.

"Then I have a suggestion." He smiled at her across the table. "Why don't we get business over with? Make your proposal, *chere* madame, and have done with it. Agreed?"

"Agreed." Drawing a deep breath, she began explaining that she'd been left the restaurant by her father, and, thanks to her desserts of exotic imported ingredients, it had flourished under her management. She finished, "Now, there is hardly an evening when every table is not filled! In short, Armand's has become everything my father dreamed!"

"You are to be congratulated, madame. For a lone woman to have accomplished so much is no small triumph." His lavish praise was quite genuine. Her success in what was traditionally a male domain was one of the qualities that attracted him to her. After all, intelligent, strong, ambitious women were infinitely more exciting, more inventive in a man's bed than clinging, dependent ones—and far more challenging. "How long has it been since you lost your father?"

"Five years." Her eyes grew suddenly moist. "I was just sixteen. I came home from convent school in Baton Rouge that summer to find bodies stacked like cordage on the banquettes. There were tar fires burning on every street corner, houses boarded up, entire families gone, wiped out by that wretched disease." She shuddered. "It was horrible. The yellow fever claimed so many lives that year! Husbands. Fathers. Innocent children."

He nodded sympathetically. The night he'd met Honey Jean-Pierre had mentioned that Monsieur Armand had succumbed in that epidemic. Honey must have lost both husband and father in quick succession, he thought. "My deepest condolences, madame. Your courage and fortitude are to be commended. And what of your mama? Did she also succumb?"

"*Maman?* Why, no! *Maman* was stricken, but with Remy's help, she recovered."

"Remy?"

She nodded. "Remy Valoir, my mammy. She and her sisters, Thalia and Maddy, were born on your plantation, you know. Thalia is your cook and Maddy your laundress.''

''Sisters? Your mammy, my cook—and my laundress? A small world, is it not?'' he teased, inclining his head. ''But go on. You said your mother survived the yellow jack?''

''Luckily, yes.''

''Yet she takes no part in the running of your business?''

She shrugged almost apologetically, he thought. ''*Maman* is from a very old, very traditional Creole family. You know the sort?''

Did he! They looked down their long, aristocratic noses at the likes of him. ''Indeed I do, madame!''

''*Maman* has no interest in the restaurant. Besides, since Papa's death, her health has been delicate. She suffers from sick headaches, too.''

He grunted. He could well imagine the old woman, dressed in black veils like a spider, scurrying to and from the confessional and the physician. An old woman preoccupied with her poor health, her past, and the husband she had lost, giving little thought to her vibrant, widowed daughter.

''Tell me more about your restaurant,'' he urged.

As she described outstripping her competitors because of her unique desserts, her earlier nervousness vanished revealing an ambitious, knowledgeable young woman. Her voice grew impassioned, her lovely face animated as she spoke of her cooking and the restaurant she loved.

''But now,'' she said, her lower lip pouting, ''I find myself in an impossible position. Several natural disasters have driven the cost of my ingredients sky-high. Since I was reluctant to pass this cost on to my patrons—my prices are already quite steep, you understand—I tried to economize in other ways.''

''With disastrous results, I take it?''

''Alas, yes. I have fallen three months behind on my payments to my grocers, and find myself without means to settle my debts. To put it bluntly, monsieur, I need a partner badly, and have no one else to turn to but you! I'm offering you a full partnership in Armand's, if you would be interested in doing business with me.''

His eyebrows rose in surprise. So, she really *had* wanted to discuss a proposition though not, unfortunately, the one he had in mind. He frowned. Was sharing her bed contingent on his acceptance of her offer?

''I see,'' he said at length. ''And exactly how much capital are we talking about, if I accept?''

She told him, glossing over the amount with her glowing projections of the fat profit he stood to make in the future, once her debts were paid off. Her delightful if transparent subterfuge brought a smile to his lips. But, although he nodded here and there and asked a great many questions, his eyes never left her face.

''The restaurant, it's very important to you. Why?''

''It was my father's dream to make it the most successful restaurant in New Orleans—in Louisiana,'' she answered. ''You see, my *grandpère* Jerome was a famous chef and restauranteur in Paris, before the family became émigrés. I suppose the business was in his blood—as it is now in mine. Their dream is one I share, Nicholas.''

Nicholas. She said his name in a husky way that aroused him. Is that how she would whisper it while they made love? He'd know very soon. . . . He asked softly, ''And is that your only reason, madame?''

''If only it were. But there are people who depend upon me for their livelihood and survival, Monsieur Sauvage—Nicholas. Though I could earn my livelihood elsewhere, without this restaurant they have nothing.''

''By 'they,' you mean your family?''

How ironic, he thought as she nodded. She'd arranged this meeting, prepared to sacrifice her pride, the independence she cherished, to continue a tradition and keep her family of émigrés together. He, on the other hand, had spent his adult life trying to put family ties and the life he'd lived behind him.

His earliest memories were not of a mother's tender, loving care, but of the procession of soiled doves, who'd raised him in their rough-and-ready fashion. Good-time gals who'd hated the gambler Jacques's "snot-nosed, grubby brat" hanging around the house when their "gentlemen" came calling. There had been "French" Lily, who'd patted his cheek and given him sips of gin for his toothache, instead of hugs and kisses. And there'd been Marianne who'd made him puff her Turkish cigars until he turned green. There'd been Doucette, Naughty Alise, Jolie, and so, so many others. They'd smelled of sex, liquor, and desperation as if it were cheap perfume, and though all were different, they'd been cursed with a terrible sameness. He'd lost count of how many had passed through his life, moving on to other men, other sporting houses, other towns, like ships in the night.

Before they crossed the parish boundaries, he knew they'd forgotten the small boy who'd prayed that this time they would stay, while knowing in his heart they never would. . . .

Silence yawned between them in the wake of his words. Honey lifted the wineglass to her lips, watching his face over the rim as she sipped. What he was thinking?

Should she have told him about Remy and her children? Would he have understood that to her the Valoirs were not unfeeling chattel to be bought and sold, but family? Not slaves, but people she loved dearly and could not bear to lose? And what of the free colored who worked for her? Where would they go?

As she stared at him, the candle flame between them blurred. His striking features softened. *It's the wine,* she thought. She was not used to it on an empty stomach. Still, she sipped again and tried to focus on his mouth.

Had those hard, masculine lips really kissed hers in the wicker gondola, high above the bayou? Had that tanned hand, splayed across the tablecloth, truly cupped her breast?

Sitting here, served by her own waiters, drinking wine from her own cellars, that day—the day she'd realized she was in love with him—seemed like a dream! She giggled.

She had the urge to reach across the table and trace his lips with her fingertips, to place his hand over her breast. . . . She swallowed. He looked so stern tonight, so dark, so handsome.

The crisp hair that waved over his collar was as black as midnight against his wind-browned face. The dark frock coat and fitted trousers made his broad shoulders appear even broader, while the snowy perfection of his high-wing collar and striped silk stock was dazzling. Perhaps she should change the restaurant's laundress, she thought, a little tipsy from the wine. But then, unless he accepted her offer she would have no laundry to worry about, except her own! She bit her lip. He just *had* to, or else she'd . . .

"Very well. I accept."

She heard him as if from a great distance. She blinked. Had she imagined his answer, or spoken her wishes aloud? "Wh-what did you say, monsieur?" she whispered.

"I said, madame, that I accept your offer of partnership," he repeated, looking amused as she blinked at him. "Raoul! Have Claude uncork a bottle of his finest champagne! Your mistress and I have something to celebrate!"

"At once, suh."

"Bring us the dessert, too, Raoul," she instructed, her laughter bubbling up. "The *special* dessert," she added behind her hand.

"Aaah, *oui*, madame!" Raoul hurried off to the kitchens.

"What's this? A special dessert for Mardi Gras?"

She laughed. He had heard her. "*Non.* It is a dessert I created just for you in the hope that there would be something to celebrate." She reached across the table and pressed her hand over the back of his. "Thank you, Nicholas. Thank you so very much. You cannot know what a relief your acceptance is—or what having you as a partner will mean to me!"

He drew her hand between his own, the ball of his thumb idly circling the back of it. "And if I had not accepted? What of your 'special' dessert, then?"

"I would have poured it into the gutters for the hogs!" she declared.

He threw back his head and laughed. "Your honesty is refreshing, *cherie.* I'm delighted such drastic measures won't be necessary! However, I do have a small condition to my acceptance."

She grew still. Was this the sting in the scorpion's tail? "Oh? And what is that?"

"Nothing you will find unpleasant, I trust. I'll explain as we enjoy our dessert. Tell me. What have you named my special creation? Nicholas's Folly? Nicholas's Ruin?"

"*Non!*" she confessed with a shy, sweet smile. "I have named it Sweet Sin, Monsieur Sauvage."

Her warm, brown eyes met his, and he cocked his eyebrow. He had not been mistaken. The lady was ready and willing to share his bed. Like every woman, she'd merely been waiting for him to meet her price. Hers was simply much higher than most. So much for propriety....

"Sweet Sin, indeed? Then I shall pray it lives up to its name, *cherie!*"

The dessert did more than that he decided after a single spoonful. The crumbly richness of the chocolate torte was offset by a hint of coffee liqueur and vanilla, then crowned with a generous dollop of whipped cream. The raspberries in the sauce burst on his lips in tiny explosions of sweet, juicy flavor, before surrendering to smooth Amaretto. For a few moments he was so lost in the delicious melange of flavors and complimenting her, he forgot what he'd meant to tell her.

"Monsieur? Nicholas! The condition?" Honey reminded him in a sharp tone. Her earlier pinched, anxious expression was gone. She appeared delighted by his lavish praises. And why wouldn't he praise her creation? It tasted like heaven on earth!

He grinned as he pointed his silver spoon at her, aware of a pleasant sensation spreading through his veins, warming his belly. "My condition is that you and I attend Mardi Gras. *Together.*"

"And?"

She looked as if she were holding her breath. Why? he wondered. Was she afraid his condition might cost more than she was willing—or ready—to pay? A smile played about his lips. He brought a raspberry to his mouth; devouring it with a noisy, greedy gusto he knew full well would ignite any number of naughty sensations in her. Sure enough, her cheeks reddened.

"There is no 'and,' madame. That is it. All of it."

"But why? Have you never seen the Mardi Gras revels?"

"Not here in New Orleans. Last February I found myself in Baton Rouge. The February before that I was up in Natchez on business. But Jean-Pierre assures me no city celebrates Fat Tuesday like New Orleans." He gazed at her over yet another luscious spoonful of Sweet Sin. "As a daughter of this fair city, *chere* Madame Armand, you must show me everything!" he murmured, drawing her long, tapered fingers to his lips.

Chapter 5

Minna was helping Honey dress when Remy came up to her bedchamber the evening of Mardi Gras. Carrying the wings for Honey's butterfly costume, she crossed the room and laid them on the woven-counterpane-covered, four-poster bed that Honey's *grandmère* Marie had brought from Paris.

"*Voilà!* How do I look?"

Honey twirled on one of the hooked rugs of natural wool, patterned with roses, scattered across the oak floor. On her upswept hair, she'd pinned a black satin skullcap with gold antennae tipped with paste diamonds. Her swirling gown was an old one, but over its satin skirts, Remy had sewn two layers of diaphanous tulle. The sunset pouring through the shutters turned the pale yellow skirts to gold.

"Lordy, lordy! Ain't you a pretty sight, chile!" Remy exclaimed, sounding breathless from the stairs.

"If I am, I have you to thank for it! Talk to me while I finish dressing." Dragging the small chaise, upholstered with pink cabbage roses on a cream background, from a corner, she pressed Remy down onto it.

"These wings are lovely, Remy," she exclaimed, picking them up from the bed and going to the window. She held them up to the light of the chimney lamp on the rosewood escritoire, where the bulky leather-bound journal in which she and her father had penned their recipes and a daguerreotype of Papa were arranged. "Your mama's so clever with her needle, Minna."

Minna giggled and twirled one of her braids. "Daddy say she worth her weight in gold, Miz Honey."

"He's right." Remy had sewn the tulle and sequins to a dainty wire frame. "Pin them on for me, would you, Remy?" Honey stood in front of the chaise and Remy got up.

"Turn 'round, then, sugar. By the by, that man's waitin' on you in the drawin' room."

"Already? Minna, my slippers! Quickly, quickly!"

"Hold your hosses, chile. He'll keep. Besides, it don't do t' let a man think you anxious. Stop twitchin'."

"Is he wearing a carnival mask?"

Remy snorted. "A mask ain't all he's wearin'!" She pinned the wings to the back of Honey's bodice. "He found hisself a costume and a half!"

She laughed. "Really? No, don't tell me. . . . He's Lord Lucifer, complete with horns and tail."

Remy's lips pursed. "You'll see soon enough. Chile, let Minna touch up them side curls."

After applying the sizzling tongs to her hair, Minna patted Honey's curls. "You all set, Miz Honey."

"Thank you, Minna, darling."

Smoothing down her skirts, she turned back to the looking glass, and was delighted with what she saw. The airy yellow gown floated about her like thistledown. The bobbing antennae and gossamer wings might even start a new fashion, *à la papillon.* She smiled and her reflection smiled back.

After all those sleepless nights, it was going to work out, she thought with a silent prayer of thanks. Soon Armand's and the Valoirs would be safe, and she could concentrate on what she loved most: her beloved cooking—and her flirtation with Nicholas.

"Look at you! It's been an age since I seen that sunny smile, baby." Remy wrapped her in a hug. "And I ain't never seen you prettier than you is tonight, Miz Butterfly!"

"Pretty enough to be Queen of Carnival?"

Remy harrumphed. "Pretty enough t' need a chaperone 'round that gamblin' man." She pursed her lips. "You run along, chile. I'll fetch my shawl."

Her smile fled. "You're not coming with us?"

"Sugar, you'll hardly know I'm there. . . ."

Standing in *Maman*'s elegant drawing room, his fists on his hips, his booted feet planted apart, Nicholas looked sinful enough to make any Creole mama swoon!

From his belt jutted a rusty cutlass that almost toppled a ginger jar as he turned to greet her. With his full-sleeved shirt showing his naked chest, a gold earring in one ear, and a strip of red cloth tied around his dark head, he was every inch a pirate.

"Monsieur *le capitaine,* welcome." Honey dropped a deep curtsey that made her tulle skirts billow around her. "Surely no bolder buccaneer ever sailed the seven seas."

He cut her a rakish bow. "My thanks, lovely butterfly!"

He kissed her hand. "Tonight, with you on my arm, I'll be the envy of every buccaneer in New Orleans!"

"Flatterer!" she came back gaily.

"Shall we?" With a pirate's swagger, he offered her his arm and led her downstairs to the place d'Armes.

Clucking like a mother hen, Remy followed them.

A sole star twinkled in the charcoal sky. The night breeze carried the scent of flowers, underscored by the faint tang of the river. The air was pleasantly cool against Honey's flushed cheeks.

"Where to, madame?" Nicholas asked. "Canal Street?"

"*Non.* Too crowded. Let's try Bourbon Street. We'll have the best view of the parade there."

"Bourbon it is," he declared.

They set off, joining knots of other revelers heading in the same direction. Remy followed and, judging by her expression, Honey knew there'd be hell to pay if they tried to lose her.

The French Quarter had outdone itself in honor of Mardi Gras. Flowers garlanded the iron-laced balconies, and the yellow, purple, and green flags of Carnival billowed everywhere. The merrymakers, whether Creole, Americano, or free men and women of color, wore gorgeous masks and sequined costumes. There were Neptunes and mermaids, centaurs and demons, each costume more fantastic, more ablaze with glitter, plumes, and jewels than the last.

She and Nicholas were swept down darkening alleys toward Bourbon Street by merrymakers, who'd formed an impromptu band of harmonicas, concertinas, and tambourines. Their noisy gaiety was contagious.

"Enjoying yourself?" he shouted over the din, grinning.

A trumpet blared. A concertina wailed.

"Yes!" she shouted back. "And you?"

His dark eyes twinkled. "Very much so."

"You see, monsieur? No one can resist the spirit of Carnival."

"Or the charming company, madame."

She looked away, breathless and unable to meet his eyes.

Desire blazed in their dark depths. Was desire mirrored in her own?

The balconies above Bourbon Street were thronged with elegantly dressed men and women sipping champagne and waiting for the parade to pass by. In the hotel lobbies, waiters were serving champagne to the revelers.

Honey found a brimming glass thrust into her hands by a devil in a crimson mask. "Drink, pretty butterfly!" he urged. "It's your last chance to make merry before Lent, *non?*" He showered colorful confetti over her.

She laughed and drained her brimming glass before Nicholas led her on, down the street.

At the next corner, the onlookers suddenly gave a roar. Turning, Honey saw an enormous papier-mâché cavalier bobbing down the street, like a balloon. It was followed by horse-drawn floats swaying around the corner like stately Spanish galleons.

"Oh, Nicholas, look! There's Penelope weaving at her golden loom! And there's the goddess, Medea, and the dragon!"

In the light of the oil lamps hanging from chains on every street corner, the lofty floats were transformed. A few spangles, a handful of sequins and they were no longer paint and paper, but a magical pageant of gods and goddesses, monsters and giants.

"Comus comes last," Honey added. "He's Rex, King of Carnival. Tonight he and his court, the Mystick Krewe, will preside over the Mardi Gras ball at the Orleans Theater. Now, you shall see how we celebrate Carnival here in New Orleans, Nicholas. Or," she amended softly, "perhaps I should call you Nick, since we're to be partners?"

The huskiness of her voice made Nick's heart thunder like a racehorse on the home stretch. What was wrong with him? He'd never let any woman get under his skin, but he craved Honey as other men craved strong drink or the spin of the roulette wheel. Did he love her? he wondered. Was it love he felt for her?

There's no such thing as love, you fool!

Like the glittering pageant before him, love was just an illusion, a pretty bagatelle as easily broken as a wedding vow. Hadn't his mother and the soiled doves at Natchez Nell's proved it time and time again? They'd all claimed to love him in their own fashion. Yet, one by one, they'd abandoned him, abandoned his father, abandoned even the men they'd whored for.

No, what he felt for Honey was only lust. Nothing more. He contemplated her lips, then dropped his gaze to her silky throat, to her lusciously curved breasts. What red-blooded man wouldn't lust after such a beautiful, experienced widow? As his mistress, she would enjoy a passion she'd never known with her Don Carlos, or her husband, he'd lay odds on it! And after bedding her, perhaps he'd be able to put her out of his thoughts—and out of his heart.

"*Sacré bleu!*" Pain suddenly lanced through his foot.

"My stars! That your foot I stomped on, Massa Nick?"

"It was, yes, Madame Valoir," he ground out, not taken in by the woman's innocent expression.

"Why, I'm mighty sorry, suh!"

"The devil you are," he muttered.

"Shall I take Miz Honey home, so you can poultice that foot?"

"That won't be necessary, *merci.*" Doubly determined to lose Honey's watchdog now, he turned back to the king's float.

Honey sighed. Remy stuck to her like a burr to a hound's pelt whenever she felt she needed protection. Poor Nick. His foot must hurt, yet he didn't show it.

The crowd parted then for the Rex's runners dressed in scarlet turbans with silver plumes. They ran alongside the float, their torches spilling ruddy light over the crowd's faces. Behind them, in time to the blaring music of a brass band, swayed the huge float of Comus, drawn by eight prancing horses draped in shimmering cloth. Their hooves clattered on the cobblestones.

On the throne high above the crowd sat the King of Carnival, crowned with gold and jewels, and cloaked in flowing ermine. Around him, gorgeously costumed dancers undulated to the rhythm of the throbbing drums. They flung confetti, metal doubloons, streamers, and bagatelles over the onlookers, as well as little paper sacks of flour that burst, scattering their contents. As shrieking children dived for pretty bead "throws," Nick caught a paper fan. He presented it to her with a flourish.

Lowering her lashes, she snapped the fan open. Her eyes met his over its painted folds, and she gasped. The raw hunger in his expression made the breath catch in her throat.

"I want you, *cherie!*" he rasped. "Now—tonight!"

The fan spilled from her fingers. Her sigh became a breathless moan of surrender as he drew her against him, crushing her breasts to his chest. The two of them were an island of stillness in a churning sea of bodies. The only sound was the wild thunder of her heart and the answering beat of his.

His lips were warm as they moved against hers, tasting, exploring. His fingers tenderly grazed her hair, her throat as he whispered, "Enough of these games, *cherie.* We both know what we want. Come with me. Let's make tonight a night to remember."

But before she could respond, a jester slammed into her, almost slamming her to the cobbled street. "Ooh!"

"Pardon me, señorita!"

"Watch out, or I'll teach you some manners!" Nick growled.

Bells jingling, the drunkard muttered an obscenity and lurched away. As Nick followed, a group of revelers separated Honey from him and Remy.

"Nick! *Nicholas!*" She tried to fight her way back to his side. But, although she glimpsed his angry face between the bobbing heads, she could not escape the crush of bodies.

Like a leaf caught by the tide, she was swept away down

the street. Her mask, headpiece, and a satin slipper were lost, her wings shredded. The oppressive heat and smell of so many bodies made her light-headed, but she dare not swoon or the mob would trample her.

When powerful arms dragged her up against a hard male body, she lashed out. ''Let me go, you brute!''

The man easily caught her wrists. ''Brute, is it, *cherie?*''

''Nick! Oh, thank God!''

''Take my hand. Let's get out of this crush!''

''Where's Remy? Isn't she with you?''

''We were separated. She'll find her own way home. What about you? You're limping. Are you hurt?''

''I cast a shoe.'' She lifted her skirts to show her white, silk-stockinged foot. ''Like a horse.''

He stared at her leg and grinned. ''Not with legs like those. Up you go, Cinderella!'' Ignoring her protests, he lifted her into his arms and headed for the banquettes.

Chapter 6

Nick carried Honey to the small door, set in a high brick wall, that led to his townhouse. After a few moments, his knock was answered by his housekeeper.

''Mercy, you back early, Massa Nick!''

''So I am, Beulah.'' In a lower voice, he inquired, ''Is supper ready?''

''Yes, suh. Just like you wanted.'' She stepped aside.

''Splendid.''

He carried Honey down a narrow passageway that opened into the flagstoned courtyard drenched with moonlight. Palm trees rattled their huge fronds against the louvers of his bedchamber two storys above, while the fountain splashed water into a mossy basin. Its burbling had soothed him during more restless Saturday nights than he cared to remember.

Skirting the lichened stone pots that squatted in his path, he started up the stairs, their iron-laced railing draped with lavender wisteria, bleached by moonlight. Its perfume was haunting, intoxicating.

"You don't have to carry me, Nick. I can walk."

Her laughter was low and sensual on the scented hush. Her warm, sweet breath fanned his cheek. The lush swell of her breasts, her rounded bottom cradled against his middle, increased the ache in his loins. Unsmiling, he looked down at her. "I know."

"Then set me down."

"So you can escape me again? Not a chance!" he declared, reaching the top of the stairs.

Husky laughter trembled on the shadows as she curled her arms about his neck, and he hastened to reach his bedchamber door. Throwing it open, he saw that the instructions he'd given Beulah earlier that evening had been carried out.

His housekeeper had lit dozens of candles which cast romantic shadows on the stucco walls. The shutters and louvers had been opened to the sounds of merriment in the street below. He could smell candle wax and peppery spices as he strode onto the balcony.

Beulah had outdone herself, he saw, lowering Honey into a chair. The table was spread with a snowy cloth. Frilly white orchids, crystal goblets, and silverware flanked plates of gold-rimmed porcelain. A silver candelabra with ivory tapers guttered in the balmy breeze scented by the honeysuckle, cape jasmine, and crepe myrtle in the courtyard.

While they sipped the chilled champagne Nick had splashed into elegant crystal flutes, Beulah deftly served the repast of fresh oysters on the half shell; a warm, crusty baguette; a steaming tureen filled with crawfish, shrimp, and crab, boiled and seasoned with peppery spices; and fresh strawberries.

"Excellent, Beulah. That will be all for tonight. Don't wait up," Nick said, moving to stand behind Honey's chair.

His tall mulatto housekeeper beamed. "You welcome, suh. Good night, suh. Madame."

When they were alone, Nick lifted Honey's hair and kissed her nape. Her loose, silky curls spilled through his fingers like honey drizzled from a spoon. They were perfumed with vanilla and strawberries and her own exquisite sweet fragrance that had invaded his senses months ago.

Still kissing her, he slid his fingers deep into the bodice of her gown, to cup her breast. He almost groaned aloud as its warm fullness filled his palm. The velvety nipple puckered between his fingers. "Eat, *chèrie.* And after we'll satisfy our other appetites, *oui?*" he whispered.

As he took the chair opposite her, Honey stuffed a piece of steaming bread into her mouth and chewed like a hungry little cat. Swallowing, she took a gulp of champagne, then selected a plump shrimp. Popping all but the tail into her mouth, she greedily sank her teeth into the crescent of succulent pink-and-white flesh. She moaned and closed her eyes. "Hmm!"

"Good?" he asked, his jaw clenched. That was a foolish question! Hard with lust, he shifted position.

"Hmm, better than good." With a blissful sigh, she dispatched another shrimp, then licked her fingers, one by one, making juicy smacking noises. "It's *délicieuse!*"

It was all he could do to stifle a groan.

"Try one, Nick. Or perhaps you'd like a strawberry, instead? Open your mouth, *chèri.* I'll feed you."

Leaning across the table, she selected a large strawberry, then dipped it in the champagne. Holding it by the leafy stem, she brought the dripping berry to his lips. But when he tried to bite it, she laughed and pulled it away and his lips closed on air. "Better luck next time, Nick!"

"I give you fair warning, madame. You are playing with fire."

"I am?" She moistened her pink lips with the tip of her tongue. "Then perhaps I want to get burned, yes?"

He watched as, slowly and deliberately, she brought the fruit to her lips, which parted to receive it. Well aware that his eyes were riveted to the glistening berry on her tongue, she closed her mouth over it, chewed, swallowed, and sighed dreamily. "Hmm. Won't you have one, Nick?"

"Thank you, no," he ground out. "You see, I have a craving for something else."

"Oh?" She offered him the tureen. "Crawfish? An oyster?"

He shot her a grin. "You!" Reaching across the table, he grabbed the champagne bottle by the neck and led her into his bedchamber.

Dropping to one knee, he drew off her slipper and tossed it over his shoulder. "That's better."

Standing, he hooked his fingers under the straps of her gown and slid them down to her elbows. He feathered little kisses over her shoulders, her throat, before turning her away from him. One by one, he freed the hooks of her gown, kissing the slender, ivory back he bared inch by inch.

She shrank from his lips, clutching the bunched satin and tulle to her breasts. He smiled. Even now, here, his elusive madame maintained her modest pose.

"Let it go," he urged, turning her to him. "You won't need clothes tonight."

He felt a frisson of pleasure run through her as he stroked her arms. Sighing, she released the gown. It fell to her ankles in a whispering cloud of tulle, leaving only her lacy underclothes and horsehair petticoat.

His groin tightened, for her nipples were tiny tempting peaks beneath her watered silk camisole. He covered first one then the other jutting nub with his mouth, dampening the fabric that was pulled taut over them, before drawing off her camisole.

Shyly, she stood before him, bared to the waist, her full, high breasts peeking through strands of her golden hair.

"How lovely you are, *ma belle* Honey! So very lovely."

Plunging his fingers into her hair, he captured her mouth in a hungry kiss, and unfastened the drawstrings of her petticoat. Lifting her, he lay her tenderly across his bed like the precious gift she was.

Stripping off his pirate gear, he knelt beside her, unfastening the lacy garters, embellished with tiny roses and ribbons, just above her knees. He rolled down her white silk stockings, then trailed the silky wisps across her body in a whispering caress. Lifting her dainty foot, he kissed her ankle, the hollow behind her dimpled knee, his hands and mouth sliding higher, until his lips met lace-trimmed ruffles.

When she guessed his intention, she stiffened in a modest display that would have driven a saint to madness.

"*Non!*" she protested. "You must not! Nick, no!"

"On the contrary, darling. I must. . . ."

She moaned as he pressed his lips over the fine muslin, imparting the damp heat of his mouth to the sensitive mound beneath it. She tasted sweet and hot as sun-ripened fruit, drenched with the nectar of desire! Sweet sin, *indeed!*

She sighed as he grasped the waistband of her pantalets and slowly drew them down over her long, white legs. The breath caught in his throat as her last garment bunched in his hand. She looked so sweetly sinful, sprawled across his bed, trying to shield her breasts and gold curls from his eyes, his hands, his lips. Her rosy blush made him harder than a madam's heart.

Whispering endearments, he lowered himself over her.

Chapter 7

The graze of Nick's lean, hard body against Honey's was like the kiss of fire. He was magnificent, all muscle, all hot, salty flesh, all *man!* When he splayed his hands beneath her hips, she made no protest, but opened eagerly, cradling him with her hips.

Gracefully, confidently, he entered her, paused when he found his way barred, then thrust again. This time he flowed into her like hot silk, pushing until he was deep inside her. The sheer and unexpected delight that followed the blunt pressure, the stinging pain, wrung a startled sob from her.

"Ah, *chèrie.* You're so ready, yet so tight, my sweet," he whispered thickly against her hair. "Has it been so long for you, then?"

She gave no answer. She was lost in the velvety, sensual slide of skin against skin, in the spiraling heat, the fluid sensations, the mutual reaching for something more, something just out of reach. But so close, so very close, she could almost . . .

With a cry, she arched to meet him, to move to his rhythm. She cried out with wonder and pleasure, gripping his sinewy buttocks as he thrust harder, deeper, increasing her pleasure until she was bent like a bow beneath him.

Then, her world stilled. A warm wave rose and rippled through her. "Nick! Oh, God, Nick!" The night exploded in a shower of gold.

"Ah, *chèrie,* yes! It was never . . . like this before!" Her name ripped from his throat like a battle cry. He reared back, his eyes closed, and she felt his hot seed spill inside her.

Rolling onto his back with her still in his arms, he sighed and she felt his body relax. She nestled close to him and after a few minutes, she realized he was asleep.

Though her limbs were languid, her body pleasantly exhausted, she could not sleep. She lay awake, listening to Nick's deep breathing, watching his untroubled face in the moonlight, aching to hear the words he'd left unsaid as they'd made love.

"I love you, Nick," she whispered, pressing her cheek to his chest. "God help me, I love you!"

Nick stared at the rust-stained sheets in the gray light that seeped through the shutters. Below his balcony a chorus of birds was joyously greeting the new day. The yeasty aroma of beignets and coffee wafted on the morning air, bringing a hungry growl to his belly.

He smiled as he fingered the corn silk curl that lay against Honey's flushed cheek. His beautiful mistress! He would wake her with kisses, then have Beulah serve them a lazy breakfast in bed. And after they would make love all day long, he promised himself.

"Honey? Wake up, sleepyhead!"

She rolled over. Her chocolate-brown eyes opened, her sooty lashes fluttering like dark moths against her rosy cheeks. When she smiled up at him, his heart lurched crazily in his chest. It was like the sun coming out.

"Hmm, you're really here." She stretched like a sleepy kitten. "I thought I'd dreamed last night. Dreamed *you.*"

"It was no dream, *chèrie.*" He caressed her cheek. "Not for either of us. Did you enjoy last night?" Falling asleep after they'd first made love, he'd then awakened and their lovemaking went on for hours, until they finally drifted off into an exhausted sleep. "I didn't hurt you?"

She sat up. Lifting his hand to her lips, she kissed the knuckles, one by one. "*Non.* You were very gentle, Nick."

"And you, my love, were delectable." He kissed the corner of her mouth. "Hungry?"

"Ravenous!"

As he turned to ring for Beulah, the sheet Honey had pulled over her slipped revealing another of the rusty stains he'd seen earlier. "What's this mark on your thigh? And this one here?"

"That? It's blood." Her cheeks reddened.

"But, what the devil—aaah! How foolish of me, your curses. Forgive me, *chèrie.* I did not mean to embarrass you."

"No, it's not my . . . It's not that." She looked down at her hands. They were curled like pale flowers in her lap. "Last night, when we . . . when we made love, could you not tell?"

He frowned. "Tell what?"

She bit her lip. "That I was innocent."

"Innocent!" He chuckled and dropped a kiss on her lips. "Come, now, how could you be innocent, *chèrie?* When an older man takes a beautiful young bride, he . . . Well, let's just say I'm quite certain Louis Armand tried his best to get an heir on you!"

"Louis Armand?" She stared at him as if he'd suddenly sprouted two heads.

"Your husband, remember? Unless, of course, the poor old devil was impotent. Is that what you're saying, *chèrie?* That your marriage was never consummated?"

"My marriage? But Louis was not—"

"Besides, you've had other lovers since his death," he cut in. "Your Spaniard, Don Carlos, comes to mind. Now, don't tell me you never shared his bed, *chèrie,* because I know better! I saw him escorting you home one morning. At dawn."

"My Spaniard—" A moment ago, her face had been glowing. It was now the color of chalk. "So that's it! You thought that Don Carlos and I—" She shook her head. "Nick, listen to me. Louis Armand wasn't my husband. He was my father, God rest his soul!"

Her words were like fists, slamming into his belly, leaving him winded. "Your father!" he echoed hoarsely.

"*Oui!* And Don Carlos is *Maman*'s beau, not mine!"

His jaw dropped. "Your mother has a beau? *Sacré bleu!* Then you're saying your *mother's* the Widow Armand?"

"Of course she is, since I've never been married."

"And the name of the restaurant is your father's?"

"Yes. Who else's could it be?"

He slammed the heel of his hand against his forehead. "By God, I see it all now. You set me up. You planned this all along, you scheming little gold digger! You played me for a fool, and I didn't have a clue until you'd played your last card!"

"What? Don't be ridiculous! There was no plan. You made a mistake, that's all."

His index finger stabbed the air before her nose. "If I did, then it was one you wanted me to make! Why else would your staff call you Madame Armand, unless it was a ruse? Explain that if you can! Why else would you allow me to call you madame, if you've never been married? Not once did you correct me, lady! Not once!"

"Why should I correct you? I earned the right to be called madame! It is a term of respect for a female chef. If I were a man, I would be known as Maestro Armand, and no one would give it a second thought!"

"But you knew what I would assume."

"I'm not responsible for your assumptions, monsieur!" she flared. "Or for the conclusions you jump to—right or wrong!"

"Who put you up to this? Why did you set me up?" But he fancied he knew the answer to that question, even as he posed it.

It was no business partner Honey had been after, but a wealthy husband. He thought he knew every trick in the damn book, yet he'd fallen for the oldest game in town!

For seven months Honey'd used her voluptuous body, her sweet smiles—even her damned chocolate desserts!—to string him along, with last night's seduction as her ultimate goal. *Mon Dieu,* who'd been seducing whom?

He'd wanted a fascinating, beautiful mistress. What he'd got was a virgin—the equivalent of a millstone around his neck! And what options had he now as a man of honor? he thought bleakly. None, none at all. If he ever wanted to do business in this city again, he had to see it through to its bitter, logical end. He had to marry her.

Honey forced herself to stand, to move limbs that were wooden with shock. Her heart was broken. He didn't love her. He'd never loved her. He'd only wanted to seduce her.

"Perhaps the women you're accustomed to would have set you up, Monsieur Sauvage, but I'm not one of them."

Gathering the tattered remnants of her pride about her like a cloak, she wound the sheet about her body. "The Ursuline sisters taught us that honesty was a virtue. I swear on my papa's grave that I had no intention of trapping you! I—I care for you, Nick!" Her admission ended on a strangled sob she could not staunch. "That is why I let you make love to me. The only reason."

His face was a stony mask of disbelief. "And you expect me to swallow that?"

"You must, because it is true," she whispered.

"What's true, mademoiselle, is that I'm obliged to offer you marriage, if I wish to continue doing business in New Orleans."

"Don't bother, monsieur. I want nothing from you, not now, not ever! Keep your money. I'd sell myself on the streets before I'd marry you!"

"Too late! You've already sold yourself, sugar. Here, in my bed! Your price was a partnership in Armand's. Remember?"

She felt the color drain from her face. "You—*bastard!*"

He grinned nastily. "Not quite, my dear. My parents had their faults, but they were married. We'll be married, too—in name, if nothing more. You may be carrying my child."

With a savage finality that tore at her heart, he took fresh garments from the armoire and dressed. "I'll summon a priest to perform the ceremony. I suppose we'll need witnesses, too.'' He scowled as he folded his stock. ''Your mother will do, for one. And that damned Delacroix for the second! It's only fitting, considering their parts in this charade, no?''

''Parts?'' She felt numb, unable to think clearly.

Thin-lipped, he straightened his lapels, buttoned his brocade waistcoat. ''It was Jean-Pierre who pointed you out to me last June as the Widow Armand. And, I suspect, your mother's reputation as a very merry widow was what led me to believe . . .'' His mouth twisted in contempt.

''What? That I—that the Widow Armand would welcome your attentions?''

''Yes!'' he admitted. ''I'll have Beulah bring you hot water and linens. Make your toilette quickly, madame—or should I say, Mademoiselle Armand.''

At the door, he turned to face her. ''And, remember, I don't intend to be your husband in anything but name. Better women than you have tried to trap me, and failed. Marriage won't change that.''

Less than an hour later, Nick and Honey were husband and wife in the eyes of God and of man. Their vows had been heard by bleary-eyed Father Rodrigo from the Cathedral Saint Louis, and witnessed by Estelle Armand and Jean-Pierre, both of whom Nick had summoned to the townhouse himself.

After the wedding certificate had been signed, he left his bride alone with her mother in the drawing room, and escorted his friend and the priest down to the courtyard. Slipping Father Rodrigo a generous donation for the poor box, he sent him on his way, then ordered his stableboy to bring Jean-Pierre's horse.

''Well, well. It would seem I won my wager, after all, eh, *mon ami?*'' Jean-Pierre reminded Nick with a chuckle, drawing on his riding gloves and donning his top hat with a satisfied pat. ''Not even a year and Belle Refuge has a new mistress just as I predicted! I wagered ten dollars that night, I believe. Or was it twenty?'' He scrunched his brow in thought.

''Ten—but I didn't take the bet, remember? And, all things considered, I'd say you're damned lucky I don't give you a black eye for your part in this morning's charade,'' he snarled.

The grin on Jean-Pierre's face vanished. ''Me? What had I to do with your blasted marriage?''

''Everything! It was you who gave me the wrong name the first time we dined at Armand's, my friend. I pointed to Honey Armand. It was you who told me she was the *Widow* Armand! You again who implied that the widow and pastry chef were one and the same.''

''It was an honest mistake, old man,'' Jean-Pierre protested, looking decidedly guilty now. ''Until this morning, I, er, I thought they were! One and the same, I mean.'' He shook his head. ''Two Madame Armands, by Jove, and enough alike to be sisters! Who'd have thought it? Her mother's a beauty, too, don't you think?''

Beauty be damned! He was in no mood to be sidetracked. ''Then you admit none of this would have happened if not for you!''

Jean-Pierre's face hardened. ''Now, see here, Sauvage. Enough's enough. No one is to blame. As I said, it was an honest mistake. But the truth is, none of this would have happened if you hadn't taken it into your head to seduce the chit. Take my advice. Make the best of things and have a good wedding night, *mon ami*—or rather, what's left of it. In a week or so I'll ride out to Belle Refuge to see how things are going, all right? Congratulations!''

He rode off before Nick could throw a punch.

Once she and *Maman* were alone, her mother's tears vanished. She threw her arms around Honey's neck and kissed her cheek. ''Oh, what a clever, clever girl you are, my darling!''

''Clever? What did I do that's so clever?'' Honey asked miserably.

"You landed yourself a wealthy, handsome husband, that's what! I couldn't have done better myself, darling. True, Sauvage has a questionable past, but more than enough lovely money to make up for it! Madame Melisse Sauvage. Oh, you'll be an adorable mistress for Belle Refuge, Melisse."

"I told you, I didn't set out to 'land' anyone, *Maman.* It was all a misunderstanding!" She wrenched free of her mother's hands. "He thought I was you! That I was the Widow Armand! He claimed he only wanted me to join him for Mardi Gras, but I drank too much champagne and the next thing I knew, I was—"

"In my bed," Nick cut in brutally.

How long had he been standing there? Judging by his livid face, long enough to hear every word her mother had said.

"And the rest, as they say, is history," he continued in that cold, dead voice that cut her to the quick.

"Please, leave us now, Madame Armand. I wish to speak with Hon—my wife—alone. Don Carlos is waiting below, in his carriage, is he not? I suggest you join him." His eyes were black ice, cold and impenetrable.

"Ah, yes. Dear Carlos. Thank you, Nicholas."

Rising, *Maman* gave her new son-in-law a dismissive nod that made her garnet earbobs swing. She swept across the room in a cloud of expensive perfume, trailing the swishing folds of her satin opera cape behind her like a peacock's tail.

When she drew level with Nick, she patted his rigid arm and murmured, "Whatever the circumstances of your marriage to my daughter, I'm delighted you've joined our little family, dear boy!"

"I regret I cannot say the same, madame. Good day." He pointedly offered her his broad back.

With a Gallic shrug, Estelle blew Honey a kiss as she made her exit.

When they were alone, Honey began, "Nick, I—"

His raised hand silenced her. "Don't bother with explanations. Your mother made everything quite clear. Tomorrow morning, I'll have my lawyer begin drafting our partnership contract. Once it's been approved and signed by both of us, I'll transfer the necessary funds from my account to yours, and your blasted restaurant will be secure."

She nodded, hating the way he looked at her, as if she'd slithered out of the bayou. Tears welled, but she was too proud to let them fall. "After our business has been concluded, what then?" She wanted to ask if she was to accompany him to Belle Refuge, but dare not with this cold rage upon him.

His lip curled. "Did you really think I would settle your debts, then retire to the bayou and leave you to your own devices?" His smile was scornful. "On the contrary, if I'm to be a partner in Armand's, I intend to be an *active* one. There will be some changes implemented, starting tomorrow."

"So soon?"

"The sooner the better. You can do your part, madame chef," he scoffed, "by cutting back on the extravagances that are beggaring *our* establishment."

"And what extravagances are those?" Let him spell them out, the arrogant brute!

"The purchase of exotic spices, of expensive European liqueurs, and sundry other imported goods."

"Not extravagances, *monsieur,* but necessities!"

"Extravagances, *madame,*" he repeated. "If the price of these goods is beyond your budget, you must curtail their purchase immediately!" To give emphasis to his words, he banged his fist on a beautifully carved table with a resounding thud.

She flinched. "Very well. And what about the chocolate?" she demanded, goading him into making an exception of his personal vice. "That, too, Monsieur Pinchpenny?"

Nick squared his jaw. "Especially the damned chocolate, madame!"

"You can't be serious! Those ingredients are the foundation of my desserts!" she protested, truly afraid now. "Without them, Armand's menu is no different than the dining rooms of the—the St. Charles or the Verandah Hotel!"

"Then you will have to find another way to make Armand's excel."

She was about to argue, then thought better of it. For Armand's future to be completely secure, their business must first be completed. She would just have to bite her tongue until it was. "Very well! My—our—patrons may dine upon custards and—and rice puddings, henceforth!"

"A wise decision. If you need to contact me, I'll be at Belle Refuge until the contract is ready for our signatures. Good day."

With a curt nod of dismissal, he turned on his heel and strode from the drawing room. Soon after, she heard hooves striking the flagstones below and knew he'd ridden out.

She did not cry until he was gone. Even so, the tears were not for herself. They were for something beautiful that had blossomed during the night, and was now lost forever.

Chapter 8

The Monday morning following her wedding and Mardi Gras, Honey had her belongings carted to Nick's townhouse. Then she had resumed her position at Armand's as if nothing had changed except her name. But, alas, it had, because since that day everything that could go wrong had!

That Monday, with half the restaurant's tables reserved for a noon luncheon, she had scorched the roux for the mushroom sauce that accompanied the beef. In the afternoon she had cremated her meringues.

On Tuesday her cheese souffles had fallen flat as flapjacks. On Thursday her bread had refused to rise and her sponge cake had sunk. On Friday she had discovered weevils in the flour and ants in the molasses, and on Saturday, caterpillars in the greens. Sunday morning the fresh cream had curdled in the milk pail!

When the wretched butter refused to churn the following Monday, she had thrown up her hands in disgust and knocked a basket of six dozen fresh eggs to the flagstones. It had taken Minna and Harriet an hour to mop up the mess. The rest of that week had been more of the same.

But the final straw had come last night. Distracted by thoughts of Nick, whom she had not seen for two weeks, she'd added too much red pepper to the crawfish-and-shrimp boil, the *specialité* of Armand's.

Her waiters had rushed like chickens with their heads cut off, bringing the diners endless glasses of water. They had filled pitcher after pitcher from the butts of fresh drinking water in the courtyard until the crisis had passed.

When she'd wailed that someone must have placed a voodoo *gris-gris,* or hex, on her, or else she was going mad, Remy had assured her she was nothing of the sort. She was lovesick and should go home, and not come back until she was herself again.

Knowing Remy was right, she had left. Her heart wasn't in her cooking anymore, and the missing ingredient couldn't be found in her spice racks, the storerooms, or at the French market. It was in her heart, which felt as hollow as a blown egg, for despite her faint hope that Nick might miss her, relent, and come back, she'd heard nothing from him.

And then, just a few minutes ago, a little servant boy from Belle Refuge had delivered a note from Nick. She glanced at it now and forced herself to finish icing the last of several gateaux before going into the courtyard to read it.

Settling herself on the bench, she read, "My dear wife,"—she could almost hear his mocking tone—"the contract has been drawn up and awaits our signatures. Kindly join me at M. Henri Bienville's offices at two tomorrow afternoon to conclude our business. My carriage will call for you." It was signed "N. Sauvage."

She bit her lip. That their partnership would soon be official should have brought her enormous relief. After all those sleepless nights the restaurant would be saved. But all she could think of was that, once the contract was signed, she would rarely, if ever, see Nick again.

He would make sure of that.

"Well, madame. You have everything you wanted now. I only hope the end justified your means," Nick said as they left Bienville's offices the following afternoon.

"It did indeed, monsieur, although the end was not the one I foresaw—or wanted. Good day." With a tight nod, Honey stepped down to the pavement, her head held high despite her low spirits, and began walking away.

For several weeks now she'd been asking God and Saint Jude to answer her prayers. They'd done so by sending her Nick. But, somehow, she'd fallen in love with her unlikely benefactor—and fallen hard. She'd hoped that seeing him again this afternoon would remind her of just how arrogant and judgmental he could be. Instead, it had made her heart ache. She'd wanted to hide from his accusing black eyes, to forget that they could twinkle with laughter, or be tender, oh, so tender, too.

"Madame, wait." Nick caught up with her. "I've hired a cab to take you home."

"Thank you, I prefer to walk."

"Madame Sauvage!" His scornful tone turned heads, she noted, mortified. "Rue Orleans is that way." He jerked his thumb in the opposite direction.

"I'll take whichever way I please, monsieur!" she hissed. Furious, she swung her bag by its drawstring, almost braining a passing pedestrian.

"On the contrary. As my wife, you'll go where I please." His hand closed over her elbow.

"Have you forgotten, Nick? By your own admission, you are my husband in name only!" Tossing her head, she marched away, her heels drumming a smart tattoo on the banquette.

Casting a quick glance over her shoulder, she saw Nick fling the cabby a handful of coins and head for her. She hurried her pace.

"Rue Orleans is back that way, woman."

"I know. But I find myself in need of fresh air—as far from you as possible!"

"You're asking for trouble, coming here," he warned as she crossed the cobblestones onto rue Iberville. "Decent women don't frequent this part of town."

"But I'm not decent, remember? I'm a 'scheming gold digger'! And trouble is mother's milk to us gold diggers! Good day, Monsieur Sauvage." She moved away from him and no longer heard his steps dogging her.

With the sun behind it, rue Iberville looked like a leering mouth, the houses crooked stumps of teeth with names on their doors: Jacqueline, Anne, Paulette, Carlotta. The shutters framed women in silk kimonos. What sort of women were they? There was a sinister cast to the shadows, too. A miasma of despair clung to the crumbling buildings and cribs.

She shivered. She'd meant to take a shortcut to the market, but had lost her way, thanks to Nick. So, rather than admit her mistake, she continued down the narrow, dirty street.

As she passed them, the women in the windows shouted crude insults that burned her ears. She walked faster, intent on reaching the far end of the street as quickly as possible.

When Nick drew level with the cribs, the soiled doves smoothed their wrappers down over their plump hips, and fluffed out their hair.

"*Bonjour,* handsome. Won't you come inside?"

"Lonely, monsieur? Come and visit 'French' Marie?" called another.

"You're wasting your time, ladies!" he snapped.

"You sure about that, lover?" asked one brassy shutter girl. She nodded after Honey's retreating back. "You wouldn't have to chase my tail to get what you want!"

"Me and half the city, sweetheart!" he retorted, softening the insult with a grin. "Thanks, but no thanks."

"Bastard!" The woman slammed her door.

His smile faded when he saw sailors staggering down the street toward his wife. Their drunken leers made his blood boil. He caught up with her as she drew abreast of them.

"Afternoon, beautiful!" one tar began. "Why don't you and me find ourselves a cozy—"

"Crawl back to Piccadilly, English," Nick gritted, shoving his face into the sailor's.

Gripping her elbow, Nick turned Honey back the way they'd come, putting himself between her and the men.

A sailor stepped forward, his expression ugly. "Hey, I saw her first!"

"Lucky cove! I *married* her! So, if you know what's good for you, pal, you'll take a walk! A lo-o-ong walk. . . ."

The sailor's eyes met Nick's, and he threw up his hands. "Right. She's all yours, mate. We don't want no trouble with you Frenchies, do we, lads?"

The men lurched across the street, headed for the delights the shutter girls had to offer.

"Let go of me," Honey ground out when they'd gone.

"The devil I will. You're not safe out alone, lady."

"That's my problem, not yours. Let go of me! You have no right!" She aimed her toe at his shin. When he stepped back, she was thrown forward, into his arms.

"I have the only right I need, *chèrie*. A husband's rights," he murmured, steadying her with his hands under her elbows.

"The right to bully me?" She shrugged him away.

"To see to your safety." It was a right he took very

seriously, he realized, frowning. The thought of another man touching her, hurting her, had made him see red.

"Ha! I was never in any danger."

He snorted. "No? Did you see those men in the alleys?"

"The sailors? Yes, of course."

He shook his head. "The others, back there."

Her eyebrows rose. "I saw no other men."

Didn't that prove his point? Taking her arm, he propelled her down the street. "They are leeches, parasites that make their living off the whores in the cribs. They're always on the prowl for fresh women. Girls have disappeared from these houses and never been seen again."

"Oh? You seem to know more than your share about such places," she accused.

"I should. I was raised in one."

"You were? Really?"

"Ah. You're shocked." For some reason, the thought pleased him, perhaps because any emotion on her part was preferable to her chilly indifference.

"Not so much shocked as . . . curious, shall we say. You give every appearance of being a—a—"

"Gentleman?"

"Well, yes," she admitted with obvious reluctance.

"I'll take that as a compliment, *chèrie*." Stepping away from her, he made a mocking half bow. "God knows, I've worked at it."

"And very successfully it would seem. Apparently, you've built yourself a very different life. Where, er, where was this—sporting house?"

He tipped his hat back. "Why do you want to know?"

She shrugged. "As I said, idle curiosity."

"Natchez. A place called Natchez Nell's."

"How quaint. And were you . . . Did you live there long?"

"Long enough to swear I'd never go back. Will you accept my offer of a carriage now?" He knew he sounded bitter, but couldn't help himself. She'd forced him to remember faces, places he'd sooner forget.

"No, thank you. But a cup of coffee would be most welcome. I confess, I feel a little . . . parched."

He shot her a long look. Then his shoulders slumped. "No harm in being civil, I suppose." He offered her his arm. "Shall we, Madame Sauvage?"

She smiled and slipped her arm through his. "Let's!"

The cafe Nick had chosen fronted the busy levee. Keelboats and paddle-wheelers were docked alongside it. As Honey and Nick sat at a little table beneath a gaily colored umbrella, the loading and unloading of tobacco and cotton bales made for a colorful, lively scene.

"You were saying, Nick?" she prompted, eying him over the delicate rim of her demitasse cup.

"I was?"

He looked as if he'd rather be anywhere but there with her, and she felt a pang of regret for the way things could have been between them. The sunshine patterning his harsh face with light and shadow brought back the memory of him looming over her the night of Mardi Gras, broad-shouldered, tanned, his eyes dark with desire in the candlelight. Her feelings for him had deepened since then, she realized. She wanted him more now than ever.

Heat flickered like summer lightning through her loins. Her breasts ached for his touch.

"Yes. You were telling me about your childhood, remember?"

He cocked a doubtful eyebrow at her.

"Something about your mother, I believe?" He'd told her no such thing, but she was determined to find out everything she could about the man she'd married, for better or worse, by whatever means. His cool announcement that he'd been raised in a Natchez bordello had shocked her, and, somehow, his lack of emotion made it worse.

"Me, talk about my mother? Hardly!" His bitter smile made her yearn to take him in her arms. "Since I can't recall her face, it's unlikely I'd mention her, wouldn't you say? Good try, *cherie!*"

Ignoring his tone, she pressed, "But she's still living?"

His jaw tightened. "I heard she'd died."

"Oh! I'm so sorry."

"Don't be. I'm not. It's hard to mourn a stranger."

"I suppose it is. When did it happen?"

"A few years back. There was a shootout in a Mexican cantina. I heard she got caught in the crossfire." Still no emotion in his tone.

"So your father raised you." Was his father like the faceless men on rue Iberville? Did that explain Nick's determination to steer her away from that area?

"I wouldn't say that." His mouth twisted wryly. "He had too many other 'children' to worry about. Fifty-two, to be exact. They never left his hands."

A deck of cards. What sort of father treasured a deck of cards more than his little son? "You despised him—"

"Clever of you to guess."

"Yet, you became a gambler, too?"

"For a few years, yes."

If he was surprised she knew, he hid it well.

"I needed a stake. I did what I had to do." He shrugged. "Surely you can understand that, *chère* madame? The trading of one's . . . talents to achieve an end?"

Let him think what he wanted, she thought, taking a sip of her cold coffee. She'd never intended to trade her virginity for his blasted partnership! She wrinkled her nose.

"A fresh cup, madame?"

"I'd love one, if you have the time. This has cooled."

Despite the challenge in her voice, he did not look away. "I do have another appointment, but I have time for one more cup."

Nick didn't want to leave Honey, not yet. He realized it somewhere between drinking a third cup of coffee he didn't want and spilling his guts about the past he'd tried to put behind him. How she'd maneuvered him into doing either, he couldn't say.

The truth was, seeing her again had thrown him. She'd

alighted from the carriage at Bienville's office looking so damned beautiful, his mouth had gone dry. Then later, as he watched her, her lovely head tilted as she examined the contract, he'd found this thoughts straying back to the night in his bed. He'd wanted to toss up her skirts, right there and then, and make love to her between the blotters and inkwell on stuffy Bienville's desk!

Ridding himself of the blasted woman had been the *last* thing on his mind!

"But surely there was one you were fondest of?" she was saying now.

She must mean the soiled doves at Natchez Nell's.

"One who was like a mother to you, I mean?"

"Hardly. They passed through my life like ships in the night. Getting fond of them only ended in grief. Mine!" He forced a rueful grin. "I learned the hard way, but I learned."

"Learned what?"

"What else? That they wouldn't be around when I needed them no matter what they said." He signaled to the waiter. "If you're done with your coffee, I'll see you home."

"Ah, yes. That 'other appointment' you mentioned."

He hesitated. "Yes."

The atmosphere between them was almost intimate by the time they reached the townhouse on rue Orleans—a result of the confidences they'd exchanged, Honey believed.

Beulah beamed when she saw them together. "Afternoon, suh, madame. You be stayin' for supper, suh?"

"Master Nicholas has a business engagement, Beulah. Just one for supper, as usual," she said before Nick could answer.

Beulah's face dropped as Honey handed her feathered hat and jacket to the housekeeper.

"I think I'll have a drink before I leave," Nick said. Scooping up the black cat that arched about his legs, he murmured, "*Bonjour,* Ace. How are you today, my friend?" He scratched beneath the animal's chin, smiling when the cat purred.

Smoothing her skirts, Honey led the way into the high-ceilinged drawing room furnished in burgundy. Its beautiful rosewood furniture was a far cry from *Maman*'s shabbily elegant pieces.

Acutely aware that Nick was watching her, she opened the doors to a tall liquor cabinet. Inside, a silver tray held a number of crystal decanters. "What can I get you, Nick?"

"Bourbon. Straight up." Still lazily stroking the cat, Nick watched as she poured his drink. In that prissy high-necked blouse, she looked as elegant as a cameo—and just as cold. He preferred her as she'd looked strewn across his rumpled linens, her hair tangled on the pillows, her skin glistening from their exertions.

She carried the drink to him, uttering only a squeak of protest when he plucked the glass from her fingers and let Ace spring to the floor.

Setting the glass aside, he framed her face between his hands. "I've changed my mind. What I want is you."

"But your drink—"

"Later."

He felt her body tremble as he drew her into his arms and carried her upstairs to the bedchamber. She was still trembling when he pressed her down onto his bed, whispering his name over and over like a prayer. Her fingers threaded into his hair as, one by one, he freed the ivory buttons of her bodice and pressed his mouth to the creamy skin he bared.

"You're so beautiful, *chèrie,*" he murmured when she was naked to the waist. He kissed her rosy breasts. "So very beautiful."

And ready, oh, so ready for him, he discovered moments later. The hot silk of her body wrung a groan of pleasure from him as he thrust forward, lodging himself deep inside her. She rose to meet him, her head falling back, her hips lifting, giving herself up to him. And nothing—nothing!—had ever felt so wonderful or so right.

* * *

Doves were cooing when he awoke. From a nearby courtyard, a deep, mournful voice sang about "crossing the Jordan to freedom." The light slanting through the shutters patterned thc stuccoed walls with bars of gold.

Honey's head was cradled on his shoulder, her slender hand nestled inside his larger one. He swallowed. That somehow trusting gesture moved him, tugged at a heart he'd thought hardened to all emotion. When had it happened? When had he started to care? When had Honey become real to him, not just another conquest, another pretty face, another few moments of pleasure?

Like it or not, she'd done the impossible. She'd wormed her way into his heart. The knowledge stirred something fragile, something vulnerable he'd buried deep inside him, where it was safe from hurt, betrayal, desertion. He couldn't let it happen! Not again—never again! He had to get her out of his life, out of his heart, before it was too late. Before he cared too much!

Honey woke to find Nick preparing to leave, and it was the morning after Mardi Gras all over again. His expression was closed, hard, his movements brusque and mechanical as he finished dressing.

"Nick? Are you going?" she forced herself to ask.

"Yes. To Belle Refuge."

"I see. And when will you be back?" She kept her tone light, casual.

"I hadn't planned on coming back. Remember? We're married in name only."

Her hand clenched the sheet. "It doesn't have to be that way. Didn't this afternoon prove anything to you?" She rose from the bed, the sheet wound around her. "It did to me. We love each other, Nick. We do! Whether it started with a mistake or a formal introduction doesn't matter. If you love me, want to be with me, we could have a wonderful marriage.

"I'm not like those women at Natchez Nell's. I will

never, ever go away.'' Despite her best efforts, panic filled her. Her lower lip quivered. ''I love you! Please, don't shut me out of your life.''

''This afternoon was lust, not love. Hell! I don't even believe in love! In a few days you'll be over me, and I'll be over you. After all, women are all the same. Like pretty bonbons. No matter how delectable, once tasted, they're easily forgotten.''

With that parting shot, he hooked his frock coat over his shoulder and opened the door. ''Good-bye, Honey.'' And then he was gone.

''That's where you're wrong, monsieur!'' she hissed, shaking uncontrollably as she heard Nick's Thoroughbred clatter from the courtyard. ''This is one little 'bonbon' you will never forget!''

Chapter 9

''There's a boy at the gate, Miz Honey. Rode his mule clear from Belle Refuge with this letter for you.''

''Thank you, Hannibal. Give him a glass of buttermilk and ask him to wait for a reply.''

She hurried through the shadowed restaurant, out into the sunlit courtyard. At last! A letter from Nick! After rattling about his plantation since March, he'd had second thoughts, she knew it!

Perched on the rim of the fountain, she withdrew a folded sheet of heavy paper. ''Madame,'' the note began, and her heart sank. ''I have received last quarter's statement of accounts. Judging by the outrageous expenses detailed therein, you have clearly elected to ignore my instructions regarding imported items. Do so henceforth, or I shall take steps to ensure that you do."

The pompous brute had again signed himself "N. Sauvage." She snorted, annoyed now. It should have been signed "I. Sauvage," as in *I* for "Ignorant!" Even a—a child knew you had to spend money to make money. How could she create the desserts that had made Armand's great without exotic ingredients? The man was an idiot! A fool!

She crumpled the letter into a ball and hurled it into the fountain. As the ink ran, so did her tears of anger, disappointment. "How dare he!" she seethed, startling the fantailed pigeons into flight. "That—that arrogant, meddling devil! He won't get away with this! Remy! Remy!"

"Comin', chile! Lordy, missy, you look fit to be tied!"

"I am!" she ground out. "Come on. I need your help."

"To do what, sugar?"

"To send something to Belle Refuge."

"Lordy! I thought you was fixin' t' murder somebody!"

"Ha! Don't tempt me."

"Massa Nick! Nathan back already, suh. He brung you somethin' from the missus, suh."

"I'll be in shortly, Thalia. Rub him down, Jim, there's a good man."

Nick tossed the stallion's reins to the groom before heading toward the house, slapping his hat against his dusty boots. A layer of cane-field dirt, rich and red, covered him, and every grain of it for as far as the eye could see belonged to him. He'd done damn well for himself, he thought. But for once the knowledge gave him no warmth, no pleasure.

Swabbing his sweaty throat with his bandanna, he strode down echoing halls of parquet, through high-ceilinged, cavernous rooms with ornate plaster friezes, where Queen Anne and Chippendale furniture made lonely little islands on rafts of tapestry or Turkish carpets. He tracked down Thalia in the kitchens, behind the house. Something delicious simmered on the black range. At her feet was a half barrel, packed with straw.

"That's it? What is it?"

"I don't know, suh. Nathan brung it t' me when he come back from N'Orleans. It's for you, suh. From the missus."

Her coy tone annoyed him. How his slaves had found out so quickly about his marriage was beyond him. But the day after his nuptials, within minutes of his homecoming, Thalia had shyly congratulated him and asked if "the new missus" would soon be coming to Belle Refuge. Thalia's crushed expression when he'd barked that Honey wouldn't be joining him had made him feel guilty. Almost.

He gingerly poked at the loose straw, half expecting a cottonmouth or a rattler to strike from its depths. Squatting on his haunches, he removed a handful of straw, then an armful or two. When nothing awful happened, he kept digging until he unearthed a domed silver platter engraved with *fleur-de-lis.* It was surrounded by chunks of ice.

Lifting the serving dish from its cold nest, he set it on the table and stared at it without touching it, his expression wary. Given the way he and Honey had parted company, he wouldn't have been surprised to find the head of John the Baptist under that silver dome, failing his own!

"You want me t' take that lid off for you, Massa Nick?"

"Hmm?" He stared at Thalia. Strange. But, except for her size, his cook suddenly reminded him of Honey's tenacious mammy, Madame Remy. Was he losing his mind? Probably. "No, I'll do it."

Thalia shrugged her massive shoulders. "Suit yourself, suh."

He lifted the lid, recoiling in horror. It was not a snake. Nor was it anyone's head. Nooo, it was something far deadlier. Something diabolically calculated to make his blood boil and set his teeth on edge.

It was dessert! And not just *any* dessert. This extravaganza reeked of imported ingredients! He drew a deep breath and caught a tantalizing whiff of vanilla, a suspicion of lemon, a luscious hint of chocolate escaping the confection.

Suspicions were all very well and good, but he had to

be absolutely certain of his facts before he accused Honey of disobeying his strict instructions.

Thalia handed him a fork. "Here you go, suh."

He frowned. Had she read his mind? Perhaps she really was a conjure woman as his field hands claimed.

The first spoonful was damning. The airy, layered lemon sponge cake was topped with a glaze that was indisputably flavored with vanilla. Its filling was chocolate, without a shadow of a doubt, a brazen half-inch chocolate ganache, laced with coffee liqueur, that made his taste buds sit up and beg for more.

"Ith dere a mote?" he mumbled, trying to look as if he didn't care.

Thalia rummaged through the straw and the melting ice. "No, suh. Ain't no love note. Just cake." She beamed at him like a huge black cherub. "Ain't that nice of the missus, Massa Nick? You apart, but she surely thinkin' sweet things 'bout you, suh."

Just cake! Huh! That was rich! This wasn't "just" cake at all. No, sir. It was a—a gauntlet tossed down on a silver plate. And it wasn't "nice of the missus," either. Far from it! This was defiance under a silver dome. His blasted wife's unique way of consigning him to the devil for the reprimand he'd sent her.

"She's trying my patience now! You hear me, Thalia? I won't stand for this—this flagrant disobedience!"

"No, suh. You surely won't stand for it, suh."

"By God, I'll—" He stopped short. Was that a smile she was trying to hide? "Are you poking fun at me, Thalia?"

"Me, suh? Why ever would I do a thing like that, suh?"

Unconvinced, he took the knife, sliced himself a generous wedge, and wolfed down every crumb. Almost immediately he felt a warm, fuzzy glow spread through his belly. A feeling of contentment cocooned him.

"*Mon Dieu,* I'll be damned if I'll stand for this," he repeated, dreamily licking a smear of glaze from his finger. Bad mistake. It tasted like her. Vanilla. That little schemer!

Setting his jaw, he sliced another hefty wedge. There was no sense in wasting all those imported ingredients. He hated waste.

"... the cost of shipping ice downriver from Saint Louis is an unnecessary expense. Had you served the *nonperishable* desserts I suggested, this cost could have been avoided."

"That all?" Remy asked.

"*Non.* But it's enough, don't you think?" Honey threw down the note and picked up the whisk. She beat the egg whites so violently they stiffened in seconds. "First, he insists I forego my imported ingredients, and now—*now,* he wants me to cancel the ice, too!" She hurled the wire whisk aside.

Minna ducked. The whisk crashed against the whitewashed wall, rattling the spoon rack.

"Only a complete dimwit would ask that of me!" she cried, grabbing a spoon.

"An' we both *know* Massa Nick ain't no dimwit, right, chile?"

Taken aback, Honey set down the spoon. "That's right," she agreed, suddenly thoughtful. "He isn't, is he?"

Remy stopped her mending. "You ask me, I'd say your plan is workin', chile. Your man, he comin' to a fine old boil!"

"Do you really think so? So soon?" Hope filled her.

"Yes. 'Else he wouldn't be stickin' his nose in the pot, remindin' you he's still 'round."

"All right, then. On to the next phase of the plan! Pass me the ladyfingers, Harriet. *Merci.* Next, the coffee liqueur, Minna. That's right, darling, soak the ladyfingers with it. Don't scrimp. Next, we fold together the cream-cheese-and-whipped-egg mixture, like so. Perfect! And now the finished creation!"

Her hips twitching, she layered the ladyfingers and creamy filling in a cut-crystal bowl, and sprinkled chopped nuts and chocolate curls over the creamy top layer.

"There! It's ready. I wish I could see his face when he tastes this. It makes the last three dishes look like something they'd serve in the poorhouse! I think this time I'll send him a note. Just to reassure my darling that I won't be ordering any more ice."

Remy giggled. "Ohhh, you bad, Miz Honey."

"Don't I know it!"

"Massa Nick? You in there?"

Through bleary eyes, he saw Thalia poke her head around the door of his study. He scowled. "Get out, woman!"

He'd drawn the draperies when the sun came up, preferring the gloom to the dazzling sunshine. He scratched his face, hearing the stubble rasp. Damned beard itched like the blazes. He reached halfheartedly for the whisky decanter on the desk at his elbow. Empty.

Yet the room reeked of liquor, stale smoke, and something despairing, sad. Last night, maudlin and more than a little drunk, he'd concluded it was the smell of *only-ness*. Loneliness. Only-ness. He gave a mirthless chuckle that was due more to the bourbon than to his pun.

"Massa Nick, suh?"

"Get out, I said!" he growled, blinking his gritty eyes.

"The—um—the missus done sent you somethin' else, suh."

Her announcement brought him out of his chair, to his feet.

"Looks like another present, suh. I'd say she miss you powerful bad, suh." Thalia winked.

"The devil she does, the scheming minx. This is just another of her extravagances, in deliberate defiance of my wishes. I'd bet on it! That woman never wanted a business partner. She wanted a pantywaist she could twist around her little finger! Take it out to the cabins. Let the children enjoy it."

"If you say so, suh."

At the last minute an uncontrollable longing filled him.

"Thalia! Wait! I, er, should at least look at it, wouldn't you say?"

Thalia beamed. "I reckon that 'ud be best, suh."

Under the domed cover lay a lavish concoction, strewn with the chocolate curls he loved. He poked his finger into the gooey, creamy top layer and sucked appreciatively. As he suspected, it contained more imported ingredients per spoonful than Honey's other creations combined. He eyed it longingly, covetously, his mouth watering, while rage simmered in his heart.

"Suh, there's a letter."

He almost snatched it from her.

As it had that night at Armand's, months ago, the fragrance of vanilla and strawberries wafted from the envelope, teasing his senses, tugging at his heartstrings, playing merry hell with his memories. The perfume conjured an image of Honey that was so powerful he could almost see her hair gleaming in the sunshine, could hear the soft splash of a fountain, the cooing of fantailed pigeons. . . . He flicked his head to clear it, then ripped open the envelope, scanning the elegant script.

"How dare she!"

"Somethin' wrong, Massa Nick?"

"I'll say! Read it aloud! Read what that—that virago's written!"

"Why, suh, I doesn't know how t' rea—"

"Whether it's lawful or not for a Negro to read, I know you can, Thalia Valoir! Now, read!"

"All right. I'll read it, if'n you say so, suh." She nervously cleared her throat and began reading fluently, ending, " 'Furthermore, I'll have no reason to purchase block ice from upriver, henceforth, since your—since your—' "

"Well? Go on!"

"I can't, suh! I truly can't. I scared, suh."

"Scared of me?"

She nodded so vigorously the fringed ends of her dark red tignon wiggled like rabbits' ears.

He cursed. "Read it, anyway."

Her mammoth breasts heaved. "It say, 'since your hard heart is more than icy enough to chill a—a wagonload of desserts,' suh." Catching his eye, she tried unsuccessfully to disguise her laughter as coughing. "You gonna go talk to Miz Honey, suh?"

"The devil I shall! We've nothing to talk about. Just hand me that spoon, woman."

After he'd sampled the luscious dessert, he instructed Thalia to give the remainder to the children and trudged upstairs to change. He tried to ignore the warm glow that filled his belly—and his gnawing hunger for more of the same.

He'd go riding, he decided. He'd ride the length and breadth of his plantation, learn every blasted grain of dirt, blade of grass, and cane stalk he owned. He'd ride through bayou, field, and swamp until it was too dark to ride. Until he was too exhausted to sit in the saddle, to think, let alone feel.

And then, after he'd ridden himself to exhaustion, he'd come home and seek oblivion in yet another bottle. Perhaps then, he could ignore just how big and meaningless this damned house seemed lately.

"It's not working."

"You don't know that."

"What else am I to think? He's been all alone out there for almost four months. Thalia says he either works himself to exhaustion every day, or drinks himself under the table every night. He should have crumbled by now, if he's going to."

"He's a mighty proud man, chile. Proud mens take longer to crumble."

Remy was right. Nick *was* proud—and more than a little afraid, too, she suspected. Afraid that, like the women of the bordello, she would leave him if he took the chance of loving her. Afraid she'd become yet another "ship that passed in the night,'' a ''pretty bonbon'' whose face he could not forget as readily as those others.

Imagining the frightened little boy he must have been growing up in a place like Natchez Nell's, her heart went out to him. Was it any wonder he doubted a woman could be loyal and constant as she would be? That any woman could love him as she loved him? And so, like a cornered animal, he'd lashed out, trying to hurt, to wound, to cut her out of his life, before she could hurt him. His fierce pride had demanded it.

She'd not come to this realization easily, however. Nick's rejection had hurt her deeply and shaken her conviction that, whether he admitted it or not, he loved her. It had taken *Maman*—surprisingly wise about matters of love and romance, now that she was to marry Don Carlos in August—to point out the obvious.

Why would ''that handsome rogue'' have married her, if not for love? Though very beautiful, her little Melisse had neither fortune nor title, Estelle had been quick to point out. Furthermore, at the great age of one-and-twenty, she was an old maid in society's eyes. Far too ancient to become a bride for the first time! So, what had compelled Nick to marry her daughter, really, if not love?

The answer was simple. Nothing. Nothing at all!

True, he'd claimed he was marrying her out of a sense of honor. Yet by his own admission, he scoffed at convention. His insistence that she might be carrying his child was ridiculous, too. A few weeks' wait when her curses were due would have proven if that were truly the case, would it not? Of course it would!

The truth was, she had brought no pressure to bear upon him whatsoever. Had, in fact, actively protested the marriage when he'd accused her of engineering it! *Maman* was right. Remy was right. Whether or not he knew it, Nick had *wanted* to marry her. Why? Because he loved her. Now, if only he would admit it to himself.

''I believe it is time for the last act of our little drama,'' she declared. ''Remy, you'll send Thalia a message. Harriet, fetch our baskets and my straw hat. I must do some marketing before we begin."

Like a general marshaling her troops for battle, she gave them her instructions, and like it or not, Nick was about to be reminded of what he was missing.

Chapter 10

"I could eat a horse this morning!" Nick declared, taking his place at the head of the long mahogany table that could have seated fifty. For the first time in many weeks, he'd enjoyed a deep, dreamless night's sleep. Consequently, he was in a good mood this sultry July morning. "What's for breakfast, Benjamin?"

"Weell, I'm sorry, suh, but we ain't got no hosses, and that's a fact!" his butler said, grinning. "We've some fine pickled pork, though, sweet ham, poached eggs, an' biscuits."

"They'll do. Pass the butter and preserves."

"Why, I'm mighty sorry, suh," Benjamin murmured, shaking his woolly gray head. "Thalia say she done used up all her preserves, suh. Maybe you'd like a little of this instead?" He handed Nick an earthenware crock.

"Honey?"

"Yessuh. Finest honey in all Louisiana! Taken from your own hives, too, suh," Benjamin added. "Belle Refuge bees, they make the best honey there is, ole massa used t' say."

Nick scowled. "Just butter, thank you, Benjamin."

"Certainly, suh. An' how's about a slice of this fine Virginia ham, suh? It's honey-glazed an' just as sweet as the mornin'!"

Suddenly he'd lost his appetite. All the talk of "honey-this" and "honey-glazed-that" had chased it away. With a curse, he flung his napkin aside and strode outside, well aware that Benjamin was staring after him.

It was dark when Nick returned from the neighboring plantation. He had spent the afternoon admiring Don Miguel's fine Andalusian horses, and the evening on Miguel's verandah listening to the crickets chirp as he sipped the Spaniard's fine sherry.

The size and emptiness of his plantation house had never been more apparent than now, as his footfalls echoed through beautiful rooms in which hung elegant crystal or brass chandeliers. Brocade draperies graced the long French windows. Plaster frescoes adorned the ceilings. Expensive European furnishings were arranged in all the rooms, every piece, every inch of fabric, wood, and glass a testament to the taste and flair that money could buy. But they were beautiful luxuries he enjoyed—alone.

As he stood there, the silence and emptiness crowding him, suffocating him, he remembered what Honey had said when he'd asked why saving the restaurant was so important to her. "Though I could earn my livelihood elsewhere, without this restaurant they have nothing," she'd said, referring to her family and her employees.

"And without you, *belle* Honey, I have nothing," he told the shadows. All his wealth and luxury were meaningless without someone to share them.

The thought filled him with melancholy. Insisting he had dined with Don Miguel, he refused all of Thalia's offers of food and retired.

Candles and lamps had been lit in his bedchamber. The French doors stood ajar to let in a cooling breeze. He stiffened as he removed his coat and unknotted his cravat. A shadowy female figure, her curves silhouetted through the filmy mosquito netting that shrouded his four-poster bed, was fluffing his pillows.

His mouth went suddenly dry. "Honey?" He sounded hoarse.

"No, suh. It's me, Suki. I was turning down your sheets, suh." She stepped into the light. She was slender, with *café-au-lait* skin and liquid brown eyes that were as shy and wide as a doe's. "Sleep well, suh." With a nervous glance at his face, she scuttled from the room, closing the door behind her.

Why had she looked at him that way? Had she expected him to force himself on her? He shook his head as he unfastened his breeches. Forcing women was not his style. Besides, he thought, stretching out on the cool sheets with his arms folded under his head, there was only one woman he wanted to bed, damn her..

That night Honey filled his dreams. Tossing and turning, he relived the night of Mardi Gras. Her perfume filled his senses as she danced away from him, scattering a trail of strawberries and shrimp in her wake and . . .

He jerked awake, sitting up to find the night had flown. Sunshine streamed through the French doors. A long, down-filled bolster was clasped tenderly in his arms. He sniffed, nuzzling the pillowcase like a bloodhound. Vanilla! The pillows, the sheets, were scented with vanilla, and something else. . . .

He followed his nose and discovered a lace pouch tucked inside the bolster. The bundle was tied with ribbons and silk roses, and filled with what looked like twigs and dried leaves.

He got up, washed, and dressed, then headed for the kitchens to have a little talk with Thalia.

"What the devil's this?" Striding over to where she sat, he tossed the small packet into Thalia's lap. "One of your damned *gris-gris?*"

Thalia picked up the offending object and began to chuckle, her huge body shuddering in the shoofly chair. "Lordy, this ain't' no *gris-gris*, Massa Nick! This here's a potpourri sachet. Fine Creole ladies use 'em t' make their linens sweet as flowers. Hmm. This one got rose petals, looks like. And strawberry leaves. Vanilla pods and dried *honey*suckle. Sure smells pretty, that *honey*suckle, don't it, suh?''

''The devil it does!''

Turning on his heel, he strode from the kitchens, turning a blind eye to the honey bees buzzing in the honeysuckle vines that grew wild near the springhouse and the stables. He ignored the glorious perfume of honeysuckle on the hot, humid air.

Nick was bone-weary when he returned to Belle Refuge late that evening. His throat was parched by dust and by the sun that had mercilessly beaten down on him all day.

Calling for a cool glass of syllabub, he ordered a bath drawn, then lowered himself into the soapy water with a grunt of satisfaction. Leaning back, he closed his eyes, and imagined Honey was with him in the slipper-shaped tub. He could almost see her luscious curves flushed rosy pink as she pressed herself against him, her breasts and hips glistening as she whispered, ''Massa Nick! Massa Nick!''

Massa? He frowned.

''Massa Nick! You sleepin'?''

He opened his eyes. ''*Mon Dieu!* What the devil are you doing in here?'' He flung a linen towel over his huge erection. ''Get out!''

Thalia chuckled as she loomed over him. ''Now, suh, ain't no call t' be shy 'round me. You ain't got nothin' I ain't already seen, sugar! Mammy Thalia done changed the soiled napkins of more boy babies than you got fingers, suh! Don't you mind me.''

As she spoke, she handed him a small crystal platter. On it reposed a wedge of chocolate torte, a triangular island in a small lake of crimson raspberry-Amaretto sauce, garnished with whipped cream and curls of chocolate. He gulped. A man didn't have to be a master chef to recognize

Honey's handiwork. It was Sweet Sin! He'd have bet hard money on it!

He inhaled and was back at Armand's again. He could hear the clink of silverware against fine china, the drone of conversation. He could see Honey in her butterscotch gown, the candlelight in her hair. He could feel her lips and her kisses as a warm glow in his heart and his belly.

He could even remember what she'd said the night of Mardi Gras, believing him asleep. "I love you, Nick! God help me, I love you!" And then, the following morning, "I care for you, Nick. That is why I let you make love to me. The only reason."

Because she cared for him, she'd said, and what had he done? He'd denied her love, turned his back on it, and walked away. It was better this way. Honey had become too important for comfort. Still was, if the truth be known. Only grief could come of caring for someone.

"What's this? I—I asked for syllabub."

"Syllabub's all gone, suh. Every last drop! Hot day like this, why, it don't last long. 'Sides, what's on that plate is better for you, suh. Trust me," Thalia murmured gently. "You want me t' scrub your back while you eat it, suh?"

"Hell, no!"

Thalia patted his shoulder and rumbled with laughter like a giant volcano about to erupt. She sashayed from the room, leaving him all alone with his erection—and the scrumptious dish that Honey had created just for him. Sweet Sin!

He sure as hell felt like sinning now, for more than anything else she'd sent him, this dish *was* Honey.

The smooth raspberry-Amaretto sauce had the delicious sweet tartness of her lips. The silky chocolate glaze was the same melting brown as her eyes. The whipped cream held just a hint of vanilla like her flawless skin. The damned woman had bewitched him! There was no other explanation for it. She had ruined him, placed a hex on him with her cooking that was so potent no other woman would ever appeal to him.

Everywhere he looked, everything he tasted or touched,

everything he smelled or dreamed of, reminded him of the blasted woman he'd made his bride. And unless he put a stop to it, he was condemned to spend the rest of his life mourning that—that extravagant, devious minx!

It was time to have it out with her, face-to-face, he decided. And what better time than now?

Chapter 11

Nick galloped down the canebreak that followed the curve of Bayou St. John which led into the city. As he rode, he swore he'd take Honey sternly to task for flouting his commands. He was her husband, damn it, as well as her business partner. She'd promised to obey him!

Entering the city and heading toward *his* restaurant, he vowed he would demand in no uncertain terms that she [illegible]ease her extravagances immediately. And if she couldn't— [illegible] more likely, wouldn't stick to a budget, he'd hire a chef [illegible] would. That would make her sit up and take notice, [illegible]od!

[illegible]ting in front of Armand's and dismounting, he looped [illegible]se's reins over the wrought-iron hitching post. Then, [illegible]de past the carriages drawn up to the banquette and [illegible]d the restaurant.

[illegible]ood evening, Monsieur Sauvage," greeted Francois [illegible]homme, Armand's maitre d'. "Your usual table, sir. Sir, wait!"

Brushing the man aside, Nick strode through the restaurant, sidestepping anyone who tried to block his path. Unsmiling, he stalked from the storeroom to the wine cellar to the ladies' dining room, in search of his wife.

Not surprisingly, he ran her to ground in the restaurant's kitchens. Her trim back to him, she was supervising Minna and Harriet as they chopped vegetables and grated cheese while she stirred a bowl.

As the kitchen staff gradually grew quiet, she turned to make a suggestion to her apprentice, Philippe Gaston, who was filleting a fish. Nick knew she was unaware that he was standing there, watching, waiting.

Several seconds passed before all conversation ceased, and all eyes, wide with alarm, were trained on him.

"Out, all of you!" he demanded.

He saw Honey stiffen, but she did not turn around. Instead, she stared down at the bowl, her hand clenched on the bottle next to it.

"Miz Honey?" Minna sounded scared.

"It's all right, darling. Run along. All of you, go on now. Monsieur Sauvage and I will just be a moment."

They gave him a wide berth, scuttling past him as if he were a madman. Perhaps he was. He'd never felt like this before.

When they were alone, he slammed the door and slid the bolt.

"Madame," he began sternly, his hands linked behind his back. "I want to talk to you."

"Of course you do, Nick."

Honey turned to face him, a wooden spoon in one ha[illegible] a bottle of Amaretto in the other, and his heart pou[illegible] like a drum. Other parts of his anatomy snapped to [illegible]tion.

Fair tendrils had escaped her topknot. With the f[illegible] hind her, the gold wisps framed her flushed face in a[illegible] That angelic innocence should have infuriated him[illegible] somehow, she'd never looked lovelier—or more des[illegible] to him than now, with that smear of chocolate on her cheek.

He braced himself. It wouldn't do to weaken now.

"I've had quite enough of your defiance, madame!" he bellowed. "And more than enough of your extravagances!"

He clenched his jaw, determined to see it through as he'd planned. Oh, Honey might shed a tear or two by the time he was done with her, but it was for her own good.

Plucking the spoon and bottle from her hands, he set them aside. "If Armand's is to be a paying proposition, then, by God, you'll cut corners, or I'll know the reason whaa-whaa-" He broke off and stared at her lips.

"Whaa, whaaa what?" Her eyebrows arched, her lashes trembled. "Go on. You were saying?"

He coughed. "Er, quite. Why I, er—" Confused, he stared at her mouth, curved now in a sweet smile, and scowled. "I'll be damned! I've forgotten what I was going to say!"

"Really? Then perhaps it wasn't as pressing as you thought."

"Perhaps not," he agreed uncertainly.

"Or perhaps there's something else you'd rather discuss?"

"Well, I—"

"Yes, Nick?"

She smiled and something inside him shattered with the faint tinkle of glass. Or was it ice?

Honey saw a nerve tick at his temple. His fists were so htly curled that his knuckles were bone-white. Finally he ind out, "I've, er, I've missed you."

r heart sang. *Oh, thank you, God!* "I'm glad to hear u see, I've missed you, too, Nick. So much!"

must have been crazy to let you go, *chèrie*."

u were—crazy, I mean." She stepped into the circle arms. "But what matters is that you're here now. long together, Nick. I hope you know that."

nodded. "In bed—at table—even in my dreams!—I ouldn't get you out of my mind!" He caressed her cheek with his knuckle and fire leaped through her.

"How strange."

"People—Thalia, for one, Suki, my butler, and others at Belle Refuge—were starting to look like people here. I guess it must have been my conscience acting up, don't you? Telling me I shouldn't have left you?"

"You're probably right," she agreed, making a mental note to thank Thalia, Benjamin, and Suki for all their help when she saw them.

"I hurt you, didn't I? By comparing you to the gals at Natchez Nell's?"

"It doesn't matter. I forgive you."

"You're nothing like them." He swallowed. "Ironic, isn't it? I was so damn busy trying to turn you into my mistress, I didn't notice I'd fallen in love with you, instead."

She bit her lip, and her eyes watered. "Did you, Nick? Do you, truly?"

His voice was hoarse with emotion as he whispered, "More than anybody or anything in my life! That's why I'm here, darling. I'm gambling my pride, my self-respect, and my future that you meant it when you—you said you loved me, too?"

She saw the fear in his dark eyes, and her own stung with tears. What it must have cost him to come here, to admit that he'd been wrong. That he loved her! Her heart sang.

"I meant it, darling. With all my heart!" She rested h cheek against his chest. "Oh, Nick, I'm so glad changed your mind."

"Prove it. Marry me," he said in a stronger, deter voice.

"But we're already married!"

"We'll have a *real* wedding this time. You'll be m of my house, the mother of my children, the queen heart!" He drew her into his arms. "I haven't had experience at loving someone, Madame Sauvage. Y have to teach me."

"I have a suspicion you'll be an excellent pupil, monsieur."

His embrace tightened. "Come home with me now,

Honey. Say you will, and I'll buy you a river of Amaretto, a mountain of raspberries!''

''But what about our restaurant? Every table is full—''

''Close early. It's high time we had a honeymoon.'' He kissed the chocolate from her cheek. ''Hmm. And soon.''

''But all those expensive ingredients will be wasted if I close early.''

He grinned. ''*Touché*. Philippe can close. Now, will you come home with me?''

''It's a tempting offer, monsieur,'' she teased. ''One I'm afraid I must . . . accept''—on tiptoe, she brushed his lips with hers—''for you see, I'm not some ship passing in the night, darling. Or a bonbon, to be easily forgotten. When you wake each morning, I'll be there. I'll always, always love you, Nick. You can bet on it!''

He said nothing. He was so hard with desire, she knew he could not speak, let alone stand. With a naughty grin, she pressed her body against his. ''Let's go home,'' she murmured.

Reaching behind her, he unfastened her apron and flung it aside.

''Nick?'' His black eyes smoldered as he began unbut-
oning her blouse from her chin to her waist. ''Nick, you
vil! What are you doing?'' She giggled.

'Making love to the chef.''

Here?'' She laughed. ''But I thought we were going
to Belle Refuge?''

ter. Right now, can you think of a more appropriate
celebrate our reunion? Or, God help me, a closer
he added through clenched teeth.

the sweep of his arm, he cleared the floury surface
ted her onto the table. ''Look at you, *ma belle!* Ar-
's most luscious dessert!''

She curled her arms around his neck. ''The only menu on which you'll find this dish is yours,'' she promised impudently, offering him her lips.

As Nick began to make passionate love to her, she offered up a silent prayer to God and Saint Jude that their marriage would always be as sweetly sinful—and as sinfully sweet as the dish she'd created for Nick with all her love.

Penelope Neri thinks that the way to a man's heart truly is through his stomach, and she believes an exquisite dish, lovingly cooked and served, will capture and keep any man's heart!

The British-born best-selling author of over twenty historical romances, Penelope knows what she's talking about. She has been preparing romantic dishes for the man in her life for the past twenty-five years and is convinced that love makes the difference in everything we do.

She is also certain that a pinch of humor is as vital in the recipe for love as trust and honesty. After all, love without laughter is like champagne without bubbles or a souffle without eggs!